STEALING
TESLA

a noir thriller of espionage

jonathan call

To Patricia...always...my wife, and best friend

Huge steel-ribbed monsters rise into the air
Her Babylonian towers, while on high
Like gilt-scaled serpents glide the swift trains by,
Or, underfoot, creep to their secret lair.
A thousand lights are jewels in her hair...

The Empire City – George Sylvester Viereck

Prologue

July 11th, 1934

NEW YORK, WEDNESDAY, JULY 11, 1934

TESLA, 78 REVEALS PLANS FOR DEATH RAY

Particle Beam Weapon Destroys Planes From Great Distance

Calls Weapon 'Chinese Wall of Defense'

From his rooms at the New Yorker Hotel, eminent scientist, Nikola Tesla, yesterday revealed his concepts for a new defensive weapon, an invention powerful enough to destroy 10,000 enemy planes from 250 miles away.

Nikola Tesla, who turned 78 years old yesterday, is the father of modern methods of generation and distribution of electrical energy. He considers his a new apparatus the most important of the 700 inventions he's made so far.

Dr. Tesla said he has perfected a method and apparatus, which will send concentrated beams of particles through the free air, of such tremendous energy that they will bring down a fleet of airplanes and will cause armies of millions to drop dead in their tracks.

This "death-beam," Dr. Tesla said, is effective at great distances and fires its force in silence. "As far as a telescope could see an object on the ground and as far as the curvature of the earth would permit it." It will be invisible and will leave no marks behind it beyond its evidence of destruction" said Tesla.

An army could be annihilated in an instant, he said, even the most powerful microscope would not reveal what catastrophe had caused the destruction.

Tesla claims this latest invention of his would make war impossible. This death-beam, he asserted, would surround each country like an invisible Chinese wall, only a million times more impenetrable. It would make every nation impregnable against attack by airplanes or by large invading armies.

Part 1

———◦———

The Teleforce Book

Seven Years Later

Chapter 1

———◆———

The New Yorker Hotel, Manhattan
October 6th, 1941 8:18 PM

THE THIEF WAS READY. Sitting in the back seat of the parked Yellow Taxi Cab, his mind ticked through each stage of the job one last time, satisfied that every detail was in place.

Turning his head, he squinted through the passenger window the glass glazed with fog. Withdrawing a handkerchief, he wiped the glass to peer through. From this side of Eighth Avenue, he had a splendid view of his target, the New Yorker Hotel, its art déco setback architecture ascending into the evening sky.

A mischievous grin creased the thief's mouth. His mark was in there somewhere, oblivious, trusting his treasure to be safe.

Not quite.

Street noises blared through the glass as the taxi idled. In the front seat, Eddie, the cab driver, was yammering about something; he had been talking nonstop for the last forty-five minutes.

Ignoring him, the thief rolled down the rear window. His gaze clambered up the hotel's forty-three stories, to where gigantic letters—four stories tall—electronically blazed the 'New Yorker' name like a crown. He craned his neck like a gawking tourist, as if seeing it for the first time. But it wasn't his first time, of course. The thief had studied every aspect of the building, even paying a couple of visits inside just to get the lay of the land. He was meticulous that way. Each job had its own nuances and challenges, but he'd had two weeks to prepare.

This job had come to his attention through a newspaper article he had read in *The Daily Mirror*. The article had showcased the perfect opportunity for a man of his skills—a lucrative opportunity. Unfortunately, that very same newspaper had also given the thief some unwelcomed press.

A clever reporter at The *Daily Mirror* had connected a series of high-end burglaries that had taken place in Manhattan over the last few months and had attributed the crimes to one individual. With no clues to the thief's identity, the reporter had nicknamed the thief, *The Smoke*, calling him 'vaporous and elusive, drifting from jewelry store to penthouse to boardroom'.

The article had highlighted the thief's uncanny ability to seep through a locked door and between the seams of a sealed safe to plunder treasure at will and then disappear—yes—in a 'puff of smoke'. Hackneyed maybe, but sensational too, and the other newspapers picked up on the moniker, creating their own hackneyed headlines, all the while adding a Robin-Hood flair to the mysterious thief.

The Smoke.

He was okay with the label, but he didn't care for the attention it provoked. Anonymity was an asset in this business; notoriety...not so much. Especially on nights like this, when The Smoke intended to seep into one of the classiest hotels in the city.

The New Yorker Hotel had opened its doors just over ten years ago in 1930. As the largest hotel in the city, The New Yorker was something of a city unto itself, with twenty-five hundred rooms and suites, five restaurants, ten private dining salons, its own beauty parlor, a forty-two chair barber shop, and a direct tunnel to Pennsylvania Station. In the bowels of its subbasements was the largest private steam-generated power plant of its kind in the nation.

The thief knew every inch of it, every floor, every ballroom, every salon, every restaurant and, most importantly, every exit.

Forty-three stories. But only one story interested him—the thirty-second.

His glance fell back to the street, taking in the front entrance of the hotel. Beneath the brushed-chrome awning, the pavement pulsated with early evening activity. The thief watched with satisfaction the stream of people floating past the amber glass doors to the hotel. As always, the city was alive. He would be just another face in the crowd. Smoke drifting by—as the newspapers might say.

One couple stopped to ogle the sandwich board sign set off to the side of the front entrance; it advertised the swing sounds of the Benny Goodman Orchestra being offered inside the hotel's grand ballroom tonight. The thief could tell that the woman wanted to catch the show. She tugged at the man's coat sleeves, cajoling him toward the doorway; but he was having none of it. Giving the sandwich board sign a disappointing frown, the two melded back into the crowd stream.

Too bad, thought the thief. They might have enjoyed kicking up their heels to the *Henderson Stomp*, or cuddling to Goodman's version of Cole Porter's sexually suggestive tune, *Let's Do It (Let's Fall in Love)*.

Benny Goodman would aid the thief tonight. No, not intentionally. The bandleader would play an unwitting role in the plot—a diversion. The thief had read that his mark loved America's big band sound, and tonight's show would be just the thing to entertain him. The thief had already taken steps to ensure it by sending complimentary tickets to his room.

All part of the plan.

Eddie, the cab driver, mumbled something from the front seat, more of an angry hiss than words.

The thief broke his gaze from the New Yorker to peer over at the back of Eddie's capped head. The driver was a non-stop talker. Apparently, the thirty dollars the thief was paying him wasn't buying his silence.

"My uncle Stanlius, once removed, was killed by the damn Krauts," seethed Eddie. "Shot him dead in the street. Right in front of his wife and kids. The bastards."

The thief caught Eddie's appalled rage in the rear-view mirror.

"He never left the homeland. Lived his entire life in Poland...in Warsaw. Made it through the Luftwaffe bombing—barely." Eddie shook his head. "Bombed the tar out of them, those damn Nazis did."

As the thief gazed into Eddie's eyes reflected in the mirror, the voice of his father echoed in his thoughts—one of the Old Man's cardinal rules:

Never use a cutout with the gift of gab—you'll be sorry, one way or another.

You were right, Pops, I'm already sorry.

Since getting into the cab an hour ago, the thief had listened to enough of Eddie Petrowski's prattling to write a biography of the guy. Eddie, it seems, was a second-generation Pole. Eddie's father worked in the garment district but drank too much and tended to bat around his mother some. Eddie had driven a cab for four years and had never stepped foot off of the island of Manhattan. He and his wife Ethyl had two children, Eddie didn't drink a drop, and claimed to have never taken a swat at Ethyl—not once, he'd said.

Yeah, he was a talker, but fortunately, Eddie fit two of the Old Man's other rules. The first being:

A stranger makes the best cut-out.

The thief had never set eyes on Eddie until climbing into his cab on the Upper East Side. Sure, the thief knew all about the cabbie now, but

Eddie would have little to offer about the fare he'd picked up on Lexington Avenue—other than the handful of lies he'd been fed.

Eddie also fit with another of Pop's rules—one of the thief's favorite:

A dimwit makes the best cutout. Don't use a nitwit, they're too stupid. And never use a halfwit, they're too smart. A dimwit is just perfect.

Eddie grew sullen in the front seat.

"Then after shooting him, the damn Krauts dragged Uncle Stanley to the side of the road and just left him in the gutter," he hissed. He wheeled around to face the thief, his forearm draped over the seat. "The sonsof-bitches are taking all of Europe. They'll be here next. Crawling right up Fifth Avenue with that goose-stepping, stick-up-their-butts march that they do. You watch! We'll both be wearing uniforms before we're through."

"Not me," spoke the thief with a tender bitterness. "I don't look good in green."

Eddie grunted. "There'll be no getting out of it. Uncle Sam Wants You—and me. We'll be fighting them for sure—either here or there. I might get off this island yet. I only hope they drop me right in the middle of Poland—for Uncle Stanley's sake."

Eddie's eyes blazed with a wild mixture of hate and vengeance.

His Polish rage had been boiling for two years—ever since the German invasion in '39—and now it spewed like lava into the cab. The thief couldn't remember the Old Man saying anything about using an angry cutout, but he was wondering if he shouldn't make up his own rule about it.

Eddie was no different than everyone else in the city—the entire country, for that matter. Fixated on the events in Europe. Emotions ran high. You couldn't escape it. Everyone had an opinion. The nation was growing war-hungry. Wanted to kick some Nazi butt.

The thief couldn't care less. Europe was over there. Let them duke it out. Why waste brain molecules on things you couldn't control?

Tonight, all he cared about was room 3227 of the New Yorker Hotel.

"They're vermin that need to be stomped out!" spit Eddie, as green neon from the street signs glinted in his wild eyes.

The thief held Eddie's stare until the wildness leeched away. The besieging Germans fading from his thoughts.

"Eddie, you do remember what you're doing for me tonight, right?" the thief asked.

Eddie blinked, confused, as the anger fell from his face.

"In the hotel, Eddie," said the thief, a bit too sternly. He gave a nod toward the building across the street.

"Oh sure," said Eddie with a dismissive wave. "I know what to do."

An uneasiness hit the thief. He had planned the entire operation to the minute. He was confident in its success—as crazy and risky as it was. However, he was staring at the one untested variable. His cutout. His dimwit. He was relying on Eddie Petrowski to perform a simple, but critical role.

"You can count on me," said Eddie.

The thief was suddenly dubious.

I don't know, Pops, maybe using a dimwit for a cutout isn't such a good rule after all.

Chapter 2

⸻◈⸻

New Yorker Hotel - The Main Lobby 8:38 PM

Maneuvering around the Benny Goodman sandwich board sign, Sergeant Detective J. Patrick Tooke stepped up to the New Yorker entrance. The doorman blazed a welcoming smile as he opened the door for him. The detective passed through the foyer into the lobby, where a well-dressed couple nearly bowled him over. Squabbling and oblivious to everyone else, the couple was in a rush to get through the doors; they brushed by without offering so much as a 'pardon us'.

Tooke shook his head in dismay. What was happening to manners in America these days?

The detective took in the luxury and liveliness of the room. Wide and bright, with looming ceilings and crystal chandeliers, a mezzanine balcony surrounded the lobby overlooking the main floor. A grand staircase off to the right twisted up to the second level. The marble flooring glimmered as smooth as glass. Recessed into the back wall was the front desk. At least twenty clerks serviced the guests with quick and efficient registration—there would be no waiting in lines at the New Yorker. Uniformed bellhops scurried about, pushing brass luggage racks or toting suitcases; while on the other side of the room, behind the concierge desk, tuxedoed men whisked back and forth, dispensing their tactful citywide wisdom. The room was bustling, flashing with activity. However, it didn't seem chaotic, but smooth and exacting, like the thrusting pistons of a V-12 Packard.

Detective Tooke blended with the room's glamor. For an Irish cop, he dressed with authority in mind. Tonight he wore his dove-gray, three-piece suit, tailored to slim his somewhat expanding waist and to help broaden his somewhat narrow shoulders. He wore a yellow tie with a matching hand-kerchief, tri-cornered in his left breast pocket. His charcoal gray fedora, with a black band, was cocked just so. His topcoat draped one arm, and in the other, he carried a folded edition of this afternoon's newspaper, which concealed a green folder tucked inside its pages.

The green folder was the reason for his appearance at the hotel—a favor for an old friend.

This wasn't Tooke's first visit to the New Yorker. He had investigated a few petty thefts during his time in Robbery Division, and on one oc-casion, after his transfer to homicide, he had looked into the suicide of a honeymoon bride, who—upon discovering her new groom compromising a chambermaid—had taken a walk out of a seventeen-story window.

The New Yorker wasn't all glamor. It, too, had its gritty side.

Down at the precinct, they called J. Patrick Tooke, Paddy. He was a second-generation Irish American, as well as a second-generation flat-foot—his father had been a cop for thirty-five years. Paddy joined the force after his stint in Europe during the Great War and had now been a blue blood himself for twenty-two seasoned years. Starting as a beat cop over in his neighborhood in Brooklyn, he eventually climbed up to the rank of Sergeant Detective here in Manhattan. Paddy had a reputation for being no nonsense, honest, and for solving cases.

Three unique gifts contributed to Tooke's success.

The first was his ability to blend. He was average height, average weight, with average looks—somewhat reminiscent of the movie actor, Pat O'Brien. No one took notice of him—as if he were the invisible man. He liked that. He wanted to be right on top of you before you even knew he was coming.

His second gift was an eidetic recall for faces. He could spot a suspect in the crowd, as if sighting through a sniper's scope. His cerebellum instantly flashing the perp's name, address, case history, rap sheet, APB's, arrest warrants, and known associates. And he had the uncanny capacity to de-chronologically age a person he may have seen twenty years earlier, stripping away wrinkles, age spots, hair loss, and sagging muscle tone to see the younger person they once had been. This gift fascinated the guys in the precinct to no end.

But it was the third gift that raised him from a beat cop in Brooklyn to Sergeant Detective in Manhattan.

The gift of observation and instinct.

He noticed things others didn't. The faintest oddity set alarm bells clanging in his head, and once the instinct kicked in, it gripped him to the point of obsession, forcing him to follow it to its natural conclusion. He never ignored it. His wife, Dottie—Dorothy Tooke—insisted that it was God speaking to him; she called it his Divine cop-voice. Dottie was a faithful Irish Catholic who went to mass daily, prayed earnestly, and ran the Tooke household with a righteous fist of iron. To Paddy, she was the voice of God.

Paddy had called Dottie earlier in the afternoon to tell her he wouldn't be home for dinner because he would be doing a favor for an old friend.

That old friend had called out of the blue, surprising him, as they hadn't spoken in years. The man had been Paddy's superior officer, back in 1918, while serving with the Fighting 69th in France. The 69th was the 'Irish Regiment' based in Camp Mills on Long Island and led by a fellow Irishman by the name of Major William Donovan—or, as he'd been called since his football days at Columbia, Wild Bill.

Wild Bill Donovan had been no ordinary officer. By the end of the war, they'd pinned his chest with all kinds of medals, including the Medal of Honor, the Distinguished Service Cross, and a couple of Purple Hearts. He was a tough SOB, always striving to live up to his notorious nickname.

Paddy heard that after the war, Wild Bill had become an attorney in Buffalo. Over the years, however, Paddy had lost track of Donovan.

Then the call came...out of the blue.

Their conversation this morning had been brief, but filled with a mix of warm and sorrowful war recollections. Wild Bill, it seems, had been following Paddy's career, surprising him with details of his police work even he had forgotten.

Donovan was now working out of an office in Washington DC called The Office of Coordinator of Information, and he was calling in that capacity to ask a special favor. He wanted Paddy to contact a man named Allen Davies who ran their operation in New York out of Rockefeller Center. Davies was following a lead concerning a national security issue and Donovan thought a local cop, who knew the city, could help. The favor came as a request, but Paddy—projecting himself back into his Fighting 69th Sergeant's uniform—took it as an order. An order he was happy to dispatch for Wild Bill.

Paddy's meeting with Allen Davies after lunch had been brief. They had met in a suite of offices in Rockefeller Center. There had been nothing stenciled on the outer door to help identify it as a government agency, and the nameless office had been hard to find because of it.

Allen Davies was a thin man with a craggy face and deep-set eyes the color of rusty shovels. He immediately used his intercom to call in another fellow by the name of Phillip Carver. After introductions, Davies proceeded to chain smoke, but never uttered a single word for the rest of the meeting.

Phillip Carver, Paddy was told, was overseeing the case. He was younger than Davies, tall and reedy, with an intense manner. He greeted Paddy with an air of impatience that signaled he had more important issues that needed his attention. He said little, giving only a minuscule amount of information about the job. Using two fingers, he pushed a green folder across the desk, saying that everything he needed to know was in the folder, including his instructions, along with a couple of photographs.

Paddy left the Office of Coordinator of Information feeling they had regarded him as something of an intrusion, and that possibly the only reason the two men accommodated him was because of Wild Bill's recommendation. Both of them had been furtive, unwelcoming, and stingy with words. Paddy spent the rest of the afternoon reading through the file while trying to decide whether he liked the two men in the nameless office.

Yet, here he was, going about a mysterious business which may, or may not, have something to do with national security. He was wondering what he'd gotten himself into.

Tooke walked up to the front desk and spoke to a clerk, showing his badge and telling the young man that he had an appointment to speak with the hotel detective, a man named John Williamson. The clerk pounced on a nearby telephone. Another clerk standing nearby had overheard the request. He had red hair, a ramrod posture, and pale blue eyes sparking with unease. After a few seconds, the clerk, as if uncomfortable in the presence of a police officer, turned and shirked away.

A minute later, Williamson appeared.

He was a tall, keen-eyed man, with a pencil mustache, and Tooke could tell that the house dick was not overwhelmed with joy that the Police Department was encroaching into his territory. Nevertheless, the man remained professional, extending his hand in welcome. After leading Tooke over to a nearby cluster of upholstered chairs at the far end of the lobby, they sat, and he asked how he could be of service.

Tooke took off his hat and rubbed his chin, uncomfortable as to how to proceed. He came right out with it.

"Mr. Williamson, we have it on good authority that a Nazi collaborator will be visiting your hotel tonight."

Chapter 3

———◦———

New Yorker Hotel, 8th Avenue, 8:48 PM

"ARE YOU READY TO earn your money, Eddie?" asked the thief.

The taxi driver turned off the engine to the cab and slapped his meter flag down. He was officially off the clock. "I'm ready."

"You know what to do?"

The cabbie nodded. "Oh, sure! Get a room, right?"

The thief cocked his head as if addressing a child. "No, Eddie, you already got a room, remember? We made a reservation earlier."

An hour ago, the thief had waved thirty dollars over the seat, asking Eddie if he was interested in a business proposition. The cab driver immediately pulled over, wondering if it involved anything nefarious or illegal.

"No, of course not," the thief had replied. "All you have to do is make a reservation at a certain hotel and then register at the desk as a guest."

"You want to pay me to sleep at a hotel tonight?" A touch of concern had graced Eddie's voice, as if fearing he'd picked up some kind of pervert. "I don't think my wife Ethyl would—"

"No," the thief had replied. "I will stay at the hotel—you will not. I just want to borrow your name for the evening."

"I don't understand...why would you—?"

"Let's just say that I am to meet a young lady tonight, and I can't be using my own name. I wish to be discreet." Truthfully, the thief wanted to limit his contact with any hotel personnel that could potentially describe him later. But Eddy needn't know that.

"A woman, you say?" said Eddie, eying the thirty bucks at the same time. It was, after all, more than a week's pay for him.

The thief had watched Eddie contemplate the opportunity with a gleam of unease pinching his face. Was the cabbie going to get judgmental on him? Would he have to strike out to find another dimwit hack with less scruples? He hoped not.

"You're married, huh?" asked Eddie.

The thief shook his head.

"Ah, but she is."

The thief gave him a practiced, bashful smile that said it all.

"I see," said Eddie. "And just in case her husband comes sniffing around the hotel register—"

"I don't want my name to be there," inserted the thief.

Understanding fully, Eddie had nodded with a conspiratorial grin.

There was no woman, of course. The thief had fabricated the story for Eddie's sake. As the Old Man would say:

Always misdirect! Make them believe a false reality—create a theater of the mind.

The thief had watched as the theater curtains had opened in Eddie's eyes.

"A married woman," said Eddie dreamy-like, as if instantly discarding his wife, Ethyl. "I bet she's pretty!"

"Beautiful," the thief had replied. "She's a natural looker, Eddie. She looks just like a woman in the movies."

"As pretty as a movie star, huh?" Eddie leaned in.

"No, I mean, she literally looks like an actual movie star. A dead ringer."

"Who? Ginger Rogers? Carole Lombard?"

The thief shook his head. "She looks like that girl in that Hitchcock movie that just came out, *Foreign Correspondent*."

"Ooo..." squealed Eddie. "She's the same girl that plays the nurse in all those Dr. Kildare pictures. She's a beauty. What's her name?...uh, I got it, Laraine Day!"

The thief snapped his fingers. "That's the girl. She looks just like her. Identical. Could be her twin sister."

"Good body, huh?"

The thief bristled, annoyed by the cabbie's vicarious need to be enticed. "Yes, a nice body," he muttered. "She's also intelligent, witty, and dignified. But it was her eyes that got to me. They shimmer silver and blue at once... like a mountain lake. They look back at you as if you're the most important thing in the universe. The moment I laid eyes on her at the World's Fair last year, I knew she was the girl for—"

The thief stopped abruptly. Without realizing it, he had drifted into truth. What had begun as an attempt to misdirect had somehow detoured into his past, leaking out like an open wound.

He had been describing...her.

Natalie.

He could barely go on.

The buried memories overwhelmed him. Her face, her eyes, and that spark of electricity that flared as their hands accidentally touched at the World's Fair. Every aspect of her manifested in the backseat with profound clarity.

The indulgence angered him. A stupid moment of unguarded weakness. He couldn't afford to be so reckless—not tonight, of all nights.

"You really love her, don't you?" Eddie had whispered, not realizing how biting his words truly were.

The thief shook away the memories, embarrassed. Gathering himself, he had said. "I...as you can see, I need to be discreet. I can't register into the hotel under my own name. But I will pay handsomely for your help."

And so, Eddie had agreed to the deal—an entire week's pay for signing into a hotel. It happened less than an hour ago, and now the thief had to remind the cabbie again of his role.

"You know what to do, Eddie?" asked the thief.

"Yeah, I know what to do," Eddie mumbled, somewhat defensively. "You want me to register and bring the key back out here to you."

The thief released an exasperated breath. How many times did he have to go over it?

"No, Eddie, I want you to get the key and go straight to the room. Take my case with you. Once in the room, you wait fifteen minutes and then bring the key back down to the mezzanine lobby to the Terminal Barbershop. I'll be inside getting a shave and you can leave the key there with me."

Eddie nodded enthusiastically. "Right, but how will you know the room number?"

"The room number will be on the key."

"Right."

Eddie's mouth twisted into a look of concern. The thief could almost read his thoughts. He pulled forty dollars from his billfold and dangled the bills in front of Eddie. He had already paid him ten dollars just for calling in the reservation.

"Pay for the room in advance, Eddie. We reserved a suite, so it should come to $12.50."

"For one night?" exclaimed Eddie, astonished. "Wow, that must be some fancy place."

"It's the New Yorker, Eddie. It's one of the best hotels in the city. This is the rest of the money that I promised you...with a little extra. Tip the bell boy well and treat yourself to a haircut after you bring me the key."

Eddie nodded. He eyed the bills, but he made no move to grab the money. The thief could tell that the cabbie's greed was wrestling with his conscience.

"You sure I'm not getting mixed up in any trouble?" he muttered.

"What trouble? You're simply doing me a favor," spoke the thief warmly. "And who knows...I might need you again next week. And the week after that."

Eddie's right eye brightened. "Same deal? Thirty smackers?"

The thief smiled with a nod.

That did the trick. Nothing like a steady income stream to sweeten the pot. Eddie swooped up the bills and stepped out of the cab.

"Eddie...you might want to leave your cap here. After all, it is the New Yorker."

"Oh, right." He tossed the cap through the window onto the front seat. He stood there for a moment in his leather bomber jacket and bowtie as if waiting for approval. "I...I don't have a suit coat...just my hack-jacket. Is that okay?"

The thief considered that. The New Yorker was a classy joint. He didn't want Eddie sticking out. The less attention, the better.

He then came to a decision that he didn't care for, but what choice did he have?

"Tell you what, Eddie, wear my topcoat into the hotel and leave the jacket here."

He was reluctant to hand over his Benson-Anderson cashmere coat, but it had to be done—Eddie needed to fit the part.

"When you come back down to the barbershop, hang my coat on the coat rack with the key in the pocket. And I'll take it with me when I leave."

Eddie nodded and grinned. "That's a good idea. You're a smart man, Mr...uh..."

Nice try, he thought to himself. Eddie had already attempted to get his name out of him with similar tricks. Ignoring the challenge, the thief handed the topcoat through the window. Eddie took off his jacket and slipped into the coat. It was a size too big for him, but not noticeably so, and it classed him up pretty well—at least good enough for a few minutes work.

He turned to leave.

"Are you forgetting something, Eddie?"

The cabbie paused and looked back stupidly. "What?"

"The case, Eddie. I need you to take the case to the room."

"Oh, right. The case."

The thief handed it through the window. Eddie looked it over, running his fingers along the Corinthian Leather and the locked clasps that held it shut. Then, as if being caught trying to figure out how to open it, Eddie gave a nervous smile and spun away. Dodging traffic, he slipped across the street toward the hotel entrance.

The thief sat back, watching as Eddie entered the hotel. An unease plagued him. How could such a simple task be so confusing to the man? It made him squirm. All of his plans rested on his cutout performing to task.

He let out a sigh.

Yes, Eddie worried him, but he had to wonder. Was that the only reason for his unease? Or was it the memories of Natalie lingering in the cab? He had mistakenly let her in. Since mentioning her to Eddie an hour ago, he hadn't been able to purge her from his thoughts.

But purge he must. He couldn't go into the hotel unfocused. Not tonight.

Chapter 4

World's Fair, Flushing Meadows, Fourteen Months ago,
August 1940

THE WORLD'S FAIR HAD *begun in '39 and was near the end of its run.
Hyped on the radio, in newsreels, and in newspapers for what seemed like
forever, I went to the Fair that day on a whim. I figured a crowd that
size offered plenty of dipping opportunities. People mesmerized by fanciful
displays make for easy targets.*

*Truth be told, I hate dipping. Pickpocket work is too up-close and personal.
Looking a mark in the eye makes them actual people and tends to scratch at
my conscience. Give me a locked safe in a darkened room anytime. It's much
easier to detach from the personal aspect of thievery.*

*They had advertised the Fair as 'The World of Tomorrow', its slogan, 'A
Dawn of a New Day'. And for me, I suppose it became just that, and it had
nothing to do with the ultra-modern exhibits on display. No, my 'new day'
came while buying a pretzel.*

*'The World of Tomorrow' didn't disappoint. An excited and diverse crowd
packed the grounds. Ironically, I became a part of the 'oblivious crowd', taking
in the exhibits with such childlike fascination that I forgot all about relieving
the unsuspecting of their wallets. Some thief I am.*

*The centerpiece of the Fair was the gigantic exhibit called Trylon and Peri-
sphere, a seven-hundred-foot-tall obelisk and two-hundred-foot-tall sphere.*

The locals gave them the irreverent name of 'the spike and ball.' The sphere inside was eighteen stories high, with moving balconies, an auditorium as looming as Radio City Music Hall.

For hours I ambled in and out of the different exhibit halls, absorbing the displays. I watched a synchronized swimming routine at the Aquacade. Johnny Weissmuller was there; he gave us his famous Tarzan yell. It was a pretty splendid show. Better be, it cost a whopping eighty cents to get in.

I was just coming out of the Westinghouse Exhibit Hall—where I'd seen a seven-foot robot named Elektro, talk, smoke cigarettes, and flirt with passing girls—when I realized I was hungry. I spotted a pretzel cart outside the doors. It was a rare vendor without a long line. I drew up and ordered a pretzel with mustard and a Pepsi Cola.

The vendor, a heavy-set Italian man with a thick mustache, nodded without looking up, his busy hands kneading dough for his customers.

While waiting for my food, I scanned the crowd, remembering the reason I'd come to the Fair in the first place—to dip. It struck me that I suddenly had no ambition for it. Everyone looked so happy. Why spoil their fun?

Then, from behind me, a deep-throated Italian accent said, "There you go."

Swinging around, I went to grab my food and instead grabbed someone's hand. A woman had been reaching for the same pretzel. A spark of electricity flared between us.

"Oh, did you feel that?" she cooed.

I turned to see the most beautiful woman in the park. She looked oddly familiar. I stood there flummoxed, my jaw moving, but no words coming out.

"Uh, I think you can let go of my hand now," she said pleasantly in an English accent.

"That pretzel is for the lady," said the Italian vendor with a growl. "Give it to her!"

I quickly released her hand. "I'm sorry, I thought he was giving it to me."

"My hand?" she asked demurely.

"The pretzel."

She smiled at me, and my heart thundered. "If you are that impatient, you can have it."

"Your hand?"

"The pretzel," she warned with a blush.

"The gentleman's food is coming," scolded the vendor. "He can wait."

The woman smirked at the rebuke, pressing the back of her hand—the one holding the pretzel—to her lips to hold back a burst of laughter. Her other hand came up to touch my shoulder as if we were sharing a secret joke. Such an intimate gesture. Her touch sent vibrations through my bones.

"I guess he told you," she quipped.

"Do I know you?" I asked. "You look so familiar."

She then released her laugh, as if she could contain it no longer. "I get a lot of that lately." She licked a dab of mustard off her fingers.

"Do you? It's not a line, I really feel that—"

"Have you been to the cinema lately?"

Her words threw me. It was as if she were asking me on a date to the—

"Wait a minute," I cried in recognition. "Are you—?"

"Laraine Day?" She was still chuckling. "No! I am not."

"Are you sure?" I asked, stupidly.

She leaned in very conspiratorial-like. "Yes," she whispered. "I'm pretty sure I would know if I were she."

"Good," I whispered back. "Actors are fakers. And I don't like fakers." I said the words as if I weren't one at all.

She laughed again, and I rode the musical wave of it. Adoring the way she seemed to enjoy laughing. She was good at it.

There was something natural about the atmosphere between us, as if something destined us to quibble playfully over a pretzel. I was entranced. Magnetically drawn into her orbit, and I sensed she was to mine as well.

She told me her name was Natalie Stevens. I told her mine—not the nickname that everyone else calls me, but my actual name. I don't know why I did that. We ended up strolling the grounds together, eating our pretzels, talking nonsense, and making fun of the occasional odd-looking person we spotted in the crowd. We flirted effortlessly. We pretended not to peek at each other. I, however, had already done a full appraisal. She was like no other woman I'd ever met.

And that's how it started.

Natalie Stevens.

A dawn of a new day.

At the World's Fair.

I never picked a pocket that day. In fact, I stole nothing for some time after.

Chapter 5

New Yorker Hotel Lobby, 8:47 PM

"A NAZI COLLABORATOR HERE at the New Yorker?" said Hotel Detective John Williamson. "I hardly think so."

Sergeant Detective J. Patrick Tooke produced his folded newspaper with the green folder tucked inside. Before opening it, he said, "First, Mr. Williamson, I need to let you know up front that officially I'm not representing the police department tonight."

"What do you mean?"

"I'm here as a favor for a friend of mine who works for..." Paddy hesitated, reluctant to mention the name of the government agency, as even he had never heard of the Office of Coordinator of Information until this afternoon. After a pause, he said, "the State Department."

Williamson was taken aback. "That's unusual, isn't it?"

"We live in unusual times, Mr. Williamson," said Tooke. "With everything happening in Europe, we need to be vigilant here in the States—to keep us secure."

"What does that have to do with my hotel?" asked Williamson, his tone icy.

"I know how mindful you are of your hotel's security, Detective Williamson," said Tooke, purposely using the man's title to telegraph a sign of mutual respect—one professional cop to another. It seemed to work as Williamson's stony face thawed some. He continued, "Everyone speaks highly of you. And I know you would do anything to keep your patrons safe."

Williamson nodded. "Of course I would. So tell me, why you are here and what has this to do with the State Department in Washington?"

Tooke unfolded his newspaper and retrieved the pale green folder, given to him by Allen Davies earlier in the day. "In the interest of national security, we would like to locate this man."

He pulled out a grainy black-and-white photograph and handed it to Williamson.

Williamson looked the photo over, nodding. "I know this man. He visits occasionally. His name is George something...George..."

"George Sylvester Viereck," said Tooke.

"Yes, that's it. Viereck. He's a writer of some sort."

"Very good, Detective. You have an excellent memory. He's a poet."

"A poet?" Williamson snickered. "He's a national security threat? How much harm can a poet do?"

Tooke gave a gentle smile. "Writers can be quite seditious."

Williamson grunted. "I suppose. But poetry?"

"Viereck doesn't just write poetry. He's also published essays and articles on fascism and the Third Reich. We believe Viereck is a member of the German American Bund movement."

"German-American Bund? What's that?"

"A pro-German group that has organized here in America. We also suspect Viereck has made trips to Berlin and has met with Adolph Hitler on occasions."

"This man does not live at the hotel!" stated Williamson adamantly. "He only visits."

"Have you seen him tonight?"

"No, I haven't seen him for a few weeks. That's not to say he hasn't slipped in without me spotting him."

"I fully understand that he may have come and gone without your knowledge. However, we have a source that tells us that Viereck will be—"

A sudden clamor arose behind them—a hearty mix of cheers and boos that echoed off the walls. Both men swung around, their professional ears perked.

But recognizing the commotion, they just as quickly relaxed.

On the other side of the lobby, coming up from the Pennsylvania Tunnel entrance, was a group of young men walking with hangdog expressions. A small crowd had amassed around them, spewing cat calls.

Paddy squinted at the group of men. "Hey isn't that—"

"Dem Bums," said Williamson with a note of misery.

"The Brooklyn Dodgers," exclaimed Paddy. "What are they doing here?"

"They're booked at the New Yorker during the World Series. Unfortunately, they lost to the Yankees tonight. Three to one."

"Say, that's Leo Durocher!" cried Paddy. He pointed to the Dodger manager slipping through the mob. "He looks different in his street clothes."

"You a Brooklyn bum, Lieutenant?" asked Williamson, a smile creasing his face for the first time.

"Sure I am," he declared proudly. "I lived at the ballpark as a kid."

"Dem Bums will be back," said Williamson firmly.

They watched as the team disappeared through the doors of the Manhattan Room Restaurant across the way. When Williamson turned back around, a new expression of cooperation graced his face—ready to do anything for a fellow Dodger fan. "Where were we, Detective?"

"Please, call me Paddy," he replied, hoping to encourage the new bond. "We were talking about George Sylvester Viereck."

"Right. As I was saying, I haven't seen him lately. He occasionally comes to visit that strange old goat who lives here."

Ignoring the note of disrespect, Tooke asked, "Which goat would that be?"

Williamson blanched. "Sorry...Paddy," he choked. "That was an un-professional remark. I didn't mean to be disrespectful towards one of our guests."

Paddy smiled with a nod.

"I meant to say that he comes to visit the elderly Mr. Tesla."

Paddy's eyes widened. "Tesla? Are you referring to Nikola Tesla, the scientist? He lives here?"

"Yes, that's the fellow. He used to be famous for something, I don't remember what."

Tooke stifled an urge to blurt out his astonishment. *He's only famous for discovering alternating current, the electric motor, and bringing light and radio to the entire world*, he thought to himself. But he said:

"I thought Dr. Tesla lived over at the Hotel Governor Clinton?"

"He did at one time, but they kicked him out. I heard he owed them money—twenty thousand dollars. He's been here for at least seven years, maybe more." Williamson shook his head. "I already apologized for my remark, but I have to say, Paddy, Mr. Tesla is an odd duck."

"Oh? How's that?"

"He has...peculiarities. He won't shake hands. He washes his own hands twenty times a day—the maids can't keep him in soap and towels. And he's fascinated by pigeons, dotes on them; he even lets them fly into his room from his balcony. And then there's the three's thing."

"What do you mean...the 'threes thing'?"

"Well, to begin with, he lives on the thirty-third floor, in room 3327...a number divisible by three. When eating, he wants eighteen napkins on the table—again divisible by three. Also, before entering the building, he walks around the block three times. That kind of thing."

"I see," replied Paddy thoughtfully. He knew of Tesla's genius and ac-complishments, but he hadn't heard of his odd behavior.

Paddy recalled while training in the Irish Regiment at Camp Mills, in Garden City out on Long Island, how he and an army buddy had used a day-pass to take a road trip in a Model T out to see the famous scientist's mysterious laboratory on the northern shore of Long Island. The laboratory was called Wardenclyff. And it was a marvel to behold. A tower built on the site stood one hundred and eighty-five feet tall, supposedly to send wireless telegraphy—others suspected more nefarious reasons. It loomed over the landscape like a gigantic badminton birdy. The sight of it was daunting. Paddy also recalled that not long after his visit, they had torn the tower down and the laboratory repossessed because of financial difficulties.

He now wondered if Nikola Tesla had anything to do with his mission tonight. If so, the dossier from Rockefeller Center was strangely missing that information.

"And this man, George Viereck, comes to see him? Mr. Tesla?"

Williamson shrugged. "Yes, that's right. They're old friends from way back." Alarm leaped into his eyes. "You don't think Mr. Tesla is involved with the Nazis, do you?"

"No...not at all," said Paddy quickly. He tried to be reassuring, but the question bothered him. His admiration for the scientist was too great for it to be even a remote possibility.

"Do you think this Viereck is going to show up tonight?"

"We're not sure. But we have a tip that he might."

Paddy glanced down at the photo of Viereck laying on the coffee table. Unease came over him. What could those two men have in common? A brilliant inventor and a fascist poet? Allen Davies and Phillip Carver hadn't filled him in on this aspect, as if stingy with secrets. They only said that Viereck might show up at the New Yorker Hotel tonight, and to call their offices immediately if he did.

"Are we done, Lieutenant?" asked Williamson as he stood. "I'm afraid I have other duties to attend to."

Tooke also stood. "I thank you for your help, Detective, and with your permission, I'd like to linger a bit and keep my eyes open. See if our tip plays out."

"Be my guest. And if you have an extra photo, I will show it to my team, so they too can be on the lookout for him."

Tooke rifled through the folder for one of the extra photographs that Davies had provided and handed it to Williamson. They shook hands, and Williamson left.

Paddy closed up the folder and sat back down. Gazing up, he realized he had a panoramic view of the lobby and the 8th Avenue entrance.

Raucous laughter arose from the Manhattan Room restaurant from across the lobby. The ball players were enjoying themselves, even if they had lost today. Dem Bums. The aroma of grilled steaks wafted Paddy's way. His stomach grumbled. With a touch of resentment, he remembered it was Monday—Dottie always made pot roast on Mondays. A fact that had skipped his mind when he'd called to tell her he'd be working late.

He reached into his coat pocket and produced his Kaywoodie Briar pipe. He gave it a couple of taps on his knee, found his tobacco pouch, and pinched a wad of Kentucky Club into the bowl. Tamping it down, he lighted a match to it, puffing its pungent vapors into the surrounding atmosphere. Chasing away the delicious smell of grilled steaks.

The room was busy; full of people, but not a soul resembled George Sylvester Viereck.

A tip, huh?

Was Viereck truly a threat to national security? Maybe. His relationship with Nikola Tesla certainly raised suspicions. Was the poet after something the elderly inventor possessed? Or was there another reason he might show up tonight?

However, the real question nagging Paddy Tooke was, why—after all these years—had Wild Bill called him out of the blue to bring him in on this? Donovan had always been a shrewd one, always operating with ulterior motives. But why Paddy? Why tonight?

And, for that matter, what pray-tell was the Office of the Coordinator of Information, anyway?

As Kentucky Club smoke swirled about his head, and with his stomach protesting, Paddy was resenting hearing from his old major this afternoon.

After all, he had enough work at the precinct to do. He didn't need to be chasing crazy poets around New York.

But then Paddy recalled another poet, one he had served with in France. The poet, Joyce Kilmer, had also been a member of the Fighting 69th. He had been Wild Bill's adjunct during a battle fought outside of Paris during the Aisne-Marne campaign near the Ourcq River in 1918. They had ravaged the Irish Regiment. Donovan lost all of his company commanders, including Kilmer—killed by a sniper's bullet. Shortly afterward, Paddy took his place working directly for Donovan, who would go on to receive the Distinguished Service Cross—the Army's second-highest decoration.

The Major had never let him down during the war—never.

So, pushing the resentment aside, Paddy relented, out of respect for his old friend.

And the moment he did...

A tiny flutter of that old gift of instinct became aroused. A nudging whisper, telling him he was here for a reason tonight—whatever it may be. The voice of the Divine Cop? Maybe...maybe not. But he was familiar enough with its language to listen.

He settled back, clenching the Kaywoodie in his teeth. He picked up the newspaper and unfurled it with a snap. Keeping one eye on the door and one on the newsprint, he immediately began missing the taste of Dottie's pot roast.

Chapter 6

Lobby Front Desk, 8:47 PM

DRESSED IN HIS DESK-CLERK uniform, Henry Blacksmith stood straight as a knife behind the front desk as he checked in an older couple from Utica. From the corner of his eye, he watched as the hotel house detective, John Williamson, approached. Blacksmith's muscles tensed. Adrenalin sharpened his readiness.

The clerk had been discreetly monitoring the meeting taking place on the other side of the room between the house dick and the police detective. It concerned him, making him wonder if Williamson might confront him. If so, he needed to be ready.

Earlier, after the officer had first shown his credentials, a small buzz had arisen among the desk clerks. Everyone was curious about the hushed conference. One of the other clerks had snickered, 'someone is in trouble now'. He had been jesting, of course, but the comment had put Blacksmith on edge, causing an escape route to unfurl in his mind.

Getting to the street would be key. The escape route had been in place since first taking the job as a desk clerk three weeks ago. However, if he became trapped, he was prepared to respond with force. Weapons concealed within his clerk's uniform would buy him time.

The couple from Utica signed the register.

Williamson drew closer. Blacksmith noticed he carried, what appeared to be, a photograph.

Tracking him out of the corner of his eye, Blacksmith's right hand edged into the opening of his suit jacket, where a special pocket, sewn into the lining, held a nickel-plated C G Haenel Schmeisser I—a tiny German-made pistol. Padding helped to conceal the slight bulge made by the small caliber weapon; the bulge was further camouflaged by the carnation boutonniere they required the clerks to wear as part of their uniform. A snap at the opening of the pocket kept the gun in place. Being no bigger than the palm of his hand, Blacksmith knew the gun was next to useless—you had to be close in and shoot point blank to do any damage—but he also knew that simply brandishing it in the open could stir enough panic and confusion to help pave an escape.

He would rather it be a Lugar Parabellum, a larger caliber gun that promised to leave a trail of carnage. But the Haenel Schmeisser would do.

Blacksmith also carried a thin razor knife strapped to his outer thigh. A zippered pocket inside his trousers made it easy to retrieve. But that too was a close-in weapon.

A third item was available to him—a vicious little thing—but it needed preparation and was to be used only for special circumstances.

This was not one of them.

Williamson came up to the desk.

Blacksmith allowed his fingers to unsnap the pocket inside his liner. The pearl handle of the pistol now available.

Williamson crossed in front of him, right past the clerk's station, giving him no notice. He flipped up the divider door built into the counter and went straight into the hallway that led back to his office.

Blacksmith let out a breath of relief. The conference with the police officer must not have been about him after all.

"Young man! Are you even listening?" came an irritated yelp from the other side of the counter.

Blacksmith turned a stabbing glance to the old couple from Utica. Being focused on Williamson, the check-in process had taken longer than necessary, and they were growing impatient. Their wrinkled faces looked indignant. He had an urge to slash them both with his razor knife.

"We would like our key, please." wailed the old man. "My goodness, does everyone have their head in the clouds here?"

Henry Blacksmith released a lethal smile and eased his hand out of his jacket. Turning around, he retrieved their key from the kiosk along the back wall, mumbled the standard spiel about having a 'pleasant stay at the New Yorker', and moved them on their way.

He glanced over to where the police detective remained seated in the corner, casually reading his newspaper. Why was he still here? Had Williamson gone to retrieve something from his office? Possibly the fabricated resume Blacksmith had used to get his job?

The photograph bothered him. Was his face on it?

The officer's presence unnerved him, but Blacksmith remained steady.

He knew from the beginning that inevitably there would be moments like this—witnessing questionable conferences that may, or may not, have anything to do with his reason for working at the hotel. The trick was to not allow paranoia to usurp better judgment. It was easy to hallucinate false alarms.

Henry Blacksmith stood just over six feet tall, with muscled shoulders, a smooth, high cheek-boned face, and eyes as blue as splinters from an iceberg. His actual name was Heinrich Carl Schwinghammer. The name, Blacksmith, being a play on words, as his German name Schwinghammer literally meant to swing a hammer—the designated job of a blacksmith. He loved the name; there was strength in it, as well as action. Aptitudes that fit him well.

Five weeks ago, he had been dispatched into the United States, via neutral Ireland, as an agent of the Sicherheitsdienst, or S.D., the secret intelligence agency of the Nazi party. It was a return of sorts, as he'd lived in the U.S. previously as a child and teenager when his father was stationed here as a low-level diplomat. This time, he entered the country alone, dying his blond hair a rusty red and using a mock passport provided by the Abwehr.

No one, but a select few, knew of his entrance into the States, and even they didn't know the true reasons of his coming here—that is, except one. The embedded agents here in New York he'd found to be lackluster. Most were members of the Amerikadeutscher Volksbund, a German-American group that espoused adherence to National Socialism. Their clout was nearly impotent, but they had some sway—like the one who had secured the job for him at the hotel. The contacts here believed he was here to work for them, but his orders came only from Reichsführer Heinrich Himmler's office back in Berlin. Orders that would hopefully culminate tonight...if all went according to plan.

Unless a certain police detective intended to unmask him.

Blacksmith stepped away from the counter and eased a look down the hallway behind him. Williamson had disappeared into his office. The door was closed.

Yes, the photograph bothered him. He hadn't been able to get a look at it. It might be nothing. But it would put his mind at ease knowing whether or not his face was on it.

His contact would arrive at the hotel soon to execute the plan they had put in place. There could be no hindrances. Tomorrow it wouldn't matter. Tomorrow, he would be on his way back to Germany. But tonight—if his cover was in jeopardy—he needed to be on the offense and not the defense.

His hand slid over the bulge beneath the white boutonniere. The Haenel Schmeisser felt tight in its cocoon. Yes, a Lugar would be better. After all, his name was Schwinghammer, and, if his life depended on it, he'd rather be swinging a sledgehammer than a ball-peen.

Either way, Henry Blacksmith would use whatever hammer necessary to get a look at that photograph.

Chapter 7

Suite 3327, 8:55 PM

THE BLACK NOTEBOOK SAT on the corner of the cluttered desk, poking from beneath a short stack of papers. An inch thick, the pages were stained and yellowed with age. On one frayed corner, the leather ply curled back as if the secrets inside had burrowed an escape tunnel.

The secrets of Nikola Tesla.

Sava Kosanovic eyed the book nervously. Was now the opportunity? Could he do it?

He sat alone in the room; his Uncle Niko had stepped away. It would be so easy to reach over, grab the book, and slip it into his attaché case. His uncle none the wiser.

It appalled him, this act of duplicity. But what choice did he have? He needed the book and the secrets within its pages.

Kosanovic glanced over at the arched doorway that divided the suite, and to where Uncle Niko had disappeared into the bedroom. How long would he be gone?

The desk with the notebook was situated across the room, near the glass doors of the sky terrace, piled with books and papers. Behind the desk was a narrow alcove with built-in shelves and cabinets. A tall safe sat wedged against the wall in the far corner, its door slightly ajar.

Sava was glad for one thing. Uncle Niko had not locked the notebook away in the safe. It usually was.

Sava—like his uncle—was Serbian but had been born in Croatia. Sava loved his uncle, but with terror raging in Europe, Sava's political alignments were increasingly at odds with his Uncle Niko's. Never, in a million years, would he intentionally hurt him. But at eighty-five, the elderly inventor simply couldn't grasp the complexities of the situation taking place back in their homeland.

Sava snickered at the irony of that thought. The vast intellect of the great Nikola Tesla, unable to grasp the complexities of something so mundane as politics. Yes, he understood the intricacies of the metaphysical world and its unseen forces...but politics? No.

Earlier in the year, on Palm Sunday, three hundred Luftwaffe bombers had assailed Yugoslavia, ruthlessly strafing the city streets of Belgrade and filling them with blood. Twenty-five thousand civilians killed; thousands more wounded.

Within days, a coalition of German, Italian, and Hungarian forces besieged the country. The Yugoslavian army was no match for such an onslaught, and the country fell. For his safety, the young monarch, King Peter, was forced to leave the country. The exiled government now operated from out of London.

Resistance to Nazi occupation arose immediately, yet even under the knuckle of Nazi rule, the country's time-worn ethnic tensions had exacerbated. A Serbian Army officer, loyal to the monarchy, named Draza Mihailovic, led the Chetniks. But a new resistance faction had also sprung up, a communist-backed movement called The National Liberation Army, led by Josip Broz Tito. Both of the factions fought against the Nazis, but they tended to war with each other too.

Hatred and confusion reigned.

Back home, Yugoslavia considered Nikola Tesla to be a national treasure. Sava could recall as a boy sitting around the kitchen table hearing the stories of his famous uncle, who had immigrated to America and made a name for himself, by working with, and challenging, the likes of other great inventors, such as Edison and Marconi.

Yes, Sava worshiped his uncle. So how could he do this to him now? Take his precious notebook?

His eyes remained riveted on it.

At forty-seven years old, Sava had eyes saddened by the burdens of war. His hands rubbed together nervously. It would take less than ten seconds to reach it and squirrel it away. Uncle Niko was busy dressing for a meeting he had this evening with a visiting professor from France.

Sava gathered the papers from atop the coffee table—including the newly signed statement from his famous uncle concerning the Nazi occupation of Yugoslavia. From the other room, he heard Uncle Niko rummaging through the closet while mumbling to himself.

Sava stood, shaking nervously.

"Uncle Niko, I'm going downstairs, while you meet with your guest," he called out. "I'll be back in a couple of hours to say good night before I leave for home."

Nikola's response was muffled.

"Okay," responded Sava, paying little attention to what he had said.

He only needed the notebook for two hours. His uncle wouldn't even miss it. The visiting Frenchman was of a different scientific field—an archeologist, if Sava remembered correctly. So, he doubted his uncle would refer to it. He rarely did. Only those within a small, trusted circle of family and friends knew that it even existed.

Leaving his attaché case open, he stepped over to the desk. A pang of guilt knifed through him. But he had no choice. His uncle had boxed him into a corner.

Glancing up, he noticed the framed Time Magazine cover hanging on the wall behind the desk, his uncle's face adorning the cover. The feature story had been about Nikola Tesla. And though it was seven years old, it was the revelations written in the article that drove Sava into the deception he so loathed to perpetrate tonight. His uncle's boast had been so...public.

During the summer of 1934, Uncle Niko had gathered news reporters to his New Yorker suite, to inform them he had conceived of a device that could end war permanently from the earth. He had, the article claimed, designed a particle-beam weapon that could vaporize armies and attacking planes from as far away as two hundred and fifty miles. He called the weapon, 'The Chinese Wall of Defense'.

The article had caused quite a stir. While some had dismissed the concept as unachievable, its potential captivated others. Whoever possessed such technology would maintain military superiority for years to come.

God bless him, Uncle Niko had taken investment money to develop the weapon. $25,000—from, of all people, the Russians. A hefty sum. And so far, he had failed to provide the blueprint designs and calculations to make the device a reality. The investors were growing impatient. They wanted the weapon now. Hitler needed to be stopped!

The role of liaison between the Russians and Uncle Niko had been thrust upon Sava. The Soviets were pressing him for results. He needed the notebook to appease them. Hopefully, it would help unlock the mysteries to the technology.

Sava had once asked Uncle Niko about the device. Could they develop it? His uncle had released a crafty smile, tapped his head, and said, "It's all in here." Then he tapped the warped cover of the notebook. "...and in here. Believe me, I can build it."

The book was a guarded treasure. Within its pages were many of the initial inspirations behind much of his uncle's research and inventions, a theoretical photo album to chronicle his discoveries, much like parents would chronicle their child's life with a scrapbook. A lifelong bachelor, these pages were Uncle Niko's babies. He never let it out of the apartment and only showed it to those he trusted most. Yes, he had allowed Sava to flip through the pages, giving him glimpses of its secrets. Most of it was beyond Sava's ability to comprehend, for though he was a clever man, with some scientific background, he was no intellectual match for the great Nikola Tesla.

That was why he needed the book now—to get it into the hands of someone who could decode it. And tonight, the opportunity to do just that was available—a small window of opportunity. It was all set up. Take the book and photograph it.

His palms were sweating. He gave the door to the bedroom one last glance. Uncle Niko had grown quiet. Was he about to come through the door?

A long pause ticked away.

Do it now!

As quick as his trembling hands could move, he shimmied the notebook from beneath the stack of papers, tossed it into his attaché case, and snapped it shut. Scooping up the case, he stepped over to the open archway.

"I'll be back to say good night, Uncle Niko," he said, his face burning with shame.

Stepping out of his uncle's suite and into the hallway, he paused, taking in a breath, his heart pounding. Now if he could just show it to his contact, get it photographed, and placed back undetected, only then would relief come.

Heading to the elevators, his case felt full of heft. He knew it was foolish to think so—the notebook weighed less than a pound—but the information it contained added to its mass. He continued to tremble, not only because of his betrayal but for the potential he carried, as if the secrets inside his case could disintegrate the very molecules of the hallway.

And Sava Kosanovic knew that, quite possibly, they could.

Chapter 8

The Main Lobby, 8:50 PM

WHEN THEIR TWO SONS were young, Dottie Tooke loved bringing the boys into their bed on Sunday mornings, to read the newspaper before attending Mass. Dottie would spread out the funny papers, gather the boys in her arms, and read through the antics of Mutt and Jeff, Li'l Abner, and Prince Valiant.

Paddy Tooke, still in his pajamas, would sit next to them, reading the rest of the paper.

Once done with the comics, Dottie would turn to the puzzle section of the funny papers, which showcased two look-alike cartoon scenes that were identical except for a few nuanced details—a monkey's tail would be upside down in one and upright in the other, a tree would be taller in this than that, a shirt button could be missing, a person smiled on one side and frowned on the other, that kind of thing. Dottie and the boys would quietly work through the hard-to-find differences and note each one.

Once discovered, they would hand the puzzle to their dad. The three of them would giggle and marvel as their father, using only a casual glance, would call out every mistake within a matter of seconds. The boys always thought he'd cheated somehow, but Dottie knew better. It was his gift, the Divine Cop-voice. That's what he did. He spotted the out of place.

With one eye on the lobby, Paddy Tooke was halfway through a news article about Hitler's all-out offensive toward Moscow, when those puzzles came to mind.

He spotted something out of place.

He had already cataloged a couple of oddities in the room. The two men in dark suits, for instance, sitting in the center of the lobby by themselves with dour expressions on their faces, their eyes drilled on the front doors. They hadn't moved in the last twenty minutes. Who were they? What could their business be?

He also noted the young woman in a green dress sitting by herself. She had set up a small office for herself, scribbling notes across papers on a makeshift desk she'd made of her briefcase on her lap. She, too, watched the room, although her eyes were more focused on the elevators.

But neither the two men nor the woman were anything compared to the odd man that had just ambled into the lobby.

Peering over the top of his newspaper, Paddy watched as the fellow came through the 8th Avenue entrance with unsure steps and the look of awe stamped on his face. Paddy knew immediately that the man was not George Sylvester Viereck, but he struck a curious chord, nonetheless. Like those funny-paper puzzles, the man didn't match the scenery.

He paused at the entryway, as if deciding to turn around and go back whence he came. His face did a series of circus tumbles until determination lit up, and he stepped forward.

Paddy studied him as he toddled across the marble floor toward the front desk, trying to ascertain why his curiosity alarm was clanging.

The first thing that came to mind was how the man was hatless. That wasn't too unusual—a lot of men went without hats these days. But Paddy could tell by the matted hair around the crown of his head that he had recently been wearing one—maybe only minutes ago. Yet, he carried no hat in his hand, either. So, what happened to it?

The second odd thing was his topcoat. It was all wrong. The brown cashmere didn't mesh with the dull white shirt and cheap bowtie beneath it. And while others may not have picked up on it—Paddy could tell the coat was slightly too big for the man—by maybe a size. A garment that stylish should be tailored to fit one's form. And yet, it didn't.

And the leather case he carried, that too, didn't fit. The man held it clumsily, as if it were a new accessory. It batted about his legs like a pennant flag in the wind. And for all the knee clunks that the case took just being walked across the lobby, its appearance was too un-battered to have been in the man's possession for too long. It looked elegant and well maintained. But not by this man!

Although, what truly set him off was the man's manner. He was nervous and overwhelmed. He didn't belong in this landscape...and he knew it.

Paddy folded his arms and puffed his pipe. He watched the man approach the front desk. A clerk came up to service him, and the hatless man bent in as if to speak a secret. The clerk nodded, turned away, and returned with a reservation ticket to register the man in as a guest.

Paddy gripped his Kaywoodie pipe and let out a snort. Yes, the man bothered him. His alarm was flaring.

Yet here was the problem: the man wasn't doing anything wrong. He was simply checking into the hotel. Yes, he looked nervous, but there was no crime in that. And yes, his dress was peculiar, but this was New York; fashion goofballs filled the city.

So why was Paddy bothered?

The things he had spotted were minor issues. Nothing to get bent out of shape over. He fought his tendency to take action. No! The man didn't need to be tailed. No! He didn't need to be questioned or detained. Leave the man be.

Besides, there were two solid reasons for ignoring the odd, hatless man: first, he was the hotel's concern, not his. And second, he wasn't George Sylvester Viereck—which was his concern.

So, battling the compulsion to follow his nose, Paddy made the undesirable decision to let the fish go...that is...until a minute later, when something else caused his instinct to pulsate into an unwavering thrum.

It came in the form of another out-of-place man.

The man entered the 8th Avenue door. Again, he wasn't George Sylvester Viereck but...

Something was off.

The man was as different from the hatless man as night from day. Paddy guessed his age to be twenty-five. He stood five-eleven, a hundred and seventy-five pounds, lean, with strong shoulders. Sharply dressed in a buff wool suit and cream-colored fedora, he carried no luggage. He strolled in confidently, his gait like an athlete. And, in contrast to the hatless man, he seemed to be in his element in the posh surroundings of the New Yorker—not intimidated in the least. He seemed to belong.

Yet a couple of minor itches gnawed at Paddy.

First, the man wore no topcoat. Nothing out of the ordinary. But having just seen the first man come in wearing a coat that obviously didn't belong to him, Paddy could picture that same cashmere coat completing the ensemble of this second man. It would fit him like skin.

The other thing he noticed was how the man scoured the room. His eyes flitted across the architecture with quick snapshots of every angle in the lobby—even landing on Paddy for a twinkle of a second before continuing by.

Those are fox eyes, thought Paddy. He's marking territory, his nose to the wind, sniffing the air for either predators or prey.

But what truly sent Paddy Tooke's gift sparking was something that happened in a flash of a second.

As the fox-eyed man had combed the room, Paddy noticed that he had passed over the hatless man registering at the front desk a snippet too quickly. And sure enough, as the hatless man was turning around with a key in hand, Paddy caught him flashing the well-dressed man a quick, subtle grin—which the second man purposely ignored, by spinning off course and heading straight toward the row of phone booths on the north wall.

It happened so fast that for a moment Paddy wondered if he'd imagined it.

But he hadn't. Those two knew each other. And they were up to something.

Yet it was his memory for faces that sealed it for Paddy Tooke.

A moment ago, their sightlines had collided for half a heartbeat, enough
time for Paddy to gather two facts about that face: first, he had never seen
it before in his life...and yet it looked eerily familiar. And second, as strange
as it seemed, he felt in his bones that the face belonged to a dead man.

Chapter 9

———◇———

The Main Lobby, 8:55 PM

THE ELEVATOR DOORS OPENED. Sava Kosanovic gave a nod to the operator before stepping into the lobby of the hotel. Kosanovic scanned the room for his secretary, Arlene Muzaric. It did not surprise him to find her making her way toward him. Her ability to anticipate his movements, as well as his needs, never ceased to amaze him.

As he awaited her arrival, he retrieved a pack of Chesterfields from his jacket and tapped out a cigarette. He snapped a flame from his silver-plated Zippo and lighted the end. He hated American cigarettes—preferring Turkish blends—but they were readily available and affordable on his wartime allowance.

He was releasing his first draw when his secretary materialized at his side.

Arlene Muzaric had a round, pleasant face. Her smile possessed a welcoming quality, which left you feeling valued. Behind the wire-rimmed glasses were intelligent gray eyes kindled with a love for life and an undercurrent of humor. She wore an olive-green dress, belted at the waist, and buttoned to the throat where a yellow floral print scarf was knotted. She clasped a batch of folders to her breasts.

Sava appreciated his secretary's energy and efficiency. Usually, her winsomeness elevated his mood. But not tonight. The stolen notebook in his attaché case darkened his mood.

She flashed him that wonderful welcoming smile, but he could only manage a tired grin in return.

"How is your uncle doing today?" she asked. "Is he well?"

Releasing a plume of smoke, he shrugged. "He didn't ask if George Westinghouse would be visiting...if that's any indication."

Arlene cocked her head. "George Westinghouse has been dead for almost thirty years, Mr. Kosanovic."

He grinned sardonically. "True, but during my last visit, Uncle Niko wondered why he hadn't been around lately."

"That poor man. He's as skinny as a rail. I'm sure it's affected his mind. He needs to eat better...get some fat on his bones."

Sava snorted a laugh. "Uncle Niko? He hasn't been fat since being weaned."

"Still, he's eighty-five years old. He needs to take care of himself."

"The man survives on saltine crackers. But it seems to work for him. He has more energy than I do."

"Your meeting got done early, I see." Arlene walked back to where she had been sitting. Sava followed. He could tell that she'd been working while she waited.

"Uncle Niko has another appointment. A Frenchman is coming by his suite," said Sava. He glanced at his watch. "Probably with him right now."

"A Frenchman?" she said, her nose scrunching up. "He wasn't on the schedule."

Sava smiled. For once, he had inside information that Arlene didn't. "He's an archeologist staying at the hotel tonight. He's been dying to meet Uncle Niko for years. The concierge set it up."

"I see." She glanced down at the attaché case. "And did Mr. Tesla sign the document?" She asked with an edge of displeasure.

Kosanovic caught the undertone in her voice and met her eye. "Yes, he signed it," he offered.

"Which one?" she asked, knowing full well that she had helped Sava draft two separate statements to present to his uncle—one that Uncle Niko would happily sign, and one that would take some coaxing. Understanding the admiration that much of Europe had for his famous uncle, Kosanovic had pressed for his uncle to release a statement denouncing the Nazi occupation of Yugoslavia. Both statements, which Arlene Muzaric helped draft, said essentially the same thing, however, one was nuanced in favor of King Peter (now living in exile in London) while the other statement encouraged the communist-backed resistance movement taking place in the country.

Sava saw a spark of fire in his secretary's face.

"Well," she asked again. "Which one did he sign?"

"The right one," said Sava, his tone defiant. They both took a seat in the chairs. Placing his attaché case on his lap, he opened it up and handed her a folder of documents.

She opened it and scanned the two pages, checking for which of the two documents contained the signature, and then smiled brightly. "Yes, Mr. Kosanovic, it is the right one."

Sava didn't smile back, letting out an exasperated breath. "It was the only one I submitted to him. After all, he didn't ask about Westinghouse."

She frowned at him. "That's an unkind thing to say, Mr. Kosanovic. After all, you know how he loves King Peter. Besides, your uncle shouldn't be used as a pawn for political benefit—especially when he's not fully...coherent."

"Sometimes, Miss Muzaric, I think you speak your mind too freely," he muttered.

She leaned in, the twinkle back in her eyes. "I'm an American, Mr. Kosanovic, we get to do that. Will the same be said of Yugoslavia if the communists have their way?"

Sava had hired Arlene Muzaric two months ago, and already she had proved to be an asset in organizing his disheveled life. Like Sava, she also was Serbian, but unlike him, she had been born in America and raised in Philadelphia. However, she spoke the Serbo-Croatian language with fluency and held a vast historical knowledge of the Serbian and Croatian peoples.

Sava appreciated her help but had noted that she held strong opinions on the tensions in Europe and Yugoslavia in particular; opinions that didn't necessarily align with his, but more so with his uncle's. It rankled him at times.

"You might also remember that you work for me, Miss Muzaric, and not the other way around."

"Yes, Mr. Kosanovic," she replied with a dash more sugar than necessary.

He ignored the condescension and handed her another folder. "Here are some more papers from Uncle Niko that need to be typed out and filed.

Leaning in to take up the folders, Arlene's eyes fell to the opened attaché case propped on his lap. Spotting the battered notebook lying there on top, she shot Kosanovic an alarmed look.

"Mr. Kosanovic, that's Mr. Tesla's private—"

"I know what it is!" he snapped.

Arlene's eyes narrowed. "But he never lets it out of his sight."

With an icy silence, Sava snapped the case shut. He could feel her judgmental glare crawling all over him. "What else do you have for me this evening, Miss Muzaric?" he asked.

When he finally glanced her way, he was met with a tight-lipped glower.

"Mr. Kosanovic, I don't like the idea of that notebook—"

"The notebook is my business, Miss Muzaric! And again, I remind you that you work for me, not the other way around."

Arlene drew back, possibly offended. Sava blew out his aggravation and quickly recovered, giving her a sympathetic look.

"I apologize for snapping, Miss Muzaric. I'm under a lot of pressure at the moment. Believe me, I will take good care of the notebook. I note your reservations. Now, what else is on the agenda for tonight?"

She relented and replied, "That *charming* Mr. Vuk Milosh is here." Acid laced the word 'charming.' Vuk Milosh was Kosanovic's Croatian liaison.

Arlene didn't care for him. "He told me he has a meeting with you tonight. I hope it has nothing to do with—"

"Where is Milosh?"

"He's waiting for you in the Manhattan Room."

"Is anyone with him?"

A glint of suspicion slipped across her face. "Are you referring to the Russians?"

Sava gave a start. "What do you know of that?"

"When I ran into Milosh earlier, four other men were with him. I'm pretty sure they were Russian. Although, he didn't introduce me. You know how Milosh can be. And he resents having to speak to you through me."

"Where are they now? The Russians?"

"I don't know. They must have rooms of their own here at the hotel. Milosh is eating alone, as far as I know."

Sava rubbed the back of his neck. "Four of them, you say? All Russian?"

"I assumed so. They didn't say much. They might not speak English, Mr. Milosh addressed them in Russian."

"Russian...and not Serbo-Croatian? You sure about that?"

She cocked her head and released a coy smile. "Well, Mr. Kosanovic, if he had spoken Serbo-Croatian I would have noticed, don't you think?"

Sava nodded.

"As it is," she continued, "I was able to pick up a bit of their conversation in Russian."

Sava's eyes widened. "You know Russian too, Miss Muzaric?" He hadn't known that—it hadn't been on her resume.

She shrugged. "Enough to stay out of trouble if the people's revolution comes to America."

Sava's eyes widened. "People's revo...?"

She shot him a wily wink. The issue of the notebook behind them, the sparkle in her eye was back.

"Ah, you tease me, Miss Muzaric."

"Maybe a little. We Americans have had our revolution, Mr. Kosanovic, and it turned out just fine. And, as far as I'm concerned, we don't need another...thank-you."

"Maybe...maybe not," Sava offered. He quickly turned away before she could respond. Talking politics with women always made him ill-at-ease—especially intelligent women who adequately challenged his own waffling stances.

"Four Russians?" he murmured.

"I believe two of them are from the embassy here in New York. Another is an older, bookish-looking fellow. He might be a doctor of some sort—at least they called him Doctor."

Sava nodded. He knew the man she meant. Dr. Boris Peshkin was the expert that Vuk Milosh had set up to examine Nikola's notes, and hopefully, make sense of them.

"And who was the fourth?" he asked.

Her face clouded. "I don't know. But I didn't like the looks of him at all, I haven't met many Russians that I like. But this guy..." She shuddered. "Creepy."

Sava swallowed hard. Vuk Milosh hadn't mentioned bringing anyone else but Dr. Peshkin to the meeting.

"Do you want me to locate where their rooms are?" she offered.

"No...I will meet with Milosh first." He turned to scrunch out his cigarette in a nearby standing ashtray. He stood. "Is that all then?"

Arlene shuffled all the files into one neat pile and hid them away in her briefcase. "Uh, there is one other thing. Dr. Fredrick Markovitch called."

"Dr. Markovitch? From my uncle's laboratory? What did he want?" Sava knew that Dr. Markovitch worked in the laboratory under the 59th Street Bridge, the one whose existence Uncle Niko closely guarded.

"He wouldn't say. He was in a panic over a phone call he'd received from a man named Kenneth Sweezy."

"I know of Sweezy. He's a friend of Uncle Niko, a writer. Sweezy has written articles about Uncle Niko. What did he want?"

"I have no clue. However, Dr. Markovitch said it was urgent. He needed to talk to you tonight."

"Tonight? Why?"

Arlene shrugged. "I tried to set up an appointment for tomorrow, but he wouldn't have it. It had to be tonight...said it couldn't wait."

Sava's brow knitted with concern—like he needed another emergency on his plate.

"I said I would call him as soon as your meeting with Dr. Tesla concluded. What would you like me to say?"

Sava grunted. "Let him know we can meet later this evening. I have another meeting after I get done with Milosh."

"Another meeting? It's not on the schedule," she said, full of suspicion.

"No, it's a private meeting." He glanced at his watch. "Tell Dr. Markovitch I can meet around ten-thirty. I know it's late, but there's nothing I can do about it."

"Yes, sir," she replied. She gathered her coat and briefcase and stood. "Will you be needing me for anything else tonight, sir?"

He snapped a curious look at her. "Do you have somewhere else to be, Miss Muzaric?"

A coy beam came into her face. "Well...I would like to go up to the room where Benny Goodman is and...you know..." Her eyebrows did a seductive dance.

Sava's face lit with shock. "Miss Muzaric...I didn't even know you had a love interest." Sava flushed.

"Love interest? Please. I wish! Benny Goodman, he's playing at the hotel tonight."

She gave a nod toward the sandwich-sign at the base of the Grand Staircase. Sava swung a look that way, taking in the musician's photo as he posed with his clarinet.

"Oh! This Mr. Goodman you speak of is a musician?"

"That's right. I thought I might kick up my heels a bit."

Sava smiled. "You dance the Charleston, Miss Muzaric?"

She threw back her head to release a throaty laugh.

"The Charleston? Mr. Kosanovic, we don't do that tired old kick anymore. We do the Lindy Hop, or the Trunky Doo, or the Jitterbug...or if you're daring..." She leaned in close; he could feel her breath on his cheek. "...we do the Rummm...ba." The word rolled off her tongue, low and seductive. "Come up to the Grand Ballroom and join me, Mr. Kosanovic. Let off some steam."

Sava's face reddened. "Miss Muzaric, you're teasing me again."

She beamed a smile. "You take life too seriously, Mr. Kosanovic."

Sava nodded, allowing that, yes, he did take life too seriously, but war and Nazi occupation did that to you. Watching this wonderful creature in front of him, he wondered if he would ever be as carefree as she.

"I'll call Dr. Markovitch," she said. "And if you need me, I'll be in the Grand Ballroom. Be careful with the Russians. I don't trust them. And please, take care of Mr. Tesla's notebook."

She spun away to head for the phone booths.

Sava watched her go, wondering if he shouldn't start looking for another secretary, one a bit more submissive and...less of a distraction.

He then turned toward the Manhattan Room.

Vuk Milosh had brought four Russians. Sava had expected one—Dr. Peshkin. He hoped they hadn't come with scheming intentions. He would never allow his uncle's notebook to be turned over to them. He needed to return it before Uncle Niko noticed it missing.

With hesitant steps, he started toward the Manhattan Room

He wasn't looking forward to meeting with Milosh. Sava had little trust in his contact from his home country of Yugoslavia. The man was prideful and politically driven. However, as much as he didn't care for Milosh...

He cared for Russians even less.

Chapter 10

———◦○◦———

The Main Lobby, 9:01 PM

ENTERING THE HOTEL LOBBY, the thief scanned the room. In the weeks leading up to the job, he had visited the hotel just to get the layout of the place and to identify, if possible, the hotel security team.

He spotted no one from those earlier reconnaissance visits.

He did, however, notice two men sitting in armchairs in the center of the lobby. Dark suits, dour faces, and watchful eyes. Their attention swept over him as he came through the door, causing his pulse to race. They gave him the once over, but they didn't appear to be hotel staff. Would he have to worry about them? Maybe.

As for other potential threats, the only other person, he noticed, was a nondescript gentleman puffing a pipe across the way. Their eye-lines had crossed briefly, and a hint of curiosity had sparked in the man's face. The fellow looked harmless, but the thief would monitor him too—just in case.

At the desk, Eddie the cab driver flashed a mischievous grin the thief's way.

Anger flared and the thief quickly turned away to avoid eye-contact with him. The idiot!

Tamping down his anger, he veered a path toward the row of phone booths along the north wall. It was time to place the call. If his mark hadn't checked in yet, there would be no point in proceeding.

Approaching the row of phone booths, his heart sank. Every booth occupied. What luck! Eight phone booths and not one available. He would now have to stand in the open. He only hoped that Eddie had the good sense to avoid contact. If Eddie approached him, he may have to forfeit tonight's operation altogether.

He edged over to an art déco davenport next to the phone booths. On the wall above was a mural painted by the artist Louis Jambor. Attempting to act as nonchalant as possible, the thief pretended to take in the beautiful work.

He felt exposed.

He fought the urge to glance back into the lobby to check if the two men in the dark suits were watching. Juices of paranoia stirred. The minutes felt elongated. From a speaker hanging on the wall, a strain of classical music played. As he listened to the lilting notes, a memory stabbed him, causing his anxiety to heighten even more.

Natalie.

The music reminded him of her.

Was that Shubert being played?

Since describing her to Eddie earlier in the evening, he hadn't been able to shake her from his thoughts. She plagued him even now. It only added to his aggravation.

———— ◆◇◆ ————

Manhattan, September 7th, 1940

"Did you study classical music at university?" I asked.

We were relaxing in her suite at the Navarro Hotel on 59th Street. She lived across from Central Park but had no view of it. That didn't matter.

I didn't need a view when she was in the room. She was enough. Simply stunning. Sprawled out on the couch, my head in her lap, her fingers combed through my hair. From a Zenith Console Radio in the corner, an orchestra was playing Shubert—at least that's what she'd told me. Otherwise I wouldn't have known.

"Shush," she scolded with a smile, pressing a delicate finger to my lips. "The music."

I grinned at the rebuke. Was it really because I was interrupting Shubert? Or was it her way of squelching a question about her past? I had violated an unspoken rule between us. I had tried to pry into who we were before we met.

Natalie and I lived in the moment. No past, no future, only now. As if time had begun with a spark while reaching for a pretzel. The two of us born at the World's Fair. Our previous lives had been lived by strangers; strangers that neither of us recognized or acknowledged.

And so, from the beginning, she spoke little of her previous self and I did likewise. It heightened the mystery between us, and I was only too happy to be untethered from my past. I lived in constant fear of being questioned about it. I knew I couldn't lie—not to her. And telling the truth mortified me. The thought of alienating her because of my criminal life filled me with dread.

Natalie was a woman in possession of herself. She carried herself with quiet dignity. She was intelligent and an artful conversationalist. The last two months had been a whirlwind of excitement. And one of change.

Since touching her hand at the World's Fair, I hadn't stolen a single thing.

I was so relaxed on the sofa, looking into her eyes above me, that I barely noticed when the music from the radio abruptly stopped and a news anchor broke in.

"We interrupt this program for a news bulletin. German planes have conducted a mass air raid over London earlier tonight. The German blitz came in the early hours and casualties are mounting as..."

A pall came over me, the world intruding.

I felt Natalie stiffen, as if bothered by that other voice in the room. I got up from the sofa and walked over to turn the radio off.

But as I placed my hand on the knob, a spark flared across the back of my fingers. Natalie's hand was touching mine. She had gotten up too and was standing behind me.

"No," she whispered. "I want to hear."

I was about to object—the intruding voice wrecking our private atmosphere—but I noticed her staring, not at me, but somewhere in the distance.

"What is it?" I asked.

Slowly, her head turned to face me.

"My home is being bombed," she whispered, almost too soft to hear.

A heaviness fell over my heart. The dread in her face so obvious. I wanted to bash the radio to pieces for making her look that way.

It was the first time she'd ever mentioned her home. I had already guessed that she was from England—her accent gave that away, but I never pictured her there. After all, we were newly born, living in the now.

But tonight, Nazi bombs were shattering that fantasy.

Emotion choked in my throat.

"I'm sure it will be all right," I offered...wondering.

The newscast ended. Shubert was playing again. She continued to stare.

Without warning, she swung around to embrace me, burying her lips on mine. Her fingernails biting into the back of my neck. The kiss was intense, fervent, full of passion.

Full of denial.

The German blitz evaporated as we clung to each other, struggling to keep our newly born world intact.

⸺◦◆◦⸺

New Yorker Hotel, October 8th, 1941

The thief shook away the memories, forcing himself to focus on the Louis Jambor painting in front of him.

No, he decided. That wasn't Shubert playing after all. It was Mozart.

From the corner of his eye, he caught someone approaching the row of phone booths from the other side, a woman in glasses, wearing a green dress. She held a briefcase and a packet of files, along with her coat. She squinted at the occupied phone booths, while impatiently taking glimpses of her watch. She, too, wanted a booth. It could turn into a foot race to the first available one.

Just then, a booth door folded open, and a chubby man in a tuxedo exited. Fortunately, the booth was closer to the thief than to the woman. He leaped toward it before she could blink.

In his rush, the thief nearly collided with the tuxedoed gentleman, surprising him. He lurched out of the way, banging into the late-approaching woman. Her files spilled across the floor. The chubby fellow shrugged at the mess and waddled off. She stood for a moment, gape-mouthed, and then shot the thief an annoyed glare. The thief, concerned about the attention brought on by the incident, slunk into the phone booth before she could comment. He released a weak smile, touching his hat brim as a means of apology.

Then shut the door.

Peering through the glass, the woman did not look happy. She was busy gathering papers from the floor, scowling angrily. He responded by turning away. Not very gentlemanly, but he needed to focus.

Lifting the handset off the hook, he dialed the memorized number.

Time to check on his mark. Time to get the ball rolling.

Chapter 11

The Main Lobby, 9:12 PM

THE FACE PLAGUED HIM—THE dead man who had just entered the New
Yorker Hotel.

Sergeant Detective Paddy Tooke clenched his Kaywoodie between his
teeth. The man with the foxlike eyes was now inside a phone booth on
the other side of the lobby. He had nearly bowled over a woman getting
there. Paddy recognized her as the woman that had set up a makeshift office
earlier. The woman wasn't happy. Her files had dumped. Her vexation was
obvious even from across the lobby as she squatted to gather papers from
the floor.

Frustration smothered Paddy. For the first time in his life, his gift for
facial recognition was failing to put paint on the canvas. That face was so
familiar...and yet it wasn't! And the fellow's name also eluded him, as if his
brain contained a sealed envelope marked *Top Secret*. He wrestled to put
the face in context. Had he, or had he not seen it before?

Added to the frustration was the pesky sense that the owner of that face
was dead. But how could that be?

And more to the point...what was his connection to the first man who
had come into the hotel moments before? The odd-looking one in the
ill-fitting coat.

Paddy stood and casually eased up to one of the square pillars supporting the mezzanine balcony and peeked around it. There at the front desk was the man in the topcoat. The desk clerk handed the man his key, and a bellhop bounced his way, sweeping up the leather case he'd carried in. The odd man appeared alarmed by the gesture and tried to grab it back. The bellboy spoke to him, smiling, and the man hesitantly handed it over. The two of them turned toward the elevator alcove. They passed the phone booths along the way, the man's gaze riveted on them.

The man and bellhop entered an elevator car, and the doors slid shut.

Paddy hurried over to the elevators, passing the phone booths without looking at them. Inconspicuously as possible, he fiddled with his pipe over a chrome-plated ashtray on the floor in the alcove, watching the needle indicator above the elevator. It didn't stop until the thirty-fifth floor.

Why was he so bothered by these two men? They were not his business.

He returned to the lobby and walked up to the front desk, showing his badge to the clerk who had served the man.

"The man who was just here, could you give me his name?" he asked.

The clerk hesitated. Another clerk stood behind him, lurking near the back hallway. It was the red-headed fellow Paddy had noticed before. He was smoking a cigarette—pinching the butt from underneath with his thumb and forefinger as if holding the legs of a spider. The redhead's eyes kindled with alertness and he quickly backed into the hallway.

The first clerk carefully eyed the badge and then looked down at the ledger in front of him. "Edward Petrowski," he finally said.

"Did he have a reservation?" asked Paddy.

"Yes, sir. Made earlier in the evening."

"He went up to the thirty-fifth floor," said Paddy, a statement, not a question.

"Yes, sir...room 3527. It's one of our suites. The reservation specifically asked for a room on that floor facing 34th Street."

"I see," muttered Paddy, puffing his pipe. "Edward Petrowski, you say." The name registered nothing in Paddy's memory banks.

The kid nodded. "Is there a problem...uh, officer?" He looked concerned, as if he was about to be arrested himself.

"No, no," smiled Paddy. "I just thought that I'd seen him before. I must have been mistaken."

Paddy turned away from the desk and returned to the chair he'd occupied moments ago, wondering what he should do? A quick scan of the room told him that John Williamson, the house detective, was nowhere to be seen.

The two men in the dark suits hadn't moved. He again wondered who they could be—members of Williamson's team? Maybe, however, they had taken no interest in either of the two men that had just entered the hotel, so they were very sloppy at their jobs, or they were waiting for someone specific. Their eyes remained glued to the entrances.

Should he talk to the clerk again? Have Williamson summoned? But what would he tell them? That he had suspicions? A hunch?

I've just seen a man wearing a topcoat too big for him go to his room, and I also saw another man—who I'm pretty sure is dead—make a phone call from one of your booths!

They would think he was crazy.

Maybe he was.

He picked up his newspaper.

The blank canvas laughed. And the *Top Secret* envelope in his mind remained sealed.

Chapter 12

Lobby Front Desk, 9:17 PM

HENRY BLACKSMITH BACKED INTO the hallway, his fret level accelerating. He put his cigarette out against the wall and dropped the butt on the carpet.

The police detective had come up to the desk again and looked right at him. Oh, he pretended to be asking about one of the other guests, but Blacksmith had to wonder if that had only been a ruse—a way of possibly comparing him to the photo he'd given to the house dick earlier.

He needed to make sure. And there was only one way to settle the issue.

He needed to break into House Detective John Williamson's office to examine the photograph.

Several minutes earlier, Blacksmith had noticed the house dick leave his office to take an elevator to somewhere in the building. Now was as good a time as any.

With quick, quiet steps, he crept down the hall to the office door. He knew he had only minutes to get in, find the photograph, and get out.

The door was locked. Fortunately, that was not a problem.

Two weeks ago, after first getting on at the hotel, Blacksmith had done a thorough reconnaissance of the hotel offices. The Registration Supervisor, Frank Delong, had an office behind the Front Desk, just down the hall from Williamson's office. Delong's office usually remained unlocked during working hours, and Blacksmith had noted the availability of a key cabinet on the wall. The cabinet contained duplicates of the hotel room keys, for when customers forgot or lost theirs. It also held a set of master passkeys, which could open any door in the hotel—used by chambermaids and valets to enter any room in the building. A week ago, Blacksmith had appropriated a passkey, made a mold of it in putty, and had fashioned his own key, which he kept on him at all times.

The key fit perfectly, and Williamson's door opened. Giving a quick glance around to make sure no one was watching, he slipped inside.

The light was off, and he took a moment to get his bearings in the gloom. He felt along the wall and found the light switch. Reluctantly, he turned it on, knowing full well that someone could come walking by and spot the light through the frosted glass window of the door. But he had no choice. He needed light to find the photo. Besides, hopefully, he would only be in here for less than a minute.

He sidled up to the wooden desk, scanning its surface for the photograph. It wasn't there. The top of the desk was orderly. No clutter and no photos. He came around the desk and tried the drawers. Locked. A silver-plated letter opener neatly aligned with the blotter on the desk. He figured he could use it to pry open the desk if need be, but he would only use it as a last resort.

Behind him, against the wall, were two metal filing cabinets. He tried to open the cabinet drawers, but all were locked, and he could see that the locking mechanisms differed from the keys to the office doors. The master key wouldn't fit.

Frustrated, he thought that he might have to use the letter opener after all.

That's when he spotted the credenza behind the office chair on the other side of the desk. On top of the credenza were two wooden trays, marked as in/out boxes. Both stacked with papers. Blacksmith fingered through the items stacked in the 'In' box and...yes! There crammed a few layers down was the photo.

He slid it out and gasped.

No, it was not his face on the black-and-white picture, yet he recognized it immediately. It was the contact coming tonight. The one person who knew of his mission—the one who had secured the job for him at the hotel. George Sylvester Viereck.

Why would a police detective be interested in him? And why tonight, of all nights? And, more importantly, could they connect Viereck to him? If so, his mission might have to be scrubbed.

Blacksmith bristled. The damn fool! It was due to all those articles praising the Fuhrer and National Socialism. It was bound to bring attention to him. It is impossible to be covert when you're so bluntly overt. He might as well have been wearing a swastika armband.

Blacksmith had first met Viereck in Germany. They had been introduced six months ago at the New Reich Chancellery in Berlin, even taking in an intimate lunch in the Fuhrer's private living quarters. Blacksmith had taken an immediate dislike of Viereck. He thought him to be pompous and overly intellectual, with an overblown perspective of his own self-importance. However, both Himmler and the Fuhrer loved the man, for a couple of reasons. First, they felt his writings could hold sympathetic sway with the American public, and second, because they saw an opportunity in his friendship with the scientific mastermind, Nikola Tesla.

Hitler, of course, wanted every military edge he could achieve. He had heard of Tesla's idea for a particle beam device that could disintegrate planes from out of the skies at two hundred and fifty miles away. He drooled at the possibility of weaponizing such technology. He would not only conquer his enemies in Europe; he would own the ether above it for decades to come.

A plan was birthed. Get an agent planted in the hotel and work with the contact, Viereck, to obtain every design formula and blueprint associated with the device, and, if possible, steal a working prototype—which Viereck adamantly claimed to exist.

Much of the scientist's real secrets, he realized, were in a notebook that Tesla guarded with a keen eye. Viereck, himself, had never looked inside the book, and Tesla had never shown it to him, but the scientist had referred to it several times in the course of their discussions.

The Fuhrer wanted the book.

The problem was that Tesla rarely left his apartment these days.

By virtue of his new job, Blacksmith had already been in the old man's suite on three separate occasions, but Tesla had been present each time, so there was little he could do but familiarize himself with the layout of the suite—the office section in particular. It was during the last visit, yesterday afternoon, that he had spotted, what he believed to be, the notebook, buried under a pile of papers on the old man's desk. He called Viereck immediately, and the two construed a plot to get it.

The plan was simple. Viereck would arrive at the scientist's suite unannounced, as he often did, and cajole Tesla up to the Terrace Restaurant for a late dinner. Viereck was confident that Tesla would take him up on the offer, as he rarely refused an evening with a fellow intellectual. Tesla loved socializing with Viereck. The scientist considered Viereck's poetry to be genius, even committing to memory several of the man's works. Viereck felt that a leisurely dinner would get the man out of the suite for at least two hours. Blacksmith, using his passkey, could then photograph the notebook, and leave as if it had been untouched.

But now...

Now a police detective was on the lookout for Viereck. He needed to call and warn him immediately.

Williamson had a phone on his desk. Blacksmith folded the photograph and crammed it into his jacket pocket—no sense leaving it around for Williamson to study further. He was reaching for the handset to make the call, when...

"What are you doing in here, young man?"

Blacksmith whirled around, his hand instinctively moving toward the handgun concealed behind his boutonniere. But he stopped short.

It was Frank Delong, the Reservation Supervisor—his boss.

A strained pause filled the room.

"Well?" snapped Delong.

"It was my break, sir. I was on my way to make a phone call…my mother's been ill and…the door was open. I saw the phone on the desk and…"

"Well, you can't be in here. This is a private office." The man's jaw firmed. "Personal calls should be made from one of the phone booths in the lobby."

"Yes sir," mumbled Blacksmith. Not one for being contrite, he did what he could to look thoroughly chastised.

Delong stepped off to the side of the doorway, giving a sweep of his arm as if to usher him out. Blacksmith took the cue and shuffled past him. That's when his boss asked a question that stopped him dead in his tracks.

"Blacksmith…I thought I read on your resume that your mother is dead?"

Henry Blacksmith swung around to face him. He was met with a hard, suspicious glare. Tension hardened between them. In a flash, Blacksmith considered his course of action. With his shoulders turned perpendicular to Delong's chest, he slipped his opposite hand into his trousers pocket, easing down the zipper inside that would give him access to the razor knife strapped to his leg.

"My mother is dead," he said. "I was raised by my aunt. And I've always considered her my mum. S…she was in a bad way when I called on her this afternoon…and I was just concerned."

Delong held his stare. Blacksmith could see him pondering. His fingers worked through the slit in his pocket, grasping the handle of the knife. He could have it out in a heartbeat.

Finally, Delong's face melted into a sympathetic look. "Okay, Blacksmith, go use a telephone in the lobby. And the next time I find you where you don't belong, it'll be your job!"

"Yes, sir." He replied.

He turned away, and stepping into the hallway, a sneer slithered across his face. The idiot! If only he knew how close he'd come to having his throat slit.

He headed for the phone booths. He needed to contact George Sylvester Viereck before it was too late.

Chapter 13

The Main Lobby, 9:17 PM

"New Yorker Hotel. How may I direct your call?" The voice was pleasant and female.

"The front desk, please," said the thief. He settled back on the red leather bench tucked inside the phone booth. The woman who had dropped her files on the floor outside the booth had left.

"One moment, sir," came the operator's voice.

A couple of seconds later, a male voice came on the line. "New Yorker Hotel front desk. How may I help you?"

"Good evening," said the thief. "My name is Pierpont Van Buren and I'm calling on behalf of the Museum of Natural History, confirming Monsieur Jean Pierre Marie Montet's arrival this evening."

A brief pause followed before the voice responded, "Yes, sir. Monsieur Montet checked in two hours ago. Would you like me to connect you to his suite?"

"No, that will not be necessary. However, can you please confirm whether Monsieur Montet received the gifts, which were left for him compliments of the museum?"

The thief had called two days prior to set up a welcome bouquet, along with tickets to the Benny Goodman Orchestra, which the thief had purchased via courier the day before—and by doing so, he had also verified the mark's room number, Suite 3227.

"Yes sir, Monsieur Montet appreciated the gesture."

"It's the least we can do. By the way, we are setting up a luncheon in his honor tomorrow afternoon, and we were wondering if Monsieur Montet is traveling with any other personnel—besides his wife, that is."

Another pause. "Uh, yes sir. Monsieur Montet has arranged for a connecting room for his security man."

The thief cringed. He thought it possible that the mark might bring his own security. A small hitch that needed to be handled, but he responded with, "Ah, excellent. Would it be possible to make sure that a third ticket for tonight's show is sent to his suite? And please bill the museum."

"Yes, Mr. Van Buren."

The thief hung up the phone. Hopefully, the guard would take the bait.

He knew from the start that this job would either be done the easy way or the...more interesting way. The easy way required the lack of a guard. But with this little nuisance, the second solution would have to be employed—the more dangerous one. Ironically, the more dangerous solution was safer in this regard: less chance of being caught. Even so, he was committed to it now, even if the guard took the bait and went to the show.

The thief had read of Montet's impending visit to New York in the *Daily Mirror* two weeks ago. Montet was a French Egyptologist. The war had disrupted his digs in the northeastern Delta Nile region, but not before he had stumbled upon the royal necropolis in Tanis of the twenty-first and twenty-second dynasty of Egypt. The inscription on the tomb was for Osorkon II. By the time Montet got there, much of the tomb in Tanis had already been plundered. Even so, he excavated several valuable items, including alabaster jars, a heart scarab, and a funerary figurine.

One other fantastic item had been excavated: a gold bracelet. The thief recalled the photo of the piece from the article. Made of solid gold, it was an elegant piece, with interlacing lines embossed with Egyptian hieroglyphics and a hinged opening. The accompanying article had said the French archeologist would be bringing it with him on his visit to New York.

The minute he'd read the article, he began making plans. He knew of just the buyer for such a priceless artifact, an old friend who dealt in antiquities. He rang him up, and they negotiated a five-figure sum for the bracelet on the spot.

Now all he had to do was get the treasure.

The thief knew each suite had a built-in wall safe—a Meilink model G7 flush mount with an 'Eagle' lock combination tumbler. The safe was a measly barrier to him. His Pops had trained him on combination locks from the time he could walk—he learned his numbers by spinning those dials.

The only hitch now was circumventing the guard. A minor setback, but one he had planned for.

The thief opened the door to the phone booth and exited. It was time to head for the Terminal Barbershop for his shave and wait for Eddie to return with his key and coat. He did another survey of the room. Still no house detectives in sight. The two men in dark suits were still in place, but their attention remained on the front entrance. So far, so good.

It wasn't until he started up the Grand Staircase, to the upper mezzanine level, that a caution shimmied up his spine.

Over the years, the thief had refined an intuitive alertness to when he was being observed. He always paid attention to it. His Pops would say:

> *Listen to the hairs on the back of your neck. They're like a thousand antennae receiving signals from the molecules of nearby thoughts.*

He paused, casually glancing over his shoulder. He caught the flash of a face ducking behind a newspaper.

The man with the pipe! The harmless-looking, non-descript gentleman.

Had he been watching? Was he going to be a problem? The neck hairs quivered. Caution flared.

Maybe.

Chapter 14

———◇———

The Manhattan Room Restaurant, 9:22 PM

SAVA KOSANOVIC FOLLOWED THE hostess as she made a weaving path through the dimness of the Manhattan Room. In the far corner, a man sat at a table pressed up against a window overlooking 34th Street, his face intense. A plate of bread and a bottle of wine sat next to a half-smoked cigar smoldering in an ashtray. As they approached, the man glanced up and stood, a sudden smile cresting his face.

"Greetings, comrade!" blurted Vuk Milosh, his arms spread, ready to embrace him.

Sava cringed at the tactless reception. He caught the hostess squish a question into her forehead—as if she hadn't heard right. Sava waited until she turned to walk away before giving Milosh a quick, stiff embrace.

"Be more discreet, Vuk," Sava said sharply. "We are in America. The people here have a low tolerance for communistic jargon."

Milosh waved away the rebuke. He was a handsome man, twenty years younger than Sava, with ebony black hair, a firm chin, crystal blue eyes, and a wry grin that reeked of superiority.

"Ach, it would surprise you how many like-minded people are here in America," spoke Milosh, in Serbo-Croatian. "They're in the government, the unions, the newspapers, and most important...in Hollywood. We have many friends here, Sava."

Sava's head swiveled around, taking in the room. "Still, I come to this hotel often, and it would not be good to be targeted as a red threat."

Yuk Milosh eyed him with that superior grin, as if being regarded as a 'red threat' an honorable consideration. He glanced at the attaché case Sava carried. "Do you have something for me?"

Sava gave a curt nod. He bent and placed the case discreetly on the floor by the table. He was not about to flaunt his uncle's notebook in a public place. He would open the case when the time was right.

"Good, Dr. Peshkin is on his way." He glanced at his watch. "Should be here any moment. I've taken a suite here at the hotel, myself. We'll look everything over upstairs. Thankfully, Natka is here. She will photograph the pages and help with any necessary translation."

"Natka?" exclaimed Sava, almost choking on the name. "You're not talking about...Natka Stefanovic?"

Vuk grinned. "Yes, Natka. She's upstairs in the suite, waiting for Dr. Peshkin."

A wave of astonishment hit Sava. His knees became weak, and he eased himself into a chair at the table. "How is that possible? I thought..."

"You thought, as I did, that she had been killed during the blitz in London. But fortunately, Natka is alive and well."

"Natka is alive?" mumbled Sava. A new joy bleeding into his system.

Sava's family and the Stefanovic's had been close friends for years, even staying in touch after the Stefanovic's had immigrated to England in the late '20s. Natka was only a girl at the time. Sava became reacquainted with Natka a decade ago, after she and her family had returned to Belgrade for an extended visit. By this time, she had blossomed into a beautiful, intelligent teenager. She called him Uncle Sava, even though there was no blood between them. She had just been accepted to the University of Prague—the same university where his Uncle Niko had studied and had made a name for himself. And like him, she would study physics and engineering. Sava was excited for her and had closely kept track of her progress at university. She proved to be a brilliant student, with a keen scientific mind and an aptitude for critical thinking.

Her studies, however, had been cut short after the Munich Agreement took effect in 1938, annexing portions of Czechoslovakia. Seeing the storm clouds on the horizon, her parents begged her to return to London before troubles escalated—a wise move, for soon the Nazi occupation shuttered all Czech universities, with many students taken as prisoners.

That's when Sava had stepped in. He arranged for her to come to New York, to work in his uncle's laboratory, while things settled in Europe.

Sava had enjoyed her brief stay in New York. She had been a ray of light, an eager learner, and one to make heads turn while strolling the city streets together. She was full of promise, making headway in the male-dominated scientific field. Even Uncle Niko took note of her contributions in the laboratory.

But then tragedy struck.

Earlier in the year, her mother had taken ill, and Natka suddenly had to return to London. It was shortly afterward that Sava got word that she and her family had been killed during the blitz. The news broke his heart. He had loved Natka as a daughter.

"Natka is alive," repeated Sava. "Thank God."

Vuk Milosh's eyes narrowed. "Thank who?"

A pause hung in the air. Sava could feel the man's self-righteous scrutiny. Even an offhand utterance to a Deity could offend a staunch communist like Vuk. As for Sava, who had been raised with a strong church background, he was not so quick to abandon the idea of a God for political expediency—even if it wasn't the same idea found in the catechisms he had memorized as a boy.

"How did Natka find her way to New York?" asked Sava, somewhat hurt that she hadn't taken the time to look him up.

Vuk shrugged. "She came with me, of course. A wife should always accompany her husband."

Shock slammed into Sava. "Wife?" he croaked. "What are you talking about?"

Vuk picked up his cigar and puffed on it. "Natka's my wife. I thought you knew that."

"No...I didn't."

"We married back when we were still students in Czechoslovakia."

Sava gulped. "I...I recall you knew each other in Prague, but..."

Milosh shrugged. "We married."

Sava remembered the day that Natka had introduced him to a fellow student named Vuk Milosh. Handsome, intelligent, and charismatic. But even then, Sava took an immediate dislike for the man, as he had also been brash, opinionated, and condescending—and an open communist. After the meeting, Sava had pulled Natka aside to ask about his intentions with her. She brushed off his concerns, stating that their relationship was purely platonic. It had left Sava relieved.

But now, sitting across from the man who'd become his contact with the freedom fighters in Yugoslavia, the thought of him being married to Natka sickened him.

Then something occurred to him.

"B...but that means that she was married when she worked here in New York?"

Vuk's grin evaporated. "Ach! Yes...we...had separated for a time. I thought our marriage was doomed." He gave a wave of his hand, "Troubles...you know. But I still loved her. It devastated me to hear she had been killed. However, I was in London a few months ago and behold! She is alive. We ran into one another. We are very happy together now."

"That is good news, Vuk. I'm glad for you both." Sava spoke the words, but without conviction. Though happy to hear that her life had been spared, he was not so pleased to learn she had married Vuk Milosh, nor that she had kept the marriage secret from him. He had thought of Natka as one who respected and trusted her Uncle Sava as a mentor and confidant. Maybe he didn't know her as well as he thought.

"She works with me now...as my assistant," said Milosh. "Her English is excellent—like a first language—as well as her Russian. She's good at translating documents, and with her scientific background...well, she's indispensable."

"Yes, yes, Natka would be an asset to any organization."

"And now that Dr. Boris Peshkin has arrived, she can work with him—help make sense of your uncle's notes."

Sava grew quiet at the mention of Peshkin. A fresh wave of guilt washed over him. Maybe Natka's involvement was good. Although—as hypocritical as it may be—he felt annoyed by her willingness to be involved in such duplicity.

Milosh leaned in and lowered his voice. "I have some things to discuss before we meet with our friends."

"Friends!" snapped Sava. "Arlene told me about the other Russians. You told me it would just be Dr. Peshkin. Who are the others?"

Milosh shrugged. "Anatoli Yakovlev is the station chief at the Russian Consulate. He and one of his associates will be with us. And our comrades in Russia thought it best that Dr. Peshkin travel with an escort as well."

Milosh poured wine into a glass and pushed it across the table to Sava. "Have you read the papers?"

Sava nodded. A grave look creased his face. "Hitler is marching towards Moscow. They say he's only two hundred kilometers away."

"It's bad, Sava. The papers have whitewashed the story. If the European public knew the full extent of the attack, it would demoralize them."

"I'm sorry to hear it."

Milosh shot a glance toward the attaché case next to the table. "Perhaps help is on the way? We certainly could use the device as soon as possible!"

Sava's eyes drifted to the case. "Yes, I hope the notebook will be helpful in the war effort."

"Our...friends are getting impatient," sighed Milosh.

Sava remained quiet, uncomfortable with the not-so-subtle reminder that his uncle was indebted to the Soviets for $25,000. He took a long draw from his wine glass, avoiding Milosh's glare. He wanted to change the subject quickly.

"And our homeland, Vuk? What is the news there?"

Vuk Milosh shook his head. "Occupation doesn't sit well with our people, Sava. Nazis everywhere. Our country is a mess. As always, we end up fighting each other as an impotent monarchy sits backs and lets it happen. It must stop!"

Milosh slammed a fist on the table, sending a clatter into the room. Nearby guests shot glances their way. Embarrassed, Sava's face reddened.

"What news have you of the exiles—King Peter and Ivan Subasic?" asked Kosanovic.

Subasic presided as the titular head of the government as the Ban of Croatia.

Milosh sneered. "Both are in England hiding and sucking at the teat of Churchill. I hope they both stay there. There is no room for the old ways anymore, Sava. Once we throw the Nazis into the sea, and the dust settles from this war, a new day will dawn on the world...a world of the people."

Sava grew quiet, wondering what that 'new day' would look like with people like Vuk Milosh at the helm.

"We don't just fight the Nazis, Sava. It's that blasted Draza Mihailovic and his Chetnik forces. They are for the monarchy. Fortunately, for the time being, Churchill is backing Tito."

"Churchill is backing the communists?" blurted Sava, astonished. "That hardly seems possible."

"Churchill is a sly old fox. He will always back the winning side, my friend. He knows that Tito and his communists have stronger forces than the Chetniks—and the people back us, of course."

Sava wasn't sure if that was true. "But still...do we trust Churchill?"

Vuk Milosh flared a wolfish grin. "As we say, 'it is okay to walk with the devil until you get to the bridge'. Churchill supplies us with weapons and intelligence. With his help—as well as help from the Soviets—we'll get to the bridge. We'll defeat both the Nazis and the Chetniks too. Once we are free to make our own decisions, we can stop kissing Churchill's backside, and align with our true friends, the Soviets."

Sava gave a weak nod of approval. He felt conflicted. Part of him yearned for a *new day* for his countrymen, while another part respected King Peter—maybe not as much as Uncle Niko, but still.

Vuk Milosh leaned in again. "I have heard good things spoken about you in the inner circles, Sava." he whispered. "Arso Jovanovic—Tito's right-hand man—has talked about making you the first ambassador of Yugoslavia to America."

"Ambassador?" said Kosanovic, taken aback.

Milosh nodded. "He has suggested you to Tito. Which means it is as good as accomplished."

A giddy wave swept over Sava. Ambassador! He liked the idea of it. He enjoyed living in New York, and such a position could assist his efforts in establishing a museum for his Uncle Niko. A smile rolled into his fleshy cheeks.

But it was a short-lived smile, as Milosh suddenly blurted, "Ach! Our friends have arrived."

Swiveling his head, Sava Kosanovic saw the same pretty hostess leading the four Russians their way.

They did not look pleased. But then, Sava thought, Russians rarely do.

Chapter 15

—◦—

The Main Lobby, 9:36 PM

PRETENDING TO READ HIS newspaper, Paddy Tooke continued watching the front doors. However, mounting frustration caused his mind to race in other directions. For fifteen minutes he'd been wrestling with the face—the dead man.

Several minutes ago, he had watched the man with the foxlike eyes leave the phone booth to ascend the grand staircase to the mezzanine level. However, halfway up, the man had glanced Paddy's way, nearly catching him in the act of spying. After reaching the mezzanine level, the man had turned into the hotel barbershop.

Had a dead man walked those stairs?

Let it go. He thought to himself. It's not your concern.

But he couldn't. Exasperated, he folded up his newspaper, placing it on his lap.

That's when the man with the ill-fitted coat showed up again.

He ambled out of the elevator alcove, no longer carrying the leather case he had brought into the hotel. He stood looking a bit lost. A bellhop was whisking by, and the man stopped him to ask a question. The bellhop pointed up to the mezzanine level, giving directions, and the man nodded his thanks and headed up the stairs.

Oddly, he, too, disappeared into the barbershop.

It was more than he could stand. Something was up, and Paddy had to investigate. He scooped up the green file, tucked it away in his newspaper, grabbed his topcoat, and scampered up to the mezzanine level.

Keeping in mind his mission for Wild Bill, he found a nook along the balustrade overlooking the lobby, where he still had a view of the front doors below. Yet, he could keep his eye on the barbershop across the way at the same time. He leaned back and again took up the ruse of pretending to read his newspaper...and waited.

Five minutes later, he caught movement by the barbershop doors. Peering over the edge of his newspaper, he saw two figures leaving the shop. But he was quickly disappointed. It was only a father and his adolescent son—both looking sharp with brand new haircuts.

However, as Paddy Tooke watched the father and young boy walk past him, something stirred in his recollections. A revelation was birthed. Paint poured onto the empty canvas of his memory. A portrait emerged. The Top-Secret envelope in his brain sliced open, and both a face and name came together.

The face of a dead man!

And Paddy knew exactly who the fox-eyed man was.

Chapter 16

—◦—

The Manhattan Room Restaurant, 9:42 PM

SAVA KOSANOVIC AND VUK Milosh both stood to greet the approaching Soviets. They looked stern and focused. Sava felt a nervous tic scuttle up his back. Milosh uttered something in Russian to the new arrivals, which Kosanovic did not understand. They shook hands and everyone took seats at the table.

"Gentlemen, I will speak in English, as Sava Kosanovic does not yet speak Russian," said Milosh, as if to hint that learning the language would soon be required. "This is the nephew of the great Croatian scientist, Nikola Tesla."

Sava nodded to them, noting that Milosh had failed to mention his uncle's Serbian heritage as well.

"Sava, this is Anatoli Yakovlev, the station chief at the Russian Consulate here in New York. He will be the liaison between us and Moscow."

Built as solid as a beer keg, Anatoli Yakovlev had a graying mustache and hair like combed steel wool. A politician's smile rolled up into his face as he nodded in Sava's direction.

"We have admired your uncle's work for some time, Comrade Kosanovic," said Yakovlev, his voice like the deep rumblings of a farm tractor. "His 'Chinese Wall of Defense' is needed. We look forward to reaping the rewards of our investment."

Sava cringed. His uncle's debt of $25,000 again intruding.

"And this," continued Milosh, "Is his associate, Aleksandr Feklisov, also from the Consulate. Comrade Feklisov worked as an engineer in Moscow but now works here in the States to...well, let's say he is in charge of recruitment."

Feklisov was a young, dark-haired man with suspicious eyes that flitted like a hummingbird, never resting on any one object for too long. "I am pleased to meet you, Comrade Kosanovic, and I am eager to learn more about your uncle's device. Although, to be frank, I am more interested in Einstein's work. I suspect the Americans may be using his theories to create an atomic weapon. Is the U.S. government focused on bringing your uncle's theories to reality as well?"

"I don't know," said Sava. "Many of my uncle's former protégées now work for the Defense Department. I cannot speak to what they are working on."

Feklisov pursed his lips, his jittery eyes squinting as if confirming a question that had plagued him. Sava felt the man had already dismissed his uncle's work as inconsequential.

Across the table, Milosh said, "And as you know, this is Dr. Boris Peshkin. He needs no introduction. His work is well known."

Dr. Peshkin's hair was a riot of exploding snow-white clumps, with a matching mustache. His rheumy, colorless eyes sat in thick pockets behind a set of round spectacles. "I am looking forward to reviewing your uncle's theories concerning the weapon," he said. "I have read his paper, *The New Art of Projecting Concentrated Non-Dispersive Energy Through Natural Media*. It was impressive in its claims but lacked much practical theoretical substance. Many holes need to be filled in for me to believe it possible."

Sava didn't know what to say to that, so he said nothing.

The older diplomat, Anatoli Yakovlev, leaned in, chuckling. "Ach! These—how you say in English?--eggheads? No? They are always skeptical. However, our great leader, Comrade Stalin, has confidence in the genius of Nikola Tesla. He believes in the device."

Peshkin bristled, "We will see."

Feklisov only glowered.

"And this," interrupted Vuk Milosh, "Is Yegor Volkov. He is here to...protect...the interests of the Soviet Union and its allies. He is traveling with Dr. Peshkin."

Turning to look at him, Sava felt his neck turn cold. Volkov possessed a face that could have been poured from molten steel, with a fierce, unsmiling mouth, and eyes like rivets that seemed to have been driven into his eye sockets. A single black eyebrow ran over the bridge of his nose as if underlining his forehead. He had slabs for arms that rested on the table like beef carcasses. So daunting was the man's form that Sava nearly gasped. Volkov offered no greeting other than a microscopic nod of his head. His eyes seemed to be elsewhere in the room.

"Well," exclaimed Anatoli Yakovlev with a clap of his hands. "I take it you have bought the needed intelligence?"

Sava nodded. "Yes, I have my uncle's notebook...here in my briefcase."

"Ach. Good, good. Now if you could be so kind as to hand it over to Dr. Peshkin, we will take up no more of your time."

Sava gulped. "Hand it over?"

"Yes, of course..." Yakovlev's eyes narrowed. "We are here to pick it up, no?"

"Well...no. That is...I didn't expect to give you the book. Only let you borrow it."

A frown fell across Yakovlev's face like a night shadow. "Borrow? No, no. We must take it with us. Dr. Peshkin must have total access to it."

"I...I'm sorry...but I can't do that. I only borrowed it. I need to return it to my uncle's room this evening. He doesn't know that it's gone."

Anatoli Yakovlev sat back in his chair, his expression grave. "This is unsatisfactory."

The flitting eyes of his associate, Aleksandr Feklisov, came to a halt, landing harshly on Sava. To his left, Yegor Volkov twisted his head just enough to level a fierce look at Sava.

Milosh interrupted. "Now, Anatoli, I told you before that we wouldn't be able to take the notebook. But we can photograph it. Natka is upstairs as we speak, ready to do so."

Yakovlev didn't respond. Lacing his fingers over his barrel chest, his eyes drilled into the table. The silence hardened like cement.

Dr. Boris Peshkin leaned Sava's way. "Mr. Kosanovic, would it be permissible to allow me to at least look the volume over? With my own two eyes?"

"Yes, of course," said Kosanovic. He was glad to be looking at a somewhat approving face, avoiding the glare of the others. "I always intended to show it to you. And let it be photographed. But I simply can't give it to you—it's not mine to give."

Dr. Peshkin shot Yakovlev a glance and gave a little shrug. "Then what does it matter that we don't have the volume? Paper or microfilm...it's the information that counts."

Yakovlev sucked in his teeth. He and Feklisov shared a look between them. Sava didn't care for it.

"My concern," grumbled Yakovlev, "is not how we obtain the information, it is that no one else obtains it. We would like the weapon exclusively. Our enemies are after this technology, too. And we can't let them get it."

Milosh peered over at Sava. "Well, he has a point, Sava. We can't let it fall into Nazi hands."

"No one else knows that the notebook exists...certainly not the Nazis," exclaimed Sava. "Besides, my uncle guards it like a hawk. He keeps it locked in a safe."

"Ah..." said the Russian diplomat, Yakovlev, "You say he guards it like a hawk. And yet..." his eyes fell to the attaché case. "There it is."

"That's different," snapped Kosanovic. "I could get it because my uncle trusts me." Even as the words crested his lips, Sava felt the bile of duplicity sicken in his stomach. He stood abruptly, swooping up the case. "If you can't accept the conditions, gentlemen, then I will return my uncle's book to his room. I'm sorry, to have inconvenienced you, but the notebook does not leave this hotel."

To his right, Yegor Voltov also stood. Sava could feel his looming form. His heat. The air over the table became taut. He felt Voltov glowering at him and dared not look that way, lest his burst of courage would evaporate into mist.

Aleksandr Feklisov leaned over to whisper into the Station Chief's ear. Sava held his breath, unsure whether or not to leave. Yakovlev gave a curt nod of his thick head.

Anatoli Yakovlev lifted his eyes to meet Sava's, the politician's smile returning. "Ach. I can see there has been a misunderstanding, Comrade. For that, I apologize." He raised a palm in Volkov's direction, and, as if the man were a puppet controlled by strings, he eased the man back down into his chair. "We are all friends here, are we not?"

Sava took in the men seated at the table, wondering if that was so.

"My dear comrade, Kosanovic, I can see how much you love your uncle," said Yakovlev. He lifted his hands with a shrug. "You respect his property. This is a good thing. If you promise me that the information will be kept from enemy hands...I take your word for it."

Sava swallowed hard. "Yes, of course. It will be safe."

Anatoli Yakovlev abruptly stood. "Good! Then let us photograph the book, so you can return it to your uncle's safe, and we can send the microfilm to Moscow."

The others stood, too.

Sava gave a weak nod of agreement. He didn't dare look at Peshkin's escort, Yegor Volkov. To be caught in the glare of the man's rivet-eyes left him terrified.

The group filed out of the Manhattan Room Restaurant. Heaviness blanketed Sava. He was now committed to handing over his uncle's secrets to the Soviets.

Strictly speaking, Sava had just become a spy.

Chapter 17

The Main Lobby, 9:44 PM

HENRY BLACKSMITH SEETHED WITH anger as he redialed the number—the third time. The air inside the phone booth was suffocating. He waited as the ringer on the other end wailed ten times. George Sylvester Viereck was not picking up.

Frustrated, he slammed the handset down on the hook. The fool was probably on his way to the hotel.

Now what?

He peered through the glass door of the booth. The police detective had disappeared. He was no longer seated in the chair across the lobby. Where had he gone?

Over at the front desk, Supervisor Frank Delong had also disappeared. Blacksmith wondered to where? He couldn't afford to have him snooping about—especially if he had an itch to recheck his resume. He might spot Viereck's name listed as a reference. Then a panic swelled as another possibility came to mind. Maybe the two of them gone into the back office together to compare notes. Was the Detective questioning his boss?

He didn't have time to dwell on it. His first concern was diverting George Sylvester Viereck away from the authorities. Possibly, the police detective intended to detain Viereck for questioning, maybe arrest him. Blacksmith had no confidence in Viereck's fortitude. He was all flash, but no substance.

If interrogated, he would break down and confess under little or no pressure, and possibly give up Blacksmith as a collaborator. Before the night was out, they both could be arrested as spies. It would mean the gallows. He couldn't let that happen...at least not until he fulfilled his mission. And that mission was going to be fulfilled tonight! Viereck, or no Viereck. He scissored open the phone booth door, but halted. Men were coming out of the Manhattan Room Restaurant across the way, and a bolt of shock hit him.

He shrank back into the booth, closing the door, watching as they headed toward the elevators.

He knew them. Or at least some of them.

He recognized Sava Kosanovic immediately. He was the nephew of Nikola Tesla. He had read the S.D. dossier on the man. Blacksmith had already spotted him in the hotel on a couple of other occasions, but he was usually alone or with that mousy secretary of his.

Of the other five men in the group, three were strangers, but two others were not. And the sight of them made his flesh crawl.

Soviets! He recognized their faces from his time as an Abwehr agent.

Six years ago, as part of a surveillance operation to monitor possible dissident activity inside German universities, he had been ordered to take in lectures conducted by visiting foreign professors. Because of his youthful appearance, he blended well with the other students. And, except for the secret recordings he had made at each lecture, he had always considered those days of sitting on hard chairs in a stuffy auditorium wasted.

But now, staring across the lobby of the New Yorker, six years later, it was paying off.

Conducting one of those lectures had been a Soviet professor of theoretical physics named Dr. Boris Peshkin. Blacksmith distinctly recalled the man's unruly snow-white hair and mustache. And there he was, plain as day, getting into an elevator car.

But it was the other man he recognized that turned his blood to ice.

Yegor Volkov. A known Soviet assassin working for the Chief Intelligence Directorate, the GRU—Russia's version of the Gestapo. Blacksmith was also familiar with his work. He had once been the personal bodyguard of Lavrentiy Pavlovich Beria, the much-feared head of the NKVD. Yegor Volkov was a ruthless killer. Blacksmith knew of three Abwehr agents the Germans suspected of having been liquidated by Yegor Volkov; each had disappeared without a trace—on German soil, no less.

He was not a man to be toyed with.

Why were they here? And what were they doing with Sava Kosanovic?

It was obvious. The Soviets were here for the device. The Death Ray.

Blacksmith grit his teeth. The operation was falling apart. Viereck was on the verge of arrest, and the Soviets were conspiring to steal the technology. It was time to take matters into his own hands. And that meant executing the contingency orders given to him by Reichsführer Himmler himself.

Blacksmith remembered clearly, six months ago, as that meeting at the New Reich Chancellery in Berlin had concluded. The Fuhrer had taken George Sylvester Viereck into the next room to show him some of the ink cityscapes that he had drawn as a young art student while attending university—one pretentious artist to another. They had left Henrick Schwinghammer alone with Reichsführer Himmler.

Schwinghammer recalled at the time how he thought Himmler resembled an accountant dressed up to look like a soldier, but he never allowed that amusement to deceive him. To think Himmler harmless would be a perilous underestimation. His eyes were as dark and lifeless as black ice.

Himmler had taken Henrick Schwinghammer aside and told him, in no uncertain terms, that if the mission proved unattainable, or if it looked like the device could fall into the hands of the Reich's enemies, they authorized him to exercise extreme unction. He was to destroy all available notes and blueprints related to the device, and eliminate any agents that could connect the Reich to the operation—including Viereck. But to ensure that no other government could develop the death ray machine, he was to terminate anyone connected with its design.

Yes, even Nikola Tesla.

It looked like that time had come. Blacksmith still held out for the possibility of getting the notebook into his possession, but he knew for certain that he couldn't let it fall into Soviet hands. He would destroy it before that happened.

However, first things first. George Sylvester Viereck would be here any moment now. His service to the Reich was no longer needed. He would have to be disposed of...and quickly. He couldn't risk Viereck being questioned by the police detective.

It would be tricky. He had to time it right. However, using his pistol or razor knife openly in the lobby would be foolish. They would catch him for sure. No, it had to look natural, and if possible, done in such a way as to not draw attention to Blacksmith.

Only his third weapon would do. Yes...the other weapon sewn into his jacket pocket.

The weapon killed silently, mysteriously...and quickly. It would take a few minutes to prepare beforehand, and he would need to be close to the victim for it to work, but if done properly, the victim would be dead and Blacksmith out of the room before anyone knew what had happened.

And if that damnable police detective was nearby, he would take them both out with a single swipe.

Henry Blacksmith swiveled open the phone booth door and stepped into the lobby to head back to the front desk. He reached into his pocket, feeling along the lining of his suit jacket. There on his right hip was the slight bulge of his third weapon. Begging to be unleashed.

Yes, he would kill George Sylvester Viereck.

And if possible, the meddling detective too.

Chapter 18

The Terminal Barbershop, 9:48 PM

THE THIEF HAD WATCHED as Eddie came into the barbershop and hung the topcoat on a hook near the front doors. Finishing up with his shave, the barber wiped the thief's face with a hot, clean towel as Eddie took a chair six stools down. A mirror ran the length of the wall; within its reflection, their eyesights crossed. With the slightest of movements, the thief shook his head to let Eddie know they were not to communicate with each other.

"Would the gentleman prefer a cologne or aftershave lotion?" asked the barber attending him.

"Neither, thank you," replied the thief.

As a rule, he avoided unnecessary scents prior to engaging in his work. Much of his work took place in a dark room, with the possibility of people nearby, who were sleeping or otherwise unaware of his presence. The thief knew that other senses, like hearing and smell, became enhanced in the dark, and he did all he could to minimize unwanted provocations—a critical lesson taught to him by his Pops. A lesson that forever scratched a sorrow deep into his soul.

He stood, and the barber whisked a hand-broom over his suit jacket. Fortunately, he wouldn't be wearing these clothes, and if all went according to plan, not another soul would be in the room with the safe. So lingering body smells were of little concern.

He walked up to the counter and waited in line, as a father and his young son paid for their fresh haircuts. He paid for his shave, tipped the barber, and—completely ignoring Eddie as he passed by his chair—took his topcoat from the hook.

He left the shop and strolled into the mezzanine lobby. He slipped his fingers into the pocket of the topcoat to ensure that Eddie had left him the key to the room. He sighed with relief at feeling it there. He pulled it out. Attached to the key was a fob shaped like the Statue of Liberty.

Perfect.

Good boy, Eddie. You were a faithful cutout.

Now he had only to bide time until his mark came downstairs to enjoy his complimentary tickets to the show. His plan was simple: enter the Grand Ballroom, relax to the Benny Goodman Orchestra, and wait for the mark to appear. And then the fun would begin. He had started the evening with two plans, one easy and the other not so easy. Upon learning of Montet's security detail, he knew he would have to do things the hard way.

Oh well, it was the more thrilling of the two plans.

Making his way along the upper balcony, he nonchalantly scanned the lobby below. He spotted the two men in the dark suits, still sitting where they had been when he'd first entered. They simply watched the entrances, as if waiting for someone. It satisfied the thief, however, that they had no interest in him.

The night was looking up. All was in place. No one was tracking his movements.

However, circling along the rail, his neck hairs quivered, and looking up, he realized why.

There, on the other side of the mezzanine, was the man with the pipe he had spotted in the lobby—the man whose eyes had crawled all over him when climbing the stairs earlier. He had moved to the upper mezzanine. Why? His head was down and turned away as if reading his newspaper, yet something was off. The man looked too casual, as if that was what he was attempting to affect. The thief could feel his scrutiny from across the mezzanine. He was watching him. No question about it.

Why? Who was he? And what should he do about it?

The thief backed away from the railing and strolled casually to the front doors of the Grand Ballroom, where a short line had formed. He could feel the man's eyes drilling into his back.

The fellow seemed ordinary enough, but then his Pops would say:

> *Be wary of the ordinary, the Brown Recluse is a bland-looking spider with a wicked bite. It's usually the commonplace things that end up biting you.*

Was he just being paranoid? Did the man with pipe suspect something? And if so, what should he do now? Abandon the job? Or continue as planned?

The thief fought the urge to turn around. His thoughts ran through the possible exits from where he stood. He could be on the street within a matter of seconds. Nothing lost and nothing gained.

But it was the 'nothing gained' aspect that gnawed at him. He had a potential buyer for the Osorkon bracelet, with a five-figure sum that would tide him over for months. And he had no alternative prospects in the queue, nothing as big as this opportunity, just penny-ante jobs. Yet every penny-ante job was high risk, low return. While tonight's job was high risk, high return. And he could use the money. Plus, he had planned the job perfectly.

And there was his leather case to consider. It was upstairs in the room. He couldn't leave it there. There was nothing in it that could directly tie him to it. However, there were tools of the trade inside the case that meant a lot to him. Tools that his Pops had given him.

He paused in front of the doors leading into the Grand Ballroom. Music pumped from within; Goodman's hit song, *'Sing, Sing, Sing (With a*

Swing)' was being played, the staccato notes of the horns blaring out the riffs. The thief reached into his upper breast pocket for his ticket—the one he'd bought three days ago.

What should he do?

Pops would say:

> *Pay attention to your gut, Prudence trumps perfect planning every time.*

Prudence.

He made up his mind. Take one last look behind him, and if the man with the pipe was watching him, he would cut his losses, get to an exit, and leave immediately. Better that than ending up in jail. As for his case, he would come back for it later in the evening. It would, however, be too late to pull off the job—everything depended upon Jean-Pierre Montet coming downstairs for the show—but that's the breaks.

Listen to your gut.

However, if the man wasn't watching him...the job was still on.

Taking a breath, the thief glanced over his shoulder.

Chapter 19

Room 3415, 9:49 PM

THE DOOR TO THE suite swung open. Natka Milosh stood there. On seeing her, Sava Kosanovic felt both a rush of joy and a pang of heartache clench his chest.

She was as beautiful as he remembered. She wore a sky-blue dress, cinched at the waist with a black sash, accenting her slender but shapely figure. Her skin was flawlessly smooth, with high cheekbones and a delicate dimple in her chin. Her hair, like polished brass, was cut to her neckline, pulled back from her face, and styled with a curl along the edge. The sparkle in her eyes was still there, but when their eye lines crossed, Sava caught a glint of defiance which hadn't been there before. It diminished her beauty by a degree.

She smiled at him, but it never made it fully into her face.

"Uncle Sava," she said, "How nice to see you again."

That felt practiced. And again, he wondered if he had ever really known the woman standing in front of him.

Regardless, he swept her up into a hug. "Oh, Natka. I thought you were dead."

She gave him a frail squeeze back. "I came close, Uncle Sava," she whispered. "Mother and Father..."

"Yes, I heard. I'm so sorry for your loss."

"Forgive me for not looking you up when I got into town, Uncle Sava. The timing never seemed—"

Sava waved the thought away. "I'm just glad to see you again. So glad." And he meant it.

Vuk Milosh and the three Russians moved into the room, past them. Milosh kissed his wife on the cheek. She received the gesture with deference, but her lower lip stiffened under Sava's gaze, as if she sensed his disapproval.

"We must get going," muttered Vuk. "If you will not give us the book, then we must get what information we can from it. Dr. Peshkin will want to take notes, and Natka will photograph the pages after we look at it."

"Yes, of course," said Sava. "But I need to get it back to my uncle as soon as possible...before he misses it."

He gave Natka an awkward glance. She looked back, confliction crawling into the creases of her forehead. Both of them seemed ashamed to be associated with such treachery—neither believing it of the other. He opened his case and laid the notebook on the coffee table.

Dr. Peshkin took a seat in the center of the sofa. Natka sat to his right, Sava to his left. Anatoli Yakovlev and his associate, Aleksandr Feklisov, pulled up chairs to face them across the coffee table. Vuk Milosh lowered himself into an armchair in the corner. Yegor Volkov remained standing near the door, his thick hands folded in front of him.

Dr. Peshkin was giddy with anticipation. He mumbled something in Russian that Sava couldn't understand. However, he caught the name Tesla in the sentence.

Peshkin reverently opened the cover, as if it were ancient parchment ready to crumble. He stared with wonder at the scratchy illustration covering the page and the notations penciled around it.

Sava heard him gasp.

"Ach...the brushless alternating current motor concept," Peshkin's voice a mere whisper. "His walk in the park...no?" He glanced up at Sava, amazement in his rheumy eyes.

Sava nodded. He had heard the story countless times, of how Uncle Niko had been taking a walk in a park, meditating on a poem by the German poet Faust about the setting sun being the death of a day, even as somewhere else in the world a new day was birthing. It was at that moment that Nikola Tesla was thunderstruck with the inspiration for alternating current, pausing on the path to sketch in the sand the concept of rotating electromagnets.

Looking at the same crude sketch in the notebook, the white-haired professor shook his head in awe. "So elegant in its simplicity. Such genius."

The room grew heavy with quiet as the man turned page after page in slow motion. Each leaf revealing its secrets and eliciting gasps of delight from Dr. Boris Peshkin.

Natka, too, was captivated, leaning in so close that her cheek almost touched Peshkin's. Sava had never seen Natka so focused.

Periodically, one of them would mumble something in Russian and point to a calculation penciled along the edge of the page. This brought a rapid-fire exchange between them. Once, after Natka had spoken, a gleam of admiration struck Peshkin, and he peered over at her as if amazed by her observation. However, another time he seemed annoyed with her postulations, waving them off as if they were gnats about his head. Natka took the rebuke with aplomb, allowing a sly smile to sneak into her face as if she understood something the old professor didn't. Sava wondered if maybe the doctor felt threatened by her youthful intelligence.

On one page, Natka squealed with excitement, tapping the old man on the knee, like a young girl showing her grandfather a discovery in the garden. Peshkin caught what she had spotted, and the two of them had a laugh over whatever was penciled there.

With each turned page, they walked through the years and decades of Nikola Tesla.

They were a little over three-quarters of the way into the notebook when Peshkin blurted: "*Stoyte!*" — Stop!

He froze in place, his hands in the air as if worshiping at Baal's altar. His abruptness caused the men across the table to lean in, their attention piqued. Sava listened to an indiscernible discussion among them in Russian. They all appeared excited.

Glancing over at Natka, Sava caught her focused on the notebook, rapt, her eyes drilled to the page in question. Absorbing. The others in the room merely mist.

Peshkin focused again on the book. He moved not a muscle for several long, tense minutes. They turned the page, and then another. His eyes wide, sucking in the information.

After what seemed to be an eternity, his hands went to his mouth as if in prayer. "Yes." Came a whisper. "It is possible. I see everything now. It needs work...but..."

A buzz of exhilaration flit through the room. Even Aleksandr Feklisov became excited, his busy eyes jumping over the pages of the notebook. "Are you sure?" he asked. "I don't see it."

"Of course you don't," laughed Professor Peshkin, giving Natka a nudge as if sharing a joke. "You are only an engineer."

Feklisov scowled at the slight.

Natka, however, did not look up. The book tethered her eyes.

Vuk Milosh leaped from his chair. "Quick! The camera. We must get it photographed."

Everyone rose from their chair...except Natka. She continued to imprint.

"Vodka!" declared Anatoli Yakovlev. "We must celebrate." He began pouring vodka into shot glasses. Vuk Milosh, grinning ear-to-ear, took a glass and kicked it back in one swallow.

Yegor Volkov, standing near the door, made no move to drink with the others.

Taking a second drink, Milosh glanced over his shoulder. "Natka!" he yelled, snapping her from her hypnotic state. "The camera!"

"Yes, of course," she replied, giving him a fierce regard at the interruption of her reading.

Sava could see her reticence as she rose from the chair, her face ashen. She went into the bedroom and came back with a camera and a tripod.

Dr. Boris Peshkin was now up and strutting across the carpet, mumbling, deliberating with himself, his face awash with new understanding.

Milosh and the two Russian diplomats celebrated.

Natka set up the tripod.

She was positioning lamps around the notebook for lighting when...

A sharp rap came from the door.

Everyone in the room became stone. Sava heard not a breath.

Another knock.

Yegor Volkov's eyes became slits. Reaching into his jacket, he produced a pistol and stepped up to the door.

A panicked voice from outside cried. "Sava Kosanovic! Are you in there?"

Chapter 20

The Main Lobby, 10:07 PM

HENRY BLACKSMITH HOVERED BEHIND the check-in desk, watching the front doors to the hotel. He needed to prepare the weapon before Viereck arrived, but another task needed attention first. He had to know which rooms the Soviets had reserved.

A lull in guest registration had settled over the desk. A shift change was coming up; Blacksmith himself would need to clock out in a half-hour. After that, his lingering presence might raise questions. But once clocked out, he would be free to take care of other business—lethal business.

Scanning the lobby, he saw no sign of the police detective. Maybe he'd left.

Stepping up to the drawer of filed reservation tickets, he began rifling through them, hurrying, before someone noticed and asked what he was doing.

Looking for Russian names, he quickly found what he was looking for. The Russian Consulate had reserved two rooms on the thirty-fourth floor, both under the name of Anatoli Yakovlev. Blacksmith was unfamiliar with the name, but he was convinced that the rooms, most likely, had been reserved for Boris Peshkin and Yegor Volkov.

Then another name leaped out from a second ticket. A Slavic name. Vuk Milosh. Again Blacksmith had never heard of the man, but Milosh had rented a suite on the thirty-fourth floor too...just down the hall from the Russians. Not a coincidence.

He memorized the room numbers, tucked the tickets back into the drawer, and stepped back to his workstation.

Four minutes later, he slipped into the employee's restroom. He locked the door and slipped out of his jacket. He retrieved the razor knife strapped to his leg and sliced an opening along the stitches of the concealed bulge in his jacket lining. From the opening, he pulled a tiny hard-shelled case, no larger than two fingers.

He set the case on the sink and opened it. He licked his lips, hesitant to touch the object inside.

It contained two glass vials, a syringe, and a man's ring, sized to fit Blacksmith's middle finger. Made of gold, the ring had a black onyx stone set in the center. Along the side of the stone was a small aperture, accessed by using a needle. The syringe filled a cavity carved out beneath the black stone. Then, by twisting the stone a quarter turn, a minuscule spike appeared on the outer rim of the other side of the ring—the palm side. A spike just large enough to make a pinprick in someone's skin.

The vials inside the case contained a proprietary form of hydrogen cyanide. Back in Germany, they called the formula Blausaure, or Prussic Acid. Once injected, the toxicity caused by the cyanide ion would bring cellular respiration to a screeching halt, literally choking the cells to death. It didn't take much. And it didn't take long. Just .06 grams was lethal enough to kill a man in just under a minute. Blacksmith recalled how Reichsführer Himmler's eyes glimmered when looking over the lethal liquid. His lips had curled into a smile, calling the fluid the 'final solution'.

Blacksmith liked the sound of that. It fit his purposes perfectly.

He would wait until he spotted Viereck coming through the front doors, come around the desk to greet him, and then shake his hand. One pinprick in the palm was all it would take. And if that blasted Police Detective was nearby...Blacksmith would introduce him to Himmler's 'final solution' as well.

A thrill surged through him. Finally, a chance to swing a hammer. A tiny one, but oh so lethal.

He lifted the ring from the case. Cautiously. One stab in his skin and he would be dead within seconds.

Carefully, he filled the syringe from one of the two glass vials. His mouth went dry as dust, but his hand was steady. He slid the needle into the aperture on the side of the ring and squeezed the liquid into it, filling it to capacity.

All he had to do now was twist the stone to produce the deadly spike. But that could wait.

He squeezed the excess cyanide back into the vial and meticulously wiped everything down with tissues, which he flushed down the toilet. He closed up the tiny case and put it in his jacket pocket.

For a moment, he stood rock still, eying the lethal ring sitting on the edge of the sink, as if afraid to touch it. Death so close to his skin. Back in Germany he had practiced making use of its deadly potential, but they had always filled it with sugar water. This would be the first time that the power of extermination would literally be at his fingertips.

He picked it up and pressed it onto his middle finger.

He would wait until the last possible moment to activate the spike on the underside of it. That's when he would have to be hyper-cautious. Simply swiping the back of his neck, or brushing his leg, or even closing his fist could prove fatal.

But now he was ready to kill George Sylvester Viereck...and possibly a nosy police detective.

Chapter 21

The Upper Mezzanine Lobby, 10:11 PM

THE FACE! IT CAME to Paddy like a flood. And instantly he knew he was on to something big. All because of a father and son exiting the barbershop together.

But before he could process his newfound information, he spotted his prey coming out behind them. Only there was something different about the man with the foxlike eyes. Paddy caught it right away.

The topcoat! The one the other man had been wearing. It now draped over the man's forearm.

They'd made an exchange.

Now Paddy knew for certain that the two men were up to something.

Paddy Tooke watched as the man pulled an item from the pocket of his topcoat and grinned from ear to ear.

What was it?

A room key! The man with the foxlike eyes had used the first man, Edward Petrowski, to get a room for him. Why?

Wasn't it obvious? He didn't want his name on the ledger below.

The man tucked the key back into the pocket of his suit coat and strolled along the rail of the balcony as smooth as an el train sliding across the city skyline, his foxlike eyes eating up the territory below.

The face of a dead man—the face that had gnawed at him for the last forty-five minutes—now had a name!

Glimpsing the father and his boy coming out of the barbershop cinched it. Funny how routine things can trigger one's memory.

Paddy recalled distinctly the day he'd first seen the face. He'd just been promoted to Robbery Division at the 68th Precinct in Bay Ridge, Brooklyn. The year was 1929—twelve years ago.

<hr />

He was working overnights—the graveyard shift. His first partner, a crusty old goat of an Irishman named Jack Leary, had been at his desk when a call came in concerning a shooting at a brownstone on 73rd Street.

"Let's go, Tooke," Leary had muttered. "Someone's stopped a burglar the old-fashioned way—with a bullet."

Leary and Paddy made their way to the neighborhood, where a small crowd had already gathered outside the house. They were let in by a houseboy who led them to an upstairs bedroom. There they found a frantic man and a woman in their pajamas and nightgown hovering over another man sprawled on a settee in the corner of the room, bleeding from a chest wound. The man was still alive, but barely.

"I heard something and woke up and found this man robbing us," whimpered the house owner. He was still brandishing his pistol. His skinny wife, as white as the sheets on their bed, looked as if she could faint at any moment. "I grabbed my pistol and...I shot him," the man uttered.

"Well now," responded Leary in his Irish accent, "Three pennies for a bullet t'is cheaper than a trial any day of the week, now t'isn't it?" He eased the gun from the man's grip and then turned to face the man leaking life all over the leather upholstery. "Well, if it isn't me old friend Harry Flynn," said Leary.

He grabbed a nearby chair to take a seat in front of the man and then reached over to take a peek behind the lapels of his jacket. Blood pumped from the wound. Paddy stood quietly behind him with an open pad, taking notes.

"You don't look so good, Harry."

"Got a hole in my chest, Jack," whispered Harry Flynn. Blood trickled from his mouth. "It's making a mess of my best suit."

"That it is, Harry." Leary patted the man's hand. "But don't you worry, the doctor'll be 'ere any minute." The words were friendly enough, but the tone was skeptical. Jack Leary peered up at Paddy. "Harry's been a bee in me bonnet for many years. He's a pickpocket. And the best second-story man in New York. Not a safe made that can keep 'im out."

Leary glanced over at the opened wall safe. Paddy too looked that way; he could see several jewelry cases stacked inside.

"Looks like you opened one safe too many, Harry."

Harry Flynn tried to smile, but it came across as a wince. "It was my shoes, Jack. Brand new today...they squeaked when they shouldn't have."

Leary looked down at the man's feet. "They look nice, though, Harry. Very shiny."

"Do me a favor, Jack, and make sure I don't get buried in them. They proved to be traitorous, and I can't abide the idea of walking eternity with them on my feet."

"Now, don't be talking of burying and such, Harry," said Leary. "There are a few unopened safes left in Brooklyn. And without you cracking 'em, I'd be out of a job."

Harry again attempted a smile, but it fell away.

Leary looked up at Paddy. "I once nailed Harry for a robbery he did ten years ago with a couple of goons from Hell's Kitchen. One of them turned on him and coughed 'im up. He did a few years upriver. But I have to say, I never caught him in the act. You be a slippery one, eh Harry?"

Harry Flynn coughed. Blood spattered.

Leary gave him a sympathetic cock of his head. "You gonna make it 'til the doc gets here, Harry?"

The man cringed and shook his head. "Don't think so, Jack." His eyes narrowed, becoming foxlike, yet full of sorrow. "Jack...tell my son...tell him...well, you know."

Leary patted his leg. "Yeah, I know. He'll be missing you too, Harry. You two being so close—his mum being gone and all."

A solitary tear snaked a path down the burglar's face and before two minutes ticked by, Harry Flynn was dead.

⸺◆⸺

But now, twelve years later, Paddy Tooke remembered the words as if spoken this morning, *'tell my son'*, and the pieces to his private mystery fell into place—the face of a dead man that he'd never seen before. Both had those same foxlike eyes. And though he had never met the boy, he remembered reading in the report that Harry's son had been about thirteen at the time—which would match the age of the man walking along the balcony perfectly.

His name was Harry C. Flynn Jr., and he was the spitting image of his father. Although Paddy recalled that the boy didn't go by Harry, like his old man. He went by the nickname his pops used for him: Buck.

Buck Flynn.

And by the time Buck Flynn had circled the mezzanine, another piece of the puzzle dropped into place, spurred by an article buried on page six of the newspaper that he'd been reading earlier—as well as the scuttlebutt around the precinct. For it came to Paddy that if the kid was anything like his old man, he was possibly looking at the notorious cat burglar that had been victimizing the upper crust of Manhattan for the past few months.

The Smoke!

Could it be? Had he gone into the family business? And...why was Buck Flynn here at the New Yorker Hotel tonight, of all nights?

Was *The Smoke* about to strike again?

Paddy huddled over his newspaper, forcing himself not to look straight at the kid. Where was he headed? Should he follow him? Keep tabs on him? He lowered his newspaper slightly to peer down into the lobby. No sign of the house detective, John Williamson, anywhere. He wondered if he should go down and leave word at the desk, informing them they had a potential thief on the premises.

He sensed Buck Flynn move out of his peripheral vision. He dared a glance as Flynn walked across the mezzanine to the doors of the Grand Ballroom. Paddy recalled that Benny Goodman was playing tonight. If Buck Flynn went inside the Ballroom, there might be other exits he could take. He could lose him.

Paddy then made up his mind. His hunch needed to be played out. He would follow him into the Ballroom.

But as he folded up his newspaper to do so, something stopped him dead in his tracks.

Down below, in the main lobby, George Sylvester Viereck was walking through the 8th Avenue doors.

Chapter 22

―――◄○►―――

The Grand Ballroom, 10:14 PM

MUSIC FROM THE GRAND Ballroom bled into the mezzanine lobby. *Sing, Sing, Sing, With a Swing* continued. The back-beat of tom-toms sounded like jungle drums pounding out a warning.

The thief, Buck Flynn, needed to know if the man behind him had him under surveillance or not. Taking in a breath, he swung a glance over his shoulder.

The man with the pipe stood next to the balustrade. However, he wasn't looking Buck's way at all. His attention was toward the main lobby below, his face full of concern. Without so much as a sneak-peek in Buck Flynn's direction, the man stepped to the top of the staircase and started down.

A shudder of relief rippled through Buck's limbs.

False alarm. The man had been looking for someone else all along.

The job was still on.

He handed his ticket to the white-gloved attendant at the door, who handed Buck a handbill of the evening's entertainment as he entered the ballroom.

Stompin' at the Savoy was now being played, its notes careening off the walls. The orchestra was situated against the far wall. Benny Goodman stood in front, holding his clarinet to his side, his fingers snapping out the beat. The band thoroughly enjoying themselves.

Round tables were clustered around the parquet dance floor, where couples swiveled to the music.

Buck Flynn stepped off to the side, where he could monitor the door. He wanted to make sure that the man with the pipe hadn't changed his mind and followed him into the room. Five minutes went by with no sight of him, so Buck glided over to the hatcheck room, where a pretty blond girl with dimples took his topcoat and hat.

His eyes never left the door.

The best thing he could do now was to blend into the throng, find a woman to dance with, and maybe sit at her table—just to lose some of the conspicuousness that he felt by standing alone. He also needed to be seated in such a way as to spot his mark when he came into the ballroom.

He then noticed a woman sitting by herself at a table against the wall, watching the band. She wore a green dress and wire-rimmed glasses. A smile beamed across her average-looking face, just enough to make her look pretty. Her foot bounced with the beat of the music.

But what caught Buck Flynn's eye was the solitary martini glass sitting on the table next to her purse, telegraphing that she was alone.

Perfect.

He took a step in her direction when he sensed movement near the entrance of the Ballroom. A hushed gasp flit through the nearby crowd. Glancing that way, Buck's breath caught in his throat. He could hardly believe his eyes.

It was her!

Natalie Stevens.

Dressed in a cream-colored evening gown, she looked as beautiful as a princess entering her throne room. Eyes from around the room turned her way. A murmur sifting through the crowd.

A shock-wave of disbelief paralyzed him for a moment.

What were the odds? It had been seven months since he'd last seen her, weeks since he'd last thought of her. His only lapse had come a couple of hours ago when he had absentmindedly described her to the cabbie, Eddie Petrowski, to manipulate him into the hotel.

And now here she was, walking into the glimmering Ballroom...shattering his life again.

Why here? Why now?

And why did she have to be so blasted beautiful?

⸺◆⸺

Manhattan, March 1941

"What are you thinking?" I asked.

We were sitting in a club called Kelly's Stables, down on Swing Street—the name everyone uses for 52nd Street. The Coleman Hawkins Combo was playing 'Body and Soul', with Joe Guy squeezing out a solo on his trumpet. When it came to music, Natalie and I were polar opposites, yet we each shared our passion with the other; it helped solidify our relationship; she taught me about classical music, and I introduced her to American jazz, which she was quick to embrace.

However, I could tell she was somewhere else tonight; her focus had drifted into some invisible region beyond the walls. Beneath the soothing riffs, a melancholy silence had crept in between us. Her glass of wine remained untouched.

I waited for an answer to my question.

She gave me a forced smile and reached over to touch my hand. "I was thinking of how happy I've been these last few months," she replied.

I tried to smile back, but it stalled. She didn't look happy at all. She looked pensive and mirthless. It was so unlike her. That vibrant smile that had caught the breath in my chest at the World's Fair had dissipated. Over the last few days, she had become distant. I sensed it. Her thoughts seemed to be elsewhere, not on us. It left me desperate.

As Coleman Hawkins finished their set on stage, I noticed her focus had moved to somewhere over my shoulder. I turned, following her sightline. Across the room, a solitary man wove his way through the tables toward the exit, his back to us. Natalie's gaze had been following him.

When I turned back, she was staring at her untouched glass of wine. Looking up, she said, "I'm not in the mood for music tonight. Would you mind taking me home?"

We gathered our things at the hatcheck counter. Outside, the March air was bitterly cold. She nestled closer, resting her head on my shoulder as we walked. She gripped my arm with force, as if trying to keep me from escaping.

I sensed eyes upon us. But every time I turned back to look, I saw nothing suspicious. I coughed it up to being a residual effect of Natalie's dark mood.

As we came to the street of her hotel, she hesitated, slowing our pace to a stroll. Her frame stiffened next to me. Glancing down, I caught a glare on her face that frightened me. She appeared to be angry with the sidewalk traffic, as if they were crowding our way—crowding our world.

She stopped in the middle of the sidewalk. Turning to face her, I reached up to touch her cheek, wondering why she looked so wretched.

"Natalie, have I done something that—?"

"Shush," she whispered. "I don't feel like talking. I just want to...I'm tired. Let's call it a night."

She pressed her face into my hand, yet glanced away, avoiding my eyes.

"I know I haven't been good company tonight," she offered. "I'm sorry. You needn't see me in. Let's say good night here." The words came out as if giving a eulogy.

She reached up and kissed me, deeply, with force...with finality, full of passion, but a dead passion, without lust or desire. She had never kissed me that way before. It left me weakened.

She pushed away, ran a hand softly over my cheek, smiled, and turned away. I watched her walk the rest of the block to the entrance of her hotel. She never turned back.

I was about to leave, but I needed an explanation. I hurried toward the hotel door, calling her name, but she'd already escaped inside.

As I came up to the entrance, the doorman was just turning around. We collided.

"Excuse me, sir," he said. "I didn't see you there."

But I wasn't listening. I was watching my world shatter inside the hotel lobby.

Over the doorman's shoulder, I could see Natalie standing next to a man in a dark suit. He was tall and slender, and though I couldn't see his face, I guessed his age to be under thirty-five. He appeared to be the same man that Natalie had watched leaving Kelly's Stables earlier.

Natalie looked broken. She was looking the man in the eye and nodding. Even from this distance, I saw tears glisten her cheeks. The man slipped an arm around her and drew her in, patting her back. An intimate gesture. Who was he? He held her for a full minute and then gently turned her toward the elevators. The two of them entered a car, and the doors closed.

The doorman was still mumbling apologies to me. Without saying a word, I stepped around him and entered the hotel. I stood in the elevator alcove, watching the needle indicator climb to Natalie's floor and stop. I waited until the needle descended. When the doors opened, the only person in the car was the elevator operator.

My throat went dry. He was up there. In her suite. I withered inside.

I waited him out. Surely he'll be coming down in a few minutes. I would confront him. Find out who he was and how he knew Natalie.

I took a seat in an upholstered chair in the corner of the lobby and waited. My eyes drilled on the elevators. Concern built into apprehension, and apprehension into anger. The fellow was taking his time coming back down.

Two hours later, I was still waiting. I noticed the hotel staff behind the check-in desk taking an interest in me, so I eventually left the hotel and took a position on a park bench across the street. I couldn't see her suite, of course. It was on the other side of the building. But I had a view of the front door, and I determined to confront that man when he came out. Rage swelled in my thoughts. The wind had picked up. Within minutes, I was bitterly cold. But I stayed.

At three in the morning, I gave up. My teeth were chattering uncontrollably, and my hands and feet had gone numb. The man never came out. He apparently was staying the night with Natalie. I stood and trudged home, thoroughly wrecked inside. My heart as frozen as my limbs.

I'd never felt so betrayed in my life.

The New Yorker Hotel Grand Ballroom, October 8th, 1941

A cauldron of emotions boiled over him: confusion, anger, hatred...love. A spasm cranked in his ribcage as if a wasp nest was exploding there. Natalie glided into the room, joy radiating from her face.

He wanted her in his grasp. To look into her eyes and challenge her cruelty. To ask the foremost question...why?

She had transformed him. Although she never knew about it. For those precious few months, he'd changed—deep to his core. So determined was he to not threaten the fragile bond of their new relationship that he'd stopped working the business. He had never told her what he did for a living—the only lie between them. So, to break the intruding power of that lie, he stopped. For six months he went completely straight.

He had meant to tell her of his repentance, but he could never bring himself to do so. The possible consequences paralyzed him with terror.

So, he silently repented and silently lived with the stains of his criminal life.

But the real reason behind his repentance was that, for the first time in his life, he feared being arrested. Going to jail would mean being separated from her, and it left him petrified.

But then she took care of that herself. Didn't she? Forsaking him the way she did.

A month later his repentance ended—a nice collection of jade from an uptown brownstone. What did it matter now? He had no one to be beholden to.

As if propelled by fury, he grit his teeth and was about to take a step toward her, when he noticed a man suddenly sweeping up to her side to take her arm.

Buck Flynn stopped cold.

Another man! Was it the same one? The one in the hotel lobby that night? He couldn't tell. He'd never seen the man's face.

As if on a roller-coaster, the rage subsided, giving way to an overwhelming sorrow. His body trembled. It was more than he could stand—seeing her with him.

But then...slowly, the scene shifted before his eyes, morphing into something unexpected. Confused for a brief second, Buck Flynn blinked to comprehend. He recognized the man at Natalie's side! And it wasn't the man from that night at all. It was Leo Durocher! The manager of the Brooklyn Dodgers.

A smattering of boos and cheers filled the hall.

It bewildered Buck.

What was Natalie doing with Leo Durocher? And then he realized. Something about Natalie was off. Her hair was darker, her stance different. And she appeared to be slightly shorter than he remembered.

And oddest of all, the people in the room...they all seemed to know her.

The woman wasn't Natalie Stevens at all! He was looking at the actress that could be her double, Laraine Day.

She looks like a real-life movie star. He had said to Eddie Petrowski earlier in the evening.

He then recalled reading in Life magazine how Durocher had married the famous actress—the couple's photograph had been in it. Her similarity to Natalie was uncanny.

His anger fell. He laughed out loud at his foolishness. He'd almost confronted a famous actress, to accuse her of walking out of his life! How would that go over? He could've been arrested as a stalker. A crazy loon.

He could have ruined tonight's perfect plan.

The famous couple worked their way through the crowd to take a seat at a table.

His face still flushed with embarrassment, Buck Flynn turned again to the woman sitting alone at her table. Compared to Laraine Day or Natalie Stevens, the woman was as plain as wall plaster, but that didn't bother him. He only needed a prop. A shield. Someone to pass the time with until his mark showed up.

He didn't mind using women. After all, he'd given himself to one once, and look how that turned out.

He straightened his tie. Time to slather on the charm.

Chapter 23

————◦○◦————

Suite 3515, 10:25 PM

THE KNOCK ON THE door persisted. A pistol had appeared. Yegor Volkov pointed it toward the door, his lips curled upon his teeth.

As if being lifted hydraulically, Sava Kosanovic rose from his seat, his heart thwacking in his chest. Did Volkov plan to shoot someone? Here in this room? Tension thickened in the air. Sava could feel everyone's eyes on him.

The man on the other side of the door had asked for him by name.

Vuk Milosh sidled up and pressed against him.

"What is this, Sava?" he whispered, his voice angry and accusatory. "Who knows you are here?"

Sava slid a glance his way. "I told no one," he said.

"Well, who could it be?"

Another knock resonated. "Mr. Kosanovic...if you are in there, I need to talk to you. It's urgent."

Anatoli Yakovlev stepped up to them. "Well...someone answer the door. We don't want a scene in the hallway."

He gave Yegor Volkov a shake of his head. A signal to put his weapon away. The assassin eased back against the wall next to the door, folding his arms in such a way to conceal the weapon inside his jacket.

Sava swung open the door, and a man rushed past him into the room. He was short, with hunched shoulders and a bald head wreathed in gray. He wore round spectacles and had a mustache as bristly as a well-used toothbrush—Dr. Fredrick Markovitch, a scientist who worked in one of his uncle's laboratories across town.

"Markovitch," cried Kosanovic. "What are you doing here?"

"I need to talk to you," the man squawked, his panic obvious.

"How did you know where to find me?" stammered Sava.

The man's face was intense. "Your secretary."

Only then did it dawn on Sava that Arlene Muzaric had told him that Markovitch had wanted an appointment with him. Something urgent that couldn't wait until tomorrow.

"I talked to your secretary on the phone and she..." He swiped at the air as if to erase inessentials from the room. "Never mind! Have you read the newspapers?" he cried, waving a rolled-up edition in front of Sava. "It's an outrage! It must be stopped."

Dumbfounded, Sava said, "You mean the German march on Moscow? What does that—?"

"No, no! Not that!...the personals. Haven't you seen the announcement?"

"What announcement?"

"Mr. Sweezy called me at the laboratory this afternoon and told me about it. It's an outrage!"

"You mean Kenneth Sweezy? The writer?" Sava knew of the man. He was a longtime friend of his Uncle Niko, an editor for Popular Science Magazine.

"Yes, yes, of course."

"What is this about?"

"It's about your uncle's papers in storage."

"What papers?"

"In his locker. Look!" He held the paper up in front of Kosanovic's face. "Manhattan Warehouse and Storage is getting ready to dispose of your uncle's papers and artifacts because of delinquency."

"Delinquency? What are you talking about?"

"He hasn't paid the bill on the storage locker. He owes $500. They always run announcements of such things. Sweezy just read it in the paper this afternoon and called the laboratory. Unless it's paid, they are going to dispose of all the items in the locker."

Kosanovic took the paper from him, reading carefully the announcement that Markovitch had circled.

"We can't let that happen," wailed the man. "Who knows what treasures would be lost?" He had taken a handkerchief from his pocket and was mopping his bald head.

"Yes," agreed Sava. "I see what you mean. Thank you for bringing this to my attention, Dr. Markovitch. I didn't even know he had a storage locker."

"He's owned it for years."

"Years?"

"A treasure trove of research."

"I will have Arlene write a check for the past due," replied Sava. "And send it over to Manhattan Warehouse and Storage."

"It has to be done right away...after tomorrow it will be too late and..."

Dr. Markovitch trailed off. His head swiveled, as if noticing the other people in the suite for the first time. They were all looking back at him, listening. His head turned to take in Yegor Volkov looming by the door. His eyes blinked.

"Oh...you have company. I didn't realize. I apologize for barging in this way, everyone. I..." He paused, cocking his head as recognition seeped into his face. "My goodness. Is that sweet Natka that I see?"

Natka stepped forward, smiling with an extended hand. "Dr. Markovitch, how good to see you again."

He swept up her hand in both of his. His face brightened. "Sweet Natka, I can't believe it...we all thought you were..."

She placed her other hand on his shoulder. "No...I survived the blitz. Barely."

"Oh, Natka. That makes my heart so glad. We all loved you down at the..." Fredrick Markovitch stopped abruptly, his eyes taking in the rest of the room. He leaned in to whisper to Sava and Natka. "My goodness, Sava, is that Dr. Boris Peshkin? The Soviet physicist?"

Sava felt his skin chill. "Uh, yes...do you know Dr. Peshkin?"

"I heard him speak once at a symposium that I attended in Europe. He spoke on the statistical interpretation of quantum mechanics...wave functions and their effect on individual systems, and such. What is Dr. Peshkin doing here? Is he here to speak with your uncle? Is he here to—?"

He stopped. Combing the room. From face to face. Question marks in his eyes. He then landed on the notebook sitting on the coffee table, his neck telescoping forward as if he were an owl spotting something curious within the forest. The tripod and camera hovered in plain view. Vuk Milosh casually stepped in front of it. But it was too late. A tremble shivered through Markovitch before he twisted away.

"I...think I must be going. You have company. I just wanted to warn you about the storage locker. You will take care of it, won't you, Sava?"

"Yes," said Sava. "Arlene will get a check over to them first thing in the morning."

"Good. It is all taken care of then."

Fredrick Markovitch did an awkward bow of his head to all in the room. His eyes averting contact with their faces.

"It was good to see you again, sweet Natka."

"You too, Dr. Markovitch," she replied, the concern obvious in her voice. Markovitch turned and left the room.

"Dammit," yelled Milosh, once he was gone. "He saw us together. He saw the notebook."

"He's harmless," said Kosanovic.

"Harmless? He's a witness."

"To what? He saw nothing."

"He saw enough to hang us."

Anatoli Yakovlev gave a quick nod of his head toward Yegor Volkov, and the man started for the door.

"No!" cried Natka. "You can't!"

Volkov paused at her plea.

"He saw us, Natka," said Milosh. "What choice do we have?"

Alarm flicked into Sava's eyes as the implied intent slammed home. "You...you don't intend to...to do him harm, do you?"

Silence filled the room, harsh and cold.

"You can't do that!" cried Sava. "The man's a brilliant scientist."

"Brilliant?" asked Feksilov. "How brilliant?"

"The man's a genius. He knows more about my uncle's work than anyone on the planet."

A look of interest flashed across Feksilov's face, which quickly turned to scorn. "We must do something about him," he said to Yakovlev. "He saw everything."

"No. He was only trying to help my uncle. To save his papers."

"Yes, we heard. That is very interesting about the storage locker. You never mentioned it before."

"I didn't know it existed until this moment."

"What difference does it make?" demanded Milosh, "If he's such a genius, he's smart enough to put two and two together. You saw him looking at the camera and the notebook."

Yakovlev's lips worked in and out as he pondered the situation. Feksilov leaned in and whispered something into his ear in Russian.

"We need to stop him before he gets to the elevators," exclaimed Milosh. "Who knows where he's headed—maybe to the police."

Natka put a hand on Milosh's shoulder. "Vuk, he's just a silly harmless man. Leave him be."

Yakovlev drew a breath as his associate backed away from his ear. Determination filled Yakovlev's glare. He pushed past everyone to step up to

Yegor Volkov. He whispered to him in Russian. The large man gave a blunt nod and slipped through the door.

Sava shuddered.

"No!" cried Natka.

"Something must be done," said Yakovlev. "He may be a silly man, but he was in the wrong place at the wrong time, my dear."

Both Sava and Natka gaped in horror at the closed door.

A sour silence filled the room.

Vuk Milosh backed up to the bar and quietly began pouring another round of drinks. Aleksandr Feksilov retreated to his chair, his face grim, his eyes bouncing.

Anatoli Yakovlev clapped his hands together, shattering the dire trance. "Now, before anyone else comes knocking, I suggest we photograph the intelligence. Moscow will be waiting for our microfilm."

Sava Kosanovic felt his blood curdle. How had the evening taken such a horrific turn? What was to happen to poor Dr. Markovitch?

Chapter 24

———◦———

The Main Lobby, 10:27 PM

SERGEANT DETECTIVE PADDY TOOKE rarely cursed. His wife, Dottie, didn't tolerate it, but gazing down into the main lobby, his tongue slipped. "Dammit." He muttered under his breath.

So focused had Paddy been on following a potential thief that he'd nearly missed his actual assignment. George Sylvester Viereck. His distracted pursuit would not please his old army major, Wild Bill Donovan. As it was, he felt fortunate to have looked down into the main lobby when he had.

The man strutted into the hotel. Looking just like his photograph, he was slender, with a graceful gait, and haughty eyes behind wire-rimmed glasses. He looked dapper—poet that he was—wearing a blue pinstriped suit, with a topcoat and black wool homburg on his head. Hooked to his arm was an ebony cane capped with an ornate silver handle.

And he walked as if he hadn't a care in the world.

Halfway down the Grand Staircase, Paddy hesitated, leaning against the banister to relight his pipe, making his surveillance of the man as casual as possible. He needed to get to a telephone right away. As instructed, he was to call the Office of Coordinator of Information at any hour of the night—someone was sure to answer. But before telephoning, Paddy first wanted to watch the man's movements, to see whether he went into a restaurant or if he would take an elevator car to somewhere in the upper reaches of the hotel.

The man did neither.

Viereck strode a determined path toward—what Paddy assumed to be—the front desk, which was currently out of Paddy's line of sight. He could, however, see Viereck's face brighten as if spotting someone he recognized. Who? Paddy could not see. Viereck lifted his cane, by way of a wave, and quickened his pace toward the unseen person.

Paddy scuttled down a few steps to get a better view of the landscape beneath the mezzanine and to spot, hopefully, the person Viereck was approaching. Several people were loitering in the lobby, but only one was coming toward George Sylvester Viereck.

And Paddy's intuition sparked.

It was a hotel clerk. Paddy recognized him from when he'd inquired about Edward Petrowski earlier in the evening. It was the tall, red-headed fellow.

Stepping from behind the front desk, the clerk was approaching Viereck at a steady pace.

But something felt off. The clerk was not behaving with the deference normally reserved for guests. He carried himself as an equal. A friend or an acquaintance. Hotel clerks were not to be as informal as that. After all, an establishment like the New Yorker adhered to something of a class system.

Paddy hurried down to the lobby floor. He was now twenty feet behind Viereck as he strolled toward the clerk. Paddy watched intently as the two men closed in on each other.

The desk clerk's piercing blue eyes darted as if taking inventory of the room. Paddy caught something of craftiness flash across his face.

No, not craftiness...malice.

Then the darting eyes landed on Paddy. The malice fell from the clerk's face like an avalanche. A hint of uncertainty registered. The tall man hesitated, as if decisions were clashing behind the man's glare.

The clerk's lower jaw stiffened. His lips firmed.

Viereck was nearly to him.

The malice returned.

He broke his stare from Paddy to turn back to Viereck.

As they neared each other, the clerk smiled and extended a hand to greet the poet.

Chapter 25

———◆———

The Grand Ballroom, 10:29 PM

A NEW SONG SIFTED up from the orchestra: *Poor Butterfly*, soft and smooth. Buck Flynn was back on task, and he felt *Poor Butterfly* was the right song to approach the woman seated alone at the table against the wall. He stepped up and asked, "Would you like to dance?"

She looked up at him, surprise glistening behind her round spectacles. A smile crested her face. She stood, and Buck laid his handbill on the table near the other chair. They found their way to the dance floor. They danced wordlessly, letting the music carry them. He kept it simple and effortless, leaving a good amount of air between them.

He hoped to connect with her. He would be less conspicuous with a partner. And he needed to be seated with an adequate view of the Ballroom entrance, to watch for his mark.

He glanced down and caught her staring at him, a hint of perplexity on her face. He smiled, and she gave him a practiced smile back.

Then she spoke, "Is this your way of apologizing to me?"

The question startled him. "Excuse me?"

"For your boorish behavior?"

A blank expression fell over his face.

The woman grinned as if she were a lynx that had trapped a rabbit. "You don't recognize me, do you?"

A rush of panic sprinted up his spine. Did he know this woman? Had they met before? Was this night ruined because he'd asked the wrong woman to dance?

The song stopped. Benny Goodman announced from the platform that the band was taking a break and would return shortly.

Buck Flynn stood dumbstruck, staring at a woman he was sure he didn't know.

"Earlier this evening," she said. "You almost ran me over, racing to get into one of the phone booths down in the lobby."

And then it came to him. It was the woman who had dumped her files outside of the phone booth. He quickly regrouped. "Yes, of course. That's why I asked you to dance. I felt bad about that."

A dubious glimmer creased her eyes. "Is that so?"

"I saw you sitting there and hoped to make it up to you."

"Hmm. Well, I haven't heard an apology yet."

"What if I bought you a drink, and we talked about it?"

She hesitated. "I suppose. One drink."

He escorted her back to the table. The woman took a seat and, as if suspecting his profession, drew her purse to the other side of the table. Buck Flynn hailed a waiter and ordered them both drinks—a sloe gin fizz for the lady and ginger ale for himself.

"Ginger ale?" she mused. "You don't look the type to be a member of the temperance league."

"Uh, no, I have a business meeting later. I need a clear head." He kept his eye on the Ballroom entrance.

"You're just like my boss. He has business at all hours too. What business are you in?"

Buck grinned. "Antiquities." A standard reply that he used for that question.

"Hmm," she said, with a dash of doubt in her voice. "Buying or selling them?"

"Procuring them...for buyers."

"You're rather young to be involved in antiquities."

He shrugged. The charm blitz at work. "It's a business I inherited from my father."

"I see."

She sat back, eying him. A pause lengthened.

"My name is Arlene, by the way, Arlene Muzaric...thanks for asking."

Buck blanched. "I'm sorry. I'm not handling this very well, am I?"

She pursed her lips and did a slow shake of her head. Their drinks arrived, and she took a long sip. Setting the drink down, she said, "This is the part of the evening when you reciprocate by telling me your name."

Buck's mind went blank. Something was unsettling about this woman. He'd expected her to be grateful for his company, yet the opposite was happening. She was merely tolerating him as if he were an amusement. Her shrewd coolness was throwing him off his game.

Her left eyebrow lifted expectantly. Still awaiting a name from him.

Glimpsing down, he caught a name listed on the handbill, the name of a musician performing tonight. "My name is Christian," he said.

"Would that be a first name or last?"

"Last name...my first name is Jim."

"Jim Christian, mmm?" Her eyes narrowed, and she startled him by saying, "A man named Charley Christian plays guitar for Benny Goodman tonight."

Buck swallowed hard. Yep, she was sharp okay. He needed to tread softly...but then again, he remembered something his Pops used to say:

Lie small to stall, lie big to awe.

"Uh...yes. Charley is my cousin," he offered—*lie big to awe.*

Arlene's eyes widened. Yes, it worked. She was impressed. Maybe even dazzled. "Charlie Christian is your cousin?" she gasped.

"Sure. We were all happy for him when he finally got his big break with Benny."

She sat back, flashed a wide-toothed grin, enthusiasm flaring behind her glasses. "Wow. I'm having a drink with Charlie Christian's cousin. Imagine that."

He tried out a sheepish grin on her, but it ricocheted. Within half a second, the wonderment fled from her face. She leaned in, the lynx glare returning.

"I don't think so!" she stated firmly.

The switch happened so swiftly it took Buck off guard. He had not dazzled her at all. And the flat-out denial rankled him. He resented having chosen her. Why couldn't the woman just be dumb and happy to have his company?

He shrugged. "You don't have to believe me if you don't want to."

She leaned in further and said, "You are not Charlie Christian's cousin, and I can prove it within the next five minutes."

A rush of concern flooded him. "How? Are you going to ask him? Go ahead." He doubted the woman would be so bold as to approach someone playing in the band.

She shook her head. "I don't need to. In fact, I don't need to talk to a soul or even leave this chair."

He shrugged. She'd called his bluff, he'd called hers—a stalemate.

She pointed at him. "I don't know what your game is, mister. But I don't like you. I don't like men who slather on the charm and make up fake names to have their way with what they think is a poor defenseless woman. And I don't like men who lie. Besides, that was all a story about trying to make it up to me for almost tackling me downstairs. You didn't remember me at all when you asked me to dance. You know what I think?"

"What?"

"You're using me!"

"Using you? For what?"

"I'm not sure, but you haven't stopped looking at the door since we sat down. Maybe you're waiting for the person with whom you're meeting tonight—your antiquities business...if that's even real. Or maybe you're waiting for a better prospect than me. But you have shown no genuine interest in me whatsoever! You're nothing but a self-centered, arrogant jerk! And I think you're up to no good."

Buck could feel the heat rising into his face. The band was returning to the stage. He needed to abandon this woman. She was getting under his skin, and he needed to stay focused on tonight's job.

"You like speaking your mind, don't you, Miss Muzaric," he said, his words tight.

She laughed. "You're the second person to tell me that tonight. I call it as I see it, *Mr. Christian*." She hit the fake name as if to stomp it into the ground.

He readied himself to rise from his chair.

She pointed an accusatory finger at him. "And don't you go anywhere just yet. I'm as anxious as you are to part company, but not until I prove my point!"

The band began to play, the first notes filling the room.

"Oh? And what point would that be?" He snarled.

"That you are a liar, and you most certainly are not Charlie Christian's cousin."

"Okay, prove it! Your five minutes are up."

She sat back, a satisfied smirk on her face. Without turning around to look at the band, she said. "The proof is on the stage. Look over my left shoulder."

Buck glanced over at the bandstand, and his face flushed. Shocked.

Arlene Muzaric gave a coy tilt of her head. "You don't look like a negro, Mr. Christian! Charlie Christian is one of the best guitarists in the nation, but he also is black. Do you still claim to be his cousin?"

Buck met her glare. His lips tightened. It had been a mistake to sit with her. It was time to leave before she caught him in any more lies. But before he could stand, she leaned in close, her face beaming, as if the lynx had snared its game. Her eyes twinkled behind her glasses.

"*Somebody Loves Me*," she cooed.

Flynn's heart constricted. "W...what?" he croaked, his shoulders tensing. "What are you talking about?"

She snickered at his discomfort. "The tune that the band is playing...it's called *Somebody Loves Me*."

Buck Flynn was speechless. For the first time in his life, his charm offense had withered on the vine. The woman intimidated him. Maybe even frightened him.

"You can go now, Mister, uh—should we keep calling you, Jim Christian? No? I didn't think so. Either way, you are excused." She waved him away. "But thank-you for the drink."

He stood feeling stupid and ashamed and angry all at once. He so wanted to say something witty and belittling to put her in her place, but words wouldn't form.

It didn't matter, however. It was time for him to go.

His mark, Jean-Pierre Marie Montet, had just entered the Ballroom.

Chapter 26

———◦———

The Main Lobby, 10:38 PM

THE TALL RED-HEADED CLERK closed in on George Sylvester Viereck. His hand extended.

Paddy Tooke sensed that something was off. His Divine Cop-Voice was screaming. The clerk's face had a gleam of ill-intent.

The poet was almost there, lifting his right hand to shake hands with the clerk.

Paddy felt in his bones that possibly Viereck was in danger. He couldn't explain it, but every corpuscle surging through his veins was on alert.

Too far away to do anything about it, Paddy was about to call out Viereck's name when...

Two men stepped between the clerk and Viereck, cutting off their greeting.

Everyone stopped. Paddy, Viereck, the clerk, and the two men. All came to a screeching halt.

One man had credentials out, flashing them in front of George Sylvester Viereck. Neither of the two men took notice of the clerk standing behind them. Paddy recognized them at once as the two men who had been watching the front entrance earlier in the evening.

The interruption startled the red-headed clerk. Behind the backs of the two men, his icy blue eyes snapped a nasty glare toward Paddy. His lips rolled back into a snarl. Then he turned and darted away.

Paddy felt compelled to follow him, but hesitated. His first concern was George Sylvester Viereck. He needed to learn who the two men were and what their interest was in the man who had been his mission for the evening. From the corner of his eye, he noticed the clerk disappearing around the corner of the elevator alcove.

Approaching the conference, he overheard Viereck saying:

"FBI? What do you want with me?" He was reading over one of the man's credentials.

"We would like to ask you a few questions, sir."

"About what? I have done nothing wrong."

Paddy could see the man's terror. He was visibly shaking.

The man flashing the credentials turned to the other and said, "Is this the man?"

The second man nodded, his eyes glued to Viereck's face. "That's him."

"If you could come with us, sir..."

"But...why? Am I being arrested?"

"Sir, we simply want—"

Paddy stepped up to the men. They all snapped a look at him. "Good evening, gentleman," he said.

The man with the credentials stepped in front of him. He stood nearly a foot taller than Paddy, with narrow, squinty eyes set into a square face. He exuded authority. "Sir, this is a private matter. If you could please—"

Tooke flashed his own badge. "New York City Police, gentlemen, and as this hotel falls within my jurisdiction, I would say it's not such a private matter at all."

This seemed to stymie the two men for a moment. Viereck looked ashen. Three law enforcement officers now surrounded him.

"Could I see your identification, gentlemen?"

The man standing in front of Paddy simmered. After a long pause, he handed over his credentials. Paddy looked it over. He was FBI alright. Special Agent Ralph Doty, of the New York Field Office. Paddy nodded and handed him back his wallet.

"And you, sir?" asked Paddy to the second man.

He was slightly shorter than the other, with cautious eyes and a narrow crooked nose.

"I...I..." he stammered.

"Dr. Fitzgerald is with me," said Agent Doty. "He doesn't have a badge."

"That's okay," smiled Paddy. "A driver's license or other ID will do."

The thin man produced a military ID card, stating that he was Boyce Fitzgerald, a private in the U.S. Army. Paddy's intuition clanged.

"Did I just hear Agent Doty call you Doctor?" he asked.

Fitzgerald blanched. "I...I'm not a medical doctor. I work in research and development."

"As a private in the army?"

"I..."

"Dr. Fitzgerald does not need to answer your questions, Detective," snapped Doty.

"Could I ask what your interest in this man to be?" said Paddy, nodding toward Viereck.

"This is a federal issue, sir," said Doty. "We are bringing this man in for questioning."

"For what? Has he committed a crime?"

The two men shared a glance.

"Please, gentlemen," said Paddy. "All I'm asking is why you are detaining this man?"

"Dr. Fitzgerald has brought us information concerning the possibility that this man has committed sedition and crimes against his country."

"What?" wailed Viereck. It looked as if the man were about to faint.

Beyond them, Paddy caught a stirring behind the front desk. House Detective John Williamson was emerging from the hallway. His head perked up as he noticed the confrontation taking place. He scurried from around the desk to come their way. He shot a hard look at Paddy Tooke as if to blame him for the minor commotion.

"Gentlemen, could I be of assistance?" he asked.

Special Agent Doty scowled at him. "Please just back away, sir."

"I will not back away!" spat Williamson through clenched teeth. He drew up nose-to-nose with the man. "I represent the interests of this hotel. I don't know what this is about, but we will not stand for disruption of this nature in our lobby!"

"Sir, we are simply taking this man in for questioning."

"I refuse to go!" yelped Viereck.

Williamson did an uneasy scan of the nearby lobby. "Gentlemen, could we please move this little meeting to my office in the back—just so we can sort this out."

The FBI agent reluctantly acquiesced, and they all marched in single file to Williamson's office. As they entered, Williamson swung his irked attention to Paddy Tooke.

"Detective, you failed to inform me you had brought a team of police officers with you. And you never told me you intended to arrest him in the middle of my hotel! I trusted you would act with discretion."

"They're not with me," offered Paddy, amused. He took a seat on the corner of the desk and pulled out his pouch of Kentucky Club, scooping his pipe into the packet. "These men are with the FBI."

Williamson's face became white. "FBI?"

Agent Doty again showed his credentials. George Viereck had taken a seat in a chair in the corner, burying his face in his hands.

"What is your interest in this man?" asked Williamson.

"This is a federal issue," said Doty. "We are not at liberty to disclose the details, but a federal warrant has been issued for him and we are bringing him in—"

A sharp knock came on the door.

Williamson let out an exasperated breath. "What now?"

He swung open the door and two men stepped in. Paddy Tooke knew them instantly. He had met with them this afternoon in Rockefeller Center. It was Allen Davies and Phillip Carver, of the Office of Coordinator of Information.

Chapter 27

————◇————

Suite 3527, 10:48 PM

THE LEATHER CASE WAS on the desk where Eddie Petrowski had left it in Suite 3527. Still steaming from his encounter with that irksome woman in the Grand Ballroom, Buck Flynn was glad to see it. It helped to make sense of the evening.

Tossing his hat and topcoat on a nearby davenport, he gave the case a quick inspection. It looked unmolested. No signs of scratches on the brass clips that would have indicated an attempt on Eddie's part to pry open the locks with a screwdriver or knife.

Good boy, Eddie. You were a perfect cutout.

The suite was roomy and plush. In the corner, on the floor, stood an art déco cabinet containing a radio. A dividing wall broke the suite into two sections: a living area and a bedroom. He imagined the bed would be one of the most comfortable in town, but he also knew he wouldn't be sleeping in it tonight.

The open drapes of the sky terrace revealed a majestic view of New York City, its skyline bursting with lights like fallen stars from the heavens. He slid open the sliding glass doors. Three pigeons perched on the railing fluttered into the darkness. It surprised him to see the birds this high up. Cold air swept up to meet him as he stepped onto the terrace. He shivered, but it felt good. That woman had gotten under his skin and the cold helped wash away his irritation and clear his mind.

As it was, thoughts of Natalie Stevens distracted him. Seeing Laraine Day in the Ballroom had been disturbing. Even now, he was struggling to push her from his thoughts.

———◄O►———

Manhattan, March 1941

I took a cab to Natalie's hotel early the next morning. Confusion and anger clogged my thoughts. I knew there had to be an explanation for that man spending the night in Natalie's apartment, but my emotions couldn't make any excuse sound reasonable. Picturing the two of them in the lobby screened my corneas with blood.

The doorman moved to open the door for me, but heated with rage, I beat him to it. I hurried through the lobby to the elevators. A car was open, and the young elevator operator snapped to attention as I entered it. He recognized me from previous visits. He smiled but must have sensed my dark mood, because the smile quickly vanished.

"Are you going up to...?" he asked hesitantly.

"Just drive," I muttered bitterly, giving him the floor number.

"But..."

"Shut the door and shut your mouth," I seethed.

"Yes, sir."

We rode up in silence. The doors opened, and I went to step out, but the operator said meekly, "She's not there."

I stopped abruptly. "What did you say?"

The poor kid looked terrified. I must have looked like a monster, angry as I was, and my eyes puffy with dark circles.

"I'm sorry, sir, but..."

"Spit it out."

"Miss Stevens has checked out of the hotel."

His words slammed into me like a hammer. "What do you mean?"

"She's gone. Moved."

"Moved? When?"

"Last night, sir."

The news made my head swim. Anger became bewilderment. "That can't be," I said.

I hurried down the hall to her apartment door and knocked. Nothing.

The elevator doors had closed. The hallway was empty. I was tempted to pick the lock but remembered that I hadn't carried my caddy of lock picks for months because of my repentance from crime.

I felt frustrated. Then, turning to leave, I noticed a painting hanging across the hallway. I lifted it from its hook. Wire was strung along the back. Using my pocketknife, I snipped a length from it. The wire was flimsy, but after doubling it up and twisting it just right, I made a suitable lock pick. It took longer because of the tool, but I breached the lock.

The apartment was quiet...and empty. Drawers and closet doors hung open. The bed left unmade. There was nothing left of Natalie. Not a scrap.

I left and rushed down to the front desk. The clerk informed me that Miss Stevens had moved out.

"Did she leave a forwarding address?" I asked.

"No, she did not."

"Did she leave any messages?"

He shook his head.

"Was there a man with her when she left?"

His face grew sympathetic. He gave a slight nod.

"What was his name?"

"I have no idea."

"Have you seen him before?"

"Only twice in passing."

I wanted to reach across the counter and shake the truth from him, but I could see his bewilderment and his fright over my heated manner. The next few days were hell. She was gone. Without a word. How could she do that? For two weeks I checked backed regularly at the hotel to see if she had returned, but to no avail. The worst part was not knowing anything about her. I had no clue where she had been working, or if she worked at all. Because of our silly unspoken rule about leaving our lives hidden from each other, it had never come up. Likewise, I had met none of her friends or acquaintances. Until last night, it had been just the two of us, alone in paradise.

And now paradise was demolished.

I never saw Natalie Stevens again. I felt utterly forsaken. It took weeks for me to breathe again, and months to tamp down the anger I felt for her.

New Yorker Hotel, Suite 3527, 10:52 PM

Buck Flynn stared out into the night. His lips tightened. He couldn't be thinking of her anymore tonight. It was too much of a distraction. He needed a clear head—especially if he intended to scale down the building from the thirty-fifth floor.

The temperature was at least ten degrees colder up here than it had been on the street. However, anticipating the drop in temperature, he had packed accordingly. Exposure to the cold would be brief, and given the physical exertion involved, he expected to produce more sweat than chills, anyway.

However, there had always been one concern that far outweighed that of the cold.

The wind.

At this elevation, it could get pretty blustery. He had never attempted an outside entrance from this height. His greatest fear was becoming a human kite. He could picture himself being battered mercilessly against the building by gusts of wind beyond his control, or worse, being swept off its face.

Fortunately, the night was calm. Oh, there was still wind up here—there would always be wind—but it was manageable.

He glanced down to the street, where cars crawled like glowing corpuscles through blackened blood vessels. It would be quite a drop. How long would it take to hit pavement? He tried not to think of it.

Heights never bothered him. His Pops saw to that.

From the time he could crawl up and open a window, the thrill of dangling on the outside of it had always gripped him. Noticing this, his Pops, instead of discouraging the risky behavior, began working with his fearlessness by teaching him safety protocols and the fundamentals of scaling. Pops had never climbed a mountain in his life, but he seemed to know how.

He showed Buck the basics of tying knots: the figure eight, the girth hitch, the Munter hitch, the Prussik knot, and so on. He taught him how to create anchor points to which to attach a top-rope, how to loop a belay, and how to rappel—first on the iron monkey-bars at the city park, and then down the side of a building from a second-story window. He also showed him how to ascend back up again using a simple Prussik knot.

Buck was a natural. And fearless. It got so he could ascend a building by walking right up the side of it. Soon he was scaling five-story buildings and rappelling back down at breathtaking speeds. By heeding his father's patient lessons, he'd never fallen...not once!

But he'd never done it from thirty-five stories up either.

Back inside, he set the case on the coffee table. He unlocked it and began withdrawing the items: a wool sweater and leather jacket, a pair of black slacks, a knitted skullcap, a pair of rubber-soled shoes, and leather gloves. Beneath them was a small canvas rucksack that held a mishmash of tools: pliers, screwdrivers, utility knife, glass-cutter, and such, all packed into pockets and sleeves.

Beneath the rucksack was a handmade leather harness. Buck had designed and crafted it himself. The belt had loops and pockets for carabiners, hooks, and pitons. The left side held flashlights—one normal size and the other a penlight. A special sheath contained a small leather caddy of lock-picking tools. His Pops had crafted those, and Buck cherished them. The only inheritance his Pops had left him.

At the bottom of the case lay three coils of ropes. Thin and lightweight, Buck had braided the ropes using a kernmantle weave of leather thongs over a core of silk cording. He treated the rope lengths with saddle soap and neatsfoot oil, to keep the leather weave supple. He inspected them regularly. His life depended on their integrity.

The thief stripped off his dress clothes and slipped into his slacks, sweater, jacket, and climbing shoes. He then took a round canister of shoe polish and smeared his face with the black paste, covering even his neck and ears. He didn't expect to encounter anyone during the climb, but if someone were to glance from their window, hopefully, they would only see a shadow amongst the other night shadows.

He put on his skullcap and slipped into his gloves, turned out the lights to the suite, gathered his harness, ropes, and rucksack, and carried them onto the sky terrace.

He secured his anchor, tying off the two strips of webbing at separate points on the railing, connecting them with a single carabiner, and then slipped into his harness, belting it tight. He looped the safety rope through the hip rings and tied it off. To keep the top rope from getting tangled, he flaked it into loops. He clipped the mid-point with a carabiner and attached it to his web anchors. He now had two equal lengths of the folded rope, the end of which he slipped into the belay device that was attached to his harness. The belay would act as a brake during his descent and give him control as he rappelled down the face of the building.

He slipped the rucksack onto his shoulders, gathered the flaked loops of rope, and heaved the entire length over the railing.

The wind was light. Thirty-five stories below, the streets continued to crawl. The city noises a faint din.

Buck Flynn swung his legs over the railing, gripped his top-rope, released his belay, and quietly sank into the darkness.

Chapter 28

———◦———

Room 1733, 10:53 PM

A SEETHING HENRY BLACKSMITH took the elevator to the fifteenth floor. The elevator operator recognized Blacksmith as a co-worker and attempted to engage him in small talk but gave up after Blacksmith scowled his way. Once the doors opened, he left without a word. He went to the stairwell and walked up two more flights, where he knew of a room that remained unoccupied for the evening. Using his copied passkey, he entered and turned on the lights.

He paced wildly. Everything had gone to hell. He never got close to Viereck. After spotting that damn police officer coming up behind the poet, an opportunity to get both men with the ring had been seconds away.

But then those two men came out of nowhere. He'd failed to realize that the detective had brought a team of men. How did he miss them?

The cop had outwitted him.

He lifted his hand to look at the ring. Cautiously, he twisted the black onyx stone a quarter turn, retracting the poisonous spike back into the band. His assassination attempt being a complete failure, he no longer needed it extended. And he didn't want to puncture himself accidentally. He was about to slip the ring off, but left it on for now. Yes, the deadly fluid inside horrified him, but the ring could also be an available weapon if needed. He could have it deployed within seconds.

He took off his jacket, went into the bathroom, and splashed his face and neck with cold water, hoping to stem his anger. In the bathroom mirror, his iceberg eyes glinted. He snarled back, smoldering. He smashed the glass with a fist. Shards exploded. His knuckles drawing a minor cut.

"*Hurensohn! Du trolltrotte!*" he yelled—sonofabitch, you idiot! He pulled a clean towel off the rack and wrapped his fist, shaking his head in dismay. Leaving the splintered mess behind, he stepped out of the bathroom into the bedroom. Loosening his tie, he flopped into a chair.

Decisions needed to be made. Immediately.

Viereck was in custody and probably spilling his guts. He would give up Blacksmith as a collaborator for sure. He may hold out for an hour or two, but not more than that. If the authorities learned that a Nazi spy was here, they would establish a dragnet. He possibly had an hour with which to work, tops.

The words of Reichsführer Himmler kept ringing his ears. *Under no circumstances can the technology fall into enemy hands. If need be, destroy everything, kill everybody.*

The presence of the Soviets vexed him. They were one step ahead. They had Tesla's nephew in their hip pocket. They may already have details concerning the weapon. How could they be stopped?

He worried about Dr. Boris Peshkin. As a theoretical physicist, his intellect could grasp the complexities and feasibility of such a device. They could have the weapon deployed in no time.

Blacksmith couldn't let that happen. He somehow had to get to Peshkin and take him out.

However, a huge barrier stood in the way of getting to Peshkin.

Yegor Volkov.

As a trained bodyguard and assassin—maybe the best that Soviet Russia offered—he would be hard to circumvent, and even harder to take out. He would be wary of any potential attack. That was his job. Blacksmith doubted he could get close enough to the good doctor to kill him.

Unless...

He had a thought.

The Soviets didn't know him by sight, and they were unaware of his position at the hotel. It would be nothing to pose as a desk clerk delivering a telegram to their suite; all he would need was one of the silver trays the hotel used for such deliveries and a fake telegram. A simple knock on their door would be enough to get inside. And once there, he would let the ring do its work. Volkov first, then Peshkin.

Yes. That could work. He just had to make one last appearance down at the front desk to retrieve the accouterments for the job.

But first, while he was upstairs anyway, he would deal with the source of all these complications.

Nikola Tesla.

He needed to get into the old man's suite and find that notebook...and if it wasn't there...

As Herr Himmler said, *Destroy everything, kill everybody.*

Hell, he just might do that, anyway.

Chapter 29

————◇————

The 33rd Floor, 10:56 PM

THE AMBIENT STREET NOISES sifted up from the street below. The wind whistled delicately. A light breeze was not nearly enough to cause any sway in his ropes. Buck Flynn was thankful for that. So far, the climb was going smoothly. The sky was clear with no precipitation. However, at this height, he could see a clot of clouds scuttling across the sky in the east, possibly holding rain.

Releasing his belay, he eased down just enough for his foot to touch the railing of the thirty-third-floor sky terrace, where he planned to tie off his safety rope.

He paused to get his bearings. When he had passed the suite on the thirty-fourth story, the lights had been out, but here the rooms were all lit up. Obviously occupied. He suddenly wished that he'd taken the time to tie off on the suite above him instead.

The curtains to the terrace doors were open, giving him a good view inside the suite. With one foot resting on the corner of the flat balcony rail, he twisted slightly to peer from around a stand of potted shrubbery clustered on the terrace. Beyond the tall plants, he glimpsed patio furniture spread along the terrace.

He took a moment to scan inside the suite. All was still. Maybe no one was home.

Gripping his top-rope, he eased down until he found his footing square on the balcony floor behind the shrubs. Two junipers, nearly as tall as he, concealed him. Peering through their branches, he gave the suite a thorough scan. Laid out the same as the room that he'd rented two floors up, this one appeared to be someone's living quarters.

To the right of the main room, an archway led to a bedroom, its window next to the terrace, the curtains drawn, but a light shining. Buck leaned over the railing to peer through the crack of the curtains, hoping to see if anyone was home, but he could not tell.

Then, behind him, on the other side of the potted trees, came a faint shuttling. Swinging around, he caught a flash of movement that caused his heart to skip. Panic surged. But then he realized the source, and he had to catch himself from bursting out laughing.

Pigeons. Ten of them, at least, scattered about, perched on the railing, pecking at the floor, and walking along the patio table and chairs.

He let out a calming breath, allowing his heart to fall back into a normal rhythm.

That's when he spotted something else that again caused his heart to spike.

Looking into the main suite, he noticed an office. A desk sat just on the other side of the terrace doors, piled with papers and files. Next to it was a table full of clutter. And beyond the table was an alcove lined with shelves and cabinets. Books seemed to be everywhere, as well as stacks of saltine cracker boxes. But the item that drew his attention sat tucked into the far side of the alcove.

A safe.

It was a Diebold triple door, standing safe. Massive. At least three thousand pounds. An antique. Buck Flynn had never seen a Diebold that old. Possibly manufactured during the last century. It stood over five feet tall with two outer doors thirteen inches thick, each with a stainless-steel handle grip. Inside, below a section of shelves and cubbyholes, was a smaller door along the lower part of the safe—a safe within the safe called an anti-dynamite box.

Buck's excitement surged.

A safe protected mysteries. Prized possessions. A closed safe seized him with curiosity; and cracking a safe was the greatest thrill imaginable.

But the amazing thing was...this safe was not even locked! One of its thick doors was ajar. Waiting to be rifled.

Buck could hardly contain himself. No one was in the room. The safe was open. It seemed too good to be true. He took a step from around the bushes, his hand reaching for the patio door handle...but then halted.

The voice of his Pops sounded in his head.

> *Plan your work and work your plan. Glittery things distract cats and babies. Stay on course. Detours waste time and for-feit opportunity.*

Buck's lips tightened. He wrestled with the logic of it. The safe was there and open, so easy. But deep down, he knew Pops was right. He'd come this far by a cleverly designed plan, and it was working to perfection. Now was not the time to take the chance on a distraction—with the possibility of arrest if things went badly.

Besides, who knew what was in that safe? It could be a boon; it could be a bust. Its contents were a mystery. The contents of Monsieur Montet's wall safe in Suite 3227, however, was not. Don't swap the known for the unknown. Don't be detoured. Too risky.

He retreated behind the junipers.

Reluctantly, he tamped down the temptation, turning away from the oh-so-available safe tucked conveniently inside the empty suite. Pushing it out of his mind, he began tying off the safety rope on the balcony railing. He gave it a tug. It felt secure. He was about to swing his legs over the railing to finish the last flight of his climb when...

The patio doors slid open, and a sharp voice cried out: "There you are! I was wondering when you would show up."

Chapter 30

———◦———

Suite 3515, 10:58 PM

NUMB AND DISTRAUGHT, SAVA Kosanovic sat in a chair, watching silently from the corner of the room as Natka Milosh carefully snapped pictures of the notebook with her camera. She appeared to be proficient with the task, as if she'd done it many times before. It saddened him to think so. His Sweet Natka had become a communist agent, trafficking in espionage and stolen intelligence. How did that happen?

Anatoli Yakovlev, Aleksandr Feklisov, and Vuk Milosh stood in a hushed conference over by the bar, paying her no attention. Feklisov occasionally shot Sava furtive glances, his jumpy eyes bouncing like billiard balls banking off of cushions.

Dr. Boris Peshkin huddled in the other corner, scribbling notes in his own notebook. His face flamed with excitement. Sava eyed him coolly, wondering with disdain if someday Peshkin's nephew would have to steal *his* notebook for a roomful of spies.

He felt he was going to be sick. What had he done? He'd violated his uncle's trust, given stolen intelligence to foreign agents, and played a part in bringing harm to an innocent man—all to help aid the war effort. But he had to wonder if his role was justified. Was the Death Ray device really possible? Would it truly help free his country of tyrants?

And was it worth the life of Dr. Fredrick Markovitch?

He cringed, wondering what fate awaited the scientist—all because the poor man tried to do a good deed.

He wondered about the new world order being fashioned by the likes of Vuk Milosh, Aleksandr Feklisov, and Anatoli Yakovlev. What would be the price for that new world? How much blood and treasure would be spilled to bring it about? And once established, would men have more freedom? Or simply reassigned a fresh set of shackles?

Maybe his secretary, Arlene Muzaric, was right. Maybe some revolutions were worthy, and others not.

Natka shot him a glance. Her face grim. Sava could tell that she, too, was wrestling with the events that had taken place in the room. It had dismayed her to witness Yegor Volkov go through the door after Markovitch. But afterward, Sava had noted that her manner changed. She became mechanical, avoiding communication with the others and going about her assignment with heartless detachment, as if resigned to the realities of what it took to win a war and change the world.

Looking back at her, for the first time in his life, Sava despised her. She was not the girl he remembered—that sweet, brilliant teenager excited about the challenges of university or that curious scientist who had brightened up the laboratory for a brief time. Her chameleon change was more than disappointing; it was mortifying. It was as if she'd molted, shedding beautiful, enthralling skin to reveal reptilian scales beneath. Deceiving. Plotting. Cold.

But in reality, Sava knew his disgust for Natka to be misplaced. He was only projecting the loathing that he felt for himself. They were the same, he and she. Sharing the same degree of treachery and culpability. Looking at her, he saw his own reflection mirrored back at him. And it repulsed him.

Vuk Milosh stepped over to Sava. "We are almost finished here, Sava. You will be able to return your uncle's notebook to him."

Sava stared out the window, paying him no attention.

Milosh took a seat in a nearby chair. He put a hand on Kosanovic's shoulder. "You mustn't dwell on it, Sava. What had to be done, had to be done."

Sava didn't respond.

"You will find, comrade, that in this business the ends justify the means. Sometimes you have to do some unpleasant things to achieve your goals."

Without looking his way, Sava muttered, "Walk with the devil 'til you get to the bridge?"

Milosh brightened, recognizing his own words echoing back to him. "Exactly! It's all for the common good."

Sava spun around, a mean glare flashing. He had uttered the adage as an indictment, not as an encouragement. "Common good?" he snapped. "What is common, or good, about killing an innocent man?"

Milosh's face darkened. "What is one man, to the subjugation of an entire continent? We couldn't let him reveal to anyone what he saw in this room. Sometimes, comrade, I wonder whether you have what it takes to bring about our purposes. This is not a game for weaklings. The sooner you realize that, the sooner our goals become reality."

Milosh stood abruptly and turned away in a huff.

Natka, who'd been standing behind him, stepped up to take his place. She held out the notebook for Sava to take. He just stared at it. Wishing he'd left it where he'd found it on his uncle's desk. Glancing up at Natka, he saw something of a spiteful glint in her eye. She tried to disguise it with a weak smile, but it was there all the same. And he suddenly realized that she held him in the same degree of contempt that he felt for her.

He took the notebook and stood.

Oblivious to the mood in the room, Anatoli Yakovlev clapped his hands together and blurted, "This has been a good night, comrades! Moscow will be very pleased. I am eager to get the microfilm to them. Soon Hitler's planes will fall from the skies like dead birds. But tonight we must celebrate. Let us all go up to the Terrace Restaurant to eat and drink. I hear they have excellent food."

Dr. Peshkin stood. "No, no. I have no stomach for food this evening. We have come upon a wondrous discovery. I must put my thoughts down...while the concepts are fresh and alive in my mind. I will retire to my room, thank-you."

The man folded his notebook and put it into a nearby briefcase. Natka handed him the rolls of film she'd just shot, and he tucked those into the case as well. Peshkin smiled at Sava.

"Please give my regards to your uncle. He truly is a genius. I regret I cannot meet the great Nikola Tesla." He patted the briefcase. "This will change the course of the war...and beyond."

He bowed and left the room.

Milosh said, "Come Natka...grab your things. We will celebrate with Comrade Anatoli."

Natka eased down into a chair. "No, Vuk...I've developed a headache. I just want to take a powder and go to bed." She slanted a look to Sava, full of disapproval, as if he were the reason for her reticence.

"But you must come," spouted Milosh. "You have to eat."

"I couldn't," she muttered, rubbing her temples. "I'm not hungry and I'm dead on my feet."

Sava put the notebook in his attaché case and snapped it shut. "I'm afraid, gentlemen, that I too must decline. I need to pay a visit to my uncle. He waits up for me."

Without looking up, he shuffled past the Soviet agents and Vuk Milosh. They quietly let him out.

Once alone in the hallway, Sava Kosanovic nearly broke into tears. He looked down at his hands as if to find them sopped in blood.

What have I done to poor Dr. Markovitch? He wondered.

Chapter 31

———◇———

The 33rd Floor, 11:02 PM

BUCK FLYNN FROZE IN place. An icy shiver knifed up his spine. The voice had stopped him cold.

Caught! Dead to rights.

"I was wondering when you would show up," called out the voice behind him.

His mind raced. Should he attempt an escape? What were his options? There were only two: up or down. Either swing out on his top-rope to climb, as quickly as possible, back up to his room; or rappel down to Montet's suite and escape that way.

Climbing up would take longer than rappelling down, of course. He was quick, but not as quick as someone running upstairs to cut him off.

Descending, however, happened in a flash. It would take seconds to reach Montet's suite. But then what? His street clothes were up in his suite. He couldn't very well run through the hotel as he was, dressed in black, black-faced, with his harness clacking away. Far too conspicuous. Besides, Montet's room had a guard stationed nearby—that was the reason he needed to use the balcony in the first place, to get in without using the front door.

Indecision.

He knew one thing...he couldn't wait to be arrested.

He heard the patio door slide shut and the shuffling of feet coming toward him. He needed to make his move and do it quick.

"I've got your food right here," spoke the person behind him.

Food?

"I would have been out here sooner, but I had company this evening."

Something wasn't right. The man wasn't speaking as if he'd just caught a burglar.

"Here you go, my darlings."

Buck heard a pitter-pattering hit the patio floor, like the sound of sleet on a tin roof. What was that?

Slow and easy, he turned his head to find a man shadowed against the brightness of the patio doors. Tall and scrawny, clothed in pajamas, he looked like a gathering of twigs and branches cobbled together into human form. He was old, had to be eighty or ninety. The skin of his face drawn tight to his skull, nearly looking cadaverous, ashen, like ancient parchment. Gnarled hands poked from the pajama sleeves. The man was strewing birdseed from a bag perched on the patio table.

He hadn't come out to nab an intruder. He had come out to feed the birds.

Concealed behind the juniper trees, Buck stayed as still as a steel girder, watching the old man, who focused on feeding the pigeons. He mumbled to the birds, calling them by name and cooing back as if speaking in their language. Some ate right from his hand.

Then another sound came from within the suite. Buck's heart leaped. Someone had entered the rooms from the outside corridor.

A voice called out: "Uncle Niko? You still awake?"

"Out here, Sava," said the old man.

The other man appeared, framed in the patio doorway. His face and form lit up by the lamps in the room. He carried a briefcase and wore a desolate expression—as if life's tragedies tugged at his face like gravity, as if on the verge of weeping forever.

The thief stayed frozen in place, thankful for the patio shrubbery. He prayed that in his stillness, and dressed in black as he was, that he was nothing but another shadow. Beads of sweat trickled from beneath his skullcap, his hand cramped from gripping the ice-cold railing.

"Ah, feeding your darlings, I see," said the second man.

The old man chuckled. "Always."

"How was your time with the archaeologist?"

"Oh, wonderful. A brilliant man. He told me of his digs in Egypt. Had to stop because of the war. Why is there always war, Sava?"

"That's a question for the ages, Uncle."

"Someday, I will give the world something to make war obsolete."

"If anyone can...you can, Uncle."

The two of them turned back into the suite, sliding the glass door behind them and cutting off their conversation.

Buck realized that he'd been holding his breath from the moment he'd first heard the voice until now. He released air through his teeth. He still dared not move, lest the men inside caught the shifting shadows on the patio.

The two continued to converse; Buck hearing nothing through the glass. To his left, a pigeon flapped its wings, taking off into the night sky. The others followed with an awful clash of fluttering wings. The movement drew quick glances from both men inside, but neither took notice of Buck dangling alone from the edge of the terrace, and they went back to their conversation.

His eyes fell to the city streets thirty-three stories below. With the icy wind swirling around his head, his blood thickened because of his immobility; he felt dizzy for the first time in his life.

Stay focused! Don't look down. He fixed his eyes on the men in the room, waiting for his chance to drop from sight.

Then something curious took place inside the suite. As the old man was shuffling his way to a chair, his back turned away, the guest swiftly snapped open his briefcase, withdrew a black notebook, and set it on the nearby desk. Then, just as quickly, as if pretending to take a seat on the corner of the desk, the man purposely spilled a stack of papers, including the notebook, onto the floor.

The old man swung around at the commotion of it, and seeing the mess, darted over to help pick it up. There was a terse exchange between the two men. The younger one—the nephew, according to their brief conversation on the patio—took on an apologetic posture. The elderly man looked distraught. Spotting the notebook on the floor, he scooped it up, clasping it to his chest as if protecting it.

The whole scenario had been so manufactured by the younger man that Buck Flynn knew instantly that something was off. He could tell that the nephew was attempting to conceal the fact that the notebook had been in his briefcase. Dropping the mess on the floor had been his way of returning it—as if he'd taken it without his uncle's knowledge.

Buck watched as the old man trundled over to the large Diebold safe in the alcove, parted the doors, set the volume on a shelf inside, and slammed the door shut, turning the handle and spinning the combination dial as he did.

Tightly sealed again.

The men continued to talk. The tension between them abated, and smiles returned. Although the younger man's smile only exacerbated his dismal expression. Buck could tell that the nephew was eager to leave the suite—the shame of the charade he'd just perpetrated obvious, even to Buck.

Moments later, the nephew kissed the old man on the neck and left.

Buck turned his eye to the closed safe. What was that all about? Why lock away a notebook like that? There had to be value in it. Stamps? Coins? Autographs? Art?

Now alone, the old man puttered about in the apartment, turning off lights and locking the front door to the apartment. And soon he disappeared through the archway into the bedroom. A minute later, the bedroom light went out too.

Buck finally took a deep breath. He had lingered far too long on this terrace. He needed to move and get his blood circulating again. And he needed to make up time. He'd nearly been caught, and he certainly didn't want it to happen again in the suite below.

Releasing his grip on the railing, he dropped down the side of the building.

He still had an Egyptian Osorkon bracelet to steal.

Chapter 32

⸺◆⸺

Hotel Detective's Office, 11:02 PM

"YOUR SIMPLE ASSIGNMENT DOESN'T seem to have gone so well," said Phillip Carver. The young man from the Office of Coordinator of Information was leaning against the office door frame, his arms folded across his chest. His boss, Allen Davies, sat silently in a chair behind a coffee table, legs crossed, a cigarette smoldering between his fingertips.

Paddy Tooke grunted at the affront from Carver. He sat on the corner of the desk, puffing his pipe. The FBI agents had already left with George Sylvester Viereck. House Detective Williamson had gone with them to help escort Viereck through a back door to the hotel.

"We've lost a key fish," muttered Carver.

"I wouldn't call having a suspect in federal custody a lost fish," replied Tooke.

Carver glared his way. "He was supposed to be our fish! Not the FBI's. Now we won't have a chance to question him until the Bureau has squeezed him dry." He glanced at Davies with a look of exasperation.

Paddy shifted on the desk. "You never told me you wanted him detained for questioning. I was to just keep tabs on him and call you."

"Nevertheless, the opportunity is past, isn't it?"

Paddy shrugged. "We're all on the same side, right?"

Carver pursed his lips and looked away as if he were dealing with a child who couldn't quite grasp adult matters.

"Which reminds me," said Paddy. "Why did you fellas show up when you did? I thought you were waiting for my phone call?"

"We've been here all evening," stated Davies flatly, his first spoken words since they had made introductions.

Paddy started. "All evening? I didn't see you."

"Exactly," muttered Carver.

Paddy bristled at the accusatory tone of that one word.

"Your observation skills are questionable, Detective Tooke. I watched your entire movements tonight."

"Is that so?"

"You seemed to be preoccupied with other hotel guests. None of whom looked remotely like Viereck."

"Hey, now look here, Carver, I don't know what this is all about, but I gave up a pleasant evening at home to come down here and stake out the hotel, on my own time. I did it as a favor for Wild Bill. I did it without fully understanding *why* I was doing it. And I did it without being fully debriefed about the potential connections the suspect has with personnel living in the hotel. And now I find out that my presence here tonight was redundant. I don't like being used...or belittled."

"You weren't redundant," said Davies.

"You both were here all evening. Why bring me in on it?"

"Mr. Donovan thought that—"

"That's another thing! I hadn't heard from Major Donovan in twenty years. Why did he contact me out of the blue? And what the hell is the Office of Coordinator of Information, anyway?" Dottie wouldn't have cared for his cursing, but by golly, his dander was up.

Allen Davies pondered, and finally said, "Mr. Donovan thinks highly of you, Mr. Tooke. The Office of Coordinator of Information is a relatively new organization, one that President Roosevelt has commissioned. As you may or may not know, the President and Bill are on opposite sides of the political spectrum—the President being a Democrat and Bill a Republican. However, the President is smart enough to recognize leadership and realizes that the country needs to be prepared in the arena of information coordination."

"Information coordination?" repeated Paddy. "Is that code for spying?"

Davies winced. "Let's just say we're involved in gathering intelligence and looking out for the best interests of our country."

"That doesn't answer the question of, why me?"

Davies slanted a look at Carver, who rolled his eyes away. "Mr. Donovan thought you would make a good recruit for the cause."

"The cause? Of what? Spying?"

"Of honoring your country and protecting its interests."

"So, this was a test? For what? A job? Give me a silly assignment and see how I respond?

"It wasn't a silly assignment," offered Carver. "Everything we do has significance."

"Significance? The man's a poet, for crying out loud!"

Davies shot him a hard look. "You know better than that, Detective. You read his file. The man is connected to the Third Reich, and possibly to foreign agents here in the United States, who may be involved in seditious acts."

"Do you have proof of that?"

"We were hoping you could bring us something during your surveillance," said Carver, a hint of disenchantment in his voice.

Paddy's face reddened. "I only saw the fella for thirty seconds prior to being apprehended by the FBI."

"As I said before, our fish was lost."

Paddy thought of something. "So, you weren't here to watch for Viereck...you were here to watch me."

They both said nothing.

Paddy stood, tapped his pipe into an ashtray on the desk, and tucked it away. "Give Major Donovan my regards, gentlemen, and tell him, thanks, but no thanks." He started for the door.

"Could I ask you one thing before you leave?" asked Davies.

Paddy hesitated. Waiting.

"A moment ago—if memory serves me right—you mentioned not being debriefed on the potential connections that the suspect has with hotel personnel. What did you mean by that?"

"Well, for instance, the connection that the suspect has with the scientist, Nikola Tesla."

Davies' right eye brightened. "You know about that?"

Paddy nodded. "No, thanks to you! It was oddly missing from the file you gave me."

Davies shrugged. "It was need-to-know."

"Well, now I know, and a briefing beforehand would've helped."

"How?"

"I could've pressed John Williamson on it. Or talked to the staff about it."

"Why do you think Viereck's relationship with Tesla is of any importance?" asked Davies.

Paddy wondered if the question wasn't another test.

"Well, I'm no expert on Tesla, but I remember reading an article in the New York Times a few years back about his concept for the ultimate weapon. A Death Ray. I know at the time it was pooh-pawed as being science fiction. But coming from a man of Nikola Tesla's stature, it has to be considered a possibility. If such a weapon is possible...he could think it up."

"Go on."

"Well, it doesn't take a genius to connect the dots. With war waging in Europe, governments would like to get their mitts on such a weapon. Germany especially. And if they know of a sympathetic poet close to its inventor, then Viereck could very well be involved in...well, let's call it information coordination, shall we?"

Allen Davies almost smiled at that.

"It's obvious that you're concerned over possible espionage taking place right here under your noses."

"Quite," offered Davies.

Tooke turned to leave, but paused. Something had been gnawing at him and he wondered if they had purposely left another key connection out of the file, or if possibly they were in the dark about it. He said, "You know about the hotel clerk too, I suppose."

"What clerk?"

"The red-headed fellow who works behind the desk."

Davies said nothing. Paddy couldn't read his expression. Carver gave a curious cock of his head.

"Is he one of your guys?" Paddy asked. "Someone else to monitor me? Or is he another one of Viereck's need-to-know connections that you purposely kept out of the brief?"

The two men shared a look. Questions in their faces.

"We have no idea who you are talking about," said Phillip Carver.

Paddy fought to suppress a sliver of a smile. "You don't know about the hotel clerk? Why Carver, it seems your observation skills are questionable as well."

The man squinted at him, more curious than offended. "Tell us about the clerk."

"It might be nothing, but..." Paddy licked his lips, suddenly wondering if it really was nothing.

"What is it?"

"He knows Viereck."

Davies sat up, his attention piqued. "You know this how?"

Paddy explained how he'd suspected the clerk of eavesdropping on him earlier in the evening and what he'd witnessed just before the FBI swooped in. Davies listened closely, but as Paddy finished, a dismissing flinch flit over his face.

"Sounds more conjecture than—"

"There are a few other things," offered Paddy. "Small things, but small things dig at me."

"What small things?"

"The man's hair has been dyed, for one thing. I could tell by his roots. His hair has grown out some. His original hair color looks to be blond, or possibly gray, but given his age, I would guess blond."

Davies shot a concerned glance to Carver and back to Tooke. "Could be vanity. If indeed the man's gone gray."

"I also saw the fellow smoking a cigarette."

"So?"

"Well, I noticed a couple of things about his hands. Earlier, when I spotted him smoking, he wasn't wearing a ring, but later, as he was coming out to greet Viereck, he had one on the middle finger of his right hand."

Davies blinked as if the information was too insignificant to even be discussing. "Detective, I don't know how—"

"I know, it's a little thing. But it bugged me all the same. The other thing I noticed had to do with how he smoked his cigarette. It was the way he held it that got me curious. When I was in France during the war, we captured German prisoners. We handed out cigarettes to them, and I noticed they held them different from the way Americans do." He glanced down at Allen Davies' cigarette dangling near his knee. "See how you hold it? Clamped between your forefinger and your middle finger? Well, this fella held it from underneath, with his middle finger and thumb, as if pinching it. It was the same way those prisoners smoked."

Davies stared back at Tooke, growing quiet. A pause lengthened. "I see," he said.

The door to the office swung open. House Detective John Williamson entered.

Allen Davies stood as if thrust from his seat. "Mr. Williamson...Detective Tooke and I have a few questions concerning a member of your staff here at the hotel."

Chapter 33

Suite 3227 Sky Terrace, 11:14 PM

THE WIND WAS PICKING up as Buck Flynn's foot touched down on the sky terrace of Jean Pierre Marie Montet's suite. It concerned him some. On the eastern horizon, a bank of dark clouds had piled up, a potential storm approaching. He hoped it would hold off for the next thirty minutes—the time it would take to open the safe, take the bracelet, and climb back up to his room.

The drapes were halfway open, exposing the interior of the rooms. The lights were out; it appeared tranquil inside. Montet obviously still enjoying the swing music downstairs.

Buck unsnapped his harness and let it fall to the patio floor. Stepping out of it, he walked to the far edge of the terrace.

Lights blazed in the neighboring suite, and the faint cadence of music droned from a radio inside. He presumed the room next door to be occupied by Montet's security man. He was glad for the radio. It would drown out what little noise he might make—although Buck could be nearly soundless in his work.

The two suites were connected, evidenced by an open doorway at the far end where amber light spilled across the floor from the guard's room. He'd hoped it to be closed, but it made more sense that it was not. His job was to guard, after all. Buck had to assume the guard was in position to watch the front door of Montet's suite. That being the case, he wouldn't have a view of the rest of the room.

Fortunately, the wall safe, embedded in the opposite wall, was out of sight of the connecting room. Buck could see it from where he stood.

Question was, would he need his lock-picking tools for the patio doors? Putting a gloved hand on the door handle, he gave it a gentle tug, splitting a slight opening. Not locked. But then why should it be? Who's going to come in from the sky terrace?

Buck smirked at the thought.

Silently, he wedged an opening large enough to slip in sideways and quickly closed the door behind him. He couldn't have the room filling with chilly air and have the guard grow curious why.

With three soundless strides, he was to the wall safe.

This would be the only time in the evening that he would need to take off his gloves. Opening the combination lock required the sensitivity of bare fingertips. He would wipe the safe of prints after. Taking off his gloves, he took a moment to warm his hands between his thighs. They were stiff from the cold.

He kept a watch on the doorway. The guard in the other suite wasn't stirring—maybe even sleeping. The radio continued. *All of Me*, by Jimmy Dorsey's Orchestra, and the enticing lyrics sung by Helen O'Connell: *All of me...why not take all of me...*

Placing his fingers on the safe's dial, he smiled at the irony.

Yes, I just might do that.

The plan was going perfectly.

The safe was a Meilink G-7. Behind the combination dial was a spindle with a drive cam attached to the far end. Surrounding the spindle were wheels, or tumblers, one for each number in the combination, and each wheel had a gate, or notch, cut into its outer edge. These gates need to be aligned perfectly for the fence to drop into. The fence controlled the locking mechanism itself. Once it dropped in place, the lock became breached, and the door could open.

Buck knew the Eagle locks had three wheels and therefore required a three numbered combination. This saved him time by not having to discover the number of tumblers.

He had a stethoscope in his rucksack but didn't bother with it, preferring instead to test his skills without it.

He gently spun the dial, clearing the wheels, and parked on the '0'. With a slow, deliberate clockwise twist, he allowed the delicate skin of his fingertips to feel for the tender tick of the drive pin—a small protrusion on the surface of the drive cam—to catch the first wheel. Delicate work. His focus funneled into a needle keenness. The surrounding room disappeared. There was only the safe. The invisible drive pin. The elusive wheels. And the nearly imperceptible nudge of wheel-flies and tumblers aligning.

He cracked it within ten minutes.

Now the part that worried him the most: the noise of actually opening the safe. While figuring out the combination produced only muffled whirs, unlatching the door meant a metal-on-metal clunk as it opened. He only hoped the radio in the other room was loud enough to cover the sound of it.

He grasped the steel handle and gently eased it down until he heard the unmistakable clonk of the door kissing open. Not too bad.

He watched the doorway for movement.

Nothing stirred.

He waited breathlessly for a full minute, unmoving, making sure no one came peeking around the door frame.

Finally, he turned back and reaching into the safe...

He found it completely empty.

Chapter 34

THE SAFE WAS EMPTY. Not even the wife's jewelry was there.

Where was the Osorkon bracelet? Had Montet left it behind in France? Or had he stored it somewhere outside of the hotel? If that was the case...why the security detail?

And then it came to him. And Buck Flynn bristled at his stupidity.

Of course! The security man. All that perfect planning and perfect execution and he'd failed to consider one critical bit of information.

The connecting suite had its *own* Meilink G7 wall safe!

Why put the Osorkon bracelet in Montet's suite, when it would be much safer in the guard's room? The bracelet was obviously there—where the security man could monitor it.

He'd just cracked the wrong safe.

What now?

He edged over to the doorway, which stood open between the suites, and cautiously peered around the doorjamb. Music became louder. A Glenn Miller tune. The room was well lit. Buck saw the bottom half of a man lying on a davenport, his shoes untied, but still on his feet.

Was he asleep? If so, he might yet get the bracelet. It wouldn't be the first time he'd cracked a safe with people sleeping in the room. Risky? Yes, but it could be done.

However, as Buck stretched his neck to get a view of the rest of the reclining man, his heart sank. The guard was smoking a cigarette while reading a paperback by Zane Gray. He was a big fellow. His jacket was off, his tie loose. He looked relaxed, but very awake.

Buck Flynn retreated into Montet's suite.

That was it. The only way to get the bracelet now was to take the guard out of the equation. But how? Create a diversion that would get him out of the suite? That would take some forethought and planning—time he didn't have. Montet could come through the door at any moment. So, what then? Try to overtake him? Buck was not one to resort to violence. His thievery was more finesse than force. Besides, the guy was big and trained to defend. Buck was not.

So, the night was a bust. All that trouble for nothing. His five-figure sum for the bracelet evaporating before his eyes. He hated walking away empty-handed.

But then a thought flit across his mind...a long shot, but a possibility. Something that might make the evening profitable yet.

The Diebold safe he had spotted in the suite above him earlier.

He already knew that the old man lived alone, and had already gone to bed, so...

Within minutes, Buck was back on the terrace and clambering up the side of the building. Storm clouds had edged in. The temperature had dropped. The winds were stronger and wet with a cold, misty rain. The gusts blew against him, causing a bit of sway in his ropes. Even so, he landed on the thirty-third-floor terrace without a problem. Not a pigeon in sight.

He unhooked his gear. The suite inside was still dark.

The Diebold would be trickier to crack, with an older, more complicated locking mechanism and thicker doors, so he retrieved his secret weapon from the rucksack—a doctor's stethoscope. Remembering also that the Diebold had an auxiliary safe inside it, which needed a key to open it, he grabbed his lock picking caddy from the harness belt and put it in his pocket. He also grabbed the smaller of the two flashlights.

Testing the patio door, he found it unlocked and slid it open.

Once inside, he took a moment to get his bearings in the darkness. Closing his eyes, he mentally pictured the layout of the room from when he'd seen it earlier. He also listened. The room lay deathly quiet. Only the soft tick-tick-tick of a mantle clock could be heard.

Opening his eyes again, the room seemed brighter. Ambient light from the city helped, casting a blue wash over the suite. The bedroom door was closed. No light seeped through the crack at the bottom. The old man was sound asleep.

Buck Flynn eased his way to the safe. With a gloved hand, he felt along its surface, confirming that it was still closed and still locked. The two steel handles rock solid. He pulled out his flashlight, turned it on, and while holding it between his teeth, he took off his gloves. Placing the stethoscope in his ears, he set to work on the combination lock.

It took longer than the Meilink G7 in Montet's suite. Buck wasn't used to the quirks of the older Diebold. The ticks were smoother and subtle. Without knowing the number of wheels the spindle had beforehand, he had to discover what he was dealing with. It took twelve minutes to learn there were four. This meant a four-number combination—the variations astronomical. He ended up turning off his flashlight, closing his eyes, and pressing the diaphragm of the stethoscope against the cool steel. Using the silence of the room, he listened for the noiseless clicks of the drive-pin against the wheel-flies inside the thick doors.

Tick, tick, tick...click.

Tick, tick, tick...click.

One by one.

The challenge tested the full extent of his abilities, but seventeen minutes later, through his earpiece, he heard the muffled snap of the fence falling into the four gates on the tumblers.

The safe was breached.

He clenched the center handles and twisted. The fat doors felt as heavy as battleships, but they parted on well-oiled hinges with nary a squeak.

Turning his flashlight back on, he scoured the shelves and cubbyholes inside, dismayed by how little he found. No gems, jewelry, coins, or bills. Papers filled most of the shelves, which excited him at first, thinking that he may have stumbled upon bearer bonds; but scanning them, he found nothing but old photographs, schematics, blueprints, and a few patent certificates—which were useless to him.

He also came across odds and ends. Small machine parts, with wires and toggles and nuts and bolts. Nothing that would be of any value—certainly nothing worthy of a safe of this fortitude.

He then remembered the notebook. The old man had treated it as if were priceless. Certainly, there must be value inside of it.

There it was! On the top shelf. Buck pulled it down and opened its pages, scanning through it.

Nothing.

No stamps, coins, rare bills, or any other collectible item was inside its leaves. Just drawings and scribbling, much of it scientific—and way over his head. Nothing but a book of formulas and designs. What was all the fuss about? The old man had treated it as if it were gold—locking it in the safe that way. Why?

Frustrated, Buck closed up its pages and returned the book to its place on the shelf.

It was looking like a bust.

Then his eyes fell to the auxiliary safe. The safe within the safe. Maybe something of value was in it.

Kneeling, he studied the door. This section was called the anti-dynamite box, and like its name implied, completely blast-proof. The locking mechanism had a steel rod running horizontally across the width of the door with an attached brass handle. A round lockset sat in the center of the safe like a stainless-steel belly button. Once unlocked, simply pull down on the handle and shift the connecting rod to open the safe.

But first, the lock needed to be breached.

Buck took out his lock-picking tools, choosing a long narrow spike, nearly seven inches long. He slid the spike into the slot. He then chose another tool, with a minuscule right-angle bend on the end, like a tiny Allen wrench. He poked this into the lock too, gently feeling his way into the inner cutaways of the locking system. A few artful twists of his fingers and the inner cutaways gave way. A breeze. Gripping the handle of the connecting rod, he pulled it down, shifted it over, and the door swung open.

His heart thumping with anticipation, he scanned the inner shelves with his flashlight for treasure. But his excitement quickly deflated.

Nothing. Only a few photographs.

Absolutely useless.

Then he spotted something. A thick gold thread dangled over the edge of the shelf. He gave it a tug and from out of a cubby-hole slid a tiny pouch.

The sack was approximately the size of a man's palm and made of cloth with a drawstring thread along the top edge. Something inside felt thin, round, and heavy. He untied the drawstring and out slipped a large gold coin.

No. Not a coin. A medal.

Finally! Something of value.

He poured his penlight over its surface. As large as an Olympic gold medal, it looked brand new. Yellow glints reflected off its face. Stamped on one side was the profile of a man's head, and on the other, the naked figure of a man standing with, what appeared to be, an angel behind him. As Buck read the inscription on its face, he realized that the embossed profile was that of Thomas Alva Edison, and the medal was an achievement award given by the American Institute of Engineers.

Buck shrugged. He hadn't heard of the organization, or that they gave out medals. Either way, it was the only thing of value that he'd come across so far. It was no Egyptian Osorkon bracelet, but at least it was something. Maybe worth a few bucks.

He stuffed the medal back into its pouch and was about to slip it into his pocket when he paused. Contemplating.

Maybe worth a few bucks.

A rare stab of morality hit him. He turned and scanned the darkened apartment. It wasn't posh. No priceless antiques. Nothing of material worth on display. As if it was nothing more than a high-rise shanty.

Usually, his marks were the wealthy upper crust, who would barely miss their stolen valuables, and which were usually protected by hefty insurance policies. Buck rarely felt remorse for their loss and even experienced satisfaction in beating their systems to keep him out.

But this felt different.

This poor old man had close to nothing of value in this apartment—he seemed to exist on saltine crackers, for heaven's sake. His only asset seemed to be a medal that he must have received years ago for some forgotten accomplishment. How could Buck take that one cherished item from him?

He couldn't. It meant nothing but a few dollars for Buck, but it seemed to be the old man's only treasure. A paltry treasure locked in a three thousand pound safe.

He reached up and placed the sack with its golden prize back on the shelf. He sighed a breath. Yep, it was official; the night was a bust. Although Pops would always say:

No matter what the take, any job is successful if by the end of the night you're sleeping in a bed on this side of bars.

Nevertheless, empty pockets never felt like success to Buck.

Reluctantly, he closed the anti-dynamite box door and locked it back up. Temptation averted.

He was reaching for his lock-picking tools lying next to him on the floor when...

He stopped cold.

A faint scraping sound thundered across the quiet apartment. His blood became ice. He knew that sound well. It was the sound of a key turning in a lock!

Someone was entering the suite.

Chapter 35

———◆———

Suite 3327, 11:38 PM

SLOWLY, BUCK FLYNN EASED up from his crouched position, his heart pounding. In the quiet of the dark apartment, the soft scratch of a key in the lock echoed like a hammer striking an anvil.

Someone was about to come through the door.

They hadn't knocked and had a key, so it must be someone who knew the old man—possibly the visiting nephew he'd witnessed earlier while hanging from the balcony.

Buck clicked off his flashlight and quietly closed the two doors of the safe until they meshed into the center with a muffled clunk—shut, but still unlocked.

He glanced over to the patio doors leading to the sky terrace. Could he get outside in time? No. Too far away. He would never make it before the door opened. His eyes darted about for a place to hide, possibly under the desk.

But it was too late.

The door cracked open, spilling light from the hallway into the suite.

Buck pulled back into the shadows of the alcove. A narrow space existed between the safe and the wall, just enough to conceal him—somewhat. He drew a breath and squeezed into it. The safe, being only five feet tall, did little to hide him. And as soon as the lights came on, he would be exposed. What then?

He waited. Heart racing.

But the lights didn't come on.

A figure slipped through the door, closed it, and stood stone still in the darkness. From his brief glimpse of the silhouette, Buck was sure it had been a man. The figure remained soundless, as if listening. But for what? The old man? To see if he was asleep? Or did the visitor suspect an intruder to be inside the suite?

Two full minutes ticked by. Flynn felt sweat under his leather jacket. Wedged as he was in the narrow opening between the safe and the wall, breathing was difficult. He drew soft breaths through his teeth. Motionless.

Then the figure turned on a flashlight of his own. The wedge of light made a tour of the room, flicking over the living area and its furniture, to land on the office portion of the suite, fixated on the desk. The figure approached it, the beam crawling over the clutter of the desktop. Buck watched as the person bent to rummage through the papers and files piled there, as if looking for something specific. With the patio doors behind him, the man's form loomed against the city lights; he was tall and lean, with quick graceful movements.

Then Buck spotted something that gripped him with panic.

Beyond the figure, Buck's harness and ropes, piled on the sky-terrace floor, were visible through the patio doors. What would happen when the man noticed the items?

But he didn't notice. His attention was fully on the desk—although he didn't seem to find the object of his search. He worked his way around to the other side and took a seat in the chair, and began opening the drawers. When this search also proved futile, he stood to pass the beam over the floor surrounding the desk and the nearby table. He then turned his attention to the shelves behind it—that is, the shelves in the alcove! The same alcove where Buck hid.

Blood thumped in Buck's ears. The swatch of light headed his way, crawling along the alcove in a slow, careful inspection of the shelves. If the fellow didn't find the object of his search soon, he would reach the safe, and possibly glimpse the very obvious thief attempting to hide behind it. Buck needed to be ready when that happened.

The light drew closer.

Wedged as he was, Buck could not prepare himself to attack—not without giving himself away. His joints had become stiff. Sweat trickled down his face. He held his breath.

The beam fell on the safe. The figure drew up to it, patting his hands across its lacquered surface, the glow of light bouncing inches from Buck's face. He was thankful for the shoe polish mask he wore.

Upon finding the safe closed, the intruder let out an exasperated breath and turned away to head back into the room. But stopped. Deliberating.

Buck wondered if the man hadn't had a delayed response to having spotted a head among the shadows in the corner. And sure enough, he twisted the shaft of light back his way.

The man stepped to the front of the safe, reaching a hand toward him.

Gritting his teeth, Buck prepared to pounce.

However, the outstretched hand vacillated inches away, then lowered to grab one of the door handles to the safe, giving it a twist and tug.

The safe opened.

Buck heard a puff of triumph escape the man's lips. He had assumed that the doors being closed meant the safe to be locked, when it wasn't.

The flashlight swept inside the safe. Seconds later, the intruder found the item of his search—the thick notebook. He pulled it from the shelf to scan its pages. Buck watched him smirk in the reflected light.

Leaving the safe door ajar, the intruder turned away, stepping into the center of the room. Buck thought he was about to leave, but he paused, as if contemplating.

Buck waited, watching...un-breathing.

The man placed the notebook on a side table near the door and moved back into the office. He began scooping up papers from the desk, wadding them into balls, and tossing them about the room. He took his time, creating a field of clutter around the davenport, chairs, and the table near the desk. He pulled books from the shelves, piling them in a heap, and adding empty cracker boxes on top.

Suspicion flared in Buck. What did the intruder intend to do? The mess didn't appear random, but calculated. He now realized that this was no friend of the old man at all, but another thief.

No, not just another thief...something else entirely.

And sure enough, to Buck's shock, the man produced a tin of lighter fluid from his jacket pocket and squirted the liquid over the piled mess and the furniture, and then...to Buck's horror, he saturated the bedroom door. The petroleum smell permeated the room, sharp and pungent, a lethal odor.

More than a thief! A murderer! He planned to set fire to the room and kill the old man.

Terror swept over Buck. He had to stop him.

Quietly, he shifted himself out of the narrow space. He stepped out, stretching to his full height, numbness hampering his movements. The figure stood ten feet away, his back to him.

A match struck. The orange glow swelling with murderous intent. The man lifted his hand back behind his ear, ready for a toss.

Buck lunged.

He grabbed the lighted flame with his bare hand, extinguishing it.

"Ach!" cried the shadow, a shrill of surprise in his voice.

He whipped around, astonished to find Buck behind him.

"Leave now!" whispered Buck through clenched teeth.

With the speed of a striking cobra, the man swung a wild fist at Flynn. Buck sensed it coming and instinctively twisted away. The glancing blow struck his shoulder. Buck used the momentum of his defensive turn to deliver a crushing uppercut of his own. It landed squarely on the man's jaw. His head snapped back. A jolt of fiery pain sparked through Buck's forearm. The solid punch caused the man to stumble back a couple of steps, but he quickly regained his balance.

Now up close, Buck could see he had misjudged the intruder's size. He was taller, heavier, with a pair of solid shoulders. His hair was reddish, his eyes like blue glass, and he appeared to be dressed in evening clothes, a flower pinned to his lapel. The man rubbed his face, shaking off the slug to the jaw.

Buck hesitated, hoping his surprise attack had spooked the intruder into fleeing the apartment.

It didn't.

The attack had enraged him. His fists tightened. His neck flexed. His body posture squared for retaliation.

Buck braced himself, waiting for the man to lunge.

But no lunge came.

Instead, the intruder reached into his trousers pocket and withdrew an object. As his arm lifted, the object glinted in the ambient city lights.

A knife.

A spidery ripple ran up Buck's spine. The man had a weapon.

But before that thought had fully formed, the intruder shot forward at lightning speed. The blade sliced an arc toward Buck's heart. Buck tilted back from it, arching his spine. But it was too late. The knife whisked across his chest, ripping an opening in his leather jacket, and slitting across his skin.

His synapses bursting with electricity, Buck leaped away, backing into the alcove and slamming into the shelves. The figure slithered closer, swaying the knife back and forth. Buck squirmed to his left, out of reach. His heart thwacking. The fresh wound hot and wet. He bumped into the safe behind him.

Then, strangely, he heard the man chuckle. And he realized why.

Buck had cornered himself, and the man knew it.

The man sprung again, this time thrusting towards his throat. Buck twisted away at the last second. The blade plunging between the opened doors of the safe.

As quick as thought, Buck swiveled around, kicking the safe door shut. Three hundred pounds of solid steel crunching flesh. Mangling finger bones.

The man cried out, "*Du Hurensohn*!" Grabbing at the door handle with his other hand, he swung open the safe, jerking back his hand, his fingers a contorted mess.

The knife fell to the floor with a clatter.

Buck swung a fist toward the man's face, but it never landed. Even in agony, he was quick. The man's knee snapped up, ramming Buck's abdomen. A devastating blow. Pain burst into his belly, exploding all the way to his spine, knocking the air from his lungs.

Buck collapsed.

Lifting to all fours, he gasped for breath. His torso was on fire—as if ribs were broken.

But then, through watery eyes, he spotted the knife lying near the desk. Ten feet away. So far away. Miles. He had to get it before the attacker did. With all he could muster, he sprung forward.

Another kick flew out of the darkness, like the swing of a polo mallet. It caught him in the face, reeling him onto his back. Sending him further away from the knife. He crumbled. His body throbbed. Twisting around, he braced himself up against the door of the safe. His breath rasping.

Then...a thought. Maybe his Pops could save him.

He felt along the floor near the base of the safe.

The intruder stepped up. Looming over him, his right hand dangling, useless.

Buck blinked, the pain blurring his vision. Why wasn't the intruder attacking?

The man, using his left hand, reached for the flower pinned to his lapel. Grabbing the boutonniere, he pointed it at Buck.

No...not a boutonniere. A tiny silver pistol.

He fired. The sound of it like the pop of a cap gun.

Buck rolled the moment he saw the gun, but not in time. The bullet slammed into his left shoulder as if bashed with a hammer. He hit the floor face down. Without looking around, he could feel the man aiming at the back of his head. In desperation, his fingers patted along the floor in front of the safe.

Yes. It was there.

Grabbing the item, he swung upward with full force.

The lock-picking tool buried into the intruder's thigh—three inches deep. Buck yanked downward on the shaft, tearing flesh and spurting blood. The man screamed. From his position on the floor, Buck coiled a leg around the man's footing and pushed. He fell like cut timber.

Ignoring the pain flaring through his body, Buck Flynn leaped for the knife next to the desk. Both men scrambled to their feet. Buck slashed madly in the darkness. He caught the man's arm that brandished the pistol. Blood spit out.

The man whimpered and backed away, limping. The metal spike jutted from his thigh. He grimaced, full of rage. Using his smashed hand, the man reached down and yanked the lock-picking tool from his leg. He threw it at Buck, hitting him harmlessly. It fell to the floor.

Buck lunged. The pistol fired. An orange flare sparking in the darkness.

The bullet slammed into Buck's chest, twisting him as he fell forward. Momentum thrust him toward the intruder. His arm swung down in an arc. Miraculously, the knife found flesh, stabbing into the man's upper shoulder.

Buck stumbled back.

The man spun away, cursing in what sounded like German. He glanced down at the hilt of the knife protruding from his shoulder. He raised the gun again.

Buck froze, unable to move.

The man pulled the trigger.

Nothing.

Frantically, the intruder yanked two more times on the trigger. But it was jammed...or out of bullets.

Furious, the man threw the gun at Flynn, smacking him in the face. Spinning around, the man hobbled across the apartment and out the door, slamming it behind him.

Buck fell to his knees. His breath gasping. His chest felt as if dynamite had exploded in it. Looking around, he found the lock-picking spike. He wiped it clean of blood on his pants leg.

Thanks, Pops. My inheritance saved me.

He crawled over to the safe, gathered the rest of his tools and stethoscope. He could feel blood filling his leather jacket. The flames in his chest blazed. His ribs tender to the touch. He knew he was in terrible shape, but his adrenaline was spiking, ordering him to move.

He came to a wobbly stance just as a slit of light appeared from under the bedroom door. The noise had awakened the old man.

Time to go.

He hobbled through the patio doors. Before closing them, he turned back, curious.

The intruder had forgotten something.

The notebook he came to steal remained on the side table where he'd left it.

Chapter 36

Suite 3433, 11:45 PM

DR. BORIS PESHKIN CLOSED his notebook and set it aside, giving it a tender pat.

Not quite finished with the calculations, yet he could see them aligning into a probable formula for the particle beam weapon. He shook his head in disbelief. He hadn't thought it possible, but he'd been wrong. He ran his fingers through his shaggy, white hair and closed his eyes. Nikola Tesla was truly a genius, as proved by his ability to simplify the complex into its most basic and utilitarian possibilities.

Peshkin now realized that the key behind Tesla's inspiration for the weapon had been the Van De Graff generator.

In 1929, Princeton physicist Robert J. Van de Graff invented an electrostatic generator that could accumulate high amounts of electrical potential, turning the extremely high voltage produced into particle accelerators, or atom-smashers. By accelerating the sub-atomic particles into top speeds, and then "smashing" them into target atoms, the resulting collisions created other subatomic particles and high-energy radiation. Tesla capitalized on this concept and morphed it into his designs for the particle beam Death Ray.

Teleforce.

That is what Tesla called it. In the notebook, there were outlines and figures for four unique inventions that together would generate the weapon.
The first was an apparatus for producing rays and energy in free air without
the use of a vacuum; the second was a method for producing great electrical
forces; the third a method for amplifying those forces; and the fourth, a
new method of propelling the tremendous force produced. The destructive
power would be fifty million volts.

And now Boris Peshkin understood it. The weapon was for real, and yes,
its development possible.

He stood and stepped over to the bar. He had forgone the celebration
earlier, choosing instead to gather his thoughts concerning the discovery.
Now he was ready to cap off an exciting evening with a drink. Picking up
the bottle of vodka, he started to open it, but stopped. No. This called for
an American whiskey—an oak-barrel-aged bourbon. After all, he was in
New York, and when in Rome...

He poured the whiskey and took a sip of the golden liquid. He licked his
lips. Smooth. Warm. Appropriate. He set the drink aside and reached into
his jacket to retrieve a cigar—a hand-rolled Quintero that he'd found in a
tobacconist shop off of 34th Avenue earlier in the day. He'd also bought
a beautiful humidor of Spanish cedar and filled it with various premier
brands of cigars. So many choices and pleasures here in capitalistic America.
He would miss the benefits once he returned to the Soviet Union. The
Politburo blamed much of the shortages on the war. But he was old enough
to remember the lack in his country long before Hitler encroached upon
Soviet soil.

He, of course, kept the humidor well-hidden at the bottom of his suitcase. His escort, Yegor Volkov, would never understand his appreciation of
such bourgeoisie pleasures.

He didn't care for Volkov. His dark, threatening presence was a constant
reminder that defection was not an option for Peshkin—not that he hadn't
given the idea some thought. If it were not for his wife of thirty-eight years,

Katrina, waiting for him back home...well. It would not go well for her if he defected.

But that didn't stop him from dreaming. The United States had plenty of opportunities for a man of his academic caliber. Any number of universities would welcome him, and if he closed his eyes, he could picture himself at Princeton working side-by-side with the likes of Van de Graaf and Einstein, and—at the end of the day—maybe smoking Quinteros together.

He clipped the end of the cigar, rolled it around on his lips, wetting the tip, and lighted it. He drew in the smoke.

Ah, yes. Such choices.

He picked up his glass of bourbon and moved over to the patio doors. Through the open drapes, the cityscape was bursting with lights. A marvelous sight and a far cry from the blackouts that were currently required in Moscow because of the Nazi onslaught. He slid open the door and stepped outside. The crisp night air felt good. The rain was coming down now, but the overhang of the terrace protected him; however, the gusty wind misted his face with an icy spray.

His mind turned to the weapon. Everything was about to change. Teleforce would give the Soviet military superiority over the fascists and drive Hitler into the sea. Firmly establishing Soviet supremacy. And who knows, once that happens, maybe prosperity would come to the communists, the same as that of the capitalists, and he would have his choice of premier cigars in the motherland. Although, he had to wonder if such prosperity was possible. Collectivism seemed so slanted against it—as if enjoying life was a crime to itself.

But one thing was certain. With this new knowledge, and his needed guidance in developing the project, his name would become a household word in Russia. Hailed as a hero. His status in the Soviet Union would equal that of Einstein in the States. Life would become much easier for him and Katrina.

He took another sip of the bourbon, appreciating its smoky flavor. Maybe there was room in his suitcase for a couple of bottles of the American whiskey as well. He would enjoy sharing the beverage with Katrina. A welcome break from the tireless Vodka.

Standing near the railing, enjoying his pleasures, Peshkin caught movement along the surface of the building to his left.

What was that?

A flag? It was too large to be a bird. He cranked his head and squinted toward the spot he thought he saw the movement. The rain whipped. A dull haze clung to the sky. Shadows from the overhanging terraces made it hard to make out forms. He wondered if his mind had played a trick on him, causing him to see things.

But no. It happened again. There, against the back-lit edge of the building, was the form of a man clinging to the brick surface about forty feet away. It looked as if he were crawling up the side of the hotel. How could that be?

Dr. Peshkin set his drink down on the flat surface of the railing, moved to the corner of the balcony, and leaned out, trying to get a better view of the most extraordinary thing he'd ever seen. A man climbing the New Yorker Hotel, thirty-four stories up! And in the pouring rain, no less.

A gust of wind swept up. The breeze whistled in his ears, loud enough to cover the sound of the door to his suite open and close, and loud enough to drown out the approach of the person behind him.

He heard nothing but wind.

All the while marveling at the sight of a man scaling the building.

In the next second, a hard shove slammed into his back and Dr. Boris Peshkin found himself thrust over the railing. He tumbled—the city lights, the swirling rain, the climbing man, all becoming a carousel of spinning flashes.

The Quintero still clenched in his teeth; he didn't even think to scream until ten stories had whipped by.

Chapter 37

—◆—

The 34th Floor, 11:54 PM

THE PAIN WAS EXCRUCIATING. His left arm next to useless. The bullet wounds throbbed as blood seeped into his jacket. Ascending was nearly impossible. Every shifting movement shot cruel jolts of electricity through Buck Flynn's body.

It didn't help that a storm had moved in. Icy rain peppered his face and gusts of wind caused sway in his ropes. One frightening blast nearly sent him hurtling around the corner of the building.

The loss of blood and the pain brought him to the brink of fainting. He grit his teeth, determined to make it to his suite.

The one factor in his favor was that his knapsack was empty of loot.

It made him mad as hell to think of it.

All this planning and work for nothing. No! Worse than nothing. He was not only coming away empty-handed; he was coming away wounded and possibly scarred for life. Never had a job gone so badly.

He pulled and shifted. Stepped up. Pulled and shifted. Stepped up. Wincing at every movement. Swallowing the knifing pain.

So agonizingly slow.

The leather thongs were slick when wet. He had to do twice the work for half the distance.

To keep his mind awake, he dwelt on the intruder. The other thief. Who was he? What did he want with that notebook? Everyone seemed to treat the book as if it were something precious. Was it worth murdering for? If Buck hadn't been there, the entire suite would be in flames at this very moment, and the old man possibly dead.

At least something of value could be said for this wasted evening. He'd saved a life.

The intruder had spoken in German. Buck was sure of it. Did that mean something? If so, what? There were plenty of German-Americans in the city, but with all the turmoil being wreaked by the Krauts over there, it certainly made everyone suspicious of them here. And it had to make one wonder whether the intruder had been German-American, or just plain German—as in...a Nazi. If that was the case, why would he be rummaging around an old man's apartment?

The notebook!

The intruder wanted it. Buck got some satisfaction knowing that when the man had left the suite, he went empty-handed. By sheer serendipity, he'd thwarted evil designs.

Buck braced his feet against the rain-slicked outer wall. He was reaching up to adjust his knot when movement caught the corner of his eye—an awkward, clumsy, abnormal movement against the murky city sky.

To his left, a shadow flickered. Turning toward it, an eerie fright shimmied down his spine.

A man was falling through the air.

In stunned silence, Buck watched the figure tumble grotesquely, end-over-end, through the night. Hands grasping at air. Legs longing for a foothold, kicking. Body contorting. Gravity yanking. The night swallowing.

So quiet.

It took a second for the man's shriek to rise and echo across the skyscrapers. A hopeless, sickening cry. A frightful sound.

The falling form funneled into darkness. Buck heard nothing of it hitting the pavement below. But it had.

By instinct, Buck glanced up to where the figure had originated. There on a neighboring balcony loomed another figure, slipping through the patio doors of the suite. The lights went out. The figure had moved fast, so fast that Buck saw nothing but a blurry silhouette through the rain. But he was sure of one thing.

He had just witnessed a murder.

Chapter 38

House Detective's Office, 11:55 PM

THE RESUME OF HENRY Blacksmith lay open on the desk. Paddy Tooke spotted it the moment he'd returned to Williamson's office. He'd slipped away for a few minutes to make a phone call from a booth in the lobby.

Allen Davies sat in John Williamson's chair as if he had commandeered the office through a coup. His dark eyes sucking the words off the pages. Phillip Carver and Williamson hovered behind him; the House Detective stricken by the possibility of a Nazi spy being among his hired personnel.

"Pretty skimpy information," muttered Davies.

"Bare bones," offered Carver. "Just enough to get hired for the job."

Paddy took a seat in one of the upholstered chairs in the far corner, smoking his pipe and staring at the floor as if lost in thought.

"We checked his references," said Williamson, his voice squeaky with defensiveness. "He came highly recommended."

Davies lifted a page from the file. "Yes, you even have a letter of recommendation from the man the FBI just arrested for sedition." His tone dripped with accusation.

"How could I know Viereck had Nazi sympathies? He's a well-known writer."

Davies grunted at that. "His writings have been clearly pro-Hitler."

"I...I didn't know that."

Davies handed the file over to Carver. "We will need to check out the addresses, identities, and telephone numbers of all the people listed on the resume. Also, verify Blacksmith's address. We need to get a team over to search his apartment immediately."

Sergeant Detective Tooke's eyes sparked. "You mean after you get a search warrant first."

Allen Davies stared back, his face like stone. "Yes, of course, Detective. After we get a search warrant."

His face was unreadable, but Paddy felt in his bones that warrants were of no significance in Allen Davies's world and doubted that one would be obtained in this case.

As if reading his thoughts, Davies said, "You understand that this is a matter of national security. If indeed this man is a Nazi spy, we need to take immediate steps to apprehend him."

Paddy Tooke blew out smoke. "I've already taken steps to do just that."

Davies's face clouded. "What do you mean?"

"I'm a detective, Mr. Davies. That means I live in the world of motives. I always ask: what is driving a person?"

Davies said nothing.

"Here, we ask, what is driving our Mr. Blacksmith? If indeed he is an enemy agent, what was his purpose in infiltrating the hotel staff? We are only speculating, but circumstantial evidence connects the dots between Viereck and Blacksmith...and then to Nikola Tesla. It's most probable they were after something he possesses."

"Obviously," muttered Davies.

"Well, understanding that motive helps us design a strategy. It's unclear if the two of them have been successful or not in obtaining the information they seek. If they did, then Mr. Blacksmith is long gone, and most likely on his way to Germany. If not, then he may be desperate enough to make a run for Tesla's room on his own."

"Yes, that makes sense, I suppose."

"So, I put in a call to a few of my men a little while ago. I have them stationed at the major exits of the hotel and I have a man on his way to stand outside Tesla's door."

Davies's face tightened. "That was quite judicious of you, detective. I appreciate your initiative. But this is now a national security issue and must be handled with discretion."

"I told my men that this was off the books, as a favor to me. I trust them with my life. They are loyal and discreet."

"Nevertheless—"

Williamson's telephone rang. The House Detective answered it. Alarm fell across his face.

"I'll be right up," he replied into the phone and hung up. "That was your man on the thirty-third floor, detective. Nikola Tesla's room has been burglarized."

Davies stood abruptly. He and Carver stepped from around the desk. "Any sign of Blacksmith?"

Williamson shook his head. "He said only Mr. Tesla was in the room."

Davies shot a glare at Tooke, who remained seated. "It looks like your hunch played out."

Paddy Tooke stared at the floor as if thinking.

"We better get up there. Are you coming, detective?"

Paddy looked up. "I'm sure you boys can take care of the situation. I think I'll hang around the lobby and see if Blacksmith shows."

"Suit yourself."

Just as Davies, Carver, and Williamson opened the office door, one of the desk clerks came rushing into the room, his face a mask of panic. He stood before Williamson as if to speak, but eyed the other men with caution.

"Sir, we have a situation that needs your attention," he finally blurted.

"Not now, I have an issue that I have to see to on the thirty-third floor."

"But sir, you really—"

"I said, not now!" Williamson snapped.

"But sir, someone has just jumped off the building."

Chapter 39

The 34th Floor, 12:02 AM

BUCK FLYNN VACILLATED ON his ropes, too shocked to move. Rain pelleted him. Wind twisted his ropes. His wounds screamed. Horror bellowed. Someone had just murdered a man

He looked up. He was near to his suite. It seemed like miles. Could this night get any worse?

Four minutes later, he clambered over the railing of the sky terrace to his room.

He lay on the patio floor for another five minutes, panting. The icy rain soaking him. The cold tightened his muscles. He unhooked his harness and crawled his way into the suite.

He stripped off his wet clothes. Each movement agony. Blood mottled his chest. He stumbled into the bathroom and into the shower. For fifteen minutes, he lay huddled in the corner, letting the hot spray wash him down, bringing warmth back into his veins. Rose-colored water eddied down the drain. Then he washed his face of the shoe polish and murky black water eddied down the drain.

He toweled off. Looking in the mirror, he saw the bullet holes, two of them, one in his shoulder and another in his chest on the right side. They both continued to bleed. The holes were tiny, as if someone had driven 16 penny nails into his flesh and pulled them out. The gun must have been a very small caliber. His jacket and sweater had helped to impede the impact of the bullets. Twisting around to look at his back in the mirror, he could see no exit holes. That meant that the slugs were still in him. Had to be. It hurt like hell.

A gash sliced across his upper chest. It wasn't too deep—again, his jacket and sweater had spared him—but it was nearly nine inches long. Blood had coagulated, but even as he dabbed at it with a towel, he couldn't stanch the blood flow. It would need to be stitched.

Black and blue splotches covered his ribcage from being kicked. Tender to the touch. One or two of his ribs possibly broken.

And his face. Swollen and red, he hardly recognized himself.

He cleansed the wounds with soap and water. They refused to stop bleeding. He needed to get the bullets out before blood poisoning set in, as well as get the gash stitched up. He wrapped his chest with a towel, securing it with tape from his knapsack. He limped back into the living room and eased himself down on the davenport. He didn't dare lie down. If he did, he knew he would pass out. He couldn't let that happen. He needed a doctor.

Looking at the ceiling, he whispered, "Well, Pops? What pearls of wisdom do you have for me now?"

Forcing himself up, he gathered his wet and soiled clothes and scaling materials and packed them away in his case. He then dressed in his suit, a slow and painful process. Already his makeshift towel bandage was bleeding through, but he had no time to redress it. He left the bathroom a bloody mess. The maid would wonder what happened here, but that was Eddie Petrowski's problem. The room was under his name.

The hallway was unoccupied.

Carrying his leather case, he moved toward the elevator doors. The stairs were not an option in his condition; there was no way he could endure the climb of thirty-five flights of stairs. He kept his hat low on his forehead, hopefully shadowing the welt on his face.

The elevator doors opened. Besides the operator, there were six other people in the car. He stepped in and found a place in the back corner to brace himself against the wall.

His goal was the tunnel to the Pennsylvania Station coming off the main lobby. Simple and direct. He could take a subway up to Lexington. Buck knew of a retired doctor on the Upper East Side—an old friend of his Pops—who was skillful and discreet. He would extract the bullets, patch him up, and ask no questions. Buck only hoped he could make it to him before he passed out. He'd already lost a lot of blood.

The elevator ride was excruciatingly slow. They seemed to stop at every other floor to let out passengers or board new ones. Each gliding halt shot tremors of prickling pain through Buck. His muscles waned of strength. His peripheral vision grew dark.

The elevator car had finally disgorged all its riders; Buck was alone with the operator. The young man shot curious glances Buck's way, but said nothing, forcing his stare away. Buck wondered why. Then, looking down, he realized that blood had seeped through his towel bandage and had stained a crimson splotch on his dress shirt. He clutched his overcoat tighter, but already blood had left spatters on the elevator floor.

The young operator said nothing.

When the doors opened, Buck lurched forward, shuffling toward the tunnel entrance on the other side of the lobby. The marble floor loomed like the expanse of an ocean. The lobby was full of people, strolling, loitering. Several were drunk, laughing boisterously. It made his head pound.

He made his way to the mouth of the Pennsylvania Station tunnel leading underground. A brass handrail ran along the tiled wall to the ramp. Buck grasped it as if it were a lifeline, steadying himself. He only hoped he could manage the stairs down to the subway.

As he was about to descend the stairs, when he felt a tap on his shoulder and a voice behind him said, "Excuse me, young man, do you have a light?"

Without turning around, Buck replied, "No, I don't smoke."

The man behind him chuckled. "That's ironic, isn't it? After all, isn't that what the newspapers call you, *The Smoke*?"

A chill rippled through him. The peripheral darkness increased.

The voice continued: "They call you *The Smoke*, but your actual name is Harry Flynn Jr. But, if you prefer, I'll call you Buck."

In slow motion, Buck Flynn eased around, spears of pain slicing through him.

A man stood there, clenching a pipe between his teeth. Blurry recognition dripped into Buck's memory. The harmless-looking fellow he'd spotted earlier—the ordinary spider who was now the Brown Recluse. Biting him.

A queer sense of relief engulfed him. Busted. But he simply didn't care.

"I...I stopped him," he croaked.

"Stopped who?" the man asked.

The connecting wires to this world snapped, severing his grip on consciousness. The Pennsylvania Tunnel caved in around him, sucking him into a vortex of spinning shadows. His legs wobbled, and Buck Flynn collapsed into a merciful land of painless gloom.

Chapter 40

Suite 3434, 12:28 AM

NATKA MILOSH SLIPPED INTO bed, turned off the lamp, and pulled the covers over her head. She shivered in the darkness. Was it from the cold? Or the events of the evening? She was on the verge of tears. How did it come to this? How did she become entrenched in such treachery? Shame burned in her heart.

Her husband, Vuk, was still upstairs with the Soviets. She was glad for his absence. Sometimes she couldn't stand being in the same room with him. He had been so heartless toward Dr. Markovitch. She feared for him. An innocent life snuffed out.

But then, was she any better? There was blood on her hands, too.

A noise squeaked from beyond the bedroom door. What was that? Lifting her head from the pillow, she strained to listen. The shivering escalated.

Someone had entered the suite.

No light went on in the other room, but someone was there. She heard the hushed scuffing of shoes on the carpet. Her heart raced.

It couldn't be Vuk. He would have turned on the light.

Footfalls pulled up to the bedroom door.

She reached over to the nightstand, opened the drawer, and felt around inside. Her fingers felt for the pistol there, slipping her finger over the trigger and pulling the gun back underneath the covers. And waited.

The door opened. The figure of a man became framed in the doorway, pausing, then approaching.

Her finger tightened on the trigger.

The man bent toward her.

"Natka, wake up."

Vuk!

She let out a breath of relief and relaxed the grip on the pistol.

"Wake up," he repeated, nudging her.

"Vuk," she whispered. "Why aren't you getting into bed?"

"Get up," he commanded. "Something has happened."

"What?" she asked, her voice laced with alarm. Her hand went to turn on the light, but Vuk grabbed it, keeping her from doing so.

"No, don't turn on the light. Just get up."

Natka got out of bed and reached for her robe lying across a chair.

"No," snapped Vuk. "Get dressed. We need to meet with our comrades."

Natka bristled. She hated it when Vuk spoke to her as if she were a simple child. She opened her mouth to ask what it was all about, but restrained herself. It would anger him and cause a reprimand. Instead, she quickly dressed in the dark while Vuk waited in the other room.

Once she met him there, he opened the apartment door a crack to survey the hallway.

"Come," he said. "It's clear."

They stepped into the hall and walked. When they reached the adjoining suite, Natka halted, reaching for the doorknob.

"No! You fool!" cried Vuk, yanking her back. "Don't touch that door."

"But you said our comrades were waiting for us, wouldn't they be in their room?"

Vuk shook his head. "We can't touch that room now. Something has happened and we can't leave fingerprints. Comrade Yakovlev was shrewd enough to reserve another room on the next floor down. They wait for us there."

He turned and strutted off to the stairwell. Natka followed. They clamored down the stairs, exited on the next floor, and came to a door. Vuk knocked softly. A slit cracked open. A face appeared—Yegor Volkov, his stony eyes full of vigilance. He ushered them into the suite.

Anatoli Yakovlev and Aleksandr Feklisov of the Russian Consulate sat beyond the hulking man, conversing in hushed tones. When Yakovlev saw them entering, he stood to greet them.

"Good, good, you are here," he said. His bear-like voice tempered with quiet caution. "Please, be seated. We have much to discuss."

They all sat. Natka eyed the men with curiosity. "What is this all about?" she asked.

Yakovlev glanced at Vuk. "You didn't tell her?"

"No," replied Vuk. "There wasn't time."

"What's wrong?" asked Natka, a nervousness clinching her voice.

Yakovlev shook his head. "It's bad, Comrade, bad. We have had a tragedy. Dr. Peshkin is dead."

Natka gasped. "No! How?"

"He fell from his suite."

"He was pushed," offered Feklisov, his busy eyes moving over her with scrutiny.

"Pushed?" exclaimed Natka. She eyed him nervously.

Yakovlev nodded. "Yes. Murdered."

Natka's shoulders slumped. "Who would do such a thing?"

Yakovlev lifted his palms. "This we do not know."

"Then how do we know he's been murdered? Maybe he just fell...or..." She stopped, as if she couldn't bring herself to say, *jumped*.

"No," said Yakovlev. "We know it was deliberate because whoever did it, also took the microfilm from his suite, and Peshkin's notebook as well."

Natka sat in stunned silence.

"We brought you here, Natka, for your own protection."

She cocked her head. "Protection? For me?"

"Yes, yes. Whoever killed Peshkin may be out to kill you too."

"But why?"

"Because only the two of you knew what was in the Tesla notebook. Only the two of you understood it."

Natka let out a breath. "Yes, I can see what you mean."

Yakovlev leaned in. "For a moment, we must put Dr. Peshkin aside. He is gone. There is nothing we can do about that. Fortunately, we got to his room before the police arrived. Volkov wiped the room of fingerprints. There was nothing else in the room to tie his death to us. The police will talk with me, of course...and Comrade Aleksandr. We had reserved the room for Dr. Peshkin. We will tell them he was nothing but a visiting dignitary we sponsored. But they mustn't know that we were here tonight."

Natka nodded.

"The stolen items become problematic for us. Two hours ago, we had the secrets for a powerful weapon. Now we have nothing."

"This is awful," murmured Natka.

"It is. But all is not lost. We still have you."

Natka shot him a stunned glance. "Me?"

His eyes became shrewd. "Yes. You read the secrets, did you not?"

"Well, yes, but I only scanned through them. Without the notebook—"

"Ach!" He blurted, batting at the air. "You are a smart woman. We believe in you."

She turned to find the other men in the room staring back at her expectantly. Vuk gave her a sly smile and a nod.

"You can do it," said Vuk. "You're my girl."

She gulped, ignoring the pandering tone. "I'm not sure what you're expecting of me."

Yakovlev leaned in, his face grim. "You will build the weapon, of course."

"Me? Impossible. The inventions and formulas associated with the weapon are complicated, and I only glanced at the notebook. Even Dr. Peshkin had to work out the nuances of it. I could never do it."

"You will do it!" stated Aleksandr Feklisov firmly. He stamped out his cigarette and stood. The jumpy eyes momentarily stilled and zeroed in on her.

Yakovlev patted her hand. "You will have some help," he reassured her.

"Help?" she croaked, almost laughing. "Maybe Nikola Tesla himself can come back to Russia with us. That's the kind of help I would need."

Yakovlev shook his head. He too stood, taking her hand and lifting her from her seat. "No. You will not go back to Soviet Russia. You will perfect the technology here. And then we will take it back with us."

"Impossible," she said adamantly, "I have no laboratory. No equipment. No engineers to help with the project."

"All that will be provided. We have learned of a laboratory that is available for our use."

Natka shook her head. "It can't be just any laboratory. It needs the proper equipment."

"This lab has all that you need."

Natka eyed him suspiciously. "Where is this laboratory?"

"Long Island. It is called, Wardenclyff."

Natka's jaw dropped.

Wardenclyff.

The name was synonymous with Nikola Tesla. Wardenclyff had been a joint project with J.P. Morgan forty years earlier—Morgan providing the start-up capital, Tesla the ingenuity. The laboratory sat on a parcel of land on Long Island; the centerpiece being a massive tower looming over the seacoast. Begun as an experiment in transcontinental wireless transmissions, the project became a profound failure. With limited backing and limited results, an impatient Morgan had pulled all funding from the project and the vision for it collapsed. The two of them parted bitterly, and the facility abandoned.

"Wardenclyff?" gasped Natka. "Impossible. It doesn't exist. It was torn down thirty years ago."

Yakovlev shook his head. "Not true. Yes, the tower above the ground is gone, but we have it on good authority that the facility extended below the earth. It was as deep as it was high. The laboratory is still intact. Fully equipped and operational. The facility has been kept secret from the public—even the U.S. government does not know of its existence."

Natka was dumbfounded. How could that be?

"So," exclaimed Anatoli Yakovlev, "In two days we will drive out to Long Island and you will begin work on the weapon."

"But you're not listening," she cried. "There is still the problem of the missing microfilm. I don't have an eidetic memory! I could never recall all that I read tonight. I only saw it briefly."

"As I told you before, you will have help."

She looked into his eyes, pleading. "The only one who could grasp the complexities of the concepts was Dr. Peshkin. And he's...he's dead."

Yakovlev took her by the hand and lead her to the bedroom door. He swung it open and pointed.

"Help!" he declared.

Natka looked into the room.

There, sitting on the edge of the bed, was a terrified Dr. Fredrick Markovitch.

Chapter 41

———◦———

34th Avenue, 12:48 AM

NEON LIGHTS BLAZED IN the city that never sleeps. Rain pelted the side-walks, an icy mix of sleet and slush. From the other side of 34th Avenue, the rain took on a veil effect, a lacy curtain of wetness.

Tucked into the shadowed recess of a phone booth, Henry Blacksmith lurked, shivering with cold and pain. The wounds in his leg and upper shoulder throbbed as if someone were twisting his flesh with pliers. But he watched with fascination the crowd half a block down the street.

Lights flashed from police cruisers and ambulances. Officers had set up a sawhorse barricade to keep the morbid crowd well back from the human bullseye at the center of attention.

A body, twisted and bloodied, lay crumpled there.

Dr. Boris Peshkin.

Thank you, Doctor.

The body had made it easy for Blacksmith to escape the hotel unnoticed. Guards watched the service entrance at the back of the hotel and the tunnel to the subway. Avoiding those exits, he chose instead to go right through the front door. He had spotted the plain-clothed police officer standing beyond the threshold, watching the throng. But the twisted corpse, a few yards away, distracted the officer too. So, Blacksmith waited for a cluster of people leaving from the lobby and shuffled out with the crowd, right past the officer as he was craning his neck the other way.

Walking past the makeshift barricade, Blacksmith had glanced briefly at the body, unmistakably that of Dr. Peshkin. His frock of white hair, pink with blood.

One less Russian. And a prized Russian at that. Hopefully thwarting their research into the particle beam weapon for a long time to come.

At least he had some good news to report.

Now, leaning against the glass of the phone booth, he seethed with anger. Everything had gone to hell. He'd failed at every point in his mission. He'd failed to kill Nikola Tesla, as well as George Sylvester Viereck. He'd failed to steal the notebook and destroy the research.

He'd failed to escape unscathed.

Surprised and usurped by the assailant in the room.

He ground his teeth. The man had come out of nowhere. As if he had seeped into the room, like a gas or mist. Like smoke. Caught off guard, his attacker gained the advantage. The opponent had been weaker, smaller, and untrained in hand-to-hand combat…yet somehow the fool had prevailed.

It wouldn't happen a second time.

Blacksmith cringed. He needed medical attention quickly. His slashed thigh had left him hobbled. The gash huge. Every step agony. His shoulder continued to bleed. His mashed hand throbbed.

After the attack, he had returned to the room that he had commandeered earlier to extract the knife from his upper pectoral muscle. His own knife, dammit! He attempted to butterfly the wound shut with Scotch tape, but it wouldn't take. His mangled hand making it difficult. Giving up, he simply wrapped himself with a towel and taped the towel the best he could. With another towel, he made a tourniquet to staunch the flow of blood from his leg. If left too long without circulation, he could lose the leg altogether. He needed help.

Ten minutes ago, he'd called one of the embedded agents—a friend of Viereck's—to come to pick him up. Hopefully, he might know of a doctor that could see to him off the books.

Headlamps flashed, and a sedan pulled up next to the phone booth. Blacksmith stepped out into the freezing rain, limping toward the vehicle.

He now had a new mission. The Soviets must not develop the weapon! Fortunately, one was dead already. Now he would take aim for the others. Gather intelligence, identify their personnel, and take them out one by one.

And someone else, too.

He vowed to find the man who had attacked him in Tesla's apartment...and put him in his grave.

Part 2

—◆◇◆—

Operation Teleforce

Fifteen Months Later

Chapter 42

———◆———

New Yorker Hotel, Friday, 8:20 AM

ALICE MONAGHAN PUSHED HER maid's cart along the corridor of the 33rd floor. She drew up to the door of the supply closet off the main hallway and fumbled in her apron pocket for her passkey. Having cleaned four suites, it was time to unload the gathered trash and dirty laundry from her cart and restock her supplies.

She paused, glancing down the hall. Two suites left before her break. She was ready to sit down for a spell. Her bursitis was acting up.

Yes, a short break would be nice.

Opening the closet door, she gave a tug on the chain to turn on the lights.

A thought struck her as she stuffed the soiled laundry down the chute. Hadn't a 'Do Not Disturb' sign had been hanging on the door of one of the remaining suites?

Maybe she should check. Her break might come sooner than expected.

Stepping into the hallway, she squinted at the door in question.

There it was. 'Do Not Disturb'. Great! Less work for her.

Back in the closet, her hands worked swiftly. Excited by the thought of an early break, she hardly noticed her bursitis. She turned off the light and pulled her cart into the hall.

Heading toward the remaining door, Alice stopped short.

Another thought nagged at the back of her mind. Hadn't the 'Do Not Disturb' notice been there yesterday too?

She cringed. Yes, it had been. It wasn't unusual for the notice to be on that door. The elderly fellow who lived there kept strange hours and rarely wanted to be disturbed. But two days in a row? That was odd.

Alice disliked cleaning that suite. The man was peculiar and was in the habit of leaving notes: *Don't touch this table; More towels next time; Don't touch my pigeon feed*, and such. He tended to demean the girls who worked the room.

Alice needed to make sure that the old man hadn't forgotten to take down his sign. Reluctantly, she stepped up to the door and rapped on it.

"House cleaning," she called.

Nothing.

She tried again. "Housecleaning."

Again, nothing.

Alice turned away, but stopped. Something didn't feel right. Maybe she should clean his suite, regardless of the sign. She slipped her passkey into the lock and cracked the door open.

"Housecleaning."

Nothing.

Alice Monaghan entered the suite. It was deathly quiet. The living room and office were cluttered as usual. Papers, files, and notebooks filled the desktop. Saltine cracker boxes lay piled in the corner. The patio drapes were open, the morning's pale winter light filling the space. Pigeons had gathered on the sky terrace outside, cooing and pecking. There were always pigeons. She hated them. The old man let them come into the suite. She was the one who had to scrub their white splotches from the floor and carpet. How do people live like this? She wondered.

She moved into the living room, listening. Nothing stirred. No one was home. Her attention swiveled to the bedroom door, slightly ajar. A light was on.

"Hello? Anyone there?" she called.

Quiet.

Alice eased over and slowly pushed the door open.

A cry caught in her throat. Alice stumbled back in shock.

There would be no early break for her today.

Wearing only a pair of black hose, the old man lay sprawled across the bed, naked and quite dead.

Chapter 43

New Yorker Hotel, Friday, 9:15 AM

HOUSE DETECTIVE JOHN WILLIAMSON stood off to the side of the brass bed, looking down at the emaciated figure. White and withered, the body looked as if recently unearthed by an archaeologist. Two other men stood next to him: Assistant Hotel Manager Joe Stanley and the Front Desk Manager, Frank Delong. They seemed captivated by the ghoulish figure, as if expecting—or fearing—a sudden resurrection.

Others were in the room: the medical examiner, Dr. H.W. Wembly, as well as a detective named Morgan, and a uniformed officer who stood in the doorway between the rooms. Everyone watched Wembly going about his duties with the corpse. Detective Morgan had already questioned the maid. He made notes in a small wire-bound notebook.

The room was eerily quiet.

Finishing his examination, Dr. Wembly stripped off his rubber gloves, disposing of them in a sack at his feet, and picked up a clipboard that he'd been filling out during the examination.

"Can we cover him up, Doc?" asked Joe Stanley.

Dr. Wembly looked up from his clipboard. "Excuse me?"

"The body, can we...?"

"Yes, yes, of course."

Detective Morgan paused from writing his notes to snicker at the Assistant Manager's discomfort. John Williamson stepped up and threw a sheet over the naked decedent.

"Cause of death, Doc?" asked Detective Morgan, his pencil poised.

Wembly looked up from his writing. "Considering lividity and rigor, he died last night around 10:30 PM. The preliminary cause of death was coronary thrombosis. A heart attack."

"Nothing that would indicate foul play?"

Williamson shot the police detective a curious glance. Alarm swelled in Joe Stanley's face.

"Now why would you ask about foul play?" blurted Stanley. As Assistant Manager, the good of the hotel came first, and unpleasant facts could not stand in the way of its reputation. "I mean, obviously the man was old. He simply passed on. Foul play indeed!"

"Just ruling out the possibility," offered Detective Morgan.

John Williamson turned to Stanley. "I think it's a legitimate question, sir."

Stanley glared back at him, shocked that he would consider foul play too.

"I'm sure you recall that business last year with the break-in of Mr. Tesla's suite," said Williamson, "as well as the arrest of Mr. Tesla's friend in the hotel lobby. We should make sure that nothing untoward has happened to him."

"Untoward?" snorted Stanley. "He was old."

"Well, the FBI has taken an interest in Mr. Tesla's associations," said Williamson, "And I think it's prudent to rule out ill intent."

The Assistant Manager's lips pursed tightly. He subtly nodded toward the police detective, indicating that hotel business was not to be discussed among strangers.

Amused by the tension between the staff, Detective Morgan turned back to the Medical Examiner and asked again, "Foul play?"

Wembly shook his head. "None that I can see. It was a heart attack."

The detective nodded, flipping his notebook closed. "Then I suppose we're done here."

Dr. Wembly said, "People from the coroner's office should be here any minute. Has the family been notified?"

Stanley stammered, "I don't know if he had a family. He was unmarried and a lifelong bachelor, so he had no children."

"Well, who should we notify?" asked Wembly.

Frank Delong spoke up. "Mr. Tesla's hotel registration card had an emergency contact person. An old friend of Mr. Tesla's named Kenneth Sweezy."

"Doesn't his nephew live in the city?" asked Williamson.

"I believe so," said Delong.

"We should contact him," said Stanley.

"I'll check on that," offered John Williamson.

Williamson started to leave. Joe Stanley stepped in front of him, grabbing him by the arm.

"Reporters will come around," he whispered. "Don't speak a word about that business last year. No sense drumming up old news and bad publicity. Keep a lid on it. And for heaven's sake, don't use words like suspicious and untoward!"

Williamson gave a nod and left.

He took the elevator down to his office. For several minutes, he sat at his desk stewing. He recalled the fiasco from last year. What an embarrassment. A Nazi collaborator arrested in his hotel. And worse...the hotel had hired a possible German spy. It angered him to think that he'd been so sloppy. Yes, it had been a different world then — the attack on Pearl Harbor had yet to happen. War had merely been a topic to banter about over a cup of coffee.

That was then. Now the country was at war. He could ill afford to be sloppy again.

Unlocking his desk drawer, he lifted a thin rubber mat at the bottom of the drawer and withdrew a card he had kept tucked out of sight. A business card emblazoned with the seal for the Federal Bureau of Investigation.

Special Agent Ralph Doty had handed it to him after placing a handcuffed George Sylvester Viereck into the back seat of his sedan. 'Let me know if anything suspicious happens concerning Mr. Tesla,' he'd said.

Williamson laid the card down by his telephone.

Assistant Hotel Manager, Joe Stanley, would not be happy.

But Williamson took things seriously now.

He dialed the number.

Chapter 44

———◆———

Navarro Hotel, Manhattan, Friday, 9:32 AM

SAVA KOSANOVIC SCRAMBLED DOWN the hotel stairs, his attaché case banging against his thigh. Behind him, trying to keep up, was George Clark, head of the museum and laboratory of RCA. Rushing out of Kosanovic's apartment, the elevator had been in use. Sava couldn't wait. Without saying a word to Clark, he made for the stairwell. Time was of the essence.

Uncle Niko was dead.

Eleven minutes earlier, Sava had been in a meeting with Clark, discussing the collaboration of a Tesla Museum, when a man named Kenneth Sweezy had called. Sweezy, an editor of *Popular Science Magazine,* informed him of Uncle Niko's death. The news left Sava dumbfounded. Yes, his uncle was frail, but he'd always been frail. In Sava's mind, Uncle Niko had always existed as if immortal. Can gods die?

Sweezy had told Sava that the Yugoslavian Mission on Fifth Avenue had been notified.

A surge of panic gripped Kosanovic. People would be traipsing in and out of his uncle's suite. Anything could be taken. He needed to control the situation. No doubt the FBI would soon be involved. He was convinced they had informants at the hotel. Plus, newspaper reporters had their own moles, eager to leak up-to-the-minute news.

Since the episode with the break-in over a year ago, the FBI had been watching the activities surrounding Uncle Niko and monitoring his associations. Sava was sure that scrutiny was on him, as well. It had made getting documents out of his Uncle's suite difficult. He also suspected his phone to be tapped.

Uncle Niko, too, had become more guarded. After nearly losing his prized notebook during the attempted robbery, he rarely let it out of his sight afterward, making it impossible for Sava to borrow again.

The police had questioned Sava the night of Dr. Peshkin's assumed suicide. Witnesses had placed him in the Manhattan Room Restaurant with the visiting professor earlier in the evening. Sava had told the police that it was the first time he'd ever met Peshkin. When asked about the Doctor's state of mind, he could only say that he had appeared normal, showing no signs of despondency—and no, the professor *did not* meet with his uncle, Nikola Tesla.

Sava said nothing of the second meeting, which had taken place upstairs.

The Russians initially blamed Sava for stealing the microfilm. Noting his reticence concerning his uncle's notebook, as well as his obvious distress over the disappearance of Dr. Fredrick Markovitch, they believed he had meddled — or worse, was a double agent.

To his credit, Vuk Milosh had stepped in to defend Sava, calling him a faithful patriot. For the first time in his life, Sava had been grateful for his Yugoslavian contact. Although it worried him to be in the young revolutionary's debt.

Hopefully, if Sava hurried, he could repay that debt today.

George Clark had insisted on coming along. Sava wished he hadn't. He claimed it was to offer support in his time of grief, but Sava wondered if a ghoulish curiosity wasn't the real reason.

Bursting out of the stairwell and into the lobby of the Navarro, the two rushed out to the sidewalk. Sava gave a hurried signal to the doorman, who stepped into the street to hail a cab.

Yes, the FBI worried Sava. Did they know of the notebook's importance? Compared to blueprints and schematics, the book looked so primitive. Easily overlooked. The hard part would be getting to it. Three hundred pounds of steel door guarded the greatest wartime secret of all. Could he breach those doors before the authorities? Maybe.

Before leaving his apartment, Sava had put in a call to a locksmith.

He had also called his secretary, Arlene Muzaric, to tell her of Uncle Niko's death and to have her meet him at the New Yorker Hotel.

A cab pulled up. Kosanovic and Clark breathlessly entered. His uncle's hotel was twenty-two blocks away. With morning traffic at its peak, it would be a long ride. Sava's knee nervously jackhammered.

The situation in his home country had not improved. Nazi occupation still existed. Royal Nationals and Communists still fought. The only change was that the communists were gaining strength.

Over the last few months, Kosanovic's wartime role had shifted drastically. He had fallen out of favor with the exiled monarch, King Peter. While working at the Yugoslav Information Center, Sava had become convinced that the National Liberation Movement was the future for Yugoslavia. Those leanings did not sit well with the monarchy.

Then last July, King Peter came to New York attempting to drum up support from Roosevelt—who had previously promised to arm the Chetniks but was now switching sides to back Tito. While in New York, the King had requested a visit with Nikola Tesla. Having finally coaxed his Uncle Niko over to his way of thinking, Sava desperately wanted to keep the king and his uncle apart. But it wasn't to be. The two met in Tesla's suite and together they wept for the motherland. Tesla pledged his support for the exiled king.

Within one hour, Sava's sway had been erased.

Tensions between Sava and the Royal Nationals increased until they finally dismissed him from his position. Without missing a beat, Sava became President of the *Eastern and Central European Planning Board*, a pro-communist group that was already making plans for a post-war Europe. Sava no longer waffled. He wanted the new Yugoslavia as advocated by the National Liberation Movement.

The cab arrived at the New Yorker. Entering the lobby, they found Kenneth Sweezy waiting for them. The three of them took the elevator to the thirty-third floor.

As Sava came out of the elevator, he saw that the door to his uncle's suite was wide open. He bristled with anger. He, Clark, and Sweezy swept into the room to find others milling about.

As introductions were being made, Kosanovic shrewdly scanned the cluttered room, landing on the desk by the patio doors. His pulse raced by what he saw, and a plan quickly formed in his mind.

Chapter 45

New Yorker Hotel, Friday, 9:58 AM

HOUSE DETECTIVE JOHN WILLIAMSON shrunk back from the others, carefully watching as Sava Kosanovic commandeered the room. Something felt off. Rather than showing grief, the nephew appeared as if he had business to conduct. Kosanovic edged over to the desk and laid his briefcase down on it.

"I see that my uncle's quarters are open for all to come and go as they please," Sava muttered bitterly.

Joe Stanley's eyes widened, panicked by the accusatory tone. "Other than the authorities, only hotel staff have been allowed in the room, Mr. Kosanovic."

"Have my uncle's possessions been disturbed?"

"No, of course not. Everything is as we found it."

"Where is my uncle now?" asked Kosanovic. He retrieved a key from his vest pocket and unlocked his briefcase.

"They have moved the body to the coroner's office," replied Stanley.

Sava opened his case and removed several sheets of paper, perusing them. "By my uncle's wishes, we will have him taken to the Frank E. Campbell Funeral Home on Madison Avenue."

Sava set the papers down on the cluttered desk next to his briefcase, fanning them out to look over. He pursed his lips, tapped the papers, and nodded as if having read something significant.

"Have the newspapers been notified?" asked Kosanovic, his head still bowed toward the desk.

The men shot glances at each other.

"Uh, I believe they have," muttered Stanley.

Sava nodded. "Okay, then. I'll prepare a statement. But I do not want them in this room."

A knock came to the door; in stepped a thin, older man. He wore a service cap and a blue-gray work uniform.

"Someone call for a locksmith?" he asked.

Kosanovic stepped from around the desk, pointing to the standing safe nested in the corner. "We need to have this safe opened right away."

Thinking of his earlier call to the FBI, Williamson stepped forward. "Can I ask why it is necessary to open the safe?"

Kosanovic slid him a suspicious glare. "Uncle Niko's will could be inside."

Williamson held his stare for a second. "Very well," he said.

The locksmith crouched before the safe, placing his hands on his knees, inspecting its locking mechanism. "It's an oldie," he muttered.

Opening his case to retrieve a stethoscope, he set to work on the tumblers.

Another knock came on the door. The group turned in unison to find a woman standing there. She wore wire-rimmed glasses, a winter coat, a scarf, and a practical hat. She looked somber.

"I'm sorry, Miss," said Joe Stanley, stepping forward. "This room is off-limits at the moment."

"Yes, but I'm looking for—"

"Please Miss, this is hotel business, and I'm going to have to ask you to leave."

With all heads facing the woman in the doorway, Williamson sensed movement behind him. He spun around to find that Sava Kosanovic had stepped back behind the desk and was scooping up his stack of papers from the clutter to stuff them into his briefcase.

"That's okay, gentlemen," announced Kosanovic, snapping the case shut. "This is my secretary, Miss Arlene Muzaric."

"Oh, I see," replied Stanley.

Kosanovic introduced Arlene to Kenneth Sweezy, George Clark, and the hotel personnel.

His suspicion kindled, John Williamson watched as Arlene drew up to Kosanovic near the desk.

"I'm sorry to hear about Uncle Niko," said Arlene.

Kosanovic was locking up his case with a key. He nodded solemnly. "He will be remembered as a great man," he said. He slanted a glance over at the locksmith crouched in front of the safe.

George Clark came up to them. "Excuse me, Sava, but I need to be leaving. I again give you my sympathies for your loss."

They shook hands, and the man left.

The group anxiously watched the locksmith working the combination dial. Williamson's eyes, however, were on Kosanovic. The secretary had taken his hand.

Kosanovic, as if uncomfortable, asked, "When am I going to meet that new fiancée of yours, Miss Muzaric?"

Arlene blushed. "He's not my fiancée yet," she said.

Sava allowed a weak smile. "No, but he will be soon. You two have been seeing a lot of each other."

She shrugged. "We'll see where it goes."

"He's a war hero I heard."

"Well, he doesn't think he's a hero. He got wounded while working with the French underground."

"The underground? But he's American, no?"

"Yes, that's right."

Kosanovic kept shooting glances toward the safe. He said, "You didn't answer my question. When am I going to meet your young man?"

She gave a mournful smile. "I had planned on bringing him to the gala next week. But, I don't know if going to a party will be appropriate, considering…" She trailed off as her eyes took in the room's somberness.

Kosanovic asked, "Gala? What gala?"

"At the Russian Consulate next Saturday. Have you forgotten? Vuk Milosh sent us invitations. It's a black-tie event to welcome a visiting dignitary from Yugoslavia."

"Oh, yes. I remember now. Arso Jovanovic is coming to New York. Will your young American soldier feel comfortable going to an event put together by communists?"

"Probably about as comfortable as me — you know my views. However, I hear they are our allies now, right?"

"War changes the world, Miss Muzaric."

"Well, like it or not, I'm making him come. I want to see how he cleans up."

"I'm sure he will make a great impression."

Given the aura of grief in the room, the hint of joy in Arlene's eyes could hardly be disguised. "He's already made an impression on me, Mr. Kosanovic. But putting him in a tuxedo should put him over the top."

Sava grinned meekly.

Startled by the sound of clunking metal, they turned toward the safe. It was unlocked.

Kosanovic stepped forward as the doors swung open. His eyes scanned the shelves.

"Thank-you. Now gentlemen, let's see if the will is here."

Kosanovic made a demonstrative search of the safe, leaving Williamson with the impression that the posturing was just a show.

"It doesn't seem to be here. I guess I will have to search elsewhere."

Williamson glanced back at the briefcase on the desk, wondering if the document wasn't located there, and that Kosanovic simply wanted an excuse to have access to the contents of the safe.

Kosanovic then pulled a stack of papers from a shelf inside the safe and turned to the hotel staff.

"If you don't mind, gentlemen," said Sava, "I would like to take a few mementos."

John Williamson's eyes narrowed. "I'm not sure we should remove any items," he offered.

Kosanovic handed the pages to the hotel detective. "As you can see, these articles written by my uncle have been previously published. The articles are public knowledge, but have personal significance to me."

Williamson shot a glance at Joe Stanley, who shrugged. "If the articles have been published, what's the harm?"

Reluctantly, Williamson handed the papers back to Kosanovic.

Sava turned to Sweezy. "Kenneth, would you like to take a memento?"

Williamson bristled. The nephew was grave-robbing right before his eyes.

Sweezy brightened. "I would be honored."

He pointed to a bound booklet inside the safe. "That booklet I helped put together for your Uncle's seventy-fifth birthday. It's a collection of commemorative letters from scientists and engineers from all over the world. Would it be possible to have that?"

Sava smiled. "I'm sure that my uncle would want you to have it."

He handed it over to Sweezy.

"Miss Muzaric, you too are welcome to a memento."

"Oh, I couldn't," she gasped.

"Please, I insist."

"I'd feel so ghoulish taking anything."

Sava shrugged. "It's all going to end up in storage."

Her eyes fell upon a small crystal vial, filled with a dark, gravelly substance, sitting on a stand near the patio doors. She picked it up.

"This is pretty," she said. "Would it be okay if I took this?"

Sava's face grew concerned, taking the vial to inspect it. "This is what you want?"

"It's pretty," she said.

"Do you know what's in this vial?"

Her face fell. "Is it some secret formula?"

"It certainly is!"

Arlene paled.

Williamson stepped forward, curious and concerned.

Sava broke into a grin. "It's my uncle's formula for healing his sick pigeons."

Arlene and Sweezy laughed. Williamson did not. Sava pressed the vial into her palm.

From behind them, the locksmith said, "There's another safe inside, down below. Do you want that opened also?"

"Yes. Wait! My uncle kept a set of keys to that smaller safe in a stand near his bed."

Sava left and returned with a set of two keys on a ring.

The locksmith used a key, and the anti-dynamite box swung open. Sava bent to rummage through the smaller compartment. Pulling a small sack from the shelf, he opened it to produce a shiny medallion.

"I don't believe it," muttered Kosanovic.

"What's that?" asked Arlene Muzaric.

"The Edison Award given to Uncle Nico by the American Institute of Engineers."

"That sounds impressive. I'm surprised he didn't have it displayed."

"It has Edison's face on it," said Sava. "Because of their history, Uncle Niko didn't want to be staring at Edison's image every day."

Williamson knew of the bitter rivalry between the two men and their falling out.

While working for Edison, he had promised Tesla $50,000 if he could improve Edison's DC motors. Tesla accomplished the challenge by coming up with twenty-four new designs. Edison, however, reneged on the deal, telling Tesla that he'd only been joking. Nikola Tesla had promptly quit.

Sava slipped the medallion back into the smaller safe, closed the door, and locked the anti-dynamite box. He set the keys on a shelf inside the safe.

Sava looked over at the locksmith. "Will you be resetting the combination to the safe?"

"I've already done that. I will give you the new combination."

"Good."

With that, Sava Kosanovic sealed the safe.

Williamson felt relieved. Nothing of importance had been removed.

Kosanovic then turned to his secretary and said, "Miss Muzaric, I will have a lot to do over the next few days and won't be coming into the office. I want you to take the time off. With pay, of course."

"Oh sir, I couldn't. I'm sure you could use my help."

He shook his head. "I feel it's appropriate to do it myself. Go home and relax. I will be in touch with you in a couple of days."

"But sir—"

He raised a hand to stop her. "I insist."

"Yes sir, if that is how you want it."

Kosanovic took up his briefcase and handed it to her. "And Miss Muzaric, would you mind taking my briefcase and my mementos with you? Just to hold on to?"

Arlene Muzaric shot him a quizzical look. "I suppose so. But won't you be needing your briefcase?"

"I have a lot of work to do here. It would just be in the way."

She hesitated, but took the items from him. She gave him a comforting hug, turned, and left the suite. Kenneth Sweezy also gave his condolences and left.

For twenty minutes, Sava Kosanovic continued to inspect the contents of the office. Williamson stayed in the room, watching every move.

Then Kosanovic announced, "I think we're done here. I will have my uncle's possessions boxed up and moved immediately."

"That won't be necessary," boomed an unknown voice coming through the door.

Everyone swung a look that way. Two men had entered the suite.

"We can handle it from here," said the larger of the two. He had a shield out. "FBI. We have orders to place these rooms under protective custody."

Kosanovic looked alarmed, but Hotel Detective Williamson sighed with relief.

Chapter 46

———◦———

Office of Alien Property, New York City, Saturday, 10:02
AM

"WHO THE HELL IS Nikola Tesla?"

With the telephone pressed to his ear, Irving Jurow sat at his desk in his small office, staring at the stack of work cluttering his 'in' box. He didn't enjoy being ordered around by a faceless, low-level government flunky on a Saturday.

The voice on the other end said, "Nikola Tesla was one of the greatest inventors of our time."

"Never heard of him." Jurow had only half-heartedly listened to the man's introduction, hoping to dispatch the caller and go home.

"Nevertheless," said the caller, undaunted, "we would like you to take immediate steps to sequester all of his earthly possessions."

Jurow sat back, wondering how long it would take to get rid of the interruption.

Irving Jurow served the New York City branch of the Office of Alien Property, a wartime department authorized with the power to seize enemy property, whether it be monies, real estate, enterprises, or intellectual property in its many forms, including copyrights and patents—the only government agency able to confiscate enemy assets without a court order.

"Was Mr. Tesla a U.S. citizen?" asked Jurow impatiently.

"He was a naturalized citizen, yes."

"Then you're barking up the wrong tree. He doesn't fall under the definition of alien property. If Mr. Tesla was a citizen of the United States and not—"

"This is a matter of national security, Mr. Jurow," stated the voice with newfound authority.

"Is it now? Then, maybe you should wait to talk to my boss on Monday."

"This cannot wait until Monday! We need to take immediate action."

Jurow bristled. "If Mr. Tesla was a citizen of the United States, then this does not fall under the jurisdiction of being an enemy custodial matter."

"And if we consider his heirs enemies of the state?"

"Excuse me?"

"Mr. Tesla was a bachelor with no children. His only living relative is a foreigner with communistic ties."

A wrinkle creased Jurow's forehead. "Well...that's a different story. If all property inherited by—"

"It's not just property, Mr. Jurow. This concerns military intelligence. We know of several patients that are of a military significance—including a wireless transmitted torpedo system and a potential particle beam weapon."

"Particle beam weapon?"

"A death ray!"

Jurow swallowed hard, a sting of alarm pricking him.

"So, as you can see, Mr. Jurow, this cannot wait until Monday. Mr. Hoover is concerned that this intelligence could fall into enemy hands."

Jurow sat up. "Mr. Hoover?"

"Yes, as in J. Edgar!"

Jurow suddenly regretted his failure to listen closer to the man's earlier introduction. "Who did you say you were with?"

"Isn't it obvious? The FBI."

A surge of panic hit him. "How can I help, Mr. Doty?"

Two hours later, Irving Jurow entered the lobby of the New Yorker Hotel, greeted by two men.

"Thank you for coming," said Agent Ralph Doty. "We only hope it's not too late. This is my colleague, Boyce Fitzgerald."

Jurow shook hands with both men.

"What do you mean, too late?" asked Jurow.

"It's our understanding that the nephew, Sava Kosanovic, has already been in the room and may have removed items."

"I see," replied Jurow, thoughtfully.

"Representatives from Naval and Army Intelligence are waiting for us. We also have a team of men to help with packing and moving. Everything needs to be confiscated."

Jurow leveled a look at Doty. "You understand I am the only one with the statutory authority to sequester property."

Doty gave a frustrated twist of his mouth. "Yes. We understand that. We just want the property out of reach. We can sort it out later. Mr. Tesla already has a locker at Manhattan Warehouse and Storage. We would like everything moved into that one location."

Doty took out a notebook and flipped to a page.

"Mr. Tesla may have possessions at other hotels around the city, including the St. Regis Hotel, the Waldorf-Astoria, and the Governor Clinton Hotel."

Fitzgerald took a nervous step forward. "We need to search those other locations as soon as possible. I was a colleague of Mr. Tesla. It's possible that somewhere in the city, a prototype particle beam weapon is being stored."

Jurow felt his skin chill. "Is this the death ray mentioned on the phone?"

"Yes, but it's not in his room upstairs, so it must be somewhere else."

"It was my understanding that this death ray was only in the conception phase."

Fitzgerald shook his head. "Mr. Tesla told me he'd built and tested a prototype."

Jurow pushed past them, heading towards the elevators. "Then we better get to work, gentlemen."

Over the next hours, they cataloged and sequestered the files and belongings of Nikola Tesla. Every scrap of paper accounted for. After crating the material, they trucked it all to the warehouse facility, including the locked three-thousand-pound safe.

They then made inquiries at the various hotels.

It wasn't until they got to the Governor Clinton Hotel, however, that they discovered the first significant cache of materials. Tesla's goods were being held in a walk-in vault as collateral for unpaid hotel bills. Ronald Wallace, the hotel manager, greeted the men.

"Mr. Tesla left our hotel owing a good amount of money," said Wallace. "We held his possessions until payment could be made. It's been ten years."

He produced a handwritten document and handed it to Irving Jurow.

"This is a note from Mr. Tesla concerning one item in the vault," said the manager. "We were told the item was worth $10,000."

Jurow read the note and terror seized him. Slowly, he eased himself down into a nearby chair.

"What is it?" asked Agent Doty.

Jurow's eyes remained riveted on the note. "Gentlemen, we may have found the prototype weapon."

Boyce Fitzgerald stepped forward. "Here? At this hotel?"

Jurow nodded. "It's in the vault."

"We need to examine it right away."

"No," he warned sharply. "Caution is needed."

Agent Doty eyed him suspiciously. "What does the note say?" he asked.

Jurow lifted his head to stare him in the eye. "That, if opened by an unauthorized person, the device is triggered to detonate."

Chapter 47

DEPUTY DIRECTOR PHILLIP CARVER stepped behind the dais situated in front of a large projector screen. Six men sat before him, clustered around the conference table, smoking, quiet and alert.

"Thank you for coming in on a Sunday, gentlemen," he said. "We have provided dossiers for each of you."

Signaling for the room lights to be turned off, Phillip Carver glanced down at his notes. Lighted by the wash of the flex-necked lamp attached to the podium, Carver had the look of a cinema vampire fresh from his casket.

The United States was now engaged in war. The Office of Coordinator of Information had undergone a name change and was now called the Office of Strategic Services, or OSS. The new spy agency was taking on an increased role within the intelligence community. Working closely with British Intelligence, much of the operational methods were modeled after MI6 and the ultra-shadowy sub-organization called Special Operations Executive—SOE. The less-than-a-year-old agency had proliferated quickly, with trained agents, tasked with gathering crucial information and lending support for the war effort.

Phillip Carver was now Deputy Director for the New York office.

The six men gathered in the room had been recruited from various military and law enforcement backgrounds and trained in a top-secret facility in Canada known as the British Security Coordination. Carver signaled to a projectionist. A wedge of light sliced the darkness. Cigarette smoke curled within the illumination like the mystical mist of a wizard's wand.

The screen displayed the enlarged face of an old man. Phillip Carver, holding a wooden pointer, slapped the screen, hitting the portrait just below the piercing black eyes.

"Nikola Tesla," he stated. "Found dead two days ago in his suite at the New Yorker Hotel. From what we've gathered, his death was of natural causes. A medical examiner gave the cause to be coronary thrombosis with no suspicious circumstances."

A voice from the darkness asked, "Any reason to believe that there could have been foul play?"

"Not from us, if that's what you're asking," replied Carver.

The room chuckled.

"However," he continued, "We rule nothing out. We do know that several foreign governments have shown interest in Mr. Tesla's theories and experiments. They were especially interested in a hypothetical particle beam weapon with massive destructive capabilities. Mr. Tesla boasted of having made a small prototype, and we have gotten word that the FBI may have stumbled upon its location at a hotel here in the city."

A murmur arose. A voice said, "You're saying there is a working model of a death ray somewhere in New York?"

"It's not been confirmed. Many in the science community dismiss the feasibility of such a weapon. Our experts tell us that Mr. Tesla, in his old age, was more of a showman than a scientist. The Germans and Soviets believe the weapon is possible and are trying to obtain it."

The screen fluttered and a new face came to the screen. Carver stepped closer to the screen and pointed.

"This is George Sylvester Viereck, a known Nazi propagandist and suspected spy. The FBI arrested Viereck last year on grounds of sedition. He was an associate of Mr. Tesla for several years and may have used his relationship to get theoretical documents from Mr. Tesla's rooms. Under interrogation, he admitted to having met with members of the Third Reich and even boasted of knowing Adolph Hitler personally. On the night of his arrest, we stumbled upon another man, who had infiltrated the New Yorker Hotel staff, and whom we later identified as a German agent. Viereck denied any connection with the man, but we have reasons to doubt those claims."

The screen shifted, and an illustrated portrait appeared—a penciled headshot.

"We have no photograph of the suspect, only this composite drawing. He was operating under the alias of 'Henry Blacksmith'. Unfortunately, he eluded capture the night of Viereck's arrest."

"Any leads on his whereabouts?" asked a voice.

"Little information has emerged concerning his current status. He may be back in Germany for all we know. We suspect, however, that Henry Blacksmith may be one, Henrick Carl Schwinghammer, a German national who lived in the States when his father was posted here as a low-level diplomat. He speaks English flawlessly, with no noticeable accent. After returning to Germany, Schwinghammer became an Abwehr agent, but now may work with the S.D., the secret intelligence agency of the Nazi party. His last name, Schwinghammer, literally means, Blacksmith in German. What information we have is in the packets we provided you."

"Do we know if he obtained the intelligence?" asked someone else.

"Our best guess is, no. On the night of Viereck's arrest, Tesla's apartment had been broken into, but Mr. Tesla was confident that nothing had been stolen. He told the FBI as much. However, that's not to say that intelligence could have been photographed and slipped back to Germany."

The slide shifted, and a collage of faces emerged.

"Our current concern, however, is the Soviet Union. Though they are currently our allies, we do not fully trust our red friends and do not want theoretical technology to fall into their hands. We believe these five men to be at the New Yorker Hotel the night of Viereck's arrest."

He slapped the screen with his pointer.

"This is Aleksandr Feklisov, a residential diplomat at the Russian Consulate here in New York. We believe he is a Soviet recruiting agent, tempting people to conduct military and industrial espionage against America. This is his boss, Anatoli Yakovlev, also from the Russian Consulate."

The pointer moved over to the face of an elderly man with a mane of white hair.

"This is—or was—Dr. Boris Peshkin, a theoretical physicist from the Soviet Union. He committed suicide the night of Viereck's arrest by jumping from the thirty-fifth floor of the New Yorker Hotel, two floors up from Tesla's suite."

"Suicide?" asked someone. "Seems a bit too coincidental."

"There was no evidence proving otherwise," stated Carver. "However, we find his death suspicious. We also find the presence of these four men at the hotel that night to be suspicious."

"Who's the creepy-looking fellow?" asked another voice.

"That would be Yegor Volkov, an agent of the GRU, Russia's version of the Gestapo. Volkov was a former bodyguard to Lavrenty Pavlovich Beria, the head of the NKVD. Volkov is a dangerous man. We believe they sent him as an escort for Dr. Peshkin, probably to keep him from defection."

"Maybe he threw the good doctor overboard," chuckled someone.

"Highly unlikely. Peshkin was under his protective care. I'm sure Volkov paid a price for Peshkin's death."

"Did these men get Tesla's secrets?"

"The British SOE are on top of this situation, and we are confident that they did not get any usable intelligence. But with Tesla's death, there has been a mad scramble to confiscate and protect his papers, and the FBI has acted quickly, using the cover of the U.S. Office of Alien Property. However, Tesla's nephew, Sava Kosanovic, gained access to his uncle's rooms."

The slide shifted and Kosanovic's face came up.

"Stationed in America, Sava Kosanovic currently resides at the Navarro Hotel near Central Park. Kosanovic has known communist contacts. He is currently the president of the *Eastern and Central European Planning Board*, a thinly veiled communist front. We suspect that Mr. Kosanovic may have removed vital papers from his uncle's room. We have a team currently monitoring Kosanovic's movements, and we are listening to his phones. As yet, he has not contacted his Soviet counterparts, nor has he dispatched any couriers with packages from his offices. If he possesses any items, he still has them on his person, or they are with Tesla's other papers in storage."

The slide shifted again. A photo of a notebook appeared.

"This is a replica of a notebook that Nikola Tesla kept on his person for decades. In it are details of his research theories. For OSS purposes, we are code-naming the book *Teleforce*, after the theories contained within it. There is a possibility that they have sequestered *Teleforce* with Tesla's effects, which are under lock and key at the Manhattan Warehouse and Storage Company, including seventy-five boxes and crates. Among the items is a large standing safe that Tesla kept in his room. Possibly, the authentic notebook is inside that safe."

"Have we searched Kosanovic's residence or his office?" someone asked.

Carver's eyes narrowed slyly. "We have searched both, but with no luck. So *Teleforce* is probably in that safe."

A hand raised. "Can we coordinate with the FBI to have a look inside the safe?"

Carver shook his head. "Out of the question. The safe is under the custody of the Office of Alien Property. Besides, the only person with the combination is Sava Kosanovic, who also can't touch it. And regarding the FBI, Hoover would never grant us permission to the safe—even if he could do so by law."

"So how do we prove whether the notebook is in the safe?" came a voice.

"That is what we are here to discuss. We would like to have a peek inside that safe somehow — even if secretly."

"Sounds like a job for a safe-cracker," said someone with a laugh. "Any thieves present?"

"We're all thieves," quipped another. "Where have you been?" And the room roared.

Ignoring the banter, Phillip Carver closed his folder. "So, there you have it, gentlemen." He motioned for the lights to come up. "*Operation Teleforce.* We need to know where this notebook is and get to it before enemy agents intercept it. And we must do it without alerting the FBI. Any suggestions?"

A hand in the back of the room went up.

Carver looked that way and let out a sigh. Of course. It had to be him.

Carver himself had handpicked most of the men in the room. Nearly all were former colleagues he'd known for years. He trusted them. The elite. However, the fellow with his hand raised was here by appointment from over his head. He was smart, to be sure, but older than the others, and therefore old-school in his thinking. Not that he disliked the man, he just thought of him as being outdated.

"Yes," said Carver, calling on him

"If you're serious about employing a thief, I know where to find a good one," said J. Patrick Tooke. He struck a match and lit his Kaywoodie pipe.

Chapter 48

———◦———

Sing Sing State Penitentiary, Ossining NY, Monday, 8:48
AM

ESCAPE!

The obituary became the catalyst for his decision. He had toyed with the idea before, though not seriously, only to pass time. Three hundred and thirty-two nights of staring at the ceiling above your bunk made you ponder such things.

He had calculated each step in his fantasy with precision; he simply never felt the urge to carry it out. After all, he had only ten months left of a two-year stretch. He could do that standing on his head. That way a fresh start awaited him, and he wouldn't have to be looking over his shoulder for the rest of his life.

But that was before he had read the obituary in the newspaper two days ago.

Now Buck Flynn was desperate to escape Sing Sing.

They arrested Buck the night of the botched New Yorker Hotel burglary—well, in the hospital afterward. He had nearly bled out by the time Sergeant Detective J. Patrick Tooke had nabbed him. Fortunately, the detective got him into an ambulance. It had saved his life, even though it meant prison.

They couldn't get him on much. He had no stolen goods on his person. However, they found his illegal lock-picking tools and scaling equipment. And given the reported break-in in Suite 3327—with obvious vandalism—they cobbled together a case of circumstantial evidence. They found blood matching his type in the room, along with an unregistered German-made pistol, whose ballistics matched the bullets in Buck's chest and shoulder.

He had desperately wanted to explain how he'd thwarted an attempted murder, but his court-appointed attorney made sure he kept quiet on that. He didn't want Buck admitting to being in the room, even if he had helped to prevent another crime.

The New Yorker Hotel had kept most of the fiasco out of the papers. As it was, other embarrassing events had elicited sensational headlines and negative publicity for the hotel. They had arrested a famous writer in the lobby for Nazi collaboration, and to top that, a Russian scientist had committed suicide by jumping from the thirty-fourth floor. Because of those incidents, Buck's shooting garnered only a fleeting paragraph in the Metro section: *Man Shot by Unknown Assailant.*

Surprisingly, there was no mention of the capture of the notorious cat burglar called *The Smoke*. That angle, too, had been hushed up.

As for the suicidal scientist, Buck knew better. The man hadn't jumped; he was pushed. Murdered. However, he relayed nothing of what he had witnessed to the authorities. It wasn't his business.

The arrest of the Nazi writer clawed at the back of Buck's mind for months. He found it more than coincidental that he'd encountered a German thief the same night they'd arrested a suspected German spy in the lobby.

But on this too, he kept quiet.

In the end, Buck Flynn copped to breaking and entry and attempted theft. He got two years, sent 'up the river' as they say, to Sing Sing in the town of Ossining, New York.

The same prison his Pops had spent five years of his life.

His Pops used to say,

Prison is a thinking-box. It gives a man time to ponder and make decisions about life on the other side of bars.

And Buck had been doing just that.

Two months after the New Yorker fiasco, Pearl Harbor got torn to shreds. Buck had been locked up in county awaiting sentencing when the news came. His wounds were still raw, and he was adjusting to the reality of facing time. But all was forgotten in an instant. Twenty-four hundred Americans killed. Naval ships and aircraft decimated. The bombing made the country mad as hell. Buck included. His fellow inmates nearly rioted after the attack.

The events 'over there' were hitting home.

For the first time in his life, Buck began growing patriotic. A whole new experience for him. Maybe it was the encounter with a flesh and blood Nazi that started it, but suddenly he wanted to serve. He was ready to carry a rifle for his country if they would have him.

But would they?

With good behavior, he might get an early release, and the first thing he planned to do, once he got out, would be to enlist. Ten months to go.

But then two days ago, he read the obit.

It stirred him. Why wait? He'd already wasted an entire year sitting in stir while the Japs and Krauts took ground.

For some reason, the death hit him hard. He hadn't even known the fellow, except for that one night, but he recognized him immediately from the photo next to the article about his death. Reading the article, he realized he had underestimated the man. Dismissed him as a nobody. But the man was a virtual hero.

And now he was dead.

Seeing him staring back from the newspaper nearly brought him to tears. He didn't know why. He hadn't cried in years, and the encounter had been so brief. But it helped make up his mind.

Now it was time for *The Smoke* to do what he did best.

To seep where others can't.

To escape.

He knew it was achievable. Partly because of the stories his Pops had told him from his own incarceration in the same prison.

His Pops had told him of the railroad that passed underneath Sing Sing, and how the train would rattle Cell Block D. One night, after consuming half a pint of Jim Beam, his Pops had drawn a crude map for Buck as he told a story.

"There were three of us," he'd told Buck. "We figured if we could get to this alley here, behind the chow hall..." he pointed to a smudge on the map, "... all we had to do was drop through this drain grate in the road and land almost atop the trestle. Then, hop the train to Albany. We'd be Scott free."

"Did you do it, Pops?" asked the youngster Buck.

"Naw," replied his dad with a wave of his hand. Then he got misty-eyed. Something Buck had never seen his Pops do before. "Johnny the Tooth—that's what we called Johnny Howser—tried taking a swing at a guard one day and took a bullet in the head from a screw in the tower." His Pops grew quiet. Wiped his eyes. "Never did talk of escaping after that."

Since being here at Sing Sing, Buck had seen the alleyway several times through the barred windows of the chow hall. The layout was just as his Pops had reported. And he knew he could make it work.

Sitting on the corner of his upper cot, Buck kept watch down the corridor through the bars. The escort would come to get him soon—a bit of good fortune that would play into his plan to escape.

"Going to the Ward today, Buck?" mumbled a gravelly voice beneath him.

Franky Babcock was lying on the bottom bunk reading a redacted issue of the Saturday Evening Post.

Franky was doing six years for armed robbery. He was tolerable as a cellmate, a little slow on the uptake and a bit braggadocios about his life of petty crime, but compared to the rest of the prison population, he was okay.

Buck hadn't mentioned the escape plan to Franky. He'd learn soon enough.

"Yeah," said Buck. "Off to the salt mines, you know."

Franky grunted. "Light-duty if you ask me."

Buck couldn't argue with that. It was a plum job, working in the hospital annex.

Ironically, it was his wounds that had helped land him the job. During sentencing, he had still been mending. Once he got in prison, he had to report to sickbay to have his wounds re-dressed, as well as go through therapy. He kept his nose clean the whole time, politely chatting up the doctor and flirting with the nurses. He ended up doing small chores around the ward and, on the doctor's recommendation, they brought him on as an orderly. He worked the ward four days a week, taking care of laundry, restocking the medical supplies, and washing bedpans.

While working there, he'd discovered a locked room only available to the doctor and the head nurse, a supply closet for prescription drugs. He had no interest in the drugs, but it was a locked door, and locked doors were a matter of personal challenge.

So, one day during the hospital Christmas party, with the staff preoccupied with presents and punch, he'd breached the lock with a letter-opener from the nurse's station. He was in and out within a minute, but not before noticing that the room had a window set in the back wall. It was a rare prison window without bars; it being inside a locked room and three stories up, they mustn't have thought it necessary.

Now, Pop's map and that unbarred window provided an opportunity.

The corridor remained clear. His escort was a bit late.

Buck slipped down from his cot. On the far wall, he and Franky had amassed a crude collage of photographs of pin-up girls, starlets, and news clippings. Buck's eyes fell to the obituary he'd taped up two days ago. The face of the dead stared back at him.

He re-read it. He still almost wanted to cry. How stupid was that? From down the hall, he heard footfalls. His escort coming.

"Who was that guy?" asked Franky from behind him. He'd caught Buck reading it again. "A friend of yours?"

Buck shook his head. "No, not a friend. Just a poor schlep who did a favor for me once."

He scanned the headline.

Former Cab Driver Dies a National Hero in the South Pacific.

Eddie Petrowski, it seemed, had enlisted the day after Pearl Harbor. And though he never made it to Poland, he found himself on Guadalcanal. He and thirty-three other Marines from D Company of the 1st Battalion had emplaced four .30 caliber Browning Machine Guns on an unnamed ridge in the Battle of Henderson Field. Two thousand Japanese forces mercilessly attacked them. By the time it was over, nine hundred and forty-five enemy soldiers were killed. Of the thirty-three Marines, only Sargent Petrowski survived. Found critically wounded, propped up against a spent Browning with nothing but a .45 pistol in his hand, Sargent Petrowski would die of his wounds five weeks later.

As the escort guard drew up to his cell, Buck sighed.

"You ready, Flynn?" snarled the guard.

"Yeah, I'm ready," Buck replied.

He reached out and touched the obituary one last time. Touched Eddie's face.

The courage of his dim-witted cutout put Buck Flynn to shame.

Chapter 49

———◦———

Governor Clinton Hotel, Manhattan, Monday, 9:42 AM

THE PARCEL LOOKED SO ordinary and docile. It sat on the shelf among the other lost-and-found clutter: suitcases, handbags, and corrugated containers of various sizes. The parcel haphazardly jammed among them.

As large as a sewing machine case, it was wrapped in brown paper and tied off with cords of jute. Dust layered its top. Cobwebs gripped the corners as if tethering it in place.

Irving Jurow, the agent from the Office of Alien Property, stood stone still. He didn't want to touch it, didn't want to be near it. Boyce Fitzgerald, standing next to him, seemed just as reluctant. His partner, FBI agent Ralph Doty, stood in the vault's doorway. That was as close as he dared to come.

Block lettering printed across its face read:

> *Property of Nikola Tesla: Danger, Do Not Open Under Any Circumstances.*

"It's smaller than I expected," muttered Fitzgerald.

Jurow had never, in his lifetime, contemplated what size a death ray would be. But yes, he had to agree; it looked smaller than the name implied.

He glanced down at the note, Tesla's warning of detonation. The paper felt hot in his fingers. A burning omen.

Fitzgerald looked at his watch. "Dr. Trump should be here any minute now."

Jurow gave a dubious nod.

After reading the warning yesterday afternoon, Jurow, Fitzgerald, and Doty discussed strategies of how to proceed with the device. The military officers wanted to confiscate it and transport it to a safe military location. Jurow, however, couldn't allow that. The laws governing sequestered property needed to be followed; the package was to be opened, its contents identified, and then legally placed with the other collected materials in the Manhattan Warehouse and Storage unit.

Boyce Fitzgerald said that someone qualified to open the device should do so and suggested a professor from MIT named Dr. John O. Trump, who directed their High Voltage Research Laboratory. Trump was the secretary of the Microwave Committee at the National Defense Research Committee. With credentials like those, Jurow agreed to commission the good doctor.

They had put him on a train last night.

The air in the vault felt thick with doom. No one talked. Fitzgerald merely paced, scrutinizing the parcel.

Fifteen minutes later, Dr. Trump arrived. He was a tall, thin man in his fifties. His slate-gray eyes took in the men in the room as if they were freshmen students he would have to dominate through intellectual superiority. He appeared confident until handed the note from Nikola Tesla. On reading it, his confidence withered some.

"Where is this thing?" he muttered.

Irving Jurow pointed to the parcel on the shelf. Dr. Trump licked his protruding lower lip, a hint of worry in his gray eyes.

"Let's get it down from the shelf," he said. "Do we have a cart that we can put it on?"

The hotel manager arranged for a cart to be wheeled in. Doty and Fitzgerald nervously took hold of the parcel and slid it out from its shelf, carefully setting it on the cart.

Dr. Trump studied the box, walking around it twice without touching it. Slowly, he backed out of the vault, his eyes never leaving the parcel. He took in a breath and turned to gaze through a hotel window. The sun sat above the skyscrapers, a thin mesh of clouds beneath it. Dainty snowflakes floated in the air. He turned back to face the agents in the vault.

"It's a beautiful day outside, gentlemen," he said. "Let's try not to ruin it."

He stepped up to the cart, and, to Irving Jurow's astonishment, pulled a jackknife from his pocket. He snapped it open.

"What are you doing?" Jurow croaked.

Dr. Trump shot him a sly smile. "You want the box opened, do you not?"

Jurow stifled a protest. He had expected a more scientific implement to be used. After all, they had transported the good doctor all the way down from MIT at no small expense.

"The right tool for the right job, my good man," said Trump, fully amused at the simplicity of it.

The others stood back. The silence was as thick as cast iron. Cautiously, Trump made a slice in the jute cording. It fell harmlessly from the parcel. A bead of sweat glistened Trump's forehead.

"So far, so good," he offered.

He then sliced a piece of tape along the brown paper wrap. With the care of a surgeon, he slit every piece of tape around the circumference. Setting the jackknife aside, he gripped the paper and gently, oh-so-gently, tore the paper away.

Beneath was a wooden box. Brass clasps ran along the lower edge, securing its lid to a platform—six in all.

Dr. Trump gave a skittish glance to the other men.

"Six clasps, gentlemen," said Trump. "I suppose they might have to be unlocked in a special order—a combination of sorts." A smile formed. "Would eeny-meany-miny-mo be too unscientific a method to proceed?"

Jurow swallowed hard at the man's lightheartedness.

Trump reached down and...

Flicked open a clasp.

Nothing.

Everyone let out a sigh. But no one moved a muscle.

Without method or fanfare, Trump unsnapped the other locks in succession. When he looked up, the wide-eyed jitters seemed to have relaxed some.

"Let's lift this lid off and see what we have, shall we?" he said.

Boyce Fitzgerald stepped forward. He and Trump withdrew the wooden top—without explosion or incident—and set it aside.

Underneath sat a metal box bolted to the wooden platform. Coils, wires, dials, and meters embedded into its face. As the others stepped forward to inspect it, a strange, unexpected noise arose within the vault.

It startled Jurow, causing his pulse to race.

The noise was a chuckle.

Dr. Trump laughed. Boyce Fitzgerald joined him. Pointing at the device with a good howl.

"What is it?" asked Jurow.

"This, gentlemen, is Nikola Tesla's final joke on the world," said Trump. "What we have here is a multidecade resistance box, used for Wheatstone bridge resistance measurements."

"It's not a death ray?" choked Ralph Doty.

"Hardly," snorted Trump. "It's a standard item found in every electronic laboratory in the country before the turn of the century. It's an antique."

Irving Jurow took a handkerchief from his jacket pocket and mopped his brow. "Then there is no death ray?" he said.

"Oh, it may exist somewhere," replied Trump. "But not here." He turned to gaze through the vault door and out the window. "So, if you don't mind, gentlemen, I think I will go outside and enjoy the rest of this beautiful day."

Chapter 50

---◆---

Sing Sing Prison, Hospital Ward, Monday, 12:30 PM

BUCK FLYNN HURRIED THROUGH his duties, folding towels, stripping the beds of soiled sheets, and replenishing the medicine cabinets. His duties nearly finished, he carefully monitored the movements of the doctor and nursing staff, and more importantly, the two screws standing at the entrance of the hospital ward.

The drug closet sat behind the nursing station, partially hidden by a wall partition. Another larger supply closet was down the corridor. Because of his duties, Buck had access to the other closet. In that room, he had hidden items to help in his plan, including a lock pick made of a portion of his bed spring.

The drug closet window had no bars, but there was an alarm connected to a klaxon horn. With this in mind, he'd secured items from the ward to help circumvent it: an electrical cord from a lamp he'd found in storage and a scalpel he'd salvaged from the trash. These he hid in a pillowcase tucked on the shelves in the large storage room.

Over the last two days, he had torn his bedsheets into strips and had braided the strips into a strong corded rope. Now wound around his waist, his shirt covered the rope. The hospital ward was three stories up. The makeshift rope was not quite long enough, so he would have to jump the last ten or twelve feet.

Buck knew he couldn't escape clad in prison stripes. Fortunately, the hospital staff had lockers in the back room with laughable locks on them. Inside one, he found a pair of trousers and a clean shirt that the doctor kept there. He stashed the clothes under a gurney in the supply closet.

At the last minute, he would grab from a coat rack near the nurse's station a hat, suit jacket, and overcoat.

The timing was important. He needed the nurses to be away from the station or occupied with tasks. Once he got behind the desk, the partition would block the guards by the door from view.

However, the most important timing issue had to do with the train.

Over the months—while creating the fantasy of escape—Buck had mentally kept track of the trains rumbling beneath the prison compound. He knew the schedule by heart. His entry into the closet had to coincide with the approach of the next northbound train. To do it right, he had to be in the closet, down the outside wall, over to the alley, down into the drainage grate, and on the trestle within minutes of the next available train.

Then the tricky part.

After leaping on top of the moving freight train, he would have to scramble to be out of sight by the time the train emerged from under the prison buildings to avoid being spotted by the guards in the tower. All within a matter of seconds.

But now he was ready.

Pretending to fold towels near the racks of linen, he glanced around. The two screws were talking with each other, sharing a laugh. Relaxed. This was light duty for them, too. Every nurse had disappeared into the wards except one, Betsy, a pretty little redhead. Easy pickin's. Buck flirted with her endlessly. She liked him.

Setting the towels aside, Buck stepped from around the wooden table to push his laundry cart past the nurse's station.

"I'm headed down to the laundry," said Buck to Betsy.

She smiled at him. "Okay, Mr. Flynn. Hurry back. We've got a date to go dancing tonight, remember?" A constant joke between them.

"Let the warden know I'll be meeting you at eight," chuckled Buck. He feigned as if he were about to leave, and turned back to her. "By the way, I overheard the doctor saying he needed you in Ward B."

She scowled. "Why didn't you say something?"

"I just did."

"I mean, why didn't you...? Oh, never mind." She gathered up a clipboard and scurried off.

Perfect.

Buck rushed into the storage room, grabbed his pillowcase with his escape items, as well as the bundle of clothes, and hurried back to the nurse's station. He effortlessly rolled over the countertop to the other side, scooped up the coats and hat from the coat rack, and, using his makeshift lock-pick, was inside the drug closet within fifteen seconds.

After re-locking the door, he inspected the window. It was awning style with upper and lower panes. Brass tabs on the bottom lip of each pane connected to the alarm. Wires ran along the sill up to the Bakelite klaxon horn on the wall. The entire setup brazenly displayed. As if advertising the alarm system would thwart escape attempts. Idiots.

Using the scalpel, he exposed the wires of the spare electrical cord to create a circuit to bypass the brass tabs on the windows. Undoing the catches, he swung the window open.

No alarm blared.

Perfect.

He shrugged off his striped prison uniform, unwound the corded rope from around his waist, and changed into the street clothes. The trousers were wide in the waist and short, but would do. The coats too were tailored for a heftier man, but much better than prison rags.

During the last fifteen months, Buck had healed from his wounds, with nothing but spidery scars remaining. However, his shoulder had taken a lot of abuse during the climb up the New Yorker that night, and because of it, and his muscles retained a tight soreness that needed stretching each morning. He would be testing the full strength of his shoulder with this descent.

He tied off his rope and took a quick survey of the area below. No one was about. He dropped the length of rope down the wall.

The window was wide, but short. He went feet first, shimmying his girth through the opening to dangle outside.

Granular snowflakes fell. An earlier snow covered the rooftops below. The air was frosty, fresh smelling and...free.

The descent felt good. His shoulder protested only slightly. Buck was in his element, a familiar activity, like an Olympic swimmer diving into a pool after a long vacation.

Coming to the end of the rope, he paused, dangling over the brick pavement below. The drop was close to fifteen feet. Farther than he had expected. Still, it was a jump he could withstand.

As he released his grip, a strange aroma floated on the wind. Pungent. Sweet. Familiar.

He hit the pavement, purposely rolling upon impact to absorb the force of it. His coat soiled some; but he would clean up later once he disembarked the train. Once he was free.

Standing to brush himself off, he could hear the approaching train in the distance.

Perfect.

Turning to make his way to the alleyway and the drainage grate that would drop him down onto the trestle...he stopped short.

Shock slammed into him.

Twenty feet away, a lone figure was leaning against the prison wall, watching him. With the collar of his trench coat popped up against the cold, he looked like a man waiting for the next bus to come by. He puffed on a pipe. The familiar aroma that Buck had noticed a moment ago.

Buck recognized him. It was the detective that had arrested him at the New Yorker Hotel.

"Going for a walk, Buck?" he asked.

Chapter 51

———◇———

Ossining, NY, Monday, 3:55 PM

THE TRAIN EASED FORWARD, a shrill whistle announcing its departure. Steam billowed from the Dreyfuss Hudson engine, engulfing the polished green planks of the platform and those lingering for the next train. Buck Flynn stared out the window as the station slipped by, the horsepower beneath him gaining momentum.

He'd made the train, but not as he'd planned. It headed south, not north to Albany, and it wasn't a filthy freight train, but the famed Twentieth Century Limited. He was riding in luxury...and in his own clothes.

J. Patrick Tooke sat across from him, tamping a pinch of tobacco into his pipe. Buck eyed him cautiously, still uncertain of what was taking place.

"You are on a short leash, boy," muttered Tooke. He jabbed the stem of his pipe Buck's way. "I'm going out on a limb for you. You better not let me down, or you'll be back in two shakes of a lamb's tail."

He spoke with authority, yet Buck caught a playful glint in his eye, hinting at the experiment yet to come.

After being nabbed by Tooke on the prison grounds, the Irishman marched him back into the building from which he'd just escaped, where two guards and the assistant warden awaited them. Then, escorted by the guards and the assistant warden, they marched to the warden's office.

Seated on a bench outside the office, Buck had listened to heated grumblings from the other side of the door as the two duped guards stabbed him with vengeful glares. After a while, they ushered Buck inside.

The warden, obviously livid, sat behind a large oak desk, refusing to stand at Buck's presence. Begrudgingly, he handed him a slip of paper.

"Mr. Flynn, you've been granted a conditional parole by the U.S. government and are released into this man's custody," he snarled. "You will be processed, and we will return the belongings with which you arrived. Goodbye, Mr. Flynn. I'm sure I'll be seeing you again before we're through."

Tooke said little as he chaperoned him through the procedures, shushing him when Buck tried asking questions.

And now they were on a train, the Hudson Valley landscape rolling by.

"How did you know where to find me?" Buck asked. "Outside the wall, I mean."

Tooke struck a match. A smile crept into his cheeks. "Your cellmate, Frank Babcock, told us you were working in the ward today, but when we got there, you were nowhere to be found. A nurse told us you'd gone to the laundry room. But no, you hadn't. So, I asked a simple question."

"Oh? What was that?"

"Are there any locked doors on the floor?" He sucked the flame across the pipe bowl. "When the head nurse pointed to the drug supply closet, I knew. Plus, I'd noticed something while visiting your cell. You made your bunk, but the bedsheets were missing. I figured there had to be a reason for that. So, while the others opened the supply closet, I slipped down the back stairs to await your arrival."

"That's the second time you've nabbed me before I could catch a train."

He jabbed the pipe stem his way. "And it better be the last. Because of your shenanigans, I had a heck of a time convincing the warden to let you go. If I hadn't possessed your conditional parole—signed by the proper authorities—you'd be in solitary as we speak."

"I'm still unclear what is happening, Detective," said Buck.

"It will be explained in New York. And I'm no longer a detective. I'm a Special Agent serving the U.S. government."

Buck blinked. "You're no longer with the police department?"

"No. I set that aside after Pearl Harbor. I was in the Army during the last war, but a bit too old this time around. However, my old Major offered me a position to get me in the game."

"You consider war a game?"

Paddy's face grew severe. His eyes bore into Buck, causing him to squirm. "My own two sons enlisted the day after Pearl Harbor. My oldest is married and had been on the police force for only two years. My younger was accepted to college. Do I consider war a game? I fought in the trenches during the Great War, and you have no idea the horrors I've seen. I'll take no chastisement about war from a man who has never been to war, young man. So keep your judgments to yourself."

Buck tightened his lips at the rebuke, ashamed for being so flippant. He turned away to look out the window.

"You claimed at your trial that you had never met him before," said Tooke mysteriously.

"Who?" asked Buck.

"Edward Petrowski."

Buck recalled that Sergeant Detective Tooke had sat through his entire trial, watching Buck with something of a curiosity, or maybe sympathy. He had testified, of course, having been the arresting officer, but word had come down through Buck's lawyer that the Detective had also requested leniency from the judge — which most likely accounted for the light sentence Buck had received.

"What about Eddie?" asked Buck.

"I saw his obituary on the wall of your cell. Why did you lie about collaborating with him? Were you protecting him?"

Buck swallowed, holding back a wave of remorse. "Not that you'll believe me, but I had never laid eyes on Eddie before that night."

Tooke grew quiet. Finally, he asked, "So why—"

"Why put his picture up? Because reading about him told me something about myself."

"Oh? What would that be?"

"That a gullible cabbie had more valor in his little finger than I have in my entire body."

A wondering crease graced Paddy's forehead. "And yet I caught you attempting to escape from prison. Where's the valor in that?"

Buck ground his teeth. "I wanted to...oh, why bother, you wouldn't believe me if I told you."

Paddy said, "Try me."

Buck stared at his own reflection in the window. The glass made it look like half of him was missing. A man without substance. That was how he felt. A shadow man. Unfulfilled. Empty. How would this police detective understand that?

"I wanted to enlist," he finally muttered.

Paddy Tooke gave a start. "Don't tell me you wanted to join the war?"

"I said you wouldn't believe me."

The cop snickered. "Well, my boy, that's exactly why I've come to fetch you."

Buck snapped his head around in surprise.

Across from him, Paddy Tooke crossed his legs, a sly grin beaming.

Buck cocked his head, wondering. Something didn't feel right. He gave a dismissive snort and turned back to the window. "My Pops would say, 'if a cop shows up with a gift, his other hand is holding a Billy club.'"

Tooke laughed, slapping his knee. "I like that. It's true, you know. We always seem to have an agenda."

Buck ignored him. Outside, the Hudson River flowed alongside the railroad track, muddy and churning with winter detritus.

"You loved your father, didn't you?" said Tooke.

"He was all I had," said Buck, "Never knew my mother; she was gone before I turned one. It was just me and Pops."

"I met him, you know."

Buck twisted a shocked glance his way. "You met my father?"

"Just once. In fact, I was at his side the night he died."

"What?" choked Buck. His chest felt as if struck with a mallet.

Paddy nodded. "They called my partner and I to a break-in. Your father had been shot as an intruder." Paddy grew somber. "But you already know that—that they had shot him, I mean."

Buck's heart thumped.

"My partner knew your father. While waiting for the ambulance to arrive, they talked like old friends who played a game of cat and mouse together. Jack—that was my partner's name—liked your father. He didn't show it much, but your father's death grieved him."

Buck could only stare.

A glint of kindness melted into Paddy's eyes. "Your father's last thoughts were of you, Buck. He wanted you to know how much he loved you."

Buck tried swallowing. His throat constricted. He turned away.

"Why are you doing this?" he asked softly.

"Doing what?"

"Giving me a second chance? It couldn't have been easy, getting that parole the way you did."

Paddy snorted. "Easier than you may think."

"But why?"

"I'm not doing it just for you. I'll be getting something out of it too."

Buck snapped him a suspicious look. "What?"

"You'll see in New York." Paddy crossed his legs. "Do you believe in redemption, Buck?"

He gave a half-hearted shrug. "I'm not sure what you mean by that."

"That a man's nature can change; that he can overcome his weaknesses. Become better."

Buck recalled the brief time in his past when he had done just that. Repented for the love of a woman. "I suppose, with the right incentive," he offered.

"You have a chance to redeem yourself. Get yourself back on the right track. Make things right."

Buck remained quiet. He then craned his neck, as if searching for something on Paddy's train bench.

"What on earth are you looking for, boy?"

"The Billy-club," he quipped.

And Paddy Tooke broke out laughing.

Chapter 52

OSS Headquarters, Monday, 7:20 PM

PADDY TOOKE AND BUCK Flynn grabbed a cab from Grand Central Station to Rockefeller Center. They took an elevator to the thirty-sixth floor. They were greeted by a woman who led them to a conference room, where she left them. Making themselves comfortable, they waited. Paddy smoked his pipe. Buck sat quietly.

Buck had noticed that the outer reception area had been without designation or description of what sort of business might be conducted in these suites. Even the conference room where they sat was stark, with only a white screen against the far wall and a projector at the other end. It set Buck to wondering what kind of operation this could be, and how this was going to get him into the war effort.

The door opened and two men entered. One carried a briefcase. Neither shook Buck's hand.

The one with the briefcase introduced himself as Deputy Director Phillip Carver. The other was older, shorter, with a furrowed face. His name was Director Allen Davies. Davies took a seat at the foot of the table, whereby he withdrew a cigarette case, retrieved a cigarette, and tapped it gently on the surface of the case. He then proceeded to ignore them.

"I will get right to it," said Carver, taking a seat across from Buck. "We haven't time to waste."

Buck sensed that the man resented being here, or resented having to deal with a known criminal. He reeked of superiority and condescension.

"The job is straightforward. It is up to you whether you take it."

"Job?" said Buck. "I thought I was joining the war effort."

Carver allowed a wry grin to form. "Is that what you were told?" He slipped a glance at Paddy. "I suppose in a way it's true. But not in the way you were thinking."

Buck waited.

Carver continued. "As I was saying, the job is straightforward. In the Manhattan Warehouse and Storage Company, is a safe. We need to break into it. Can you do it?"

Buck gave a start, flabbergasted. Had he heard right? He cautiously looked at the faces in the room. Carver stared back expectantly. Davies, at the end of the table, looked distracted, uninterested. Paddy, on the other hand, nearly smirked with delight.

"Could you repeat that?" asked Buck.

Carver let out an exasperated sigh. "We want you to break into a storage locker and then into a safe. Can you do it?

"Is this some kind of trick?" he asked.

"No trick, Mr. Flynn," replied Carver. "We have gone to great lengths to get you out of prison. We would like you to help us—if you think you're up to it."

"You want me to steal something for you?"

Carver shook his head. "I didn't say that."

"You just said that you want me to break into a safe."

"Yes, that's right."

"But you don't want me to take anything?"

Carver laced his fingers together. His face bent toward the table surface, as if carefully choosing his next words.

"We *do* want you to take something," he said. "But we need to ensure that no one suspects the safe has been opened or that the item in question disturbed. When you close the safe, it must look exactly as it did when you opened it."

"I'm confused. Do you want me to steal something or not?"

"Not steal exactly...swap."

"Swap?"

"That's right." Carver retrieved his briefcase and pulled out an item to place it on the table.

Shock rippled through Buck Flynn.

It was a notebook with a tattered black leather cover.

He'd seen that notebook before. Unmistakable. He'd almost stolen it once before—and had prevented someone else from doing so. He stared, wondering if this was some kind of trick. He glanced up to find Paddy giving him a curious squint. A thin smile formed in the corner of his mouth.

Phillip Carver tapped the notebook.

"Inside that safe is a notebook like this. This is a replica. We want you to take it and replace it with this."

Buck's mouth went dry. He felt they were entrapping him, trying to get him to admit he had opened the old man's safe. And he certainly didn't want to be tricked into another crime that could compound his prison sentence.

Paddy leaned in. "Is something wrong, Buck?"

Buck said nothing.

"Something about that notebook bothers you?"

Carver shot Paddy a questioning glance.

"Why should it?" asked Buck with a shrug. "It's just a notebook."

"You look as if you recognize it," said Paddy.

"How could he?" snapped Carver. "Our forensic team just created it this morning."

Paddy Tooke sat back, clenching his pipe between his teeth. "That's right," he said, eying Buck. "You couldn't recognize it. It's brand new."

Buck's stare drifted to the notebook. It didn't look brand new. It looked well used. It had to be the one. Although it had been dark that night, and he'd only scanned it briefly. Maybe it was different. But what they were asking felt all wrong.

"Where did that come from?" he asked.

Carver said, "From our Research and Development lab."

"And it's just like the one in the safe?"

Carver nodded.

"How did you replicate it? If the other one is in the safe?"

"We used..." he paused, his eyes narrowing. "That information is need-to-know."

"I don't get it," he said. "Why replace the one in the safe with a replica?"

"Well, it's not an exact replica," replied Carver. He began breezing through its pages. "We have painfully replicated every aspect, every pencil stroke, every word, every number and formula, even every smudge. There are a few nuanced differences. We purposely altered some calculations and drawings."

Buck nodded. "I get it. It's the same, but different. You want to throw someone off. I suppose in the original there's a formula for a top-secret weapon," he chuckled. "You guys have seen too many Charlie Chan movies."

No one laughed. They only stared back, somberly.

"Wait a minute! You aren't kidding." Buck sat up.

"We don't kid about national security," said Carver, "or weapons of mass destruction."

"Mass destruction? What is this all about?"

"We can only tell you what you need to know to conduct the operation. Are you willing to help or not?"

Buck grew quiet. He was being squeezed. He didn't trust these men. And he could tell they didn't like him, except maybe Tooke—but that too could be an act.

He stood abruptly. "I think you've brought here me under false pretenses," he said.

A snide snort sounded from the end of the table. Buck glanced down at Allen Davies, who was blowing a smoke ring toward the ceiling. .

"You don't say much, do you?" sniped Buck.

Davies leveled a glare his way. "Young man, the only words I have to say are to your prison warden, recommending how many years we need to add to your current sentence."

"Are you threatening me?"

"No, Mr. Flynn, promising." He smashed his cigarette out on the table surface. "If I have to put you back on a train to Ossining, you won't be seeing daylight until long after the war has ended. As it is, while in this room, you have already been told more than I'm comfortable with."

Buck glowered at him. The noose tightening. "I don't like being set up. You're trying to entrap me."

"No, we're asking you to make a swap for us."

"I won't do it. You'll only arrest me afterward."

"Then I guess we're done here," snapped Davies, standing. "We'll arrange for your trip back to Sing Sing."

Buck whipped a glance at Paddy, who was rubbing his chin in disappointment.

Davies stepped up to Carver. "I never liked the idea of using a common thief in the first place," he snorted.

"It was Tooke's idea," chimed Carver.

Paddy set his pipe down on the edge of the table and stood. "Gentlemen, could I have a word with Mr. Flynn alone for a moment."

Carver glared at Tooke. Davies gave a minuscule shrug. Carver stood, and the two men left the room.

Once the door closed, Buck said. "Is this where you try to win me over with a fatherly lecture?"

"No, this is where I call you an asinine idiot. You are being given an opportunity here."

"Opportunity? You told me I would be going to war. You lied."

"No, I did not! I said you would be joining the war effort—big difference."

"War effort? Stealing for my country? I'm being set up."

"You don't realize how important this is, Buck."

Buck snorted. "I was all ready to go straight."

"Yes, I saw your version of going straight. Escaping from a state prison is a great way to start."

"Don't throw that in my face. I was doing it for a reason."

Paddy took in a breath and hooked his thumbs into the front pockets of his vest.

"I like you, Buck," he said. "Even as I was arresting you, I liked you. And do you know why?"

Buck said nothing.

"I think you're a better man than your actions."

"What the hell does that mean?"

"You say that you want to go straight. Well, I believe you. But so far, I'm the only one who does. I believe in you because of what happened in that hotel room last year."

Buck grew quiet.

"Something went down that you never told us about. The room was a mess. Saturated with lighter fluid—as if someone were planning a major fire. I don't believe it was you. You're not the killing type. And you didn't shoot yourself with that pistol either. You were there...I'm convinced of that. But someone else was too. And I suspect it was a German spy posing as a hotel desk clerk."

Buck blinked. His jaw fell.

"Ah-ha! I knew it," exclaimed Paddy. "You stopped him from lighting up that room, didn't you? You prevented a murder. You mumbled as much before passing out. But you did something else that night, Buck. Unknowingly, you prevented a powerful weapon from falling into enemy hands. That notebook. You recognized it! You saw that book in Nikola Tesla's apartment."

Buck averted his eyes.

Paddy shook a finger at Buck. "I bet you've already opened that safe once before."

"What if I did? That doesn't mean I want to go back to that life. Not when our boys are being killed over there."

Paddy stepped up and placed a hand on his shoulder. "Okay, you expected a fatherly lecture; here it comes. Your actual father left you something, Buck. It wasn't much, but he left you a set of skills—skills others don't have. Any other time, I would attempt to keep those skills in check. But times being what they are, your country needs those skills."

Buck grew quiet. He met Paddy's eyes.

"Besides," said Paddy. "You owe me."

"Owe you? How?"

"Ever wonder why your arrest never garnered more publicity than it did? It's because I told no one that I had arrested *The Smoke* that night. I kept it to myself. I told my wife, Dottie. We had a good laugh about it, but it stayed our little secret. Sure, I could have dug into those previous burglaries and gathered enough evidence to put you away for a long time. But I sensed something in you. That you're a better man than your actions."

"*The Smoke,*" said Buck, a wry smile emerging. "Who's that?"

Paddy grinned back at him. "Apparently, he's an idiot who doesn't know a good thing when he sees one. The U.S. government needs the services of...*The Smoke.* You'll get a full pardon and your criminal record expunged. That's a pretty good way to go straight."

Buck peered down at the notebook and back up to Paddy.

"Well, let's get on with it then," he said.

Chapter 53

⎯⎯⎯⎯⎯◦⎯⎯⎯⎯⎯

Manhattan, Tuesday, 9:45 PM

THE LONE FIGURE SHUFFLED down West 43rd Street, the collar of his topcoat popped up against the chilly night air and his hat low to shadow his face. He maneuvered through the sparse evening crowd, determined, but hobbled with an obvious limp. No one paid him any attention. The streetlamps cast a blueish tint on the street; steam vapors rose from the gutters.

He came to a dress shop recessed back from the sidewalk; closed for the evening, its lights out and its doorway darkened. He pulled back into the recess to blend into the shadows, to watch.

Across the street was a tavern called Pete's Hidey-hole. A Pabst Blue Ribbon sign fizzled with dimming neon behind filthy windows. As dives go, they didn't come any seedier than Pete's Hidey-hole. The clientele were beaten-down men and bloom-off-the-rose women, who simply wanted to drink anonymously and melt into the woodwork. It was the perfect place to be invisible. And the perfect place to conduct business away from prying eyes.

That's why Henry Blacksmith had chosen it for the meeting.

He had come early to monitor the arrival of the other participants. From his position, he had a perfect view of the street.

Henry Blacksmith now went by the name of Henry Stewart, reluctantly forsaking his Schwinghammer pseudonym. He'd also changed his appearance, going back to his natural blond hair and sporting a pencil-thin mustache—just enough facial hair to change the shape of his face. He also now wore a pair of wire-rimmed glasses.

Blacksmith had three objectives for the evening, two critical to his current needs and one to quench a curiosity.

He'd read about the death of Nikola Tesla and decided to step up the plans he had been plotting for the last year.

A sedan approached, slowing as it neared the tavern.

Blacksmith flexed his fingers, releasing the tension in his tendons. His razor knife at the ready in the left-hand pocket.

Over the past year, he had re-oriented himself to using his left hand. He had lost mobility in his right after getting it smashed in the safe door. It got pretty mangled. Two of his fingers, the pinky and ring finger, were as hard and gnarled as tree roots jutting from a riverbed. Useless.

After the attack in Nikola Tesla's apartment, they took him to a doctor with Nazi sympathies, who had a makeshift office in the back of his living quarters. The doctor knew his business but couldn't patch up Blacksmith enough to keep his leg from seizing up occasionally. The major muscle in his upper thigh—the rectus femoris, according to the doctor—got shredded by the weapon used to stab him. He assumed it had been an icepick. Totally hobbled? No. But his limp was obvious.

These days, Blacksmith fearlessly wore the onyx ring at all times on his left hand, primed with the Prussic acid poison. Of course, he left the deadly spike retracted, but had practiced rigorously to engage it at a moment's notice. He could now do it in a flash.

The approaching automobile pulled into an open parking spot a few yards down from Pete's Hidey-Hole. Two men got out and entered the bar. He recognized one as his contact from the German American Bund.

Blacksmith snarled at the thought.

He had no respect for the members of the movement here. They were impotent fools, all talk and no action. And it was the talk that worried him most—loose lips, sink ships, and all that rot.

That's why he'd moved into his own apartment. In the prior months, he'd been living in Brooklyn with two couples who were Bund members. They sat around the house plotting works of subversion that never grew wheels. He became worried that their boastful, yet empty, threats would draw unwanted attention. So, after his wounds had healed, he took a place of his own here in Manhattan, to be closer to the action and position himself to gather intelligence concerning his unfinished business.

He'd made headway during the last month. Not only was he tracking the movements of the Soviets, but had recently cultivated a key asset connected to Nikola Tesla. An asset who could bring him within reach of the plans for the particle beam weapon.

He suspected the Russians were working on a secret project here in the United States, right under the nose of the American government, but he had yet to discover where. Two weeks ago, he had followed a car driven by Yegor Volkov to Long Island. In the car was a man and woman he'd yet to identify. He had followed in a taxi. Unfortunately, he'd lost them outside of Queens.

The problem for Blacksmith was mobility. Following the Soviets in a taxi had been a disaster. The driver grumbled the entire trip and, through his ineptness, had lost track of Volkov's vehicle. The incident had left Blacksmith seething, and he'd come close to killing the driver just for spite.

Hopefully tonight he would fix his mobility problem.

He hobbled across the street and entered Pete's Hidey-hole. The room was narrow, dingy, and filled with cigarette smoke. A bar ran along the left-hand wall, with people squatting on stools. Small booths with torn red vinyl seats dotted the other wall. Absorbed in their alcoholic beverages, the handful of customers never even peeked at the new visitor.

Blacksmith slithered to a back booth where his contact and the other man sat waiting. Both had glasses of beer in front of them.

"Ah, Henry, you're here," said his contact.

Blacksmith's lips tightened at the use of his name and stared daggers at the man to let him know of the mistake he'd made. The idiot. Looking a bit frightened by the glare, the man rose to shake hands, but upon touching the deadness of Blacksmith's gnarled fingers withdrew his hand immediately.

Turning toward the seated man, the contact said, "This here is...uh," and wishing to avoid a second faux pas, he fumbled for a new name, "Uh, Joe."

Blacksmith simply nodded toward the man whose name was not Joe at all.

"Sit down and have a beer," said the contact a bit meekly.

He remained standing. "Do you have it?" he asked.

The seated man nodded.

"I would like to see it," said Blacksmith.

Joe gave a nervous flinch. "Not here," he protested.

Blacksmith gave a nod toward the rear of the building. "This place has a back door to an alley. We can have some privacy there." Blacksmith had come to the joint on two other occasions, to familiarize himself with its layout.

Joe's eyes hardened on Blacksmith, suspicion swimming all over his face. "Okay," he muttered, although much reluctance lived in that one word.

The two men followed Blacksmith down a claustrophobic hallway, past the restrooms, and out through the back door.

The alley opened into a narrow cobblestone driveway enclosed on three sides, barely wide enough for a delivery truck. The area was lit by a solitary bulb above the back door. Discarded furniture and rubbish filled the space. The soiled air smelled of garbage, automobile oil, and urine.

"Let me see it," said Blacksmith.

The man called Joe hesitated. "You got the money?"

Blacksmith gave a blunt nod.

"Show me."

Blacksmith glared back.

"No offense, mister, but I don't know you. I need to know you're good for it."

The Nazi contact nudged Joe with his shoulder. "Don't worry. He's good for it."

"I wanna see the money," he demanded, never taking his eyes off of Blacksmith.

Blacksmith let out an exasperated breath and pulled two twenties from his right-hand pocket, waving them in the dim light of the alley. His left hand fingered the razor knife in his other pocket.

Joe nodded at the sight of the bills and quickly swiped them from Blacksmith's hand. He then reached behind him and pulled a handgun from beneath his jacket.

Blacksmith watched warily, ready for a double-cross.

Joe, sensing he was dealing with a feral beast, eased the weapon over to Blacksmith.

"It's a Colt Model 1903 Pocket Hammerless," offered the man. "It's used, but works just fine. The serial number has been filed off."

Blacksmith took the weapon over to the light bulb near the doorway to inspect it. It looked worse for wear, but everything was in working order. And although it was an American gun, it had more stopping power than that itty-bitty thing he'd lost in the struggle last year. He still preferred a Lugar, but it would do.

The first of three objectives achieved: get a handgun.

"The magazine is empty," said Blacksmith with obvious disappointment.

The man called Joe hesitated. "I brought a box of cartridges. Five bucks extra."

"That's pretty steep, isn't it?"

The man shrugged. "Do you want them or not?"

"Let me see them."

Joe withdrew a box of cartridges from an inside pocket, handing them toward Blacksmith.

Blacksmith tucked the Colt away in his topcoat and used his gnarled hand to take the box from the man. As the exchange was taking place, he casually brought his left hand out, as if to handle the box with both hands, and lightly tapped the top of the other man's hand just behind his knuckles.

"Ow," yelped the man. "You must have a burr on your ring. It just pinched me."

Blacksmith allowed a smile to creep into his face. "Sorry."

The very next second, the man called Joe, stiffened with a violent jerk. His face contorted. Shocked. Opening his mouth to speak, his rolled-up tongue filled the gap like a glob of raw meat, choking out his words. Froth oozed from between the blockage. His eyes widened as if to explode from his eye sockets. He staggered, his arms spastic with flailing.

"Charley," cried Blacksmith's contact, suddenly forgetting that his friend's name was Joe, "What's wrong?"

The man's shoulders snapped back as if yanked from behind by cords. The froth spewing.

The contact's face paled in the dim light of the alley as the other man contorted wildly, only to fall as if boneless onto the grimy cobblestones. He continued to writhe with choking grunts for ten seconds until seizing up into a silent, lifeless ball.

The contact kneeled next to him.

"What's wrong? What happened?" he simpered.

Blacksmith stepped up, reached out, and brushed his left hand across the back of his contact's neck. The man felt the prick and swept a mean glance his way.

"What the—?"

"That's for using my name," muttered Blacksmith.

Two minutes later, the contact lay crumpled next to his buddy. A sickly silence filled the alley.

Objective number two achieved: test the ring. Quench the curiosity.

Blacksmith cleaned the two men of their wallets. He found gas rationing cards on both men and tucked them away in his jacket. He took their money and then, after patting down his contact, came to the last thing on his list.

Car keys.

Objective three: fix the mobility problem.

Chapter 54

Manhattan Warehouse and Storage, Tuesday, 10:45 PM

THE MANHATTAN WAREHOUSE AND Storage building loomed over 7th Avenue like an impregnable fortress. Square, squat, and nine stories tall, it possessed towering twin battlements sitting atop the north and south corners, with supporting corbels beneath, and, what appeared to be, machicolations slotted between them. The overall image was of a fortified castle.

Staring at it, Buck Flynn wondered if its security system included boiling oil.

Flynn and Paddy Tooke sat across the street in Paddy's '39 Nash LaFayette sedan, watching the sparse foot traffic. A few cars lined the otherwise quiet street. Kentucky Club smoke filled the Nash's cabin. Buck had his window rolled down to allow fresh air in.

"For future reference," Buck said, "I stay away from smoking before...uh, making an unannounced visit."

Paddy glanced at him. "Oh, yes, of course. That makes sense." He rolled down his window and tapped out the remains of his pipe on the door panel. "This is good for me, Buck, working with you like this. It helps to understand the criminal mind. Gives me an all-new perspective."

"Glad to help you out that way," he muttered.

On the seat between them sat a rucksack containing items needed for the job.

Two hours ago, Paddy had surprised Buck with his Pop's lock-picking set, which they had confiscated the night of his arrest. How Paddy got a hold of the kit he didn't say, and Buck didn't ask. "I'll be taking those back once the job is done," warned Paddy with a grin.

Fat chance, thought Buck. When this was over, he would do everything in his power to keep his Pop's inheritance.

The other item in the rucksack was the fake notebook—if it was fake. Buck still wondered about that. They had said it was a replica. But if the original remained in the safe, and had been all along, how did they copy it? Were they able to get their hands on it somehow? And if that was the case, why not make the substitution then? Or just keep the original? That would certainly keep its secrets out of circulation.

He still suspected a trap. He did not trust Phillip Carver or Allen Davies. He could tell that they were master chess players, and he needed to be on his toes to avoid becoming one of their sacrificial pawns. Gazing at the building, he wondered if other exits existed that he could reach, if things inside went badly.

"It looks like Harrington has made it to his post," said Paddy. He was craning his neck to look up into the fifth-story window of the building across the street from the warehouse.

Buck glanced that way in time to catch two signal flashes of a flashlight.

"Keep your eye on him. He'll let you know where the guards are during their rounds."

Buck had never worked with a team before. His jobs had always been solo projects, carefully thought out and planned to the minute. So, it was a fresh experience working with others; not one that made him comfortable.

Although, he was learning there were benefits to working with a team. Carver had provided three extra men to help with what was being called *Operation Teleforce*. Paddy Tooke was in charge, but surprisingly, the Irishman had informed the others that, because Buck was the expert in this kind of work, they were to take advice from him during the operation.

Carver had also provided a set of blueprints of the Manhattan Warehouse and Storage building, including a schematic of the alarm system. It would have taken weeks of research for Buck to nail down such information, but for the OSS team, it took less than ten hours.

One man Carver provided was a technician named Robert Markham. They designated him to disarm the alarm. At first, Buck balked at the offer, saying that he handled the alarms himself. Markham then demonstrated his vast knowledge of modern systems and his ability to circumvent them, convincing Buck that his expertise would be an asset.

The team had also provided information concerning the night watchmen's schedule. They had spent two nights staking out the Manhattan Warehouse and Storage Building. They had the security routine down pat.

Buck had to admit, these OSS fellows were quick to forecast and execute a plan of action. For someone who took his time to plan out a job, this was happening at whirlwind speed.

"Almost time to go," said Paddy. He checked his watch for the time.

Across the street, one of the front doors swung open, and out stepped a uniformed watchman.

"Just like clockwork," said Tooke.

The guard carried a Billy club and wore a holstered pistol. He haphazardly scanned the street, not noticing the members of the team along the block, and began a clueless stroll southward.

"Let's go," said Paddy. "We have about twelve minutes before he completes his circuit around the block."

He and Buck were out of the car and across the street in seconds. Robert Markham, who had been sitting in another car down the street, met them. Immediately, they set to work on the doors.

Buck worked the lock while Markham disabled the alarm using a piece of electronic equipment that Buck had never seen before. He watched with fascination until Markham gave the go-ahead nod.

Another team member, Theodore Pelt, stood on the corner under a lamppost, pretending to read a newspaper as he watched for the guard encircling the building. He nodded an all's-clear signal.

Tooke, using his flashlight, signaled Agent Arthur Harrington in the fifth-floor window across the street. Harrington returned three quick flashes. Harrington would use binoculars to track the movements of a second guard making rounds inside the building. Three flashes meant that the guard was on the third floor. Harrington would continue to communicate with Buck during the operation.

Yes, working with a team certainly had its benefits.

Markham stepped back. "Good to go," he said, and swung open the door. All was quiet inside.

"Be safe, son," uttered Paddy, his eyes full of concern. "Remember to leave the safe exactly as you find it. Exactly!"

Buck nodded and turned to enter Manhattan Warehouse and Storage.

Chapter 55

Manhattan Warehouse and Storage, Tuesday, 11:07 PM

Buck was on his own now. Well, almost. If a window was available, he would communicate via the signal flashes with the agent across the street. He hoped he could trust the information to be accurate. His senses percolated with suspicion, wary of a trap, and ready to bolt at the first sign of a double-cross from the OSS.

The room in front of him was dimly lit. A chill was in the air, despite the gentle whirring of heat being blown through floor vents. A large wooden service counter, shaped in a U, sat on the other side of the tiled floor, similar to a bank counter.

To the left was a hallway lit by sconces affixed to the wall. He entered the hall, passing by an elevator—using it was out of the question as the guard upstairs would hear it. He would have to take the stairs. Tesla's locker was on the fifth floor.

Coming to a staircase, he peered up its zig-zagging rise. No guard in sight. He ran up to the second floor and waited on the landing. Three minutes later, a door above him opened and closed, followed by the footsteps of the guard plodding up to the fourth floor. The surveillance team had accurately predicted that the guard used the stairs going up, but took the elevator down, once his rounds were complete.

Buck continued to follow the guard until coming to the fifth floor. He then breached the lock and quietly slipped through the door.

Now to find the locker. The only available light came through a large window at the far end of the main hall. He needed rooms, 5J and 5L.

Buck scurried down the hall and peered out the window. Pulling a flashlight from the rucksack, he signaled the OSS man in the building across the street. Harrington signaled back. The inside guard was now on the sixth floor.

Turning away from the window, Buck began his search for the lockers. Two hallways down, he found them. Situated halfway down the hall, each locker had a roll-down metal door with a combination lock on a hasp.

According to the blueprints, an inside door connected lockers 5J and 5L, therefore he only needed to open one of the garage doors to access both lockers. Choosing one, he set to work on the combination lock. It took five minutes to unclasp. The door opened with a muted clatter, but the guard by this time was on the seventh floor, far from any noise he made.

The locker was huge. The two spaces together occupied nearly six hundred square feet. There were stacks of boxes, crates, file cabinets, laboratory equipment, and machine parts. The connecting door to the second locker was there. But thankfully, he didn't need it. The safe was on this side of the partition.

The Diebold stood at the mouth of the locker as if the movers had dropped it the moment it crossed the threshold. He couldn't blame them. It weighed three thousand pounds.

Squatting before it, Buck worked the safe's dial. He hadn't opened a safe in over a year; however, this had been the very last safe he'd cracked and remembered the numbers as if it were yesterday. He twisted out the combination.

It didn't work.

Was it the same safe? It had to be.

He tried again. Nothing. They had changed the combination.

Fortunately, one tool provided to him was his own stethoscope. He began listening for the tumblers, already knowing that the safe had a four-number combination.

He closed his eyes, listening for the faint ticks. His focus drilled into the task, his fingertips awake with sensitivity, like the whiskers of a cat twitching to the softest vibration. Within the bulk of steel, he felt the pin of the drive cam catch the first wheel.

Twenty minutes later, he was in.

Swirling his flashlight over its shelves, he searched the safe. It looked the same as when he'd first opened it, except for two noticeable differences: stuffed into a cubbyhole, was a set of keys—they hadn't been there before—and...

No notebook.

He scanned it again to make sure. Nothing. It wasn't there.

Carver had stressed the importance of keeping the safe exactly as he'd found it, which meant *not* leaving the dummy notebook if the real one wasn't there.

Then he remembered the anti-dynamite box—the safe-within-the-safe down below.

Reaching for the lock-picking kit, a thought came to him. *The set of keys.*

He grabbed them, and sure enough, one fit the auxiliary safe. He searched inside.

Again, no notebook. However, he found another item that had been there the first time he'd opened this safe.

The gold medal. The one with Thomas Edison's profile on it.

Taking it out of its sack, the gold felt heavy in his palm. He recalled the last time he'd held it, along with the guilt he'd felt over stealing the old man's only treasure. Did he still feel guilty? The old man was dead. He wouldn't be missing it now, would he?

They had implored him to leave the safe *exactly* as he'd found it, with no trace of his having been here.

It was just one item. What would it hurt?

Dropping the medal back into its sack...he stopped cold.

A noise clanged.

Hallways away, the main door to the floor had opened and closed with a bang.

The guard was returning for another set of rounds.

He quickly closed the axillary safe, locking it. Setting the keys on a nearby crate, he snapped his flashlight off, listening for the approaching guard.

Still a good distance away.

He closed the safe door with a quiet clunk.

Reaching up, he pulled down the locker's metal door. Slowly. Excruciatingly slow. The noise screeching faintly against the walls of the hollow hallway.

The footsteps padded through an adjacent hall.

The door needed to be down before the guard turned the corner.

Halfway, however, the door froze as if jammed. Buck tugged, but it wouldn't budge. Panic surged. He couldn't see the obstruction in the darkness. He felt along the bottom edge for blockage. Nothing. Reaching up, he felt along the rail frame for anything stopping the castors. Nothing.

The footsteps grew louder.

The Diebold safe obscured the right-side rail. He scrambled over the safe to the other side and again ran his hand along the rail frame.

There!

The door had caught on a stack of files. They teetered. If he had forced the door down, the entire stack would have tumbled, making a heck of a noise and a heck of a mess. Carefully, he dislodged the top box and quickly crawled back to the other side of the Diebold.

The footsteps were now loud claps on the tiled floor. The guard whistled a tune.

Grateful for the extra noise, Buck eased the door closed. The outside hasp would be without the combination lock, but hopefully pass the test of a casual glance.

He held his breath in the inky darkness. Beads of sweat peppered his forehead.

The footsteps turned down his hallway, drew up to the locker, and...

Passed by without pause, the guard whistling joyfully.

Three minutes later, Buck heard the faint sound of a door slamming.

Twenty minutes after that, with the safe and locker closed up, Buck waited by the window at the end of the main hall for the 'all's clear' signal from across the street, and ten minutes later he was back on 7th Avenue heading for Paddy's Nash.

Once inside the car, he let out a breath.

Peering over at Paddy, Buck found him clenching the steering wheel white knuckled as if petrified. Sweat glistened beneath his fedora.

Paddy swallowed. "I don't know how you do it, Buck. I nearly had a coronary just waiting outside for you. I can't imagine what it must be like inside."

Buck shrugged. "It was a breeze. But the notebook wasn't in the safe."

Paddy flexed his jaw. "That's not good. Where could it be?"

Buck gave a shake of his head. "No clue."

"You left everything exactly as you found it?"

Looking him straight in the eye, Buck was about to give a confident nod when something came to mind.

He hadn't. He'd forgotten something.

The set of keys to the anti-dynamite box! He'd never put them back inside the safe. They were resting on a nearby crate.

His mind recoiled at the possibility of returning inside — and with it, a second chance of being caught. All over a set of keys.

He flashed Paddy a forced smile.

"Exactly as I found it," he lied.

Chapter 56

———◆———

OSS Headquarters, Wednesday, 8:37 AM

"WILL I BE FREE to go my way today?" Buck Flynn asked.

He and Paddy Tooke rode alone in the elevator, heading to the thirty-sixth floor. Paddy shrugged as he watched the indicator needle ascend through the floor numbers.

"I don't know...I suppose so."

"What do you mean, you suppose so? I did my part. It's not my fault that the book wasn't in the safe. We had a deal."

Paddy grit his teeth. "I only know that Deputy Director Carver left a message at the hotel this morning saying that he wanted the two of us here by 9 AM."

It had been a long night for Paddy Tooke, tossing and turning in a strange bed. For the second night in a row, he had slept at a nearby hotel, bunking with Buck Flynn to keep a watchful eye on him. Phillip Carver didn't want the young thief slipping away before they were finished with him. Paddy hated hotels and two nights away from home had left him irritable.

His mood was further darkened by the phone call he had made to Carver the previous night. Paddy debriefed him on the empty safe and Carver had raged, cursing, while asking questions in a tone that seemed to blame Paddy for the notebook's absence. At one point Carver had asked, 'did your trained monkey perform to satisfaction?' The comment rankled him, considering the risk Flynn had taken; but he held his tongue.

He felt he was playing referee between two feuding opponents.

Paddy slid a look Buck's way. The foxlike eyes stared back defiantly. It was hard to read him. The man was clever—thief that he was. He could affect a mask for any circumstance.

Like last night.

When asked about leaving the safe 'exactly as he'd found it', Paddy had caught a minuscule flinch, leaving him to wonder about Buck's truthfulness. His intuition thundered. Paddy wanted to believe in him. But he was a thief, after all, and a very convincing chameleon.

The elevator doors opened, and a young woman named Gilda greeted them.

"Mr. Carver is expecting you in the conference room, Mr. Tooke."

"What about me?" asked Buck.

Gilda gave a measured smile. "You are to follow me, sir."

Buck frowned. Hesitating. The hope of being released from his commitment evaporating. The woman led the way, and Buck reluctantly followed. Paddy noticed an agent stationed in front of the door that they led Buck to. Carver's way of keeping him in check.

Paddy arrived at the conference room. Inside were the other OSS members of the Teleforce team, sitting grimly. Robert Markham, Theodore Pelt, and Arthur Harrington each nodded Paddy's way but remained quiet.

He took a seat at the end of the table and was withdrawing his tobacco pouch to load his pipe when the conference room door swung open. Phillip Carver entered, carrying what looked to be a set of rolled-up blueprints. Two other men came in behind him: Director Allen Davies and a stranger. Carver set the blueprints aside and took his place behind the dais. The other two took seats in chairs against the wall, away from the group.

Carver gave a cough, signaling that he wanted all eyes on him.

"We suffered a minor disappointment last night," he offered, "but new intelligence has surfaced that verifies that *Teleforce* is still in play. We want to take another swing at it. It will be trickier, but it can be done."

He signaled for the lights to go out. Robert Markham stood to run the projector.

A slide shifted, showing a man exiting a building. An embossed sign on the brick façade behind him designated the building to be the Navarro Hotel.

"We have been monitoring Sava Kosanovic, Tesla's nephew. Because we did not find *Teleforce* in the safe, we think Kosanovic took it prior to the FBI confiscating his uncle's belongings. We took this photo yesterday. Kosanovic is headed to Nikola Tesla's funeral at the Episcopal Cathedral of St. John the Divine. The mayor spoke at the service, with over two thousand people in attendance."

The screen flipped through a series of photographs of the funeral service and various faces in the crowd. The scene shifted to people leaving the church to get into cars for a funeral procession. The next slide showed a snow-covered cemetery with a row of automobiles parked along a lane. Two men huddled together next to the limousines, one clearly being Sava Kosanovic.

"They buried Tesla at Ferncliff Cemetery in Ardsley, New York. In this photo, Kosanovic is talking with a man we have identified as Vuk Milosh."

The slide flipped again, revealing a close-up of the young man. He was handsome, with dark hair, a square jawline, and a cocksure grin.

"Vuk Milosh is Serbian, and a known member of the National Liberation Party. He works directly for Arso Jovanovic, Josip Broz Tito's right-hand man. We just learned that Milosh has been living in the U.S. for over a year on a temporary diplomatic visa. We are trying to verify his current address. He's not listed in any of the hotels in the city. Our best guess is that he's staying somewhere on Long Island—although not confirmed."

Carver stepped closer to the screen.

"We know Milosh was a political agitator at the University of Prague in the late 1930s, and a leader of the communist youth movement." The slide shifted. Still at the cemetery, this slide showed Sava Kosanovic talking with a young woman with wire-rimmed glasses. "We have identified this woman as Arlene Muzaric, Kosanovic's secretary. She too is of Serbian descent but was born in Philadelphia. Other than working for a suspected communist agent, we have not affiliated her with any communist organization. She is, in fact, a registered Republican." The slide clicked to a city street outside a brownstone. A series of three photos showed Sava Kosanovic exiting a limousine to enter the building.

"These photos taken this morning show Kosanovic going into Arlene Muzaric's residence. The two were headed to another smaller memorial service for Nikola Tesla being held at St. Sava Serbian Orthodox Cathedral. He was only stopping to pick up Miss Muzaric for the event."

The next photo showed the two of them coming out of the brownstone and down the steps toward the waiting car.

"Does anyone notice anything different about Kosanovic?"

Before the others could respond, Paddy Tooke said, "He's carrying a briefcase he didn't have before."

"Very good, Mr. Tooke. From our interview with New Yorker Hotel Detective John Williamson, we understand that, on the day of Tesla's death, Sava Kosanovic had given his briefcase to his secretary to hold for him. We thought nothing of it at the time."

"Is *Teleforce* in the briefcase?" asked a voice.

Carver nodded. "We believe so. His secretary had it on ice at her place."

"Was she aware of that?"

"That we don't know. But this is where it gets interesting. Kosanovic gets into the car with the briefcase. He goes to the memorial service with Miss Muzaric and..."

The slide shifts showing him standing in front of the church steps emp ty-handed, Arlene Muzaric at his side.

"No briefcase," said Carver. "Now notice the other man getting out of the same car."

"Vuk Milosh," said Paddy Tooke. "They drove together."

"Yes," said Carver. "He'd been in the car along."

"But he has no briefcase either," offered someone.

"Correct."

"Who's the other woman with Milosh? The pretty one?"

"We have not identified her yet, but that's not important. This is where we follow the bouncing ball."

The slides shifted rapidly.

"After the service, Kosanovic goes nowhere near the car that brought him. He takes a taxi home. Arlene Muzaric gets in her own taxi. However, Vuk Milosh takes the car with the missing briefcase still inside. Curious, our men prudently followed Milosh. Wasting no time, he goes directly to the Russian Consulate, at 7 East 61st Street."

A new slide showed Milosh exiting the automobile in front of the Russian Consulate, a briefcase in his hand.

"And there, gentlemen, is our missing briefcase. Vuk Milosh took it into the Consulate with whatever intelligence it contained. We now believe that *Teleforce* is in Soviet hands."

Paddy felt an air of dismay in the room.

Carver nodded for the projector to be turned off. The lights came on.

"Here's our problem. Our sources tell us that Anatoli Yakovlev, the Russian Station Chief, is going to London in two days on a transport plane. He will take a diplomatic pouch, which might contain the technological designs for the construction of the *Teleforce* particle beam weapon."

The men at the table cast glances at each other, the anxiety obvious.

Arthur Harrington asked, "Can we get a warrant, based on the evidence we have, to search the Consulate?"

Carver shook his head. "Legally, the Russian Consulate is off-limits. For all sense and purposes, the building sits on Soviet soil."

"Can we apprehend him before he leaves the country?"

"I'm afraid not. He has diplomatic immunity, and anything inside the pouch is protected."

"Two days," murmured Theodore Pelt, "then nothing can be done. They can walk out of the Russian Consulate with everything they need to build the weapon."

Carver glanced up from his notes. "It's not hopeless. We still have two days. And I believe we have come up with a workable operation to swap out the *Teleforce* notebooks."

"How, if we can't search the consulate?" asked Pelt. "We can't get in and we don't even know where to look for it."

"We can't search the consulate legally," offered Carver. "But all's fair in love and war, and all that."

Paddy Tooke leaned forward. "Are you suggesting that we break into the Russian Consulate?"

"We don't have to, Mr. Tooke, they have invited us in."

Chapter 57

———◦———

Hanover House Hotel, Manhattan, Wednesday, 9:02 AM

HE WAS CLEANING THE gun when a knock came on the door.

Henry Blacksmith sat in his sleeveless undershirt. Stripped down in pieces, the Colt Model 1903 Hammerless lay spread out across newsprint atop the rickety table. The smell of gun oil hung in the air.

The interruption startled him. He'd never had a visitor. Suspicion swept in. Was it the police? Had they connected the bodies in the alley of Pete's Hidey-hole to him somehow? Impossible. He'd been extremely careful.

He quietly cursed the uselessness of the dismantled gun.

The one-room walk-up at the Hanover House Hotel was a shabby place, with worn floors and water-stained walls. The hotel, known to accommodate transients, did not ask questions of their guests. In the two months he'd been living here, he'd never spoken to any of his fellow inhabitants, and they left him alone.

He stood and took up his razor knife, holding it hidden near his thigh as he stepped up to the door. He leaned against it but left it closed.

"Who is it?" he asked.

"Mr. Stewart, you have a phone call," came a male voice from the other side.

Phone call? Who would be calling him? Who knew he lived here?

"The telephone is on the landing at the end of the hall," muttered the voice.

He waited until he heard the person turn to plod down the hall before cautiously opening the door.

The hall was empty.

He slipped the razor knife into his trousers pocket and eased down the hall, wary of a trap. His muscles tense, his eyes watched each shut door, as if expecting them to burst open. They didn't.

When he got to the phone on the third-floor landing, no one else was about. Lifting the handset to his ear, he said, "Yes?"

"Henry...it's me."

A rush of anger flooded him. He recognized the voice immediately.

"It's me, Henry...George. You know, George Sylvester—"

"I know who it is!" he spat. "How did you get this number?"

"One of our friends gave it to me."

Obviously one of the loose-lipped national socialists who'd helped him recuperate. He wished he'd killed them all.

"I'm calling from prison...here in Ossining," replied Viereck. "They let us call out once a week."

The fury inside grew. The idiot had to know they tapped the prison phones.

"Did you hear about the death of my cherished friend?"

"Yes." He snorted. Blacksmith knew he was referring to Tesla. Two days ago, he had watched from across the street as the FBI confiscated Tesla's belongings and loaded them onto trucks. He still hadn't found out where they had taken the materials.

"The item that he had...the..." Viereck paused, as if choosing the right words. "The science book."

"What about it?"

"Have you been able to return it to the library yet?"

Library? The man thought he was being clever, talking in code, yet it would only draw attention to their conversation. Blacksmith wanted to reach through the phone and throttle him.

"No," he replied tersely. "It's unavailable."

"I may know where to find it," said Viereck. "His nephew may have borrowed it. I saw his picture in the newspaper."

"I know that!" snapped Blacksmith. Yes, he knew all about the nephew, Sava Kosanovic.

"I just thought that if you were to focus your attention on—"

"I am well aware of the situation and have made plans accordingly."

"What plans?"

"Plans!" he stated with firm finality.

"Good, I knew you would be on top of it."

"Is this the reason you're wasting your weekly phone call?"

"No, there is another matter." Viereck paused. "Remember when I first got to the prison? You had concerns about another inmate here? You wanted to be kept abreast of his...status."

Blacksmith stopped cold. He remembered okay.

After the attack in Tesla's room, he determined to learn the identity of the man who had assailed him. And promised to kill the bastard.

Initially, he had mistaken the mystery man to be a bodyguard for the old man. Yet, after combing the newspapers for a headline about the hero who had saved the life of Nikola Tesla, he had found nothing. Which made him wonder. Why was there no mention of the incident? He checked the obituaries, thinking that possibly the man had died of his wounds. Nothing.

Then he caught an item buried in the metro section about a man being shot at the New Yorker Hotel by an unknown assailant. They had arrested the man for suspected burglary. The arresting officer, of all people, was Sergeant Detective J. Patrick Tooke.

The man he'd fought with had simply been another thief—in the wrong place at the wrong time.

His name: Harry C. Flynn Jr.

Over the next couple of months, Blacksmith followed the trial of Flynn in the newspapers, disappointed that none had carried a photograph of the man. He longed to know what Flynn looked like, as his blackened face had made recognition impossible.

That December, according to the papers, they sentenced Harry Flynn to two years. Ironically, to the same prison that welcomed suspected spy, George Sylvester Viereck.

Yes, Blacksmith was eager to hear any news of Harry Flynn.

"What about him?" asked Blacksmith.

"He's no longer with us," whispered Viereck.

"What!" he exclaimed. "His sentence can't be up yet!" Blacksmith had liked the fact they had incarcerated his prey; it kept him on ice until such a time that he could reach him.

"No, he wasn't due to be released for another ten months. He got sprung."

"How?"

"My sources say that a man from the government took him out of general population."

Blacksmith grew quiet. Flynn could be anywhere now. Had he slipped through his fingers? "Do you know who the government man was and why he took him?"

"I don't know why, but I know his name. Oddly, he has the same last name as the police detective who helped pinch me. Tooke."

Blacksmith gave a start. Tooke? The same man who had arrested Flynn? The same man who had thwarted Blacksmith's attempt to kill Viereck that night?

Blacksmith had tried to keep track of Detective Tooke as well, but that same December, the man had disappeared—retired from the police department, they had said. Vanished. And now he shows up to spring Harry Flynn from prison? Why? Did he really work for the government now?

Blacksmith hung up the telephone and walked back to his room.

He tried to piece it together. Why would Tooke help a convicted thief get out of prison? Did it have something to do with the thief being in that room last year? Blacksmith recalled how the man had materialized out of nowhere. He hadn't been there, and then he was! He also recalled the unlocked doors to the safe that night. Had he been there to steal the technology for the weapon all along?

Was Harry Flynn a thief or a spy? Had his prison sentence merely been a ruse? A way to cover up blundered espionage?

He walked over to where a large tapestry hung across the dingy wall. He unhooked the top left corner and let the fabric drop. Beneath was a collage of photos, news clippings, maps, and book pages. A spider web of thread connected people and bits of information.

For months Blacksmith had studied the life of Nikola Tesla, combing articles and books about his inventions and relationships with notables throughout the decades. From working with Edison in New Jersey to helping Westinghouse light the Chicago World's Fair, from installing generators at Niagara Falls to working with J.P. Morgan and the failed experiment of Wardenclyff. All of it laid out on his wall.

Where did the thief fit in?

Blacksmith had also gathered intelligence concerning the Russians and Yugoslavians and had taken steps to infiltrate those associated with them. Even this afternoon he would meet to have lunch with an asset he'd been cultivating. And come Friday night, that asset would give him unprecedented access to the Soviets—right through the front door! He knew they were up to something out on Long Island. He didn't know what yet, but he was close to uncovering it.

But had he missed something concerning Tooke and Flynn? Maybe the two of them could lead him to the plans for the particle beam weapon quicker.

The key to finding Flynn was finding Tooke.

An idea came to him. Why hadn't he thought of it before? It was so obvious.

When he had learned of Tooke's retirement from the police force a year ago, he had assumed that the man had left the city—didn't they all retire to Florida these days? But that had obviously not been the case. He was still here in New York, possibly with a wife and family. He needed to find his address and pay him a visit.

Blacksmith took a seat at the table. His nimble fingers quickly assembled the components of the Colt.

Just like assembling a handgun, the pieces of his plan were coming together. The Soviets identified. Asset cultivated. And now...

He slammed the magazine into the gun, taking aim...

And now, he needed to aim his sights to finding Tooke and Flynn.

Chapter 58

———◆———

OSS Headquarters, Wednesday, 10:16 AM

"INVITED INTO THE RUSSIAN Consulate?" asked Paddy Tooke. "How?" All the men in the room sat forward, their interest piqued.

Deputy Director Carver stepped behind the podium. "On Saturday evening, just before Anatoli Yakovlev's trip to London, the Russian Consulate is throwing a soiree for a small delegation from the National Liberation Party of Yugoslavia. Arso Jovanovic, Tito's lieutenant, will visit, along with members of his team."

Carver located a page in his notes.

"It's a catered, black-tie event," he said. "The consulate has hired a local catering company. We are currently taking steps to infiltrate the catering team, so we can have an inside man."

"Doesn't sound like much of an invitation to me," offered Harrington.

"No, not so far, does it?" said Carver with a Cheshire grin, "However, they offered the invitation, and here is proof."

Carver stepped over to the man sitting next to Allen Davies, who reached into his jacket pocket and handed Carver a stationery envelope. From it, Carver withdrew two vellum cards. At the top of each card was the embossed seal of the Russian Consulate.

"These are two invitations to the gala," said Carver.

"R and D come up with those?" asked one man.

"No, they are the real deal. And they give us an opportunity to be at the gala. Political alliances have recently shifted in occupied Yugoslavia. President Roosevelt and Wild Bill are moving our support away from the Chetniks to Tito and his Liberation Party. The communists are doing a better job of killing Germans. And because of our new commitment to Tito, we have arranged a strategy meeting with the visiting Jovanovic."

Carver handed the invitations back to the man sitting next to Allen Davies.

"Gentlemen, I would like to introduce our point man in that new relationship, Marine Lieutenant Walter Brookfield."

Tucking the invitations away in his jacket, the man arose and stepped forward.

Carver said, "Lieutenant Brookfield retains his rank as a Marine, but has been working as an OSS agent in occupied Yugoslavia. Until recently with the Chetniks, but because of our shift in support, he...well, let's let him speak for himself."

Brookfield stepped behind the podium. He stood over six feet and as straight as a ruler. His narrow face had slashing dimples, like commas, around his mouth, and his hazel eyes possessed a shrewd glint.

"As Deputy Director Carver mentioned, I was working with the Chetnik leader, Draza Mihailovic. I spent six months with his guerrilla forces, creating havoc for the thirteen Nazi divisions stationed in Yugoslavia. However, we're now shifting efforts to providing arms and supplies to Tito's troops, as well as continuing guerrilla warfare against the Nazis."

A hand went up. Theodore Pelt. "I thought Churchill didn't want us involved with Yugoslavia?"

A thin smile emerged between Brookfield's commas. "True. He feels that we Americans might muck up the relationships he's developed with the National Liberation forces.

"So we're going to subvert Churchill's efforts?" asked someone.

"Not at all. But we do plan to work on the sly under his nose. I have already spent time with Arso Jovanovic, and while he's in town, he wanted me to meet some of his Russian friends."

"That's unusual, isn't it?" asked Theodore Pelt.

Carver stepped up next to Brookfield. "Yes, Ted, it is, but war makes for strange bedfellows. The Russians are our allies now. And that's why they've invited Lieutenant Brookfield to the gala on Friday evening. It's our golden opportunity."

Arthur Harrington leaned forward, his focus on Carver. "Okay, I get they have invited Brookfield to the party, but how does that help us? We don't know where the notebook is. It would take days for him to search the whole consulate."

"Actually," offered Carver. "We have intelligence that helps to pinpoint where the notebook might be located."

"I'm sure the Commies will monitor Brookfield," said Pelt. "How will he be able to get to it?"

"He won't. Lieutenant Brookfield is to be our diversion. Remember, we have two invitations."

"So who's going in with him?" asked Harrington.

Snapping a sharp look Paddy's way, Carver replied: "Mr. Tooke's trained monkey, of course."

Chapter 59

———◆———

Wardenclyff Laboratory, Long Island, Wednesday, 10:32
AM

HE WAS ALONE TODAY; the others gone — except for the beast. The underground building was soundless, like a buried casket. But to Dr. Frederick Markovitch, the place always felt like a tomb where hope evaporated into the surrounding dirt. For over a year, they had buried him here. So oppressive and cold it was maddening.

He rummaged about his makeshift apartment, searching for the one tie he owned, the same tie he wore the night of his kidnapping. Fifteen months with one tie. Stained and threadbare, but he needed it to look official. His friend, his only friend, would be here soon.

He was glad the others were gone. Their absence made the secret visit more special. And his friend always shooed the beast from the room. A gesture Dr. Markovitch appreciated.

There! The tie hung on a nail in the back of the closet. He grabbed the miserable accessory and was out the door, twisting a knot in place as he scurried down the hall toward the main laboratory.

Dr. Markovitch lived alone at the end of a tentacle that branched out from the main laboratory. His captors had cobbled together a room for him, furnished with a bed, a dresser, a chair and table, an electric hotplate, and two lamps.

It was a bleak existence. Depressive. But today a sliver of excitement gripped him.

He had news to share with his friend.

He entered the main laboratory. The room was enormous, as large as a gymnasium, but that only magnified its oppressiveness. He peered around, hoping the beast wasn't lurking somewhere, but he saw no one.

The others had left yesterday afternoon—something about attending a special function in the city. They didn't invite Dr. Markovitch, of course. He never went on excursions. Left behind, as always. Entombed to conduct his experiments in isolated misery.

If only they would take the beast, Yegor Volkov, with them. A constant guard, the man embodied menace. He terrified Markovitch, and so he avoided him as much as possible.

He saw nothing of Volkov in the unlit laboratory; but his essence, seen or not, haunted the underground facilities.

For fifteen torturous months, Markovitch had lived three stories below ground. The only way to stay sane was to focus on the work. So that's what he did. Day and night. He'd become disconnected from life's cycles and rhythms. There were no clocks, only devices to measure time for the sake of experiments. What did time matter, anyway? Without sunrise and sunset, there was only existence—sleeping, eating, working.

Yes, they had let him out a few times in the beginning, when they saw that confinement affected his mood and ability to think...and therefore his productivity.

He recalled the first time they had let him go outside. The exhilaration of climbing the spiral staircase to the upper level, to enter a room where the generator pumped air into the levels below. The chugging machine seemed like a living beast, and the heat it radiated had soothed the constant chill that seeped into one's bones below.

Above ground, the cement block building was only a remnant of what had been a magnificent structure of modern science: Wardenclyff. The windows, now sealed with cement blocks, made him yearn all the more for the outside world. Giddy with the anticipation of seeing grass and sky again, he felt like a child opening a gift on Christmas morning. Choked with emotion, the door opened and...

Light. Glorious light.

The air had been salty with ocean scents. So fresh. The sky vaulted with frightening endlessness. He'd forgotten what it was like to stand without a ceiling overhead. They let him walk and sit and touch and absorb. They gave him a picnic lunch. The cheese sandwich and Royal Crown soda so much tastier in the open world.

After, it was hard to return underground. To be buried again. He could hardly take the steps to do so. But the beast was there to help him along. Yegor Volkov. The shadow haunting his miserable life.

They used the visits to the surface-world to incentivize him. And at first, it worked. The endless hours in the lab now had a reward attached. But the second visit outside had been less satisfying. The third, a disappointment. The fourth, disheartening. Why glimpse the unattainable? It was like smelling a feast yet never eating of it; like desiring a woman yet being forbidden her embrace.

It was better to expunge it from his thoughts.

The laboratory, three stories down, possessed *one* venue for natural light: a square shaft, twenty feet on each side, carved into the ceiling. The shaft rose to the ceiling of the cement block building above ground, where hydraulic doors could open to the sky, like a telescopic observatory.

The shaft was an elevator of sorts, where a rusted metal platform, generated by electric motors, lifted from the ground floor of the laboratory up through the hole in the ceiling three stories above. No one knew why the lift was there or what they had used it for in the past.

Months ago they had tested the workability of the platform out of curiosity. The motors worked, and the platform did rise, but they hadn't used it since. However, during the summer, they opened the hydraulic roof to let in fresh air and light. Until they found it made Dr. Markovitch idle.

He would stand on the unused elevator platform, gazing at the sky above, watching the clouds, as if at the zoo looking at caged animals, or rather, as if he were the caged animal watching passing life.

Soon after, they left the roof closed.

It was better to keep him focused on the work.

Walking through the laboratory, he paused to inspect the latest incarnation of the weapon — the one hidden under the tarp. To admire it. The machine was a dazzling mishmash of brass and steel, glass and wires, of wheels, cams, tubes, diodes, and flanges, the latest generation of a long line of machines fabricated over the last year. Its predecessors had fizzled with failure, to be discarded to the boneyard of machine parts stacked in the back room of one of Wardenclyff's tentacle hallways.

Dr. Markovitch stroked a section of the machine as if it were a living thing needing affection. Would this be the incarnation to come to life? Surging with electricity like Frankenstein's monster?

Yes, my child. You are the one. Patience, my dear.

He couldn't wait to tell his friend his news. He would be so pleased.

He turned away and rushed to the other end of the laboratory, to where the metal staircase corkscrewed up toward the surface. Tilting his head, he waited, like a dog anticipating the appearance of his master.

In these moments, Dr. Markovitch almost forgot that he was, in fact, a prisoner here. Life before Wardenclyff seemed like a dream. Unreal.

The change in his psyche took place five months ago, at his lowest point. He was experiencing extreme discouragement over the project's continual failure, as well as mental fatigue. He was in crisis. Breakdown was inevitable.

Then came a visit from the man who would eventually become his only friend.

The Russian, Aleksandr Feklisov.

The head of the particle beam project, Dr. Natka Milosh, had been gone. Dr. Markovitch was glad for her absence. They had been squabbling over the direction of the project, both exasperated by the constant failures. Tempers flared.

Dr. Markovitch had been brooding, feeling desolate, possibly suicidal, when Aleksandr Feklisov showed up with a box of cannolis. The gesture surprised Markovitch. He had always been afraid of the man with the jumpy eyes. Feklisov put him at ease and took it upon himself to brew a pot of coffee for the two of them.

Then he did a surprising gesture.

Perhaps sensing the intimidation of the ever-present Yegor Volkov, the beast, Feklisov dismissed the bodyguard so they could be alone.

The two of them drank coffee and ate the pastries. The man was warm and complimentary and quite interested in the progress—or better, lack of progress—of the work. They talked of Nikola Tesla. Feklisov curious about Dr. Markovitch's association with him, eagerly listening to his stories of working side-by-side with the great man for two decades, a man Markovitch loved like a father.

Feklisov asked poignant questions and listened to Markovitch's concerns over the direction of the project and the constant head-butting with Dr. Natka Milosh. Markovitch knew of Feklisov's background as an engineer, but was taken aback by his intellectual capacity to grasp the complexities of the theoretical physics connected to the apparatus they were attempting to build.

His opinion of the man changed that day. No longer was he his captor, but suddenly his friend and fellow collaborator. Finally, he was being treated as a human being.

That day Aleksandr Feklisov said something that changed Dr. Markovitch deep within his chromosomes.

"You have a mind like Nikola Tesla," he had said. "You can outwit this project without him."

It had nearly caused his heart to stop. He had likened him to his brilliant mentor. Feklisov prodded him to apply his own analytical conceptions into the project.

"Forget Tesla...be your own man."

That night, while lying in the dark on his cot, he recalled something Nikola Tesla had once said:

Innovation without execution is hallucination.

That was the key. Don't simply think of concepts. Think like Tesla. Be Tesla. Execute. And if necessary, do it without Dr. Natka Milosh.

Feklisov's visits continued after that, showing up every other week, always when Dr. Milosh was away, always bringing cannolis, and always taking the time to sit and talk. Markovitch looked forward to those visits more than climbing the spiral staircase to experience the great outdoors. They became two minds, communicating on a unique level.

Dr. Markovitch knew the man to be a communist, but that never came up. Politics be damned. Science and progress were all that mattered. The weapon. That was all that mattered. The meetings always spurred him.

Feklisov gave him the freedom to be himself. To trust his instincts. To execute the innovations that stirred within.

Their visits took on a conspiratorial air. They were engaged together on a secret project. Out of sight of the others. Kept under the tarp. They bantered ideas, talked of variations, and sketched schematics. Feklisov gave his engineering input. He bolstered him. Left him feeling significant. Told him his name would be as great as Tesla's.

And now he was ready to accept that mantle.

The good news he had for his friend.

In the upper reaches of the cavern, he heard doors opening and closing. Footfalls on the metal stairs. He was coming.

Dr. Markovitch nearly squealed with delight, as if his lips would burst with the news. Feklisov appeared, waving down at him. Under his arm a pink cardboard box. Cannolis.

"Hello Doctor," called Feklisov from above. "I have good news."

Markovitch started. Blinking. *No, I'm the one with good news*, he thought.

"We've finally got Nikola Tesla's design notes for the weapon," said Feklisov. "We will have them in your hands within two days."

Markovitch felt his chest clench.

No! This can't be. This makes my news irrelevant, he thought. *Nikola Tesla would now get the credit. Five months of work evaporated. I've become inconsequential. Tesla's shadow.*

"With the notebook," said Feklisov, "We will now be sure to build the machine."

Dr. Markovitch withered into angry silence.

The notebook be damned.

His good news: the weapon was nearly complete. The preliminary tests were successful. It would be operable within days.

Chapter 60

―――◆―――

OSS Headquarters, Wednesday, 9:40 AM

THIRTY-SIX STORIES UP. NEARLY the same height as the New Yorker Hotel climb.

Buck Flynn gazed through the window, watching the shifting traffic on the street below. The empty room behind him was quiet. A table and four wooden chairs sat in the middle of the tiled floor. Lining the walls were gunmetal-gray file cabinets, each with a keyed security lock at the top—a thin barricade for a thief of his skills.

He had no interest in breaching OSS secrets, however. He was only interested in leaving this place. He didn't trust these people. He'd kept his end of the bargain. They should keep theirs.

He glanced back at the door. A guard stood outside. This may not be Sing Sing, but Buck remained a prisoner.

The window in front of him was unlocked. A window to freedom. Outside, a narrow ledge extended across the face of the building. It was less than a foot wide, but he knew he could navigate it. He could shuffle his way to another unlocked window on this floor.

Should he do it?

He turned away from the temptation to take a seat in one of the wooden chairs. Frustrated. It was the fourth time he'd toyed with escaping. Part of him wanted to do it, just to show them he could. They were dealing with *The Smoke*, after all. Even locked rooms with guards couldn't contain him. Nearly forty-five minutes had passed since they'd left him in here. What was the holdup? They must be deciding what to do with him now that their gamble didn't work out. Probably making plans to send him back upriver. He doubted they would simply let him walk away.

Five minutes later, the door swung open, and Paddy Tooke entered the room. He took a chair at the table. Buck sensed his reticence immediately. He looked conflicted. Buck braced for the bad news.

"We still need your services," Paddy muttered.

"But—"

"Just listen to what I have to say," he said.

Buck bit off a retort, sat back and crossed his arms.

"We believe we know where the notebook is."

"Believe? It's not confirmed?"

Paddy shook his head. "Not 100%, no."

"Great! If I open enough safes, I should stumble upon it, eventually."

Ignoring his impertinence, Paddy said, "While it's not confirmed, we have good evidence pointing to its location."

"Where?"

Paddy leaned forward. "I can't give you the location until you accept the job. I will let Deputy Director Carver explain that to you. However, it's important to tell you that the operation will be more involved and...riskier."

"Riskier how?"

"I'll be honest, Buck. The risk is in being caught. You'll be going into the belly of the beast, and no lackadaisical warehouse guards this time. I'm talking actual spy work. And if you get caught, you'd be on your own. The OSS would disavow any connection with you."

Buck blinked. "I'd be hung out to dry?"

Paddy nodded.

"And if I don't accept the job?"

A silence hardened between them like iron bars.

Buck drew in a simmering breath. "Never mind. I know what will happen."

Trapped again, he thought.

Buck abruptly stood and wandered over to the window. He gazed over the street traffic again. Breaking and entry didn't feel like serving his country at all. He should've escaped earlier when he had half a chance.

"So, the choice is Sing Sing or doing a job that could get me arrested for spying. Either way, I could end up back in prison."

"You'd be doing it for your country, Buck," Paddy offered.

"Yeah, that's the same line you used the first time."

The choice was tough, but fairly obvious. If he chose Sing Sing, Director Allen Davies would extend his sentence somehow—at least until the war was over. However, taking the break-in job—even with the possibility of being arrested as a spy—his prospects of clearing his name and eventual freedom were better. And if things went badly, his chances of slipping through OSS fingers would be better.

Yes, an obvious choice.

Swinging around, he said, "Okay...what's the job?"

Chapter 61

OSS Headquarters, Wednesday, 9:58 AM

FLYNN FOLLOWED TOOKE TO the conference room. They entered to find Allen Davies, Phillip Carver, and another man huddled around the table, studying a set of blueprints unfurled across its surface. The men looked up as they came through the door.

Allen Davies straightened himself, giving Buck a stony look. "All right then," he said. "I'll let you, boys, at it. Keep me posted on the progress, Phil." And he promptly left, leaving Buck to feel that he was the reason for the departure, as if he were diseased.

Carver introduced Flynn to Walter Brookfield. The man gave him a kindly smile and a firm handshake.

"Glad to meet you, Buck."

Buck eyed him cautiously. The fellow seemed genuine, with a quiet strength and sharp eyes, but Buck wasn't ready to trust anyone working here just yet.

Carver said. "We believe we've located *Teleforce*. Our intelligence tells us it's within the walls of the Russian Consulate here in New York City."

The muscles in Buck's neck tightened. "You want me to break into a foreign consulate?"

"You won't have to break in. You'll be going through the front door."

Walter Brookfield leaned in, smiling. "How would you like to go to a party with me?" he asked.

Buck shot him a look. "If you're asking me on a date, Lieutenant, I prefer girls."

Even Carver chuckled at that. "Flynn, you and Brookfield will go to a gala being held at the consulate on Friday evening. Once inside, we have to get you into position to swap out the *Teleforce* notebooks."

"So, the mission is essentially the same."

"Yes, that's right," Carver pointed to the table. "These are the blueprints for the building at 7 and 9 East 61st Street—the Russian Consulate."

"My goodness," cried Tooke. "Where did you dig those up?"

"We got them from the original architectural firm who supervised its construction thirty-eight years ago. The Russians have only been at this location for the last four years."

Carver pointed to a series of rooms on the second floor, just to the right of the main staircase.

"This suite of rooms are the offices of the station chief, Anatoli Yakovlev, and his staff. This larger room is Yakovlev's private office. We believe *Teleforce* is in that office."

"How can you be sure?" asked Buck.

"We can't. It's an educated guess based on intelligence. According to our sources, after the Russians moved into the building, they purchased a free-standing safe from a local office supply company, which was delivered and installed in that office. Yakovlev's secretary signed the delivery receipt. So, we're banking on *Teleforce* being locked up there."

"Do we know the make of the safe?" asked Buck.

"We do." Carver finger-walked through a stack of papers, producing a crumpled receipt. "According to the supply company, it's a Shaw Walker model."

Buck rubbed his chin. "Most Shaw Walkers have a solid brass Eagle lock. If it has a butterfly knob at the center of the dial, its manipulation resistant.

They are more difficult to crack. I'll need some time and my stethoscope for sure."

"Whatever you need, we'll provide."

"So how do I get to it?"

Carver glanced up at Buck. "Somehow, we need to get you away from the party, up to the second floor, and into those offices."

"Will the doors be guarded?" asked Buck.

"Of course, Mr. Flynn. You didn't think this would be easy, did you?

They spent the rest of the morning studying the blueprints and discussing how to penetrate the Station Chief's offices on the second floor—none of which seemed reasonable. They dismissed some of the simplest options, such as walking straight up the grand staircase or using other stairwells in the building, as they assumed them to be guarded.

Buck said. "Even if I get to the second floor, two doors will need to be breached: the outside office and Yakovlev's door."

Carver shot him a challenging glance. "Can you handle that?"

Buck shrugged. "The locks aren't a problem. However, I see three obstacles. The first is exposure in the hallway, here," said Buck, pointing to the blueprints. "It'll take at least a minute to breach the lock to the outside office. It would help to know the make and model of both locks."

Carver jotted down a note. "We'll try to find out."

"The second problem would be an alarm. Is the building wired?"

Carver nodded. "Yes, they contracted with an alarm company in the city to put in alarms. But seeing that you will already be inside the building, we only need to worry about internal alarms."

"A schematic of the system would help."

Carver again jotted a note. "Robert Markham could circumvent the alarm system." He then looked up. "And the third obstacle?"

"Guards, obviously. We've already talked about that."

Carver nodded. "That's our major dilemma. We have to assume they will station guards outside the offices. We can't harm them, and we don't want our fingerprints on any aspect of this operation. It needs to appear as if we were never there."

"Can we drug the guards?" asked Brookfield.

"Doubtful," said Carver. "As I mentioned, it can't look suspicious."

"How about a diversion?" asked Paddy. "Something to distract the guards?"

"The Ruskies will be wary of any tricks. It would be better to circumvent the guards altogether."

A potential solution was scaling the outside walls and going through a window. Buck pointed to a first-floor balcony just off of the ballroom where the gala was to be held.

"I could climb up from there," he offered.

"Not without being seen," Carver said. "The gala will be crowded, and guests might use the outside balcony."

"I could scale down from the roof," Buck said. "But I would need my ropes and harness."

"Too much equipment to smuggle in," snapped Carver. "And getting to the roof could be problematic with the stairways being guarded."

By lunchtime, frustration had stymied the team. Irritated by the lack of progress, Phillip Carver scooped up the blueprints and left in a huff. "We're looking at this all wrong," he yelped over his shoulder. "We need to think three-dimensionally."

Buck and Brookfield shot quizzical looks to Paddy sitting off to the side, quietly puffing on his pipe.

"Don't look at me," he said. "I don't have a clue what that means."

That afternoon Carver remained absent, so the others took a break from brainstorming to cover other essential details. Buck's cover story for attending the gala with Walter Brookfield would be that he was a fellow military officer being recruited for the work in the Balkans. With that in mind, Brookfield worked one-on-one with Buck for two hours, giving him a crash course on military jargon and protocol.

Halfway through the session, a tailor interrupted them. He measured both Brookfield and Flynn for the formal wear to be worn to the gala. They needed to look the part. Earlier, a spirited discussion had erupted on whether the men should wear military dress uniforms or tuxedos. Carver was adamant that Flynn should not wear a uniform. He felt uniforms would be too conspicuous, as well as aggressive and intimidating. He wanted them to blend. Brookfield conceded the point with a shrug. However, Buck got the impression that Carver's actual concern was a civilian thief besmirching the honor of the uniform. Unacceptable.

Once the tailor left, Paddy Tooke stepped in to continue with the training. Using available photographs, he helped Buck memorize the faces and names of the key Russians and Yugoslavians. When the photo of Sava Kosanovic flashed, Buck recognized him immediately, recalling seeing him in his uncle's suite with the notebook as Buck dangled from the sky-terrace outside. Little did he know then the role that the notebook would come to play in his life.

He mentioned none of this to Paddy.

Brookfield then drilled Buck on phrases of greeting in both Russian and Serbo-Croatian languages.

"You don't need to get these down perfect," Brookfield told him. "We'll keep it simple. Just enough to get by."

The sessions were intense, but not unenjoyable, the mood less oppressive because of Phillip Carver's absence. Brookfield was patient and encouraging. He oozed confidence — as if burglarizing a foreign consulate was a matter of course. Buck was growing to like his new partner and felt that, together, they just might pull this thing off.

It became late and, with no sign of Phillip Carver, they called it a night. Exhausted, the three men left OSS headquarters for the hotel to get some rest. They had only one more day of preparation until the gala. On the elevator ride down, silence thickened in the air, as if all were thinking the same thing, the major hole in their plans.

They had yet to discover a way to get to the second story of the consulate.

Chapter 62

OSS Headquarters, Thursday, 7:30 AM

THE NEXT MORNING, BUCK Flynn and Paddy Tooke entered the conference room to find Phillip Carver and three other men huddled around the table. Their backs were to them, obscuring the object of their attention. A heated discussion was taking place.

"I tell you, I've added it up," one man was saying. "And we are missing one hundred and twenty square feet."

"Well, where the hell did it go?" snapped Carver. "It couldn't have just disappeared!"

"That's just it...somewhere along the way it has!"

"The laws of physics demand that it cannot just vanish. Find it!"

"What's going on?" asked Paddy.

They all swiveled around, exposing the object of their attention. A balsa model of a building.

Carver, as if annoyed by the intrusion, said. "Finally, you're here. Your boy needs to look at this."

Buck bristled at the slight, but kept quiet. The two of them stepped up to take in the miniature creation sitting on the table.

"This is a model of the Russian Consulate," said Carver. "Built to scale by our Research and Development team."

"Ah, thinking three-dimensionall," said Paddy, recalling Carver's comment from the day before.

Buck marveled at the lifelike construction. Extremely detailed, the model had four cut-away sections representing each of the four floors. Every aspect faithfully reproduced. Windows, doors, stairways, balconies, halls, and vestibules; even window treatments and possible color schemes were matched. They had furnished the model with tiny tables, couches, desks, kitchen stoves, and in the living quarters on the top floor, beds and dressers. They even positioned a grand piano in the ballroom on the first floor.

"You did this since yesterday?" asked Buck.

"That's right. We're hoping it will help us find a way into Anatoli Yakovlev's office."

"But how did you do it?"

It looked as if it had taken years to build.

"We had the original blueprints, of course. However, renovations took place over the years. We accessed city building permits, contacted local construction firms, and merged the renovations into this working model. We also contacted interior design firms, electricians, plumbers, painters, furniture stores, and office supply companies who have done business with the Consulate. We have a pretty good idea of how it's been furnished. In fact, we now know exactly where the safe is."

He pointed to a long, narrow closet inside Yakovlev's office. A tiny safe sat in the back.

"According to the records at Shaw Walker, they installed it there. However, we have a problem. Somewhere along the line, we've lost one hundred and twenty square feet of space."

"Does that matter?" asked a voice from behind them. They all turned to find Walter Brookfield standing in the doorway.

"Ah, good morning, Lieutenant," said Carver. "And to answer your question, yes, it matters. We want you and Mr. Flynn to know where you are at all times, and the evaporated space is located smack dab where Anatoli Yakovlev's office is situated."

Carver pointed to a suite of rooms on the second floor, just to the right of the staircase.

"By our calculations, the missing square footage is somewhere near here."

"Maybe the Russians did some secret remodeling," offered Paddy Tooke. "If so, that could account for the missing space."

"It's possible. Originally, this complete area was a large den for the master of the house. They added wall partitions four years ago to break up the space. They could have done some construction without our knowledge."

Buck could see how a three-dimensional mock-up might familiarize them with the layout of the place, but was skeptical that it could magically offer a plan to break into the offices. Scanning the model, his eyes naturally went toward the various exits it presented. His Pops would say:

Doors and windows. Know them well. It can mean the difference between capture or freedom.

He memorized every exit point, in case things went badly, or if necessary, to elude the OSS itself.

"We have a bit of good news," offered Carver. "We've got Arthur Harrington planted inside the catering company as a waiter. He's training with the catering company as we speak." Carver glanced at Brookfield and Flynn. "It's likely they will frisk you when entering the gala, we're hoping Harrington can stash the fake notebook and other implements beforehand and have them waiting for you inside."

That sounded reasonable enough, but Buck still wondered how they planned to get him up to the second story and past the guards.

The discussion turned to getting Flynn away from the party unnoticed. Brookfield knew that the visiting Yugoslavian, Arso Jovanovic, was expecting a discussion on covert strategies. It seemed reasonable to suggest meeting privately with him and the Russians. Brookfield could infer that Flynn's clearance was still pending, giving him an excuse to remain behind at the party, and hopefully providing the opportunity to slip away to conduct the operation.

At a point in their discussions, a man came rushing in to whisper into Phillip Carver's ear. Carver nodded, and the man left.

"We may have something concerning the missing square footage," he said. "We've found a cabinetmaker who did work for the original owners of the house—work off the books, without building permits. Our men are rounding him up."

An hour later another agent came in, handing Carver a sheet of paper, which he quickly perused. "Bring him in," he said.

Escorted by an agent, a petrified elderly man entered the conference room. The old fellow was frail-looking, with white hair, and a bristly mustache; he wore work trousers with suspenders and a thick brown jacket. His rheumy eyes blinked with fright.

"Gentlemen," said the agent escort. "This is Mr. Otto Eklund. He used to own Eklund Cabinetry over in the garment district of Manhattan."

"I...I no longer own the business," the man choked in a Swedish accent. "I sold it years ago. I've done nothing wrong. Why am I being arrested?"

Carver snorted a laugh. "We're not arresting you, Mr. Eklund. On the contrary, you may help us. Several years ago, you did some work for..." He glanced at the sheet of paper handed to him earlier. "...for Mr. John Henry Hammond, at 7 East 61st Street."

The man went white. His knees nearly buckled. Carver, fearing he would topple, sat him at the table and poured him a glass of water. Eklund gulped it down. His eyes fell on the miniature model sitting on the table, and he trembled.

Carver asked, "So, Mr. Eklund, did you do work for Mr. Hammond?"

He shook his head, "I can't talk of it, sir."

"Why is that?"

"I...I promised never to speak of it."

"Speak of what? The work you did?"

"I refuse to speak of it. I know my rights! It's in the Constitution. I studied to become an American citizen."

"No one wishes to violate your rights, Mr. Eklund, but we need your cooperation," said Carver with more force than necessary. "We know that during the fall of 1919, you worked for Mr. Hammond under the table. Must we examine your income tax records to see if it was claimed or not?"

The man looked stricken. "God help me," he yelped. "Please, I will pay the taxes. Mr. Hammond told me it would be alright. We wouldn't get caught. I can't go to jail! I have a wife and family."

"Nobody's putting you in jail, Mr. Eklund."

"I don't want to get Mr. Hammond in trouble. He was good to me."

"According to our records, Mr. Hammond died ten years ago. This has nothing to do with him."

"Dead?" he mumbled.

Paddy Tooke leaned in, a curious twinkle in his eye. "Wait a minute! When was the work done?"

Carver shot him an annoyed look. "Fall of 1919."

"And they did the work in Hammond's den?"

"That's right."

A smile grew on Paddy's face. "I think I know what this is all about. Can I have a private word with Mr. Eklund?"

Carver shrugged, palms up, as if handing the dilemma over to him. He and the others stood and moved to the other end of the table.

Paddy took a seat next to Eklund. They huddled in hushed conference. After a few minutes, the old man nodded shamefully, burying his face in his hands. Paddy consoled him with pats on the back. After several more minutes, they stood to inspect the model, Otto Eklund pointing to sections on the first and second floors.

Finally, Paddy turned to the others, beaming.

"Gentleman, wonderful news," he exclaimed. "Not only have we found the missing square footage, but we've also uncovered the perfect path into Yakovlev's office." He shot a wink at Carver. "However, I've given my word that we will not prosecute Mr. Eklund for breaking the law while working for Mr. Hammond during the fall of 1919."

Petrified, Otto Eklund exclaimed, "I'll never do it again, promise."

Chapter 63

OSS Headquarters, Thursday, 12:43 PM

PHILLIP CARVER'S EYES NARROWED suspiciously. "What laws are we talking about?" he asked.

"Specifically?" smiled Paddy Tooke, telegraphing that he was thoroughly enjoying himself. "The Volstead Act. Or, as you may remember it: Prohibition."

"Prohibition?"

"That's right. The Volstead Act of 1920 outlawed alcohol across the nation, making some people upset — and desperate. You've heard of speakeasies? Well, some people stockpiled beverages. And some of the well-to-do built their own form of a speakeasy in their own house. Wet rooms you could call them. And that, gentlemen, is why our Mr. Eklund was hired."

"He built a room to hide booze?" asked Carver. "And he's frightened of going to jail for it? Doesn't he know they repealed Prohibition in 1933?"

Then, as if on cue, the room burst out laughing, an uproar. Otto Eklund, at first startled by the reaction—and jail no longer a threat—joined the hilarity.

"Ja, I built the room," he chortled.

Carver threw an arm around him. "My good man, you have done your country a great service. Show me this room you built to hide Mr. Hammond's booze."

Everyone crowded around the model as Otto Eklund pointed to a spot just to the left of the walk-in closet inside Yakovlev's office.

"This was once open space," he said. "Mr. Hammond had me close this section off...for the whiskey."

He pointed to a ten-by-twelve section in the far corner—one hundred and twenty square feet.

"How is it accessed?" asked Carver excitedly.

Eklund smiled proudly. "The room is behind bookshelves that I built along this wall. These shelves pivot on a center axis. When it is closed, it is locked tight. Unmovable. There is a release on the third shelf." He spread his arms. "Voila! It opens."

"Fantastic!" exclaimed Carver.

"It gets better," said Paddy Tooke. "Tell him about the dumbwaiter."

"Oh yes," cried Eklund, excited now to be boasting of his handiwork. "The dumbwaiter from the kitchen was used to deliver the whiskey. It's here." He pointed to a wall inside the secret room.

Carver's jaw dropped. "Are you saying that we have a dumbwaiter shaft from the kitchen into a hidden room with a secret passage into Yakovlev's office? This is fantastic." He glanced over at Flynn. "Young man, what do you think of that?"

Buck smirked. "Sounds like the easiest job I've ever—" he pulled up short, realizing what he was about to confess. "Uh, sounds good to me," he offered.

And again, the room broke out laughing.

Chapter 64

Brooklyn, New York City, Friday, 6:45 AM

THE HOUSE LOOKED RATHER ordinary. Squished between the other houses on the block as if insignificant, it almost disappointed him. The ordinariness. He expected something grander, or more mysterious. But no. It was bland. Ordinary.

From across the street, Henry Blacksmith sat hunkered low in his stolen automobile, watching. The car was older than he preferred — a '34 Ford Deluxe Coupe. Rust crusted the wheel-wells and the front fender had a dent, but it drove smooth enough, even if the engine ticked a bit. He couldn't complain, it had only cost him a few drops of Prussic acid.

He'd swapped out the license plates with another Ford he had found parked on the street — anything to keep the vehicle from being tied to the two dead men found in an alley behind Pete's Hidey-Hole.

The street was quiet. It was that kind of neighborhood. An older, family-oriented, Irish ghetto. People minding their own business. No one took any notice of him.

As for the stakeout, this was his second attempt. He'd spent several hours here yesterday without success. His target never showed. And so he returned this morning.

He shivered. The winter sun was cresting, adding a pale light to the morning chill. The car was off, therefore no heater. He hated wasting gas. As it was, he'd use one of the stolen gas rationing coupons already.

On the seat next to him was a paper sack filled with items he'd brought to subdue the target: ropes, a handkerchief for a gag, a bottle of prescription sleeping pills, as well as a bottle of chloroform.

Using chloroform wasn't like the movies — knocking out your target by covering their mouth with a drenched handkerchief. That was a Hollywood gimmick. No, it took several minutes to administer, and you needed to be careful. Chloroform could be lethal. A choke-hold worked better. Yet, he brought the drug just the same.

Also laying on the seat was the 1910 Colt.

He was growing impatient. Last night he had hoped to catch the target coming home from work. He gave up after midnight, to return this morning to catch the target going to work. But no. It was as if his target didn't live here at all. Had his target had moved?

Someone lived there, that much he knew. Last night lights had switched on after dusk and went out around ten. The blinds remained drawn, preventing him from peering in. And even now, interior lights were ablaze.

Yes, someone was inside.

He glanced at his watch. He was running out of time. He needed to prepare for tonight. Maybe his target had been inside this whole time. He decided to take a chance and knock on the door.

He tucked his handgun into his belt, buttoning his topcoat over it. Grabbing the paper sack with the items in it, he got out of the Ford. The street was empty. Crossing over to the front stoop, he set the paper sack off to the side and rang the bell. From inside, footsteps came his way. He eased his left hand into the opening of his topcoat, near the pistol grip. The door swung open.

A woman stood there, older, but still pretty, with lovely brown eyes. Her auburn hair, streaked with gray, was piled into a bun. She wore an apron and was using it to dry her hands.

"Can I help you," she asked.

For a brief second, Blacksmith stood dumbfounded, surprised that a woman answered the door. But then an idea slithered into his brain.

"Hello," said Blacksmith. "You must be Mrs. Tooke."

"I am," she said, with a guarded tone.

"I'm looking for Detective Tooke, ma'am."

She hesitated. "He's not available at the moment."

Blacksmith knew instantly that the detective wasn't home. "You don't know me, Mrs. Tooke. I'm new down at the precinct. I'm told your husband was one of the best detectives in the city. He's missed terribly," he said with a bright smile. Her guardedness melted some. "Well, we found some items belonging to him he must have left behind when he left. As your place is on my way to work, I thought I'd swing by and drop them off."

He reached down and picked up the sack, holding it up for her to see.

"Why, that's very thoughtful of you," she said, flashing a trusting smile at him. "Won't you come in for a minute, Mister...uh?"

"Stewart. Henry Stewart," he said, stepping across the threshold.

Chapter 65

———◦———

OSS Headquarters, Friday, 8:14 AM

"YOUR NEW IDENTITY WILL be Lieutenant John Humphrey Clark, U.S. Marine," said Phillip Carver, as he handed Buck a wallet and a set of dog-tags.

They had ushered Flynn and Paddy Tooke into Director Allen Davies's office first thing in the morning. Carver and Walter Brookfield awaited them there. They sat in leather chairs across from the Director's desk. Davies, quiet and smoking, sifted them with his brooding eyes. Brookfield looked pensive.

Opening the wallet, Buck found a driver's license, Social Security card, and military ID. It also contained some cash, gas rationing cards, and plastic sleeves with photographs: some of an older couple, some of a pretty woman with dark hair.

"You need to commit the data to memory," said Carver. "Date of birth, social security number, dog-tag number, all of it." He handed him a slip of paper. "These are the names of your parents, siblings, and fiancée, as well as your military unit and superior officers. Your backstory is that you and Brookfield went to college together at Ohio State and joined the Marines together after Pearl Harbor. And because of your friendship, he is recruiting you for work on the Yugoslavian front."

Carver explained his family situation and about the girl he was engaged to back in Mt. Vernon, Ohio. During the briefing, Brookfield remained quiet and sullen.

"This stuff looks authentic," said Buck, looking over the wallet. "Did R and D make these items?"

"They're real," muttered Brookfield, staring at the floor. "So are the people in the photographs — Joe and Mary Clark, the parents; and Cora Wallace, the fiancée." He looked up, a sadness glistening his eyes. "John was my friend and classmate. We played football for the Buckeyes. Four days ago, he was killed in the South Pacific."

Buck nearly choked at the revelation.

"I suggested using his information for the operation. He would have wanted it that way."

A hush fell over the room.

Then, for the first time since entering the office, Allen Davies moved. Leaning across his desk, he pointed a bony finger at Buck Flynn. "If you do one damn thing to dishonor that soldier's name, I will make the rest of your existence a living hell."

And Buck did not doubt that he would.

An hour later, Arthur Harrington stopped by to meet with the team in the conference room. Now embedded into the catering staff, he was on his way to his new job. This would be his last opportunity to coordinate issues concerning the operation. His job was to smuggle in needed equipment, including a pair of coveralls for Buck to wear during the operation — after all, he couldn't very well climb the dumbwaiter shaft in his tuxedo.

Carver provided a leather satchel for Buck to use during the job; in it would go the fake *Teleforce* notebook, Buck's lock-picking tools, a flashlight, stethoscope, and gloves. The satchel would strap to his chest, giving him easy access to the items within the cramped space of the dumbwaiter shaft. Carver also threw in a few rolls of blank photographic film.

"They probably have already photographed the notebook. Check the safe for film canisters and swap out the rolls with the blanks. Under no circumstances can the film leave the country with Yakovlev."

Earlier, while studying the consulate model, they had discovered a mop closet under a stairwell near the back exit. Located just outside of the kitchen, it was close to where the catering company would park their van in an alley. Harrington thought the closet made a good place to stash the items.

Harrington would also play a role in creating a diversion in the kitchen. Research and Development had developed an innocent-looking loaf of bread. Made of a granular explosive material, nicknamed Aunt Jemima, it possessed an incendiary cartridge. When placed on a hot stove, the flour material would explode, creating a small grease fire. Hopefully, the distraction would give Buck time to slip into the dumbwaiter shaft unnoticed.

Research and Development also brought gifts for Flynn and Brookfield—two packs of cigarettes.

"I don't smoke," said Buck.

"You do tonight," demanded Carver.

The R and D men revealed a secret inside the cigarette pack.

"This cigarette at the front of the pack is called *The Stinger*," said one man. "It's a single-shot .22 caliber firearm. Not as good as a real gun, but helpful at close range."

He then demonstrated how to use the cigarette-shaped gun.

"The filter tip is the trigger. Clamp the cigarette with the middle and ring fingers, and using the forefinger and thumb, fire the weapon by twisting the filter."

The weapon let out a small pop as it fired.

Buck and Brookfield practiced for an hour. Each Stinger carried only one ordinance and had to be discarded after one use, but there were several to play with. A fascinating device, however, Buck saw little practicality in it.

"The weapon is only to be used in extreme emergencies," reiterated Carver. "As I've said, OSS fingerprints cannot be on this operation. And there had better be a pretty damn good reason before firing up that tricky gizmo."

He said it to both Brookfield and Flynn, but his icy eyes had been on Buck the entire time.

The formal wear arrived in the afternoon, and they made final alterations. A barber showed up to give Flynn and Brookfield each a haircut and a shave. Now dressed and trimmed, the two men looked quite dashing.

With preparations complete, two hours remained before the gala. *Operation Teleforce* was a go.

Chapter 66

———◆———

Russian Consulate, New York, Friday, 5:45 PM

ANATOLI YAKOVLEV WAS EUPHORIC. The meeting with the Vice Council had gone well. Walking toward his office, he smiled to himself. He had given the Vice Council good news — the same good news he would take to London after the gala.

For two years, Yakovlev and his team had been running agents on several fronts within the United States, gathering intelligence critical, not only to the war effort, but to the future of Soviet Russia. His hard work was now paying off. Within the scientific field in particular. His spies stood on the threshold of obtaining information concerning, not one, but two, weapons of mass destruction coveted by Moscow.

Yakovlev carried a set of files for the diplomatic pouch and his trip to England. He would leave immediately following the gala. Once in England, he would relay the information to Moscow via courier.

For months Yakovlev had been monitoring activity taking place in various research facilities across the United States—the University of California at Berkley, the University of Chicago, Princeton, Columbia, and others. He had ears everywhere. Physicists across the nation were collaborating on something connected to the U.S. government. He suspected it involved the development of an atomic weapon.

His latest bit of intelligence had to do with the Army Corp of Engineers. They had rented space here in Manhattan, contracting with an engineering firm called Stone and Webster. Everything hush, hush.

Yes. It had to be an atomic weapon.

Knowing the players was key. Then penetrate, recruit, and gather intelligence. And that was something Anatoli Yakovlev and his team certainly knew how to do.

The particle beam weapon was a good example. They now possessed Nikola Tesla's personal design notes—delivered by a mole they'd networked, Sava Kosanovic. The original schematics would accelerate the work on Long Island, guaranteeing the project's success.

This afternoon, the lead scientist had photographed the notebook into microfilm—for the second time. Back-up, lest anything happened to the original notebook. Not that anything could happen to it. He had locked it in his safe until its transfer to the Long Island facility tonight.

The microfilm, however, was going with him to London, to be relayed to Moscow for analysis. The film canisters sat on his desk, waiting to be packed into the diplomatic pouch.

There would be no losing the information this time.

Entering his office, Yakovlev found his secretary clacking away at a typewriter.

"Are you still here, Miss Noskov?" he asked. "I thought you'd be getting ready for the gala."

"I should be done in twenty minutes," she answered, without looking up from her typing. "Did your meeting go well?"

"Very well. The Vice Council was pleased. Is everything set for my trip?"

"Yes," she responded. "Your bags are by the downstairs service entrance outside the kitchen. Your documents and visa are on your desk, along with a flight schedule, tickets, and your London agenda notes. The pouch is ready to be packed."

"Good. You have done well, Miss Noskov."

She gave him an austere smile. "You have a visitor waiting in your office."

He glanced at his watch. "A visitor? I need to get to my apartment to dress for the gala. Who is it?"

"Comrade Aleksandr Feklisov. He needed to speak with you before your trip. He made it sound urgent."

He frowned. "Urgent? Comrade Feklisov will attend the party tonight. Couldn't it have waited until then?"

She shrugged.

Everything was going so well. Was Feklisov troubled about something?

Passing his secretary's desk, he entered his office. Feklisov stood by the window on the far wall, leaning on the sill, smoking a cigarette as he looked out on the city.

"Aleksandr, what a surprise," he said. "You're too early for the party, comrade. It isn't for two hours yet."

"Party? Oh right, I'd almost forgotten." He mashed his cigarette out in the ashtray on the desk.

"Tito's adjunct, Arso Jovanovic, is in town. We must welcome him. You will be there, yes?"

"Yes, of course. We must make our Yugoslavian comrades happy."

"After the war, we will need new coalitions for the new world order. Tito is an important fish."

Feklisov nodded. He moved around the desk to take a seat in one of the upholstered chairs on the other side. "I understand the Americans are coming tonight."

"Yes, that's right." Yakovlev took a seat and placed the folders aside. "A young marine who had been running guns for the Chetnik guerrillas will now run guns for Tito. He's coming to meet with Jovanovic."

Feklisov arched his chin, giving the Station Chief a dubious stare. "Is he coming alone?"

Yakovlev shrugged. "We sent two invitations. I'm sure he'll be bringing a guest, maybe a woman friend."

Feklisov's lips thinned as he considered the information.

"How goes our weapon development?" asked Yakovlev. "I hear you have been visiting our facility on Long Island. What's the progress?" Yakovlev leaned forward, eager to hear the news.

A rare smile creased Feklisov's face. "Dr. Frederick Markovitch has been a great asset — better than expected. He's quite brilliant. Being locked below ground for so long has had its toll on him emotionally, but I have given him special attention, to motivate him."

Yakovlev's face brightened. "And the weapon?"

Feklisov shrugged. "It will help to have the notebook."

"Yes," said Yakovlev, rubbing his hands together. "I will turn it over to the lead scientist tonight, so it can be in Dr. Markovitch's hands tomorrow."

Feklisov's face grew somber. He retrieved a cigarette case from his jacket pocket and withdrew a cigarette.

"Something troubles you, Aleksandr. I can tell. What's so urgent that it couldn't wait?"

Feklisov arrested his jumpy eyes long enough to level a stare at the Station Chief. "Anatoli, I'm here to tell you that a spy will attend your gala tonight."

Yakovlev chuckled as he sat back in his seat. "Is that all? Of course, spies will be at the gala. We expect it. We live amongst spies. I consider every guest coming through the front doors to be a spy."

"I trust your judgment in such matters, Anatoli. However, this spy intends treachery against us."

Yakovlev laughed out loud. "What spy doesn't? Come, Aleksandr, you need to be more specific."

"Where is the Tesla notebook right now?" he asked abruptly.

Yakovlev blinked. "It's locked away."

"Where?"

Yakovlev pointed to a closet on the side wall. "It's in my safe, in the closet."

"You're sure?"

"Absolutely. I put it there myself."

"Who knows the combination?"

"Only myself and my secretary."

"Will it be guarded tonight?"

"Of course. A guard outside the door at all times."

Feklisov nodded.

"Now, what is this about?"

Feklisov pointed to a lone file folder sitting on the corner of Yakovlev's desk.

"What is this?" asked the Station Chief.

"A report that I've put together," said Feklisov.

Yakovlev picked up the folder. "What is in it?"

"Proof."

"Proof of what?"

"Read the report, Anatoli."

Yakovlev opened the folder and scanned through it. His heart sank at its revelations. Turning to the last page, he stared at a photograph of the person spoken of in the report. "This can't be," he muttered.

"I'm afraid it is."

Yakovlev sat back, rubbing his chin. "Are you sure?"

Feklisov nodded.

"What we should do about it?"

Feklisov stared at him resolutely. "I have given this some thought, Anatoli. Because of the treachery involved, I have come to one conclusion."

"Which is?"

"We must send a message. Do not toy with Soviet Russia!"

"What do you suggest?"

Feklisov's eyes became as still as Yakovlev had ever seen them. Mean, steady slits.

"Elimination," said Fcklisov calmly.

"Elimination?"

Feklisov nodded. "The sooner the better. Make the problem disappear."

Yakovlev steepled his fingers, deliberating. He swiveled his chair away from Feklisov to stare out the window at the New York City skyline. Feklisov waited, patiently smoking his cigarette. After a full two minutes, he swiveled back. "Yes, Comrade, I agree. The problem disappears tonight."

He pressed an intercom button.

"Miss Noskov, place a call to Yegor Volkov at Wardenclyff laboratory on Long Island. We require his presence at the gala tonight. Oh, and tell him to come armed."

Chapter 67

———◆———

Russian Consulate, New York, Friday, 8:48 PM

THE TAXI TURNED DOWN East 61st Street, pausing behind a short line of automobiles disgorging passengers at the steps of the Russian Consulate. From the back seat, Buck Flynn peered through the window, watching the Soviet flag flutter above a wrought-iron balcony on the second story, the hammer, and sickle so flagrant. The sight left him troubled. Buck had never been overtly political, but communism frightened him. It was a ruthless system. Subjugating or killing those opposed to it. The antithesis of freedom.

"Funny, us being in bed with the Commies," muttered Buck.

Next to him, Walter Brookfield calmly smoked a cigarette.

"The expediency of war," replied Brookfield. "Wouldn't have been my choice; Wild Bill's neither. But in Yugoslavia, the Commies are good at killing Nazis. Their forces are stronger than the Chetniks."

The taxi pulled up to the front steps and the two men got out. Brookfield paid the fare.

"You ready?" asked Brookfield. Dressed in his tux, he looked suave and unflappable, nothing like the guerrilla warrior Buck knew him to be.

Buck nodded solemnly.

They climbed the steps and presented their invitations and credentials to the uniformed guards. Entering the consulate, Buck Flynn officially became Lieutenant John Humphrey Clark USMC.

He felt like a fraud.

The Soviet guards directed them to a cloakroom. They were frisked, but with deference, as if the guards were reluctant to impose the indignity on visiting guests. Two elegantly dressed women took their overcoats.

Inside the looming main hall of the consulate, guests milled about, wearing gowns and tuxedos. Across the marbled floor, the grand staircase swept up to the second story — the reality of the miniature model in front of them. Guards stood at the foot and the top of the stairs.

"Guards are right outside of Yakovlev's offices," muttered Brookfield under his breath.

Buck gave a silent nod, his eyes combing the upper level.

They entered the double doors leading into the ballroom. Attendants in tails stood on either side. They stood on a landing at the top of marble steps leading down to the main floor; a brass handrail bisected the center of the stairs. The ballroom was spacious, with high ceilings. Crystal chandeliers spread a warm, buttery glow over the room. A flocked-velvet, scaled damask pattern covered the walls. The drapes were gold, edged with rose cording, and tied off with tassels.

On the far side of the room, glass double doors led to an outside balcony.

The OSS model-makers got it near perfect.

A string quartet played in the back corner near the grand piano. Several couples danced.

"It's showtime," muttered Brookfield under his breath.

Buck nodded, but his fox-eyes were busy taking in the exits, including the balcony doors and the swinging doors to the kitchen. Every escape route noted...just in case.

Brookfield led the way, descending the few steps to the main floor. Buck followed.

A woman came up the steps on the other side of the rail. Dressed in a creamy yellow gown, she moved with measured dignity. Her hand slid along the brass rail; her other hand lifted the fabric of her dress to keep it from scraping the steps. Her brown hair piled elegantly on the crown of her head, her countenance bright and clear under the chandelier's warmth. If not for the wire-rim glasses she wore, thought Buck, she would be stunning.

In passing, she glanced up at him and smiled, her gray eyes keen and joyful. Buck smiled back. But then...

Shock jolted him. He froze in place.

He knew her.

Behind him, the woman also paused, hesitant with the same reaction as he — she knew him too. He felt her twisting around for a second look. He fought the urge to glance back.

Who was she? He couldn't recall. Her face so familiar, yet vague.

After a heartbeat of indecision, he continued down the remaining steps. Brookfield was waiting for him. "I say, you look like you've seen a ghost."

"Worse," said Buck. "I think I've met that woman behind us before."

Brookfield's eyes remained flat, composed. "That's not good. She could blow your cover. Where did you meet?"

"That's the thing. I can't remember. She looks familiar, but..."

And then it came, his memory sparked by the woman's glasses.

The splendor of her attire and the style of her hair had tripped him up, but suddenly, he pictured her without the getup, stripping her down to her plainness—to just the glasses.

It was the woman he'd met that night at the New Yorker Hotel, in the Grand Ballroom. He had danced with her to the Benny Goodman Orchestra. The sharp one who had gotten under his skin after she had exposed his lies.

"I remember now," he muttered, lost in the memory of it. "I met her over a year ago. It was a brief encounter. One dance, one drink."

"Then maybe we're okay. She probably won't remember you."

Buck shook his head. "Not this woman. She's too smart. She'll remember okay."

"Then we'll have to avoid her."

"Of all the places to run into her. Why would she be here?"

"Is she Russian?"

Buck shook his head. "I don't think so. She sounded American to me. But we only had a few minutes together."

"Just keep a lookout for her and stay out of her way. The last thing we need is someone creating a scene."

A waiter carrying a tray of Champaign goblets drew up to them. "Hello, fellas," he said under his breath. "Welcome to the party."

Arthur Harrington was hardly recognizable in his tuxedo tails and stiff white collar. He bowed demurely, offering the tray of drinks to them. Brookfield took two goblets, handing one to Flynn.

"How goes it?" whispered Brookfield.

"Everything is set. I've got the tools stashed in a closet by the back door." He lifted his eyes to Buck. "Let me know when you're ready, and I'll lead you to them."

Buck nodded. Harrington turned and scurried away.

Brookfield took a sip of Champaign as he scanned the room. He pointed with his drink toward a cluster of people standing next to a table near the dance floor. Two men wore olive-colored uniforms instead of tuxedos, their chests bedecked with medals and slashing Sam Browne belts.

"That's Arso Jovanovic there, talking with Anatoli Yakovlev," said Brookfield. "The one in uniform. Yakovlev is the barrel-chested one."

Buck recognized the men from the photographs he'd studied.

"It's time for introductions," said Brookfield. "Use the few words of greeting I taught you. I'll try to get them away from you as soon as possible. It was their idea to meet with me tonight, so it shouldn't be a problem."

They moved toward the group. Buck glanced back to the ballroom entrance steps. The woman he'd recognized was nowhere to be seen. He sighed a breath of relief. Now if he could only avoid her for the next half hour.

As they approached the group, Buck recognized a third man from the debriefing photographs: Aleksandr Feklisov, the agent suspected of recruiting industrial spies in America. A fourth man stood near them, turned away, and talking to a group of women.

Arso Jovanovic spotted them approaching. A smile of welcome beamed. "Walter! You have come, my friend," said the man in Slovic-accented English.

Brookfield embraced the revolutionary as if they were long-lost brothers, and the two exchanged rapid-fire greetings in Serbo-Croatian. The Russians looked on with dark smiles. Buck couldn't tell if they understood the conversation or not.

"Please, let me introduce you to our hosts," said Jovanovic in English.

He made introductions to Yakovlev and Feklisov, who also greeted Brookfield in English. Though both were warm and welcoming, Buck sensed an undercurrent of hesitancy in their shared glances.

"And this," said Brookfield, "is Lieutenant John Humphrey Clark. I am recruiting him for our work in Yugoslavia."

Buck greeted them with his practiced Russian greeting. The Soviets eyed him with guarded uncertainty. Feklisov, particularly, seemed aloof, his lips tightening. He had eyes like a jittery hummingbird, never making eye contact. His Pops would say:

Never trust a man who won't look you in the eye. Like a dog circling behind you, they usually intend you evil.

"Will you be making a trip to Yugoslavia, Lieutenant?" asked Jovanovic.

"If all goes well," said Buck. "I'm currently unavailable because of my current posting here in New York, but we are working on that."

Brookfield shot him a wry smile of congratulations. So far, so good.

"Ah," said Jovanovic. "If you are stationed in New York, then you must meet my associate. He works for the Eastern and Central European Planning Board. Vuk!" he shouted. "Come meet our friends from the U.S. Marines."

The gentleman standing off to the left turned to face them. Vuk Milosh. Buck recalled his photo too. Tall, handsome, with a confident smile.

"Vuk is in New York too," said Jovanovic, "but in the past, he helped coordinate supplies and flights out of London. He has been doing excellent work."

Vuk Milosh feigned a modest bow of his head at the compliment, but Buck sensed a smugness gushing beneath it.

Walter Brookfield leaned in. "The three of us should get together to talk. The British are protective of the work they're doing with your underground. Our goal is to not overlap efforts, or offend our British friends by encroaching on their territory."

"Yes," said Milosh. "We mustn't offend Mr. Churchill." The tone was scornful.

Jovanovic laughed uncomfortably.

Brookfield said, "Because of British interests, we can't bring flights into your country. However, we have strategies to ship supplies and arms to your forces from southern Italy. It's a relatively short boat ride over the Adriatic Sea to western Yugoslavia. A supply link via Vis Island could be possible."

Buck watched as the interest of the men brightened. They shared glances and head nods.

"We need to hear of these strategies," said Jovanovic. "We have time to talk this evening, but it must happen soon. I will leave tonight for London, along with Comrade Yakovlev."

"Then let's talk right away," offered Brookfield.

Jovanovic turned away to confer with the Russians. They nodded with subdued whispers. Buck felt Feklisov watching him, warily.

Turning back, Jovanovic said, "It is set. We will use the library across the main hall. We will have privacy there. I've asked our Russian friends to join us if you don't mind."

"I welcome them," offered Brookfield. Turning to Buck, he said, "I'll be gone for a while, Lieutenant. Will you be okay by yourself?"

Buck gave a courteous nod.

"Your friend will not be joining us?" asked Milosh, surprised.

"Not this time," smiled Brookfield. "His clearance isn't approved yet. Plus, his Russian and Serbo-Croatian language skills are not yet up to our conversation. He can stay and enjoy the party."

"Ach," said Milosh. "We can't leave Lieutenant Clark alone without knowing a soul. Let me introduce him to my comrades. He will be in excellent hands with them."

Buck cringed. Brookfield's face fell as well. They had hoped Buck would have this time free to slip into the kitchen unhindered. Now he would have to come up with an excuse to break away.

Milosh tapped the shoulder of a woman standing behind him; she was in the middle of a conversation with other women huddled there.

"Natka, I have a chore for you. A pleasant one."

The woman swung around, a smile gracing her face.

Buck's heart splintered like glass. She was stunningly beautiful. As beautiful as Laraine Day. But it wasn't Laraine Day.

It was Natalie Stevens.

His Natalie.

Chapter 68

———◇———

Wardenclyff Laboratory, Long Island, Friday, 9:02 PM

NOTEBOOK BE DAMNED! THIS is my machine. I will give it life.
The gloom of the laboratory encased him like ice. So absorbed in his work was Dr. Markovitch that he had failed to notice that the beast had left hours ago. His hands trembled as he delicately twisted the Allen screw into the housing—trembling not from fear, but rage.

It became essential to finish the weapon before they brought him the book. To prove to them he didn't need it. This was his work! His alone. *They want a death ray. I'll give them one. This is my child. I am its father. I am teleforce!*

He torqued the hex screw perfectly. How many times had he done this? How many housings? How many Allen screws? Countless.

But this was the machine that mattered. His child. Every aspect designed and machined by him. Yes, the theories were Tesla's, but the nuanced concepts were all his.

For nearly a year he'd played the role of lapdog, submitting to the theories, blueprints, and designs of others on the team, listening patiently to their postulations, but secretly cringing at their futile hypotheses. They had no intellectual breadth. And it infuriated him that they rarely listened to his suggestions. As if he were insignificant. As if working two decades with Nikola Tesla accounted for nothing.

The team comprised the lead scientist and two laboratory assistants, who only came in four days a week. Also on the team were two machinists and an engineering electrician. But Markovitch considered them lab rats. Robots who did what they were told. Oh, they offered advice now and then—they weren't total idiots—but they had no capacity for critical thinking. However, *they* were not the problem.

Dr. Natka Milosh was the problem.

That the woman was brilliant was undeniable, but the project was beyond her. He constantly corrected and challenged her work. They argued constantly. She could not receive his input graciously or heed his suggestions—almost as if she were trying to thwart his efforts rather than learn from his experience and talent.

The sweet little girl he remembered from two years ago had vanished. In her place was a driven, egocentric tyrant, who demanded things be done her way. Several months into the project, Dr. Markovitch came to realize that, if left to her way, the project would never come to fruition.

Fortunately, his friend, Aleksandr Feklisov, had stepped in. Freeing him to build *his* version of the machine. Feklisov always came when Natka was away. As if he, too, understood her limitations. Feklisov believed in him—believed he could be as great as Tesla.

And now he was ready to enter that greatness.

He snickered to himself. The Allen screw tightened just so. The adjustment made. Such a minor aspect of a complex machine, but the most important aspect because...it was the last.

This latest generation was all his. Every part fashioned by him. Every wire connected by his own hands. Every concept his. This was his particle beam weapon now. His Death Ray.

The notebook be damned.

The machine was complete.

Chapter 69

———◆———

Russian Consulate, New York, Friday, 9:21 PM

THE MARBLE FLOORING BENEATH Buck's feet melted like quicksand, engulfing him into a swirling, gritty darkness. The surrounding gala dissipating.

Natalie.

She stood right there. Close enough to touch. Real.

At the calling of her name—Natka—she had twisted around to face them. Their sightlines collided. The smile broadcasting from her beautiful face shattered instantly. Recognition sparking. The world erupting.

The telltale aftermath brought a heartbeat of confusion. What did he see there in her face? Shock? Fear? Confusion? No. It was something different altogether.

Panic.

Her silver-blue eyes shimmered with subtle, quiet panic. Her lower lip quivered. She swallowed. Her elegant throat undulated as if to capture the panic and force it back down into her belly. She stood paralyzed, as if afraid to blink.

"This is my wife, Natka," Vuk Milosh was saying somewhere in a distant world. "And this, darling, is Lieutenant John Humphrey Clark. The rest of us are taking a meeting and I thought..."

He trailed off as if noticing the invisible galaxies igniting between the two of them.

"Do you know one another?" he asked wondrously.

Buck caught the minuscule shake of her head, nearly imperceptible. Yet he comprehended. A secret, unspoken language communicated via wavelengths between them. She did not want this man—her husband!—to know of their past. The panic detonating.

Buck fought to recover.

"No," he uttered, with a hollow catch in his throat. "But she looks so familiar. It startled me."

Vuk Milosh leaned in. "Like maybe a movie star, no?"

Buck wrenched his eyes from Natalie to look directly at him. To look anywhere but at her. "Yes, that must be it."

"People say she looks like some actress. I don't see it. But then, I don't watch American movies. They bore me."

Buck's heart was misfiring, like an automobile engine with a thrown timing chain. The room suffocating him.

Milosh turned to Natalie. "Would you make the Lieutenant welcomed while we take our meeting, darling?"

Natalie, who hadn't yet found her voice, nodded, forcing a smile.

"Dance with my wife," cried Milosh with a slap on his back. "She's an excellent dancer. Please, go! We will be back in no time."

The three of them stood there, awkwardly not moving, an uncomfortable tension building. Walter Brookfield, standing with the other men, looked stern, as if bothered by Buck's inaction. He jutted his chin as if nudging him onto the dance floor.

Buck swallowed. He turned to Natalie, his eyes drilling into hers. "Would you like to dance...*Mrs.* Milosh?" he asked, hitting the Mrs. part of her name with a hard edge.

Catching the irritation in his voice, Natalie's lips tightened, her eyes narrowed; however, she bowed her head demurely and extended a hand to accept the invitation.

He reached out and...

...touched...

Her hand. Her skin. Her warmth. The spark of contact quivered through the tendons of his arm like the hum of a tapped tuning fork. It grew. A stuttering vibration swelling to a crescendo. An inward earthquake. As if the two of them had collided violently. He felt her shudder beneath his touch. And together they moved toward the dance floor.

Glancing over his shoulder, Buck watched the group leave the room. Aleksandr Feklisov, however, hesitated. His flitting eyes scoured the two of them. He then stepped over to speak to a man lingering near the far wall, a thick hulk of a man. Buck recognized him from the photographs. His face could have been hammered into shape on an anvil.

Yegor Volkov, the assassin.

As Feklisov spoke, the man gave a blunt nod. And Feklisov slipped away.

On the dance floor, Buck and Natalie came up parallel to each other, their faces averted, as if afraid to look at each other. Placing a reluctant hand on her hip, he lifted his other to grasp hers, and leaving a canyon between them, they stepped. Together they merged into the music. It felt familiar. The rhythm of their movements. Their bodies in tandem. In the past—a millennium ago—they had danced on several occasions. It felt as if they'd never stopped.

After a few eternal minutes, Natalie finally spoke.

"Harry, you're hurting me."

He snapped an angry sneer at her.

Harry! Everyone else called him Buck. To her, he'd always been Harry!

"Hurting you?" he seethed.

"My hand, Harry. You're squeezing it." Her voice strained, almost choking.

Glancing at his hand gripping hers, he found their fingers entangled as a knot of flesh, white and throbbing from a lack of blood. He hadn't realized how hard he had clamped down on her. He eased his grip.

"Thank you," she whispered.

"Sorry," he muttered, turning his head away.

A quiet hardened between them. The music insignificant. The surrounding dancers mist.

Finally, she said, "This is awkward, isn't it?"

Buck said nothing.

"You're angry.

Silence.

"You have every right to be, Harry."

He snapped back around. "You left."

"I had to."

"You're married!"

"Yes."

"Were you then?"

For a brief second, a look of pain crested her face, but then disappeared. A resolve tightening her features.

"Yes," she said.

"Why didn't you tell me?"

"I...I couldn't. I wanted to. But I couldn't bring myself to do it."

"So you lied." The minute the words left his lips, he remembered his own lie. The lie of being a criminal.

"I didn't want to ruin it," she breathed.

"Ha," he choked. "Ruin it! We couldn't have that! Luckily, it all worked out."

"You don't understand."

"What's to understand? You were a married woman. You had an affair. Got it out of your system. Made up with hubby. End of story."

"Don't make it sound cheap."

"Wasn't it?"

"No. It wasn't like that."

"Sounds pretty cheap to me."

Her lips thinned; her jaw jutted. She turned her head away. A new silence hardened. He could hear her breathing over the music. Finally, she said:

"I...we...Vuk and I were separated at the time. We were planning to divorce."

"Ah, but you worked things out. I'm happy to hear it." He gazed beyond her, refusing to look at her face. Fearing to look at her face.

"Harry...things happened that..."

"Save it," he snapped. "I don't want to hear about your marriage woes."

She had been looking up at him, but now her eyes dropped. They continued to dance, gliding in rhythm to the ruse they were both carrying out.

Suddenly, she was looking up at him again. "Harry, why did Vuk call you John Humphrey Clark?"

It was his turn to panic. He'd almost forgotten about the job.

"Vuk said you were a Marine Lieutenant. Harry, why do you have an assumed name?"

He glared down at her. "You mean an assumed name like Natalie Stevens, Mrs. Natka Milosh?"

She studied him, unflinching. "There's a reason for that."

"Oh? I'd love to hear it sometime."

The music stopped. It relieved Buck. He released her.

Natalie reached up and touched his arm. He wanted to brush it away. He couldn't. The hum was there again, working its inward violence.

"Harry, could we talk for a moment?"

He knew he shouldn't. He needed to do the job. He needed to find the kitchen. Do the business and get out. He hated standing here, on this dance floor, surrounded by communists, being watched by a ruthless assassin, while a perilous job awaited his attention.

But Natalie was here.

She looked about. "There's a balcony over there through those doors. Could we go outside for a few minutes, just to talk? I'd like to explain some things."

"What does it matter now?"

"Please. I need you to understand something."

He glanced over at Yegor Volkov, still lurking near the far wall. He was watching them. He had eyes like death, as if possessing no moral voltage whatsoever. Buck shuddered.

"Please, Harry. Before Vuk and the others come back."

Buck shrugged and followed Natalie through the glass doors to the balcony. The frigid January air met them. Biting. Harsh. Natalie shivered next to the railing.

"It's colder than I expected," she offered, grasping her shoulders for warmth. She turned to him. "My name is Natalie Stevens. At least it was when I grew up as a little girl in London. That part is not a lie."

Natalie had come from England. That much he knew. Her accent made it obvious. Neither had shared their pasts during those whirlwind months. That was part of the attraction. Each possessed veils of mystery. Both caught up in the moment. Living in the now. Buck had not wished to reveal his criminal past, and she seemed just as reluctant to talk of hers, so they avoided it.

"But that wasn't always my name," said Natalie. "I was born Natka Stefanovic, in a village in Yugoslavia, called Gospic. My family immigrated to London. We changed our name to make us sound more English. At seventeen, I returned to Yugoslavia for a short time before attending the University of Prague in Czechoslovakia. I used my Serbian name during that time—again to fit in. That's when I met Vuk."

She turned away. Her body shivered from the cold.

"It was only five years ago, but it seems like a million years have passed," she muttered. "I was young, naïve—just a girl. He was charming and charismatic."

"And a communist," said Buck bitterly, folding his arms across his chest.

She firmed her lips and nodded. "Yes. A communist. Before I knew it, we were in love. Or at least what I thought was love. It wasn't until much later that I realized it wasn't."

"You married him."

She nodded, a tear glistening along one of her eyelids.

"We were only a month into the marriage when I realized the mistake I'd made. He loved his politics more than me. He was angry all the time. At the world. The monarchy. The social injustice. He had little emotion left for me. I moved out. I was still going to university, so I focused on my studies. Then Hitler established the Munich Agreement, annexing portions of Czechoslovakia. There were demonstrations. Students were shot. My parents begged me to come home to London before the troubles escalated. Truthfully, I was glad they did. It gave me an excuse to break away from Vuk."

Her body was shaking now from the cold, or maybe from emotional upheaval. Had he been standing with any other woman, Buck would have offered his jacket. But this was Natalie Stevens. The one who had demolished him. Let her shiver.

She turned back to him. "So, I moved back to London. That's when Uncle Sava contacted me and offered me a job in New York."

The name startled him. "Wait! Are you talking about Sava Kosanovic? He's your uncle?"

Surprise struck her face at Buck's recognition of the name. "No, he's not actually my uncle, just an old family friend. What do you know of him?"

Buck turned away. He couldn't have her reading his face. The more he learned, the less he trusted her. He needed to divert the subject. "Not much. So, you came to New York. We met at the World's Fair. How did you find your way there?"

"Yes. We met outside the Westinghouse Exhibit. I was working there. Remember?"

Buck knew she worked at the fair. He had assumed that she had been working a counter or hawking souvenirs, but now he wondered. She had been so evasive back then.

"What were you doing at the fair? What was your job?" he asked.

Wonderment came into her face. She chuckled. "That's right. We never talked about that, did we? We were so caught up in finding each other, our lives before meant nothing, as if the world began the day we met."

Buck ground his teeth. *And died the day when you left,* he thought.

"I am a trained theoretical physicist, Harry. Uncle Sava arranged for me to work in the laboratory of a man named Nikola Tesla. Have you ever heard of him? He just died a few days ago."

Buck nearly choked. The veils coming off. "Yes, of course."

"Because of his connection to George Westinghouse, we were asked to take part in the Westinghouse Exhibit at the World's Fair. I conducted electrical experiments for the crowd. The kind of things Nikola Tesla did years ago to amaze people." She turned to him. "Then we met—you and me."

The night chill crawled down his spine.

"At that pretzel cart, remember? We both reached for the same pretzel...and our hands touched."

His chest clenched. He had purposely blockaded that memory for over two years. Untouched. Locked within his own inward safe, whose combination he never wished to crack.

"I'll always remember that first touch," said Natalie. "It felt more powerful than the electricity in all the experiments I was conducting combined. I knew at that moment what they mean by love at first sight." Her voice choked. Her lower lip tremored. "I felt the same thing when you touched me inside the ballroom a few minutes ago."

Air eluded him. "You left," he whispered.

He watched her face weave through a set of painful expressions. Tears blotted her cheeks. She clutched her shoulders tightly now, to keep her body from quaking from the night cold. She glanced back through the balcony doors.

"We're being watched," she whispered. "Could we step over to the corner of the balcony, out of sight?"

Buck backed up against the far railing. Natalie drew up near to him. Pressed herself against him. The hum throbbing. Her face close to his. So close.

"Could you hold me? Please?" she asked, her voice soft and pleading. "It's cold."

He reached his arms around her as if compelled to do so; as if controlled by an unseen force; as if he had no other choice or will of his own.

"Harry, no more lies," she whispered, her breath warm and soothing across his cheek. He trembled, absorbing her quivering. "I can't take it any longer. For the last two years, I've been living a lie. I've done horrible things. I've got to trust somebody. Please, Harry, I've got to trust you."

He stood, waiting. Embracing. Riding the hum.

"Harry, I'm a British agent working undercover."

Chapter 70

—◆—

Outside the Russian Consulate, New York, Friday, 9:45
PM

PADDY TOOKE SAT HUNKERED down in the front seat of his '39 Nash LaFayette, watching the front doors of the Consulate half a block away. The activity had thinned. Most of the guests had already arrived, however, the occasional taxicab or limousine continued to drop off late-comers. With each arrival, he noted the license plate number, along with a brief description of each guest. He wrote the information in a small spiral notebook. Some guests he recognized from photos he'd seen during debriefings. They positioned another agent on the other side of the consulate doing the same thing, except that agent also had a camera with a telephoto lens attached.

The air inside the Nash was chilly. Condensation fogged the windshield. Occasionally, he wiped it clear with his handkerchief. Wishing to remain as inconspicuous as possible, he refrained from turning the car on to make use of its heater. Wrapped around his neck was the green wool scarf Dottie had knitted for him last year. He also brought a thermos of hot coffee. This was a comparative luxury to the bone-chilling winter he'd experienced in the trenches in France during the Great War. He'd survive.

He retrieved his Kaywoodie and tobacco pouch from his pocket and began filling his bowl, spilling a few tobacco flakes on his scarf. Brushing them off, his thoughts went to Dottie. He'd tried calling her at home late this afternoon, but she hadn't picked up. Out shopping? Maybe. Yet before leaving for his stake-out, he'd tried calling again, and she still hadn't answered the phone. It concerned him. Dottie was a homebody. However, with Paddy gone for most of the week, she may have grown lonesome and went to visit their daughter-in-law. She often did that, with their son off to war and all. He'd call over to her house later tonight, just to check.

He tamped the tobacco into the bowl, wondering how Buck was doing. The boy appeared unflustered, as if breaking into a foreign consulate was business as usual. He hoped he wasn't too confident. The consequences of being captured were unthinkable. They would arrest Flynn for espionage, and there was nothing Paddy, or the U.S. government, could do to help him. He would be in the hands of a merciless regime who had no qualms about using torture to extract information from a captured spy.

He struck a match to light his pipe, just as the passenger door swung open, startling him. A man wearing a trench coat slipped in. Phillip Carver.

"How goes it, Tooke?" He set something down on the seat between them, and then vigorously rubbed his hands together for warmth. He looked earnest and alert as he stared through the fogged windshield.

"Pretty quiet now," replied Paddy. "I've got a list of plate numbers and a handful of names of people that I recognized."

"Good. Pelt is doing the same thing on the other side. I know it's tedious work, but you never know when this kind of information will come in handy down the road."

Paddy nodded as he drew flame across his bowl.

Pointing to the item on the seat, Carver said, "I brought a walkie-talkie for you. That way you can give us a heads up if anything happens. Nothing of Brookfield and Flynn, I take it?"

"No word yet. But they've only been in there less than an hour. It'll take time to find the right moment."

"Yeah, it's early yet. Let's just hope your trained monkey can do the job without getting his ass arrested."

Paddy glared over at the man. "There's no need to be insulting the boy, Deputy Director. He is sticking his neck out for us."

Carver grunted. "He's a criminal, Tooke. A thief. He comes from bad blood. I read his file. His old man was a thief, too."

"Buck's his own man," offered Paddy. "And men can change."

Carver's eyes narrowed. "Not men like that."

Paddy said nothing.

"Which reminds me, once this is over, do you want to ride back with him?"

"Ride back with whom?"

"Flynn. On the train."

A concern flooded Paddy. He glared across the cab of the Nash. "What are you talking about?"

Carver, sensing Tooke's discomfort, allowed a thin smile to emerge. "You know that we're sending him back, right?"

"To prison, you mean?"

"Of course to prison, Tooke. We can't let him roam free. Not with all he knows about *Teleforce*. He's a security risk."

"But we told him—"

"I know what we told him! But be realistic. He's a criminal that knows too much. Prison is the best place for him. Besides, I've taken care of it."

"What do you mean?"

"I've got a team ready to apprehend him the moment he comes through the front door of the consulate."

"You're going to arrest him?"

"Contain him. We don't want him slipping away. Our guys will take him down immediately. We need to secure *Teleforce*, of course. But after that, we'll isolate him. I've arranged for a temporary cell until we can get him back upriver."

"Does Brookfield know of this?"

"No sense dragging him in on it. He has enough to think about tonight."

Ire flared in Paddy. He couldn't believe what he was hearing. "I gave the boy my word of clemency."

Carver shot him a snide look. "He's lucky he's only being arrested. Davies wanted to eliminate him as an intelligence threat completely!"

Paddy nearly choked. "You mean...?"

"Look, Tooke, this is national security we're talking about. We can't have some low-life criminal blabbing how he helped the U.S. government steal secrets from the Ruskies. It was either put him on ice in prison or take him out. He's fortunate to be going back to Sing Sing."

Paddy ground his teeth. He didn't like it. Not one bit.

"So, do you want to ride along with him or not? A couple of other men will travel with him, to make sure he doesn't try anything, but you're welcome to go too. I know that using him was your idea and all."

Paddy released a plume of pipe smoke. "I'll go. It's the least I can do for the boy."

"It was a good call on your part—using him, that is. I'll make sure that you get full credit once the operation is successful."

Paddy grunted, "I didn't sign on with you boys for the credit."

"Nevertheless, you've done outstanding work here."

And with that, he slipped out of the automobile and disappeared down the street.

Paddy stewed. Anger heating his body. He didn't like double-crossing the boy. He felt as if they had handed him the role of Judas.

You're a better man than your actions. He had told him.

It hadn't been a glib statement, or a tool of manipulation, just to get the boy to do his bidding. He believed in Flynn. Believed he wanted to turn things around and make things right. The poor kid thought he was serving his country with the chance to have his record purged.

Paddy let loose a low-grade growl. Maybe there was something he could do before they put him on that train. Maybe he could talk Carver and Davies into giving Buck a chance. He doubted it. Those two men were not in the mercy business.

Across the street, a car was backing into a parking spot. Paddy readied his notebook. He tried to copy down the license number, but mud covered the plate. A solitary man got out of the vehicle. He walked around to the trunk and opened it. After bending out of sight for a flash, the man closed the trunk lid, turned, and hurried toward the front steps of the consulate. Huddled against the cold, he stepped under the lighted awning. It wasn't until he was halfway up the stoop that Paddy caught a fleeting profile of the man.

And his gift for faces sparked — alarm, as well.

Chapter 71

Russian Consulate, New York City, Friday, 10:02 PM

ASTONISHMENT SLAMMED INTO BUCK Flynn.

"You're a British agent?" he croaked.

Natalie's arms had slipped around his waist; she was clutching at him, their chilled bodies quaking together, syncopating, merging. Over her shoulder, the glow of the gala poured through the glass doors onto the balcony's stone floor. Not a soul in sight. He feared the doors would suddenly swing open, shattering this moment of brutal honesty. He pictured Yegor Volkov stepping out, catching their embrace. He pictured him with a pistol.

Natalie nodded against his chest. "Yes, I'm with the British Special Operational Executive."

Buck swallowed. The SOE. Churchill's Secret Army. The OSS equivalent.

"How? When?" he asked. "Were you an agent when we met?"

"No. But that's why I disappeared so suddenly. If you recall, the war was heating up in Europe. We both did our best to ignore it. It didn't affect us. We were selfishly in love." She ground her face into his chest as if to blot their sins from her memory. "But then two things happened that changed everything."

She tilted her head back to look into his eyes.

"First, Hitler invaded Yugoslavia. My home country. Everyone in the laboratory, here in New York, crowded around the radio to listen to the announcement—many of my co-workers were from Yugoslavia. Around that same time, London too was being bombed. My other home."

"Yes, I remember," Buck said softly.

Without asking, Natalie withdrew Buck's handkerchief from his tuxedo jacket and dabbed at her eyes.

"Then, one day, a man knocked on my door and my world changed forever. He was from the British Embassy here in New York. He told me that the London blitz had killed my parents."

She turned to stare off into the bleak, gray skies above New York, leaning her head against his chest.

"It devastated me. He brought me the news in person for a reason. He was an SOE agent. They knew of my background: my schooling, my broken marriage, my employment with Nikola Tesla. They also knew that I was a naturalized British citizen. He'd come to recruit me to work for the British government. I was to travel back to England immediately to begin training. They had a special assignment for me... involving my estranged communist husband."

In his mind, Buck pictured the man greeting Natalie in the lobby of the Navarro Hotel. How they'd gone to her apartment that night, and never came out.

"That's why you left?"

"Yes, Harry. That's why. It happened so quickly. They ordered me not to tell anyone—not even you. They knew all about us, Harry. They had been following us. The man told me things about you too, things that shocked me at first. He said you couldn't be trusted."

Buck felt his chest clench. His lie surfacing.

"He told me about your father's criminal record. They showed me your expenses and how you lived in a luxury apartment in Manhattan, with no visible means of support. No job, no trust fund, or inheritance. No investments. Yet you always seemed to have money. I didn't want to believe him. But the evidence was so...convincing. He said you were a common thief. They had no proof. Only questions about you I couldn't answer."

Buck couldn't say a word.

"I felt...betrayed." She spoke the word as if ashamed to utter it. Her head was down, her eyes averted. "As if I didn't know you at all."

Buck now regretted not coming clean with her from the beginning. His sins stretched between them like razor wire around a prison wall. He wanted to tell her he'd meant to confess; but knew it would ring hollow. The words shriveled on his tongue.

Natalie continued, "So I left. I flew to London that very night and began my SOE training that week. They leaked a cover story that I had been killed with my parents in the blitz. Two months later, they got word that Vuk was in London. They arraigned for us to *accidentally* meet at a restaurant that he frequented. They set it up for me to be inside the restaurant before he arrived, to make it look like he had stumbled upon me. He had no clue. He was ecstatic to have found me again, and I pretended to be happy to see him but played hard to get. It was a role I played according to the psychological profile they'd compiled on him." A thin smile graced her face. "Acting. Just like that actress I supposedly look like."

She clutched tighter to him.

"I hated it, Harry. Pretending that way. After you...after knowing genuine love. I barely pulled it off. I tried to forget you. I lived in constant fear of Vuk seeing through my charade. Whenever he...touches me...I..." Her voice trailed off; he felt her shudder against him. "I despise him more than ever. I despise them all. I constantly remind myself that it's just a job. For God and country. That somehow I'm saving lives."

Buck stroked her back. Her shivering had abated some, their shared warmth spreading. He felt the wetness of her tears on his shirt.

"It's been horrible, Harry. For the past year, Vuk and the Soviets have kept me isolated. I've been working on a secret project in an underground laboratory out on Long Island. This is the first time in months I've been out amongst people."

"What kind of project?"

She snapped him a fearful look. "It's a weapon the Soviets are trying to develop. I've been trying to subvert their efforts, but I don't think it is working. Another scientist has been working with me, but I suspect he's been building his own version of the weapon."

"Where?"

"A place called Wardenclyff."

Buck had never heard of it.

"Because they've kept me isolated, I've lost contact with my British handler — the man who recruited me. The last time I saw him was over a year ago at the New Yorker Hotel. We haven't communicated since."

"The New Yorker?" asked Buck, shock catching in his throat.

"Yes. That night I smuggled microfilm to him with Nikola Tesla's designs for a secret weapon. That night I—"

A new panic flashed across her face. No. Not panic this time. Something more intense, something raw. Sorrow! Deep and convulsing. As if her soul were in agony.

"Oh, Harry. I'm so ashamed. I judged you for what those men told me you were, but I'm much worse."

"Don't say that."

"You don't understand. I...I've done something terrible."

"You've done what you had to do."

"But Harry, I murdered a man!"

"What?"

Natalie was near hysterical. Her eyes wide with naked fear. "Last year...here in New York. I pushed a man off a building. A Russian scientist. I killed him! I did it to keep him from bringing a devastating weapon back to Soviet Russia. I didn't know what else to do."

Shock blasted Buck. His throat went dry. The vision of a man falling through the night sky re-emerged. It had been Natalie he'd spotted that night on the balcony. She was the one who'd pushed that man to his death.

He worked his jaw as if to speak, but before he could say anything...

The glass doors swung open and someone stepped onto the balcony. Buck and Natalie quickly separated and swung around.

"Aha! There you are!" cried a woman. "I've been looking for you, Mr. Jim Christian!"

Alarm filled Buck. It was the woman in the yellow dress he had spotted earlier, the one he'd recognized. She marched right up to them and planted herself, a glint of triumph on her face.

"I knew I had seen you before," she stated, shaking a naughty finger at him. "I just had to remember where!"

Then, spotting Natalie hovering behind Buck, she drew up short.

"Dr. Milosh? I'm sorry, I didn't realize it was you."

"Hello, Miss Muzaric," said Natalie.

Buck was stunned. The two women knew each other.

He glanced at Natalie, amazed by how quickly she had recovered from her near breakdown. Her shoulders squared, her head high, she looked the epitome of dignity. The transformation instantaneous, as if she'd stepped onto a stage and into a role she'd played a thousand times. She gave Buck a practiced smile and made introductions.

"Lieutenant Clark, this is Arlene Muzaric. She works for my Uncle Sava."

Buck couldn't believe his luck. Everything was falling apart. First Natalie, and now his cover was about to be blown by a woman he'd only met once before—and a woman who worked for a known communist agent. He extended his hand as suspicion blossomed behind the woman's glasses.

"Lieutenant Clark, huh?" she uttered.

The woman's eyes bounced from Buck to Natalie and back again. Natalie must have caught the gleam of skepticism in the woman's glare.

"I'm sorry. Have you two met?" asked Natalie.

But before either of them could answer, the doors to the patio swung open again, and a man stepped out. Tall, broad-shouldered. Dressed in a tux. Blond. Wearing glasses.

"Arlene? Someone told me you were out here."

Arlene Muzaric swiveled around. "Oh, you've finally made it. I was getting worried."

The man drew up to them, a limp in his gait. "Sorry I'm late, darling. Car trouble."

She turned to Buck and Natalie and said, "This is Henry Stewart, my guest for the evening."

The man reached out to shake hands.

Buck flinched. Dumbstruck.

It was the man he'd fought in Nikola Tesla's apartment.

Chapter 72

Russian Consulate, Friday, 10:17 PM

IT WAS THE EYES. Icy blue. Calculating. And beneath the surface, an unmistakable layer of hate. His appearance had changed. He was blond now and wore a Clark Gable mustache. But it was the same man. Same build, same razor straight posture...

...but the eyes. Buck would know those eyes anywhere.

Shocked to be so near the Nazi spy, Buck quickly recovered to shake hands, repulsed by the act of touching him. Beneath his grip, he felt the wooden stiffness of the man's two fingers, as if they were dead appendages glued to a living hand. Further proof it was the man he'd fought. Buck himself had smashed those very fingers in the door of the Diebold safe.

The other man quickly withdrew his mangled hand and said: "Sorry about the dead fish grip. War injury."

Looking him straight in the eye, Buck said, "Is that so?"

Arlene Muzaric laced her hands around the man's arm, nestling closer to him. "Henry fought with the French resistance in occupied France. He was injured there. He took shrapnel in his leg from a German grenade."

The man's eyes locked on Buck as if challenging him to question the story. The icy blueness freezing a bit more.

Buck wondered about his presence here tonight. Was he here for the notebook? Or something else? He also wondered about his relationship with the woman. Was she a Nazi sympathizer, too? Or worse, a Nazi spy? Or had she been duped by the man's charms? She appeared genuinely smitten. She had the glow of a woman in love. But how could this woman, who had so easily seen through Buck's pretense a year ago, be taken in by this man?

"Darling, this is Lieutenant Clark," said Arlene Muzaric. "Although, I was just saying that when I met him last year, he went by another name, didn't you?" The same lynx-like grin he remembered from that night was there. She was enjoying his discomfort.

"A different name?" said Stewart, curiosity registering in his face. "Why would that be?"

"Probably his way of picking up girls," said Arlene.

Buck could feel Natalie tense up next to him.

"I think you have me mixed up with someone else," offered Buck, attempting to disarm Arlene with a smile. "I don't recall ever meeting you before."

Her eyes hardened into a dubious glare. "Oh, no. I remember it. Not that you left an impression on me. I forgot all about you the next day. But that night sticks out for other reasons."

"Where did you meet?" asked Stewart.

"We met during a Benny Goodman show, didn't we, Lieutenant?"

"Benny Goodman?" said Stewart, a questioning glimmer swept into his face.

"Yes," said Muzaric. "At the New Yorker Hotel last year. I remember it distinctly because that same night I met another man, who ended up jumping off the building to his death."

Natalie let out a gasp. Buck shot her a glance. Her eyes were wide, petrified. A new panic flit across her face. She stared back, as if attempting to wrestle a bit of logic into her mind. He could tell her trust in him was waning. Quickly.

"You were there?" she asked, her voice weak. "Why?"

Buck wanted to lie. He wanted to say anything to keep her trusting him. He wanted to deny ever being at the New Yorker Hotel, or ever meeting this other woman before.

But she was standing right there.

The Nazi spy was watching him.

Buck stepped toward Natalie, lifting a hand for her. She shrunk away. Disbelief crawling all over her. New doubts surfacing.

"Last year, this man told me his name was Jim Christian," Arlene Muzaric was saying. "Told me he worked in antiquities."

Buck swung on her. "I told you, we've never met before!" He tried keeping the anger from his voice, but it was there—enough to cause Arlene to back up a step.

"It was you!" she stated firmly.

Buck sensed Natalie slip past them. Escaping.

"Excuse me," she muttered. "I must get back."

She headed toward the patio doors. He was losing her.

"Natalie, wait," he cried.

"Natalie?" said Arlene. "You must be mistaken. Her name is Natka."

Just as Natalie reached the glass doors, they swung open. A tuxedoed waiter stepped out.

"Phone call for Lieutenant John Humphrey Clark!" he cried.

Natalie eased past the waiter to disappear into the ballroom. Buck stared at her fleeting form.

"Phone call for Lieutenant Clark!" said the waiter again.

"That would be you, wouldn't it?" said Arlene Muzaric.

"What?" stammered Buck.

"The waiter is calling for you. Or have you forgotten your name, Lieutenant?"

Buck glanced at the waiter. It was Arthur Harrington, glaring with anger.

Chapter 73

———◆———

Russian Consulate, Friday, 10:25 PM

"Where the hell have you been?" snorted Harrington under his breath. He carried a silver tray under his arm as he led Buck through the crowded ballroom. "I was thinking you had skipped out on us."

Buck's mind was swimming. The evening was unraveling. First Natalie. Then being identified by that woman. And then, of all things...the Nazi. Everything had happened so fast, he'd forgotten about the job.

What else could go wrong?

"I got waylaid," he offered.

"Well, you've got a job to do, fella. We didn't bring you here to get women's telephone numbers or to consort with the Russians."

Harrington led him through the swinging doors of the kitchen, bustling with activity. Chefs, waiters, and dishwashers, all occupied and ignoring them.

Once on the other side of the room, they slipped behind a partition to enter a wide stairwell; a set of stairs in front of them, and to the right, an outside exit. Through the door window, they could see an alley with automobiles and the parked catering van. A coat rack ran along the wall, and beneath it, near the exit, were three suitcases.

Harrington listened at the foot of the stairs. A hollow hiss echoed in the stairwell.

"We need to be careful," said Harrington under his breath. "There's a guard stationed on the second-story landing, and two more guards are just outside the back door."

Harrington stepped into a small niche to the left of the stairs. Opening the door to a storage closet nested beneath the rise of the staircase, he tugged on a chain to turn on the light. They entered, closing the door behind them. The cramped space was filled with brooms, mops, pails, and shelves of cleaning solvents. On one shelf was a wadded bundle. Harrington retrieved it and handed it to Buck.

"Here are your coveralls and tools. Give me a minute to set up the diversion. You'll hear a small explosion from the Aunt Jemima bread that will start the fire. That's when you come in. Everyone should be distracted. The dumbwaiter is right around the corner. I've already checked it out; the doors open freely, but there's no dumbwaiter car, just an empty shaft. Will you be able to handle the climb?"

Buck nodded.

"If you fall, you'll end up in the basement. Who knows what you'll land on."

"I won't fall," said Buck.

Unrolling the bundled coveralls, Buck found the leather satchel containing the fake notebook and his tools. He took off his tuxedo jacket, hung it on a nearby peg, and began putting on the coveralls over his dress clothes.

Harrington cracked open the closet door to peer out.

"You're on your own now, pal. Good luck," he said and left.

After buttoning up his uniform, Buck cinched the satchel to set firmly on his chest. He put on the gloves. Easing out of the closet, he turned off the light behind him. He gave a glance up the stairs, listening for movement. Everything was quiet. He paused behind the partition wall, listening.

A minor explosion popped at the other end of the kitchen, followed by frantic yelps. Total commotion.

Coming from around the partition, he glimpsed a cluster of flames licking across the stove and countertop on the other side of the room. He saw only the back of heads. Everyone turned toward the minor catastrophe, some hurrying to dowse the fire.

Perfect.

Thankfully, Arthur Harrington must have had an unguarded moment—the dumbwaiter doors were already split open. The dark space beyond was barely wide enough to accommodate a man. The inside shaft was paneled with wood. A cable dangled uselessly.

In one fluid motion, Buck slid into the shaft. Entering backwards, he braced against the far wall, pressing his feet against the opposite, wedging himself in. Nothing but air beneath him. It was cramped and awkward, but doable. He shimmied up far enough to slide the doors shut, encasing the shaft in darkness.

It had taken less than ten seconds from the moment of the explosion to closing the doors.

He listened. Somewhere above him, a thin wind blew through the tunnel, like the deep notes of an oboe. The air was cool and musty. Outside the dumbwaiter doors, the din of the kitchen commotion continued. Making use of the noise, he began his climb.

Pushing aside the dangling cable, he crab-walked up the tunnel. Using the cable for leverage was out of the question; he didn't trust its integrity, or what sort of rusty machinery could tumble down if yanked upon.

The going was slow, inch by inch, pressed against the walls, shuffling his feet and hands along the paneled surface. The wood was smooth and hard to grip, especially with the slick soles of his dress shoes. He wished he'd brought crepe-soled shoes for the climb. Glancing through his legs into the funnel below was a black abyss. One slip and he could fall into whatever mystery lay below.

Halfway up, he ran headlong into a mass of spider webs. The gossamer wrapped about his face like a death shroud. Frantically, he snatched away the clinging mesh and almost slipped in the process. He didn't care for spiders much. In the inky darkness, he imagined—more than felt — the creatures scuttling over his skin and into his garments. He pushed through. Real or not, the thought of spiders in his clothing quickened his pace.

A few minutes later, he came to the second story and to the sealed doors of the hidden whiskey room. Running his fingers along the indentation of the door frame, he found the slit in the center and attempted to pry the doors open, but they wouldn't budge. Time had encrusted them shut. Opening the satchel cinched to his chest, he blindly felt inside for a tool to wedge open the doors. It took several minutes of balancing precariously over the abyss before he got them parted.

The room beyond was pitch black. A mystery hole. The air was a few degrees warmer, but stale, like gathered dust. It smelled like the passage of time. Buck unwound himself from the shaft and crawled into the room, thankful to be out of that cramped space. The imagined sense of crawling spiders remained on his skin.

The room was as quiet as an after-hours library. He heard nothing of the gala taking place a floor below. Otto Eklund, the cabinetmaker, had told them of a light switch on the far wall. Whether the lightbulb would work after all these years was another question.

He retrieved a small flashlight and sliced a wedge of light, dazzlingly brilliant after the intense darkness of the dumbwaiter shaft. Shapes of furniture stood before him. Maneuvering around them, he edged to the other side of the room and found the light switch. To his relief, the lights came on.

The room was cozy and seemingly unchanged, as if mystically transported from another time, with leather chairs beaded with brass buttons, footstools, side tables, and humidors. An oak cabinet, with its doors ajar, exposed decanters, and bottles of aged whiskey, getting older by the minute. A teak wine rack ran along the facing wall, filled with dozens of bottles of both reds and whites. Surprisingly, the room was neat. Even with a coating of dust and a few cobwebs, it looked much as it would have the last time someone sat here sipping bourbon while smoking a cigar.

Turning his attention to the connecting wall to Yakovlev's office, it surprised Buck to find bookshelves on the inner wall. He had assumed that only the outer wall would have shelves; but hundreds of books were inside as well.

Moving to the left end of the unit, he reached up to feel for the catch on the third shelf and depressed it. A distinct snap sounded, unleashing a lock from somewhere within the frame. Lightly pressing on the shelving unit, he felt it give way. It was working! The wall pivoted under his fingertips.

Turning off the light in the whiskey room, he pushed open the unit just enough to peer through.

He was looking at Anatoli Yakovlev's office.

The lights were out, but the drapes were open, allowing the ambient glow of the city to wash into the room. Yakovlev's desk sat in front of the windows, an attaché case open on its surface, and next to it, a purse-like object, which had to be the diplomatic pouch. Files were stacked next to it, and what appeared to be a row of votive candles sitting along the edge of the desk.

Buck stepped into the office, pausing, listening. Quiet.

Gently, he pressed the unit back into place, locking the shelf into the wall. Leaving it open would arouse suspicions if perchance a guard stumbled in.

He found the door to the walk-in closet.

Was it locked? Twisting the knob, it opened beneath his touch. He entered, feeling along the wall for a light switch, and clicked on the lights. The closet was deeper than it was wide; the dimensions being six feet by ten, with ten-foot ceilings. A row of suits and clean shirts hung on hangers along one wall, a couple of topcoats hung on pegs near the door. Jammed against the opposite wall was a small dresser. The room was orderly.

Shelves lined the back wall, stuffed with office supplies, file boxes, and folded garments. And beneath the shelves, sitting on the floor...was the Shaw Walker safe, a squat gray box.

He kneeled before the safe to study the dial before beginning the process of discovering how many wheels it had. Using his stethoscope, it took nine minutes to learn he was dealing with a four-number combination. He'd been hoping for three. It took twenty minutes to crack it. After the last tumbler fell into place, he paused before opening it. Biting his lip.

The last three safes he'd cracked—Montet's wall safe and twice with Tesla's Diebold—had been a bust each time. He'd come away with nothing. A dry streak. He wondered if that would be the case this time. If so; then what?

He tugged the door open.

There! Right on top. The *Teleforce* notebook!

He quickly swapped out the books, replacing the real with the fake, and tucked the confiscated notebook into the leather satchel strapped to his chest.

He was about to close the safe when he recalled Phillip Carver's warning: 'Check for microfilm. The film cannot leave the country.'

He needed to substitute the blank rolls in his satchel for any canisters he came across.

Inspecting the contents of the safe, he found papers, files, a couple of velvet-covered boxes that possibly held jewelry, and even a pistol with a box of shells...but no canisters of film.

Then it came to him.

Earlier, when first peering into the office from the whiskey room, he had spotted what he thought to be votive candles sitting on Yakovlev's desk. Could those have been film canisters?

He closed the safe, turned off the closet light, and opened the door to peer out. Squinting into the dimly lit office, he focused on the desk. He barely could make out the items sitting there. Coming out of the closet, he eased into the center of the room toward the desk. His heart quickened.

Yes! The candle shapes were film canisters. Perfect. He would swap out the blank film and, hopefully, no one would be the wiser until the pouch reached Moscow.

Taking a step, he abruptly froze. A tiny noise fractured the quiet.

Light sliced across the crack at the bottom of the office door.

Someone was coming in.

Chapter 74

---•◦•---

Russian Consulate, 10:57 PM

IT WAS HIM! IT had to be!

Suspicion flamed across Henry Blacksmith's thoughts like fire licking over dry grass. He sat resolutely at his table; his gaze drilled on the swinging doors of the kitchen on the far wall of the ballroom.

The man had disappeared into the kitchen half an hour ago. Why?

Blacksmith had carefully monitored the traffic in and out of the swinging doors the entire time. The man hadn't returned yet.

Fortunately, Arlene, sitting next to him, was oblivious to his focused attention at the moment; she was prattling away in Russian with the woman sitting next to her. He hoped she stayed preoccupied. Arlene was sharp and would certainly detect his distraction if she were to become mindful of it. He had learned early on that she had an inner radar for falsehood. It had taken all of his skills as a trained manipulator to seduce her and keep her deluded. If she suspected that his attention was elsewhere, she would wonder why for sure.

For the most part, he had her wrapped around his little finger—the fool probably thought she was in love with him. Wheedling into her orbit had been fairly simple. While tracking Sava Kosanovic's movements, Blacksmith had discovered that the man's plain-looking secretary was a single woman living on her own in New York.

A situation in which Blacksmith saw an opportunity.

He had followed her for days, to get a grasp of her routine and interests, and had noticed that two days a week, Wednesdays and Fridays, she went to a local USO center to work with GI's, who were getting ready to ship out or were returning from war. The USO center offered dances and other social activities to help bolster the morale of the servicemen.

Blacksmith was able to secure an army uniform. A few extra bucks purchased him a Purple Heart medal. And after a bit of research, he concocted a believable story about being wounded while working with the underground in France. He had the limp and scars to prove it!

He then melted into the USO crowd, staying well away from the other returning veterans, who might discredit his story. And he waited, allowing her to come to him.

And she did.

He quickly found her to be shrewd and not taken in by false charm. She had aptly disarmed other GI's who attempted to pick her up. She saw through aggressive approaches. So, he bashfully brooded, playing the role of a traumatized and damaged soldier, barely talking to her at first. She responded with tender sympathy, taking him on as a project. Slowly he allowed her to fall under the pretense that she was coaxing him out of his shell, reviving him, and giving him hope. It worked. Within two weeks, a relationship developed; she being fully convinced by her role in his rehabilitation.

Asset cultivated.

And now his hard work was paying off.

He shot a glance down the length of the table, to where Sava Kosanovic sat a few chairs away, laughing with other Yugoslavian guests. Tonight, Blacksmith had officially met Nikola Tesla's nephew. A relationship that could lead him to the plans for the weapon.

Unless a better opportunity arose.

He again turned his sights on the kitchen doors.

Wishing to keep a clear head, he'd been nursing a vodka tonic for the last thirty minutes. The glass remained half full. He was growing impatient. The embers of a low-grade anger kindled inside him.

Where was the man who disappeared? And why is he here?

It was the thief! It had to be. The one who had thwarted him from stealing the plans for the weapon last year. From the moment he'd met Lieutenant John Humphrey Clark, an alarm had gone off in his head. He caught the man's hesitation to shake his hand, as if reluctant to do so. He'd also caught a glimmer of recognition sparking in the man's face. A momentary shock that lasted a blink, but was unmistakable. The man knew him, and yet...Blacksmith didn't know the man.

The encounter confused him at first. Until Arlene mentioned meeting him at the New Yorker Hotel—the same night of the attack! That's when the coin dropped, and the realization came to him. It was too much of a coincidence.

And now the coincidences were stacking up.

The call from George Sylvester Viereck two days ago, informing him of Harry C. Flynn's release from prison, and now here he was at the Soviet gala, and, according to Arlene, under an assumed name no less! It was all too fantastic. *Why was he here?*

Tesla's notes. It had to be. That's what had placed the thief in Tesla's apartment. So it stood to reason that his presence at the Consulate tonight meant the notes were nearby! *But where?*

The thief knew! But where had he gone?

The kitchen doors swung open. A waiter came out with a tray of food. No thief.

The other clue that sparked Blacksmith's suspicions was how the waiter had led him into the kitchen to receive a telephone call. Why there? Blacksmith knew of a telephone sitting on a pedestal table in the main entry hall. Wouldn't that have been the logical place to take him? Or even into the library across the hall.

But no. The waiter had led him into the kitchen.

And he hadn't come out.

Another coincidence to be added to the others.

The chamber music filling the ballroom added to his irritation. Russian compositions! He hated the stiff, bland melodies of the Russian composers. They were childish noise compared to the legendary German composers of his heritage.

Another shovel of coal added to his inward seething.

He caught movement by the ballroom entrance, five men coming through the double doors near the front steps. He broke his gaze from the kitchen doors to consider them. They appeared jovial yet somber all at once. An odd collection of guarded men bunched together, smiling, yet wary of one another. Blacksmith recognized the two Russians immediately, Yakovlev and Feklisov, whom he knew to be stationed here at the Consulate. He also recognized the man wearing a Yugoslavian uniform: Arso Jovanovic, a Communist leader associated with Tito. Arlene had mentioned that he would be here tonight.

The other two men were question marks. The tall, suave-looking gentleman, who seemed to be the center of attention, Blacksmith had never seen before, but the other one, the handsome fellow with the dark complexion and smug expression, he had. But where?

The five men paused on top of the landing to shake hands with each other, as if they had just conducted a bit of business together. Blacksmith leered at the group, his thumb caressing the onyx ring on his left hand. What would it take to swipe the whole bunch of them? To leave them all writhing and foaming on the ballroom floor?

Blacksmith then noticed Feklisov stepping away from the group to signal someone stationed on the main floor. Yegor Volkov. Blacksmith had noted the assassin earlier in the evening.

Volkov came up to meet Feklisov, who whispered something into the assassin's ear. Volkov gave a blunt nod and turned his gaze to a table a few feet away from where Blacksmith sat, pointing to a guest sitting there.

Feklisov again spoke into his ear. Volkov nodded and moved back down to where he had been standing prior.

Blacksmith wondered about the exchange. Instructions of some sort.

The group of five men dispersed. Feklisov and Yakovlev siphoned away, moving toward the grand staircase. Jovanovic and the tall man stepped over to the bar situated to their left. Their conversation continued, the tall man nodding to whatever Jovanovic was saying. However, his attention appeared to be elsewhere, his eyes combing the room as if looking for someone.

The last of the five—the vaguely familiar one—came down the steps in a confident stride, making his way to a table off to Blacksmith's right. It was the same table that Volkov had pointed to moments ago. The man walked up and bent to address a woman seated there, stroking her shoulder as he spoke, an intimate gesture that caused her to recoil some. Blacksmith recognized her as the pretty woman they had encountered out on the balcony. The one they'd caught standing with the thief. She had ducked out, upset about something. Blacksmith had forgotten all about her—being distracted, as he was, by his encounter with Lieutenant John Humphrey Clark.

But now, staring at her again, it nagged him that she too looked familiar. But from where?

The man hovering next to her cast a glance around the room, as if looking for someone. A questioning squint came into his face. He asked the woman a question and her answer came as a shrug, but Blacksmith noted a sense of fret in her expression, maybe even fear. The man took a seat beside her. That's when the woman also glanced around, as if she too had lost someone in the crowd.

Everyone seemed to be looking for someone. Could it be the *same* someone?

Off in the corner, Yegor Volkov stood like granite, watching the couple at the table, his hooded eyes tethered to them.

Then it hit Blacksmith! The synapses of his brain connecting the three of them—Volkov and the couple at the table. They had all been in the car that he had tailed to Long Island in a taxi. Volkov had been driving, the other two had been passengers. The cabbie had lost them in Queens. And now...here they were again.

Who was the couple? The woman had appeared cozy with the thief out on the balcony. What was her relationship with him? He had called her by name...what was it?

He nudged Arlene. "Who is that?" he asked, pointing with his drink toward their table.

Arlene looked past him. "That's Dr. Milosh."

"No, not the man, the woman."

Arlene gave him a perturbed smirk. "I'm talking about the woman. That's Dr. Natka Milosh. You men can be so chauvinistic. It's the twentieth century! Women can be doctors too, you know."

"Hey, I've met my share of female medical doctors," he said with forced contrition.

"I'm sure you have. But she's not a medical doctor. She's a physicist."

Blacksmith nearly spilled his drink. "You don't say? Russian?"

"No, she's Serbian. From Yugoslavia."

"A friend of yours?"

"Not really. She's an old friend of Mr. Kosanovic's. Their families knew each other in Yugoslavia."

"Ah, and now she works here in New York?"

The corner of her mouth squished as she thought. "Not in the city. From what Mr. Kosanovic told me, she's been working in some old laboratory out on Long Island."

Long Island? The coincidences were stacking up. A physicist with connections to Tesla working on Long Island. Where?

With as much control as possible, Blacksmith asked, "Doing what?"

"How should I know? What's with all the questions concerning Dr. Milosh?" Arlene's eye narrowed with suspicion. "You know she's married, right? That's her husband sitting next to her, Mr. Vuk Milosh. I mean, I know she's pretty, but—"

"Hey," he said, nuzzling closer to her, "I'm just interested in your friends, is all. Out on the balcony, you seemed to know her and I'm interested in anything connected to you, Arlene Muzaric."

"Is that right?"

"And besides, she doesn't hold a candle to you in the looks department."

She gave him a hard, dubious glare. He'd gone too far, and he knew it. Her radar for falsehood was flaring. He needed a divergence.

"Can I get you another drink?" he asked.

She scowled. "Okay, but don't be flirting with Dr. Milosh on your way there."

He smiled and stood. "Never."

He turned away and his smile darkened. His gaze riveted on Natka Milosh. A physicist connected to the Tesla family, working on Long Island? Being chauffeured by a Russian assassin? Coincidences. Coincidences.

Doing his best to conceal his limp, he started for the bar. Suddenly, he sensed movement to his left. Turning that way, he found Yegor Volkov barreling towards him. The assassin's face determined and hostile.

A rush of panic hit Blacksmith. He quickly flicked the spike of his poison ring to readiness.

The Russian would be dead in seconds.

But ten feet away, the brute veered. Brushing past him, the assassin went straight for Vuk and Natka Milosh. His sights hadn't been on Blacksmith at all.

Volkov bent to whisper to them. The two exchanged puzzled glances, hesitating. The assassin's face hardened with irritation, and reluctantly, they both stood. Natka gathered her purse. Volkov ushered them toward the front exit. An odd parade. Vuk Milosh leading, smug and strutting, Volkov following, fierce and watchful, and Dr. Natka Milosh between them with a look that could only be described as petrified.

Blacksmith watched the trio leave. What was that about? Where were they going?

He twisted a glance around the room.

The thief still hadn't returned from the kitchen.

Chapter 75

Russian Consulate, 11:05 PM

BUCK FLYNN FROZE IN the middle of the floor, his sinews taut with tension. Voices, muffled, guttural, and distinctly Russian, were coming from beyond the office door. He glanced at the film canisters on the desk. Ten feet away. Might as well be miles.

Keys scraped against the door lock. They were coming in.

No time for the film. And no time to make it to the pivoting bookshelf, unlock it, open it, and hide away inside. He had but one option.

The walk-in closet.

With four silent leaps, he made it back to the closet. He was just closing the door behind him when the office door swung open. Lights blazed awake in the outer room, creating a slit of illumination at the bottom of the closet door. Huddled in the darkness, he heard at least two men in mid-conversation. Loud, brash, Russian. He understood not a word of it.

The voices hovered in the center of the room, near the desk. Then Buck heard the sound that he dreaded most.

Footfalls approaching the closet door.

The approaching man's voice grew louder. An icy chill swept over Buck. The closet door was about to open. With nowhere to hide, except behind the hanging clothes, he pulled back into the darkness. Waiting. His heart thundering in his throat.

The door swung open.

Buck's breathing stopped.

The silhouette of a man stood in the rectangular slash of the opening. Big, rotund. Bear-like. Anatoli Yakovlev.

The station chief continued to speak to the other man behind him, his face towards the office, and because of that, he hadn't yet spotted Buck lurking in the back of the closet.

Panicked, Buck wondered what he should do once the lights came on. Fight? There were two of them. Could he overtake them both? Doubtful. He may have the element of surprise, but he also knew a guard stood outside the office door. He couldn't possibly take all three of them. His only means of escape was to get to the dumbwaiter shaft inside the whiskey room. Little or no chance of that happening.

Busted! The mission a failure. They would arrest him as a spy on Soviet soil. Carver had warned him that if caught, the American government would disavow the mission and any knowledge of the burglar known as Buck Flynn.

He braced himself for a last-ditch charge the moment the closet light came on.

But it didn't.

The silhouette paused in mid-speech with the other man. As he did so, the closet door drifted close, leaving a thin slit of an opening.

A moment's reprieve.

Buck moved quickly. Using the narrowness of the closet, he braced his body across it lengthwise, feet against one wall, hands against the other, and shuffled up toward the ceiling—a stretched-out version of his climb up the dumbwaiter shaft. Just as he made it to the crown molding, the door again swung open, and the lights came on. Exposing him.

Anatoli Yakovlev came waddling into the closet, still in conversation with the other man, his face focused toward the floor. He went directly to the Shaw Walker safe and kneeled his bulk to open it, oblivious to Buck's presence above him.

Buck Flynn remained stone. His muscles strained to remain suspended. His breath seizing in his lungs. The air near the ceiling was hot and stuffy. Sweat formed beneath his coveralls. His hands become slick. Beads of perspiration peppered his forehead.

The Russian Station Chief twisted the dial on the safe as the flow of Russian conversation continued.

Buck waited. Watching. His arms quivering.

Halfway through the combination, Yakovlev twisted around to speak emphatically to the man outside, using his hands to dramatize his words.

Open the safe already! Screamed Buck in his mind. Sweat from his forehead gathered into a pool at the bridge of his nose.

Anatoli Yakovlev turned back to finish the combination. Placing his hand on the handle, he yanked down to unlock the door.

The sweat between Buck's eyes became a shimmering bead. Helplessly, he felt it give way to gravity, streaming down the length of his nose to form a liquid drip. He fought to keep still. His arms shaking.

The drop fell.

It plummeted toward the Russian's hand that gripped the safe's handle.

At the very last second, Yakovlev pulled open the door and turned around to respond to something the other man had said.

The drop splashed silently onto the floor in front of the safe.

Yakovlev replied to the man and turned back, reached in, and grabbed the fake *Teleforce* notebook. He stood and left the closet, turning off the light, but leaving the closet door slightly ajar.

Buck could hold his position no longer. If he didn't begin descending, his sweaty palms would give way. Carefully. Slowly. Quietly. He shuttled down to the floor. He lay prone in front of the safe for a full minute, forcing his labored breathing to come in hushed bursts. Listening.

After a minute, he curled into a crouch and edged toward the front of the closet to peer through the slotted opening of the door.

He had only a partial view of the desk. Anatoli Yakovlev stood there, talking with the other man, who remained out of view. Yakovlev was filling the diplomatic pouch with files. Then, to Buck's dismay, he scooped up the tin canisters of film, stuffed them in, and locked the bag.

Buck stifled a groan. The film was now in a politically protected bag, ready to be smuggled into Soviet Russia. The designs for the weapon on their way to Moscow.

Squinting, Buck could see the fake notebook sitting on top of the desk. Yakovlev hadn't packed it into the diplomatic pouch.

A knock came on the office door. Yakovlev glanced up and muttered in Russian. Buck had no view of who was at the door, but heard it open and someone entered. A rapid-fire exchange took place, indistinguishable Russian. Shadows striated along the carpet as figures approached the desk. As they came into view, Buck recognized Vuk Milosh and Aleksandr Feklisov.

The three of them appeared to be arguing. Yakovlev and Feklisov barked at Milosh as if accusing him of something. Milosh shook his head and waved his arms in adamant denial of whatever charge they were leveling his way.

Yakovlev grabbed a file from his desk and thrust it toward Milosh. Scanning the pages in the file, the man's body language morphed. His proud, erect posture deflated, his shoulders slumped, his expression melted into dismay. He eased himself into a nearby chair, eyes fixated on the file.

Another knock came on the office door. Yakovlev trilled his fingers in a come-hither manner. Shadows again striated across the carpet but halted just out of Buck's view.

Milosh, still sitting, ripped his eyes from the file to look up at the unknown visitors. Rage flashed. Leaping from his chair, he grabbed one and yanked them violently into view. A woman in a powder blue evening gown.

Natalie!

Milosh shouted at her in a foreign language, shaking her by the shoulders. She cowered before him, her face downcast.

Buck's initial reaction was to burst from the closet and rush to her aid, but he fought that urge, knowing he could do little to help her. It would only make matters worse.

Milosh waved the file before Natalie's face, spewing a barrage of fearsome shouts. Natalie said not a word. Then he struck her. Backhanded. He put his entire body into it. The sound blasted into the room. Buck felt its vibration from twenty feet away. Natalie crumbled to the floor.

It was all Buck could do to restrain himself from exploding from the closet. His body trembled with rage.

Standing over her, Milosh threw the file folder at her depleted form. The pages coughed up and fluttered like confetti over her body. Natalie sobbed.

Buck ground his teeth. His fists balled up.

Anatoli Yakovlev stepped up to Milosh and placed a hand on his shoulder, as if to console him, and muttered something. Unable to raise his face to look at the Station Chief, Milosh sneered and gave a nearly imperceptible nod.

Yakovlev turned to the other, yet unseen, figure in the room. And without saying a word, he gave a tick of his head toward Natalie. The gesture, quiet and innocuous, had the chilling authority of an executioner.

Yegor Volkov stepped into view.

He reached down and grabbed Natalie by the front of her gown, effortlessly lifting her to her feet as if hauling a bag of garbage. Natalie found her legs...wobbly and shaking.

A brief conversation ensued. Natalie kept her head down, unresponsive. Milosh had turned away as if she were no longer of any consequence. He said little during the conversation. Volkov said nothing.

Yakovlev then reached over the desk to pick up the fake Tesla notebook and handed it to Yegor Volkov, speaking instructions to him. He finished buttoning up his diplomatic pouch and closed his attaché case. As the others moved from view, leaving the room, Yakovlev came strutting towards the closet.

Buck quickly pulled back, flattening himself behind the row of suits hanging there. He had no time to climb the wall again.

The door swung open.

Without turning on the light, Yakovlev reached in to take a topcoat hanging on a peg at the mouth of the closet and a hat next to it. He then closed the door behind him.

In the darkness, Buck waited. Listening. A minute later, he heard the office door close, and the room fell quiet.

He waited another minute before stepping out of the closet into the darkened office. The pages of the file, which had spurred the drama in the room, remained strewn across the floor. He bent down to gather them together. The words written in Cyrillic letters, inscrutable. But one page had a black-and-white photograph of a woman stapled to it: Natka Milosh. Natalie Stevens.

They'd found her out. Obviously, she'd been exposed as a British agent. But what were they going to do with her now?

Decisions needed to be made, and quick.

The microfilm was in the diplomatic pouch. Those canisters could not get back to Russia. If Buck hurried, he could catch up to him and possibly steal them back. He was well-practiced in the art of pickpocketing and sleight of hand. His Pops had trained him well. If he could get within proximity of the Station Chief, there's a chance he could steal the canisters.

But first, he needed to rescue Natalie. She was in grave danger.

He had to get down the dumbwaiter shaft immediately.

But before that, he had to open that closet safe one more time.

Chapter 76

---◆---

Russian Consulate, 11:14 PM

THE TALL, SUAVE GENTLEMAN at the other end of the bar was troubled. Blacksmith sensed it. He had lost a modicum of composure.

While waiting for Arlene's drink order, Blacksmith watched as the man conversed with Arso Jovanovic in an unfamiliar language—possibly Serbo-Croatian—and he had caught the slight change in the fellow's body language.

Earlier, the man had appeared confident, in control, at ease. But as the minutes ticked by, Blacksmith caught the man scanning the room as if looking for someone who wasn't there. His mouth tightened with each scan, a subconscious mannerism that betrayed a growing concern, or a sign of impatience.

Arso Jovanovic remained oblivious to the change, prattling away.

Casually, Blacksmith edged closer, frustrated that he didn't understand the language.

Just as the bartender handed him Arlene's drink, Blacksmith saw a doorman step up to Jovanovic to speak into his ear. Jovanovic nodded.

Turning back to the tall man, Jovanovic, speaking in English, said, "Ah, my friend, it is time for me to depart. Comrade Yakovlev has an automobile ready to take us to the airport. I look forward to seeing you soon in my homeland."

The two shook hands. "Be safe," said the tall man. "Our countries have much work to do."

Blacksmith was stunned. The tall man was an American. Until now, he'd thought him to be Russian, or possibly Yugoslavian. What did that mean? The thief was also American. Were they together?

Two other uniformed men appeared. Associates of Jovanovic. The three of them left through the ballroom entrance. Peering through the opened ballroom doorway, Blacksmith spotted Anatoli Yakovlev greeting the Yugoslavians near the base of the grand staircase. Dressed in an overcoat and hat, Blacksmith could tell that the Russian was leaving the gala — *headed to the airport*, Jovanovic had said.

Standing beyond the Station Chief, Blacksmith spotted Yegor Volkov. With him were Vuk and Natka Milosh. Both looked stricken. Blacksmith sensed the tension between them. One side of the woman's downcast face was flushed red, as if recently slapped.

Were they all going to the airport?

A waiter rushed up to the tall man at the end of the bar. He looked concerned, possibly peeved. He whispered to the man. Blacksmith sensed a hint of familiarity between the two—something beyond a waiter/guest relationship, as if acquainted with each other. They both looked toward the kitchen doors.

The same doors Blacksmith had been watching for the last hour.

Blacksmith recognized the waiter as the one who had taken Lieutenant Clark into the kitchen for his phone call.

They were connected. All of them.

Keeping his back to the men, he edged closer, listening intently.

He heard only indistinguishable whispers that were heated...and in English.

Through the ballroom doors, the group of Russians and Yugoslavians were moving, heading down the hall toward the back of the consulate.

Blacksmith watched them disappear. The coincidences plagued him.

The thief.

Americans.

Russians and Yugoslavians.

Yegor Volkov.

A female physicist.

Long Island.

Laboratory...

Wait! Laboratory. Long Island.

He closed his eyes for a moment, picturing the collage on the wall of his room at the Handover Hotel. Images floated in front of him. History. Photos. Tesla. Long Island.

And it clicked. It had been staring him in the face all along.

Blacksmith now knew what he had to do.

Chapter 77

Russian Consulate, 11:40 PM

GOING DOWN THE DUMBWAITER chute was faster, but more dangerous. Anxiety pulled at him like gravity, creating a reckless hurry that nearly caused him to slip more than once. The shaft was dark and slick; a cold nip blew up from below, but Buck Flynn was sweating beneath his coveralls.

He needed to find Natalie before harm came to her. The lingering question was: where were they taking her? To another room in the consulate? Or were they taking her off-site? Either way, Buck doubted he could rescue her without igniting an international incident.

Deputy Director Carver would not be happy.

Within the darkness of the shaft, he came to the kitchen level. The dumbwaiter doors were closed. Caring little if anyone saw him, he jimmied them open without even listening for activity on the other side. He jumped through the opening. The kitchen staff was cleaning up. Fewer people were about, most focused on their tasks; all except one startled woman who had been standing nearby. She flinched at his sudden appearance. Squishing up her eyebrows in confusion, she spun back to her duties.

Buck rushed around the partition leading to the stairwell. The space was chilly, as if the exit door had recently opened. No one was about. The cough of a car engine revved from out in the alley. Sidling up to the back door, he peered through the glass to find that two automobiles were pulling away. Only the panel van for the catering company remained.

Was Natalie in one of those cars? It was hard to tell. Each had occupants in the back seats, but all were unidentifiable in the darkness.

Glancing down, he realized the suitcases that had been there previously were gone—loaded into the car for Yakovlev's trip.

They were driving away! Possibly with Natalie. Did they intend to take her back to Russia?

What should he do? Should he locate Brookfield to explain? That would waste precious minutes. The cars were leaving now. And even then, would the OSS even care about Natalie's fate? He had switched the notebooks...mission accomplished. The original was in the satchel strapped to his chest. After stressing how OSS fingerprints needed to be nowhere near the operation, the OSS might look upon Natalie's situation as an unnecessary entanglement. Carver and Davies would abandon her in a heartbeat if it meant walking away clean.

No! He needed to catch the cars now. It jeopardized his deal for clemency, for sure, but Natalie needed rescue. Her life was in peril.

Would there be guards in the alley? Would he have to battle them?

Time to find out.

He swung open the door and stepped into the alley. No guards. They must have left with the autos.

He caught the taillights of both cars blinking to turn left onto the street.

He burst into a run. The alley was a block long. His legs churned like pistons. The crisp night air attacked his lungs, tightening the satchel cinched around his chest. Halfway there, he could see that he was too late. Both cars turned in the same direction, out of sight. By the time he got to the end of the alley, they were already a block away, their taillights merging with the other taillights of the city.

Now what?

The front entrance to the Russian Consulate was half a block to his right. Taxis lined the street. He had to follow the Soviets, even if it was in a cab.

Starting toward one of the taxis, he spotted a better alternative. Across from the Consulate stood two men that he recognized as OSS agents. They were watching the front doors as if waiting for someone. Surely, they would help him follow Natalie.

He took a step off the curb to head their way. But stopped short.

An even better option sat directly across from him.

Paddy Tooke's '39 Nash LaFayette. He could see Paddy sitting low behind the steering wheel.

Rushing over to the Nash, he flung open the passenger door, startling Tooke.

"My goodness, boy! Where did you come from?" he exclaimed.

"Quick, we need to follow the Russians to the airport," yelled Buck.

"What are you talking about?"

Buck pointed down the street to where the taillights were escaping. "The Russians have the microfilm for the weapon...they're getting away."

"Buck, I don't know if—"

"Go! If we catch them, I can get the film back."

"How?"

"I can pick pockets. If we can distract them..."

"Buck, Deputy Director Carver—"

"They've captured a British agent!" screamed Buck.

Tooke stared back at him. "How do you know that?"

The muscles in Buck's body bunched. The cars were getting away, nearly out of sight. "Please, Paddy, believe me on this. I'll explain on the way," he pleaded.

Tooke's lips firmed tight. "You're bringing us a mess of trouble, boy."

He turned the key in the ignition and pulled into the street.

Chapter 78

Wardenclyff Laboratory, 11:46 PM

"IT IS DONE," HE whispered.

The hollow vastness of the lab remained unresponsive. Dr. Markovitch failed to notice. An unfettered glee washed over him, causing him to cackle with delight. He wanted to dance and leap with abandon. To shout and sing and whoop.

The machine was complete.

He shot a forgetful glance about the laboratory, longing to include the others in his moment of ecstasy — even the beast. But of course, the laboratory was empty. Had been for hours. Or was it days? He couldn't remember. Only ghosts loomed there. It didn't matter. This was his moment. His machine. It would be crass to include others in his achievement.

They would celebrate his majesty soon enough.

For now, he would luxuriate in the moment by himself. He had built it himself, dammit; he would rejoice by himself. Even Tesla hadn't done this. Sure, he proposed it. But had he built it? No!

I did it!

Nikola. My father. Your genius is mine.

I am Tesla! You and I are one.

He strutted around the machine; chest puffed. Behind his round spectacles, his eyes gleamed with vanity, admiring its streamlined design, the contours...its majesty.

Nearly fifteen feet in length, the apparatus, in reality, was four machines in one. Each part critical to the functionality of the whole.

The first aspect of the machine he called the *Womb*. It gave birth to the electromagnetic beams. This had been the tricky part all along. He needed to create beams without the use of a high vacuum; to be produced in free air. He accomplished this by engineering a vacuum tube with one end open to the atmosphere, allowing the accelerated projectiles to be conducted into the air through a valvular conduit. Tricky yes. But not unachievable for a man of his genius.

I am Tesla!

The second aspect of the *Teleforce* weapon generated powerful electrical forces. Sixty million volts! The forces used to propel the particles. The current upon which the beams would ride. He giggled to himself. He called this part of the machine *Old Sparky*, after the electric chair, which had created so much debate in the war between AC and DC currents at the turn of the century, as well as the war between Edison and Tesla. He thought himself quite clever to have named it such. However, the original *Old Sparky's* power was limited; it only killed men one at a time; this could kill thousands.

Rise Teleforce. Rise.

The third aspect he called *The Surger*. A high potential terminal that took the electrical forces created by *Old Sparky* and magnified them, much as a speaker amplifies sound, increasing and sustaining the voltage to dazzling levels. Numerous bulbs of insulating material surrounded the exterior of *The Surger*. Inside each bulb was an electrode of thin sheet metal that had been rounded and exhausted to the highest vacuum capacity.

I did that! My hands. I'm its creator.

And the fourth aspect of the machine was the best of all.

The Gun.

The nozzle projected tremendous electrical forces. An intense concentration of energy in minute, highly charged particles fired from the tubular barrel in a single row—the beam no thicker than a pencil—and with no dispersion whatsoever, so that the concentrated ray could travel great distances with no loss of energy.

I am Apollyon. Destroyer.

The exhilaration. The triumph. Aleksandr Feklisov would be so proud. His friend and collaborator. He couldn't wait to reveal it to him.

He only needed to make sure it was fully operable. Yes, he had made tests all along, documenting each successful stage. But now it was time to bring it to life.

Dr. Frederick Markovitch reached down and flipped the first toggle switch to awaken his machine.

A glorious electric hum resounded. The apparatus vibrated.

Electricity surged.

It was alive.

Chapter 79

Manhattan, New York, 11:52 PM

"THEY'RE TURNING ONTO THE Queensboro Bridge," yelped Buck Flynn. He was leaning forward, hands on the dashboard, his face nearly touching the windshield. "I can still see them. Hurry."

Paddy Tooke remained quiet and tense, both hands gripping the wheel. His eyes squinted at the stream of taillights in front of them. He wasn't sure which ones they were following, but he pushed the Nash for all it had, weaving in and out of traffic. They took the corner approaching the bridge fast enough to tilt the car.

"Why would they be going to Queens?" cried Buck. He couldn't keep the panic from his voice. All he could think about was the danger Natalie was in.

"They'll be going to the New York Municipal Airport," said Paddy evenly, using his cop voice to ease Buck's anxious state. "That's where Yakovlev's transport plane will leave from."

"We have to catch them before they leave," said Buck.

"Tell me again about this British agent they're supposed to have captured?" asked Paddy.

Buck glanced his way. Shadows of passing bridge girders flickered over Paddy's face. Buck could read the skepticism imprinted there.

"It's a woman," said Buck. "Her name is Natalie Stevens. She's married to that Milosh fellow."

"Vuk Milosh?"

"Yeah, that's the one." Buck's teeth ground together. The image of Milosh smacking Natalie infuriating him.

"How do you know she's a British agent?"

"She told me."

"Oh? Just like that?"

Buck heard the doubt drenching his voice. He turned from Paddy's glare. "I knew her before."

"Before what?"

"Before all of this," said Buck, with a wave of his hand. "She was my girl once. And when war broke out in Europe, she left to become an agent for the SOE."

"Your girl? You just said she was married to Milosh."

"Yeah, that's right," muttered Buck bitterly. His face felt tight.

Paddy grew quiet. Buck braced himself for a wave of righteous judgment. But all Paddy said was, "And she was at the gala?"

Buck nodded.

"That's quite a coincidence, isn't it?"

Buck snapped around. "What is that supposed to mean?"

Paddy shrugged. "It must have been surprised you to find her inside the Russian Consulate."

"It nearly stopped my heart. I thought my cover was blown."

"It sounds like it was blown. And you're sure she's a British agent?"

"I'm sure," he stated firmly. "That German spy was there tonight too—Blacksmith."

Paddy merely nodded. "Yes, I watched him go in. Tell me everything that happened inside."

So, Buck told him. He started at the beginning, from encountering Natalie, to being confronted by Sava Kosanovic's secretary, to shaking hands with Blacksmith, to watching the Russians expose Natalie as a spy and smacking her around.

Once he finished, Paddy asked, "What did Walter Brookfield say to all this?"

Buck remained quiet.

Paddy shot a glance at him. "Wait! You left without telling him?"

"I had to. Natalie..." He didn't finish, anguish overcame him.

They were gaining on the two cars. They were less than a hundred yards behind them. Buck's pulse raced. He was trying to think of a way to save Natalie and yet get to the rolls of film from the diplomatic pouch at the same time. Was it even possible?

Suddenly, a tinny voice screeched from somewhere within the car: *"Tooke! Where the hell are you? One of my men saw you take off."*

Buck's eyes fell to the walkie-talkie laying on the seat.

It was Phillip Carver's voice.

He glanced up at Paddy.

"I better answer that," said Paddy. "We're already in enough trouble."

Buck quickly scooped up the device, pulling it away from Paddy's reach. "I can't let you do that," he said.

"What are you talking about? We've got to let them know what's happening."

"And what do you think they're going to tell us to do? They'll tell us to stand down."

"Deputy Director Carver would want us to get the microfilm back from the Russians," reasoned Paddy.

"Yes, he would," Buck agreed. "But Carver would also be willing to throw Natalie to the wolves. It's best we don't answer him."

"Buck, be reasonable. Carver is in charge. I'll have to answer for all this."

"They're turning!" cried Buck, pointing beyond the windshield.

But he was only half right. One vehicle was turning; the other kept going straight.

"The first car is turning toward the New York Municipal Airport," said Paddy.

"Well, where the hell is the other one going?" shouted Buck.

Paddy squinted through the windshield, watching the taillights separate in different directions.

Buck's confused mind scrambled for an explanation. Why would they be splitting up? Why would one car be going to the airport and the other not? It made little sense.

Then it hit him. Of course! They're not taking Natalie to the airport at all. They had planned Yakovlev's trip long before they'd discovered Natalie to be a spy. The arrangements set. They couldn't smuggle her through customs and onto an international flight. Security would be tight. They had no intention of taking Natalie back to Russia.

Which meant they had other plans for her. Buck shivered at the thought.

"Follow the other car!" screamed Buck. "The one that went straight."

Then Paddy did something that nearly caused Buck to jump out of his skin. He pulled the Nash off to the side of the road and parked.

"What are you doing?" yelled Buck. "They're getting away."

"We have a decision to make, Buck," said Paddy calmly.

"Decision?" he wailed. "Follow that car!"

"Tooke!" squawked the walkie-talkie. *"Where are you, dammit! Your trained monkey has disappeared."*

Ignoring the voice, Buck cried, "That other car has Natalie in it."

"Maybe, but the car going to the airport has the microfilm in it," said Paddy. "We need to make the right decision about this."

Buck wanted to scream. He shot a glance down the road. The taillights of the second car were tiny red stars slipping away.

"Tooke, answer me!" yelled Phillip Carver's tinny voice. *"Brookfield can't find Flynn. He's gone!"*

The taillights were getting smaller. Buck had no choice. Reaching into the leather satchel strapped across his chest, he fumbled around the Tele-force notebook to grab the item he'd taken from Yakovlev's safe.

The pistol.

"Follow. That. Car." said Buck Flynn, his eyes narrowing. The pistol pointing at Tooke's chest.

Paddy glanced down. "Aw, you don't want to be going and doing that, boy."

"I said, follow that car."

"Or you'll shoot me?"

Buck's hand shook. He stole a glance down the road. The taillights were pinpricks.

"You really love her, don't you?" whispered Paddy.

"Please, Paddy," Buck whispered back, his eyes wet. "They held her hostage for over a year. We have to save her."

"She's an SOE agent. She knew what she was getting into."

"We owe it to her."

"But the microfilm."

"The hell with the microfilm. They're going to kill her!"

"Tooke, respond, dammit! Where's Flynn? Where's that notebook?"

The night swallowed the taillights. Gone. As if they'd never existed. Buck let out a groan. They'd never catch them now. Paddy glanced down the road. His lips firmed.

"Do you even know where they're taking her?" he asked.

"No," he choked. His body trembled. "And now we lost them sitting here arguing."

"She didn't tell you anything that would be a hint—"

"Wait," cried Buck. "She said something about a laboratory. It's on some cliff."

"There's a thousand cliffs on Long Island."

"She told me the name...what was it? I think it was Warren's cliff."

"Wait," said Paddy, leaning in. "Did she say Warren's cliff? or Wardenclyff?"

"That's the place! Wardenclyff."

"Impossible. Wardenclyff was Nikola Tesla's old laboratory. They tore it down years ago."

"But she told me she's been working there for over a year."

Paddy became pensive, rubbing his chin. "The tower is gone for sure. But I suppose there could still be a laboratory underground."

Buck felt a spark of hope. Paddy was thinking it through. He flicked a look through the windshield, searching the road. His hope vanished. "Oh Lord," he coughed. "They're gone. And I don't know how to get there. She didn't tell me."

Paddy sat back. "Well, fortunately, boy, the fellow you're holding at gunpoint knows exactly where it is."

Buck looked down at the pistol. He'd forgotten about it. He instantly dropped it on the seat as if it had become electrified.

Paddy put the car in gear and pulled out into traffic. The Nash gained speed.

"The microfilm's important," uttered Paddy.

Approaching the turnoff for the airport, Buck's heart palpated. His breath choking in his throat. He gripped the armrest of the passenger door.

Paddy zipped past the turnoff, staying on Route 25A.

He glanced at Buck. "But so is a human life."

Buck pressed a hand against his chest as if to subdue the convulsion taking place behind his ribs.

"While stationed at Camp Mills, I once drove out to see the tower. It was a magnificent piece of work for its day."

"Thanks, Paddy," he whispered.

"Don't thank me yet. Wait until we've saved your girl." Paddy shook his head. "Phillip Carver will be plenty pissed."

"I wouldn't have shot you," said Buck weakly. "You know that, right?"

"The truth is; you couldn't have shot me." Paddy Tooke grinned at him across the darkness. "The safety was on the entire time, you idiot."

Chapter 80

⸺◦⸺

Wardenclyff Laboratory, Saturday, 12:09 AM

A CERULEAN GLOW CRACKLED from the nozzle of the gun, a short burst of power—the length of a rifle barrel—fizzing with lethal energy. Bright. Thin. Hot. Beautiful.

Wearing a pair of welding goggles, Dr. Markovitch gazed upon it rapturously. He so wanted to touch it. Feel it on his skin. Watch it dance with the molecules of his hand. But he wrestled that foolhardy thought back into its cage. It would be insanity to touch it that way, to stroke it, to feel its caress.

Disintegration loomed in that beautiful, innocent glow.

He prudently dowsed it, powering down the machine and with it the temptation to play within the glorious beam he'd created.

Success! The machine worked. But it had yet to prove its purpose. He had desperately wanted to lengthen the beam and strike an object, but did not trust the full-throttle capacity of the weapon within the confined space of the laboratory. The beam could wreak havoc. And possibly bring down the walls and earth around him.

No, he needed open space.

And a target. Something to obliterate.

An idea crawled into his skull. And he cackled with delight. Of course. Why hadn't he thought of it before? He needed to get the machine out of the laboratory, and the answer was right there in front of him.

The elevator lift.

If he could wheel the machine onto the steel platform, he could use the electric motors of the riser to raise the weapon through the shaft to the cement house three stories above him, and then open the hydraulic ceiling doors to the night sky.

Yes! Once in the open sky, he could have his choice of targets.

What shall I destroy? A plane? A ship? A building?

His hands shook with anticipation. His eyes wild with glee.

"Ah!" He whispered to the ghosts in the room. "I know the perfect target. It makes sense. It comes full circle. It's meant to be."

He rushed across the laboratory floor and into Natka's office. Against the right-hand wall stood a bookshelf. He scoured the titles, finding the book he needed.

An atlas.

He thumbed his way through the pages until landing on a certain section.

Perfect! The map had a special inset for New York City.

He wrote down the specific coordinates, the longitude, and latitude to the exact minutes. Geopolorazation. Coordinates to be programmed into the weapon. Aiming the gun with precision. Pinpointing the target.

The New Yorker Hotel.

That's where it all started. His abduction. His recruitment. His journey to glory.

Nikola Tesla resided there.

My father shall see my glory.

He closed his eyes and howled at the irony of it.

Strangely, no one had bothered to tell Dr. Markovitch that Nikola Tesla had died seven days ago.

Chapter 81

Wardenclyff, Saturday, 2:15 AM

NATALIE KNEW SHE WOULD soon be dead. They'd told her as much back at the consulate. The others in the automobile shot occasional glances her way, lethal glances. Anger filled the car like concrete. The radio off. No one talked. No sound. Just the whir of the tires...and thick, soundless hate.

She felt hopeless

There was little chance of escape. She sat wedged between two men in the back seat of the sedan, the guards that had been standing outside the back door. They were large, scowling men. Their eyes lacked mercy. Much like Yegor Volkov, who sat in the front passenger seat like a rock sculpted to resemble a man.

Vuk drove. His hate intense. Smoldering like lava.

They were almost to the laboratory.

How quickly things had changed tonight. Like an earthquake shifting the plates of her earth. Disruption. For a few enchanting moments, she had been enjoying the gala. Fooling herself into believing that there was a life beyond her pretense. She hadn't been in a social setting for months. Her circle of associations being limited and well-guarded. For those few brief moments, she had been free to chat about inane subjects like gowns, jewelry, and hairstyles with the other women.

Then, with a tap on the shoulder from her husband, her world imploded.

Harry.

She had never expected to see him again. Ever. She thought of him every day. And since returning to New York, she often fantasized about encountering him on the street, playing the scene in her mind. How they would spot one another, their eyes locking, the crowd and traffic evaporating. How they would slowly walk toward one another and then fall into each other's arms. The World's Fair all over again. He would sweep her up and carry her away from everything—from spying, from pretending, from communists, from death rays...from Vuk.

But it hadn't happened that way. It had been a disaster. Now she was angry with herself for running out on him while out on the balcony. She'd done it again. She'd left him for a second time. Without explanation, without saying goodbye. Driven by fear and suspicion. Their last moments on earth together, and she'd ruined it.

And now, in a few minutes, she'd be dead. But he would live on...always wondering whether or not she loved him.

The automobile turned onto the gravel road leading to the Wardenclyff laboratory. The moon was a sliver in the endless winter sky. The stars so much brighter here than in the city. The cement block building was silhouetted just ahead. Cold and harmless-looking. Like a forgotten storage facility. Her final tomb.

They pulled into the parking lot. Wordlessly, the men got out of the vehicle, dragging Natalie from the backseat. She attempted to resist, even though she knew it to be pointless. Upon seeing her drag her heels, Vuk stepped between the two men holding her and hammered a vicious punch straight into her face. Pain blasted through her cranium. Her head snapped back. She crumpled with a groan.

"Move, traitorous bitch," he spat.

Blood spurt from her mouth. The world spun. A tight ringing screeched within her skull.

Vuk stood there, his lips curled back in a cruel grin. A gleam of satisfaction in his eye. She loathed him. A heartless monster. Her husband. If only it had been him she'd pushed off the building that night. She could live with that.

He turned away, withdrawing keys from his pocket to unlock the door to the building. But something caused him to stop short. He twisted a quizzical glance over his shoulder at Yegor Volkov.

"Do you hear that?" he asked.

Volkov said nothing, his eyes tightening into mean, curious slits. Maybe he was listening, maybe not.

"That hum...do you hear it?" repeated Milosh.

Natalie, drooping bonelessly between the two guards, lifted her head. The dull ringing from being punched had subsided, leaving a new sound, one she thought only she could hear. But Vuk heard it too. A metallic droning layered over an electric hum. The noise struck her as being familiar. What was it? It resonated from within the building, growing louder, as if coming towards them.

Then she realized. Someone was running the elevator lift.

A new noise pierced the night. A grinding scrape. Like corrugated tin being dragged over a concrete slab.

"What the hell is that?" yelled Vuk Milosh, backing away from the locked door to gaze at the building.

The two men restraining Natalie grew nervous. They yanked her back toward the car, their heads swiveling spastically in search of the noise.

Then, from the roof of the building, a stream of light split the darkness, casting a yellow glow around the area.

The entire group backed up to the automobile, staring upward.

"What on earth!" yelled Milosh. "Someone is opening the roof doors."

The split of light grew wider. Shadows played across the top of the building. Warm air billowed from the crack, hitting the chilly night air to create clouds of steam. An image emerged from the building. Rising like a phantom from damnation.

"It's Markovitch," said Milosh, stepping closer. "He's trying to escape."

Natalie focused her blurry vision to squint at Dr. Frederick Markovitch riding the lift up from the opening in the roof—a set of welding goggles pushed back on his forehead. She blinked with wonder.

On the platform next to him rested an enormous piece of machinery, gleaming and ominous. A science-fiction ray-gun come to life. The massive barrel, ringed with chrome tubing, pointed straight upward as if to do battle with the hosts of heaven.

The electric motors screeched to a halt. The noise fell away, leaving a sickly hush. Then, from his perch, Markovitch spotted the people grouped below in the parking lot. He cocked his head, curious. Recognition came.

"Ah, Dr. Milosh," he yelled down. "I'm so glad you've made it for the ultimate test. And you've brought guests. Reporters? Good, good. They too shall bear witness to my genius." He laughed, loud and wild. With a dramatic flair, he waved his arms over the device, like a model presenting the newest sedan at an auto show. "I introduce to you my very own child...the Teleforce weapon."

Natalie, propped up between the two guards, stared in disbelief.

Milosh stepped forward. "Markovitch," he yelled. "Come down from there. Instantly."

Markovitch gave a mocking snort. "Come down? I think not. I must first test my weapon...my child." His visage turned angry, as if thrown by a switch. Moving to the edge of the roof, he shook a finger Natalie's way. "You couldn't do it, sweet Natka. You failed at every turn. You wouldn't listen to my advice. You treated me as if I were a child. Like dirt beneath your shoe. So, I built it myself. My way."

"He's gone mad," she whispered.

"Shut up," sneered Milosh.

Markovitch straightened himself, shoulders back. "And now you will see my glory...my genius. Gentlemen...and sweet Natka, I now shall give you, Teleforce."

And with that, he clamped the goggles over his eyes and flicked toggles across the face of a panel jutting from the side of the mechanical beast.

A bright hum resounded.

"Wait until you see the beam, Natka," cried Markovitch over the noise. "It is so beautiful."

"Markovitch...get down from there," screamed Milosh.

Ignoring him, Markovitch's hands continued to play across the face of the panel.

The hum increased in pitch. High and piercing. The platform vibrated. Power pulsated from the roof. Natalie felt tremors beneath her feet.

Milosh turned to Volkov and jammed the laboratory door keys into his hand. "Get that fool down from there," he yelled.

"Watch, sweet Natka," yelled Markovitch.

His arm yanked down on a lever and a new electric noise cackled in the night, sending shivers across Natalie's skin. A brilliant blue beam erupted from the nose of the gun, shooting up toward the stars. As far as the eye could see.

The birth of a death ray.

Chapter 82

———◦———

Long Island, Saturday, 2:32 AM

PADDY TOOKE SLOWED THE car to a crawl to squint at the roadway tapering off into the darkness. They were approaching an intersection. The road signs were sparse out here in the country, as if the turnoffs were a secret kept between the locals.

"The place has changed in the last thirty years," offered Paddy quietly.

The juices in Buck's stomach churned. Acid came into his throat. He noticed a hint of confusion creasing Paddy's forehead. "Please don't tell me we're lost," he croaked. "I thought you've been here before."

Paddy was quiet, intense, watching the road.

Buck tried to remain calm, but a brutal unease clamped down on him. He had no control over the situation. No idea where they were, or where they were going. It felt as if they'd been driving on Route 25A forever. He kept looking for a cliff; but had to remind himself there was no actual cliff — Paddy had told him so. The landscape was flat, and they were at least a mile inland from the ocean. He kept thinking the laboratory had a tower, but then recalled that Paddy told him the tower had been torn down decades ago.

It was useless. He didn't know what to look for.

The countryside was unlit, mysterious. They hadn't seen another car for miles. Frustration and worry were shredding his hope of finding Natalie.

To make matters worse, the Nash was merely inching along the road as Paddy's eyes combed the area, looking for landmarks. He looked befuddled.

"Can't we go faster?" wailed Buck. "We'll never catch them."

"Going faster will only get us lost at a quicker rate," retorted Paddy. "Patience, boy."

But Buck had left all of his patience back at the Russian Consulate. He was grateful Paddy had followed the second car, yet angry that they'd let the car get away from them while talking it over. The hope of finding Natalie was being dashed.

They were lost...and going excruciatingly slow.

Something caught his eye. A flash.

Bending his neck to peer up through the windshield into the night sky, Buck saw a thin line of glowing blue light piercing the ether above them, as if someone had stretched a lit tightrope from earth to heaven.

"What is that?" he asked.

Paddy stopped the car in the middle of the road to glance where Buck was pointing.

"What on earth?" muttered Paddy, astonished.

Paddy's eyes tracked the beam down from where it seemed to emanate behind a nearby stand of trees. Beyond the trees lay the faint impression of a gravel road leading from the highway.

"We may have found the laboratory," said Paddy, as he released the clutch. "But I have a very bad feeling about it."

Chapter 83

Wardenclyff, Saturday, 2:42 AM

"My beam. Isn't it beautiful, sweet Natka," shouted Dr. Markovitch over the sizzling clamor. "So beautiful."

Natalie stared, dumbfounded, at the horrific image. The fool had done it. Without the notebook. Without her help. Without Tesla. He'd built the particle beam weapon. All her efforts to thwart the project had been in vain.

But then, everything had been in vain, hadn't it? Her sham marriage to Vuk, leaving Harry, joining the SOE...and, oh Lord...murdering a fellow scientist. All in vain. No one could stop them now.

"Will you look at that," whispered Vuk, mesmerized.

Dr. Markovitch stepped to the edge of the roof, bending slightly as if to tell them all a secret.

"And here's the good part," he yelled down. "In a few minutes, my father, Nikola, will see my beautiful, splendid beam."

An icy terror poured over Natalie. "W...what do you mean, Dr. Markovitch?" she stammered.

If Milosh, standing nearby, had heard her, he didn't show it; his eyes remained fixated on the streak in the sky. Captivated by the sight, the men restraining Natalie slightly relaxed their grip on her.

"I have programmed the beam," said Markovitch. He glanced at a dial on the panel. "In exactly eleven minutes and twenty-seven seconds, the beam will strike its target at full capacity."

With a thrust of her shoulders, she shrugged away from the two men holding her and took one brazen step forward. "What target, Dr. Markovitch?"

"Why the New Yorker Hotel, of course!"

"What?" cried Natalie. "Have you gone mad? You can't do that."

"I must do it," replied Markovitch indignantly. "My father, Nikola, must see my beam."

"But you will kill hundreds of innocent people," she shouted.

Milosh, suddenly realizing Natalie's movements, grabbed her by the neck and thrust her backward, slamming her into the side of the car. "I told you to shut up!"

Natalie wobbled, but stayed on her feet. A sharp pain radiated through her shoulder.

Upon the platform, a shadowed figure appeared on the far side of the apparatus, climbing through a hatch on the roof. Yegor Volkov.

Natalie straightened herself. She could tell that Dr. Markovitch appeared to be wrestling with the words she'd just spoken to him. A bizarre specter of madness, he talked to himself, his hands gesturing in spasms as if attempting to reason out the logic of murdering hundreds of people with his creation.

She needed to coax him into turning off the machine. She shot a fearful glance at Vuk. Chances were high he would strike her again, but she had to convince him to help stop this awful weapon.

"If I can get up on that roof, I may talk him out of this," she said to Vuk. "And I could stop the machine."

Vuk cocked his head at her, wonder seeping into his eyes as if she'd just spoken blasphemy. His lips curled into a wicked grin. "Stop it? It sounds like an excellent test to me."

Natalie gasped. "But all those people."

Vuk shrugged. "Casualties of war."

"It's murder."

"It's war!"

Natalie felt nauseated, repulsed by this creature of evil that was her husband. How could she have ever allowed herself to be beguiled by his charms? To marry him? To let him touch her? She shivered.

Dr. Markovitch was shouting again. He had decided. "No, sweet Natka. I can't let you deter me. Nikola must witness my beam. He would want it that way."

Yegor Volkov was circling from around the backside of the weapon, crouching low, drawing closer to Markovitch.

Natalie again stepped forward. "Dr. Markovitch," she shouted. "Uncle Niko can't see your beam. He's dead."

Markovitch jerked, startled at the news. "Dead?"

"Uncle Niko died of a heart attack a week ago."

From behind her, Milosh raged. She felt his heat coming toward her, the crunch of his shoes on the gravel. "That's the last time I'll tell you to shut up, bitch," he spat through clenched teeth.

Grabbing her by the hair, he twisted her in a violent circle before slamming her to the gravel. She struck the ground hard, bits of stone embedded in her flesh. Her gown tearing.

Milosh withdrew a pistol from his jacket.

"Nikola is dead?" cried Markovitch from the roof. "This can't be."

From the ground, Natalie lifted her head. Wiping gravel from her cheek. She could tell that the particle beam had moved, systematically lowering and twisting on its axis. The machine was drawing a bead on its distant target. The fiery flame intensified, sparking with dancing molecules, hot and full of voltage.

On the roof, Yegor Volkov closed in on the doctor. Fifteen feet away.

From her peripheral vision, Natalie became aware of Vuk pointing a revolver at her head. She turned his way to stare into cruel eyes.

"Goodbye, dear wife," he hissed. "Volkov was supposed to do this job, but I'm glad it's me instead. You made a fool of me and it gives me great pleasure to kill you."

The gun barrel appeared massive. The world warped, the laws of perspective melting into strange angles. She only saw the dull gray noses of bullets nested in the cylinder. The hammer cocked back.

From some distant land, Dr. Markovitch cried out, his voice wailing. "My father, Nikola, will never see my beautiful beam. Natka, look at it. Its beauty draws me. Watch me touch it."

Milosh hesitated. The words he'd just heard startling him. Both he and Natalie slowly turned to see Dr. Markovitch stepping toward the nose of the gun. His hands up, as if worshipping the unearthly glow.

Volkov was nearly to him.

A cry choked in Natalie's throat. She went to scream but...

It was too late.

As if to embrace the fiery stream of light, Dr. Markovitch stepped into it.

A horrible crackling hiss. A sickly illumination. A vibrant pink mist burst in the air. An eerie dandelion of exploding wetness; it carried along the length of the beam like a cloud. Then nothing. As if Dr. Markovitch had vanished by the swipe of a magician's wand.

A tremor of horror flitted through Natalie.

Vuk Milosh gasped at the sight. "Son of a—"

Yegor Volkov stood on the rooftop, stunned, covered with the damp red remains of Dr. Markovitch.

The particle beam weapon continued to lower, searching for its programmed target. Only minutes left.

Natalie needed to stop it. She was the only one who could. She snapped her gaze toward her husband. He gaped at the empty space that had been Dr. Markovitch, dumbfounded. The pistol drooped in his hand. She needed to move—quickly.

But before she could react, something else was taking place. Changing everything.

Chapter 84

———◆———

Wardenclyff, Saturday, 2:54 AM

FOR PADDY, THE GREATEST drawback to having a Divine-Cop Voice speaking to your inner-man is that others cannot hear it, nor can they comprehend the ability if they aren't used to its mysterious sway. Dottie comprehends it. She not only recognizes the gift but encourages its manifestation.

Others...not so much.

From the moment they had spotted that streak of naked electricity in the sky, Paddy Tooke's inner warning system clanged. Everything in him screamed caution. He tried to relate that caution to Buck Flynn, pleading for restraint and discernment; but the young man ignored the Divine warning. Distress raged. Compulsion ruled.

As Paddy pulled the Nash into the mouth of the driveway, Buck exploded from the car like a quarter horse bursting from the starting gate. He rushed up the gravel road, stolen pistol in hand, before Paddy had even turned off the engine. Paddy's first panicked concern was whether the boy had remembered to flick off the pistol's safety. Then he worried whether the gun was even loaded?

Paddy leaped after him, his own handgun drawn, scurrying to catch up. The boy was fast. Paddy whispered harshly, ordering Buck to slow down so they could attack the situation shrewdly. Buck ignored him. Distress for the female British agent blinded him.

They came around the last corner of the driveway, where a thin stand of leafless trees helped to conceal their presence. Buck hesitated—finally—staring at the bizarre world before them. Paddy caught up. A small gravel parking lot lay spread out in front of a one-story block building set at the other end. A solitary automobile was parked there.

But it was the scene on top of the building that gave them pause.

A curious apparatus on the roof sizzled and hummed—the source of the electric stream slicing the night sky. A man stood next to the machine. And although Paddy and Buck were too far to hear, they could tell he was shouting to people in the driveway. Four people stood there. Two men cowered near the front bumper of the car, clearly frightened. Standing between the vehicle and the building was Vuk Milosh and a woman dressed in an evening gown. Paddy recognized her from the photos of Nikola Tesla's funeral — a woman the OSS had failed to identify and hadn't thought significant. A woman he now knew to be Milosh's wife — and, according to Buck, a British agent.

Then, two frightening things happened instantly.

First, Milosh ruthlessly grabbed the woman by her hair, twisting her full circle, as if heaving a shot-put and cruelly hurled her to the gravel. Then, as if to execute her, he leveled a revolver at her head.

But it was the second thing that almost stopped Paddy's heart cold.

The man on the roof, standing next to the machine, exploded into a vivid pink puff of smoke. Gone.

Paddy had no time to be shocked. Buck sprang toward the scene.

"Cover the men by the car," he yelled over his shoulder.

Paddy grabbed for him. But Buck was already running pell-mell toward the building. Paddy's inner alarm raged. It didn't feel right. Raising his weapon, he moved cautiously toward the men standing by the car.

Buck smashed into Vuk Milosh's blindside like a blitzing linebacker. It was a powerful collision. Buck put his shoulder into it, driving the other man face-first into the gravel. Milosh's revolver skittered across the driveway. Somehow, Buck remained upright. His pistol came up, leveled at the man sprawled in the dirt.

Buck's sudden appearance startled the two men by the car. It bought Paddy Tooke the time he needed to be on top of them.

"Don't move," he yelled.

They froze. Hands in the air.

"You got 'em covered over there, Paddy?" shouted Buck.

"Got them," he answered, his nerves on edge.

The woman on the ground stirred. Raising herself slowly from the ground.

"Harry? Is that you?" she asked, shocked by his sudden appearance.

"It's me," he answered. "You okay?"

Vuk Milosh squirmed in the driveway, turning around to face his attacker. He squinted at the silhouette brandishing the pistol.

"Clark?" mumbled Vuk Milosh from the ground. "Lieutenant John Clark? What are you doing here?

Natalie stood, trembling. "How...how did you find me?"

Buck shrugged. "It wasn't so hard. Was it Paddy?"

Paddy didn't answer. His alarm was screaming. It had been too easy. Something wasn't right.

And suddenly he knew why.

In their haste, they had failed to notice a fourth man standing on the roof, lost in the background of the dazzling ray gun. Because of the angle of his position, Paddy couldn't physically see him, only his shadow playing along the surface of the driveway.

And that shadow was taking aim with a pistol.

Shots rang out.

Two bullets struck Buck Flynn square in the chest. He groaned. Staggered. And collapsed to the gravel in a death sprawl.

Chapter 85

———◇———

Wardenclyff, Saturday, 3:01 AM

"Harry," screamed the woman.

Paddy gasped.

Buck lay twisted in the gravel, motionless.

Then havoc broke out.

Paddy sensed that the woman—so exposed in the open—was next to die. He leaped away from the two men he'd been guarding to shoot recklessly up toward the roofline. He hoped to draw fire away from her. With luck, he may hit the shooter. But he was firing blind, and both shots went wild. However, as he moved into the driveway, the angle of his position changed, and he could now see the man standing on the edge of the building, aiming at the woman below.

Yegor Volkov, the Russian assassin.

Startled by Paddy's rushing form, Volkov hesitated for a heartbeat, as if deciding which target to take out first, the weaponless woman, or the man firing at him. That pause was just long enough for Paddy to take aim and shoot. The bullet struck him in the upper torso, twisting him around. Volkov's handgun flung from his grip, bouncing along the rooftop and off the building. The large figure flailed for two seconds and then stumbled backward, toward the machine, falling out of sight onto the platform.

On the ground twenty feet away, Vuk Milosh scrabbled across the gravel toward his own revolver.

The machine continued to buzz and hum.

To Paddy's right, the woman dove toward Buck's body. No! Not his body...the pistol lying on the ground next to him.

Hearing gravel kicking up behind him, Paddy spun around to find the two men he'd been covering charging hard.

Milosh reached his revolver.

Even in her gown, the woman was quick and nimble. She tumbled across the driveway, swept up the handgun, and rolled up into a firing stance. Her SOE training obvious.

Paddy swung his weapon toward the rushing guards. Both were yanking handguns from their jackets. He fired one shot.

Behind him, husband and wife swept up their weapons simultaneously.

The woman pulled the trigger...

Nothing.

"Damn," she screamed.

Buck had left the safety on.

Milosh fired.

The bullet hissed past her, barely missing, the wind of it lifting strands of hair.

Paddy's shot blossomed a hole in the chest of the first guard. He fell instantly. The other hesitated before bringing up his gun.

The woman fumbled to find the safety of the unfamiliar pistol. Milosh fired again. The bullet grazed her jacket, tearing away threads.

Paddy fired again. The impact struck the second guard square in the face. He dropped—dead before hitting the ground.

The woman raised Buck's pistol again, taking aim.

Paddy swung his weapon around.

She fired. Paddy fired...his last bullet...the shots resounding as one.

A bullet slammed a hole into Milosh's forehead, his face a mask of surprise. He fell like a sack of wheat.

Seven seconds of complete chaos...then quiet. The only sounds remaining: the rasping of breath from Paddy and the woman...and the continuing electric drone of the weapon.

"You okay, ma'am?" asked Paddy.

"Yes," she choked. "I...I just killed my husband."

He laid a hand on her shoulder. "It was my shot that killed him," Paddy said, wondering if that was the case. "You were defending yourself."

She looked up at him, forlorn. "I know."

Paddy glanced over at Buck Flynn, stretched lifeless in the gravel. His heart sank.

"Harry..." whimpered Natalie. She took a step toward the body but stopped short. She trembled. Turning to Paddy, tears in her eyes, she said. "The weapon needs to be stopped immediately. It's programmed to strike the New Yorker Hotel any second now."

Paddy's jaw dropped. "Can it reach the city from here?" he asked.

"There's no dissipation of energy with a particle beam weapon. It'll reach. But we need to hurry. There are only a couple of minutes remaining on the timer."

Paddy shot another quick look at Buck's body, and the two of them rushed to the laboratory door.

The woman twisted the knob. Locked.

"I forgot," she cried. "The door self-locks when it closes. Volkov had the only set of keys. Now I'll never get to the machine in time."

Overhead, the noise of the weapon changed. They felt the change in the vibrations of the building and the thrumming of the gravel beneath their feet.

Paddy's God-voice was screaming.

Chapter 86

Wardenclyff, 3:04 AM

THE DARK FELT DEEP — like a well plummeting into forever. He scaled the darkness, clawing at the well's black walls. Toiling. Aiming for the glimmer of light at the surface.

Opening his eyes, he saw stars blinking in a liquid sky. His chest throbbed as if his sternum had exploded. Breathing was laborious. He wanted to move...or at least test movement, to see if it was possible.

Buck Flynn lifted a hand to his chest, his fingers spider-walking over the damage. Two bullet holes. The tips of his fingers slid into the cavities. Dry. Papery.

With winded breaths, he propped himself up on his elbows to peer down.

No blood.

The satchel strapped to his chest was split open. The Tesla notebook inside, shredded by the bullets. Flipping open the top flap, he reached in behind the notebook and withdrew the caddy containing his lock-picking tools, bent and misshapen...two slugs burrowed into the caddy's leather.

Thanks, Pops...my inheritance saved me again.

He became aware of the earth trembling beneath him and of voices riding an electric hum. Twisting his head toward the building, he spotted

Paddy Tooke and Natalie Stevens attempting to open a locked door. Paddy was swinging at the knob with the butt of his gun.

"I can unlock that if you want me to," he offered, still propped up on his elbows.

The two of them swung around, stunned by the sound of his voice.

—◦—

Helping him to his feet, Paddy wanted to hug the boy, but there was no time. Seconds mattered. The particle beam weapon grew perilously level with the earth, the streak of hot light nearly touching the treetops. Celebration over Buck's resurrection would have to wait.

Even with bent tools, it took mere seconds for Buck to breach the lock of the laboratory door. As it swung open, Paddy's inner alarm continued to clang. Something felt very wrong. The doorway appeared to be the open throat of a gigantic snake waiting to swallow them whole.

The three of them burst into the building. Following Natalie, they sped through a labyrinth of passageways leading to the riser shaft. A catwalk surrounded the open space. Three stories below was the floor of the laboratory; above them stretched the bottom of the riser platform, merged with the ceiling of the block building. Powerful vibrations pummeled the structure as if attempting to jostle the building to dust. The electric whine had become ear splitting.

"That ladder leads up to the roof," shouted Natalie above the noise. She pointed to the metal ladder bolted to the wall on the other side of the catwalk.

Rushing over, Paddy Tooke climbed up first, throwing open the hatch and scrambling through the hole. He stood, but his legs wobbled with the thrusting roof. The particle beam weapon shook violently as if the machine were a captured animal attempting to break free of its restraints. The smell of ozone filled the air, hot and crisp. Up close, the beam was brilliant...blinding...baking him with heat.

He then noticed two things.

First, Yegor Volkov was nowhere to be found, only splotches of blood where he had fallen.

But the second thing Paddy noticed made his skin prickle with fear.

The far corner of the riser platform was coming undone from its moorings. The heads of busted bolts bounced along the corrugated surface of the metal floor.

Paddy spun around just as Natalie popped her head through the open hatch, her face a quivering blur as the roof pounded and shook.

"Back!" he shouted. "Back down."

"I need to stop the machine," she yelled.

"It's too late...the platform's about to go. Get. Out. Of. The. Building."

"But—"

"Get out!"

He pushed her head back down the hole. A tremor struck, knocking Paddy off his feet. Falling backward onto the platform, he watched helplessly as the hatch slammed shut in front of him.

The platform lurched. The far corner dropped a foot off-kilter, its anchorage breaking away. The machine tilted with the angle of the slant, the beam slicing upward, piercing the sky. The massive apparatus shimmied toward the incline of the busted corner.

Scrabbling to get a foothold, Paddy realized he needed to move or be crushed by the sliding weapon. The machine screeched along the metal floor. He lurched out of the way, ducking beneath the beam.

As the fiery light sliced the air behind him, he frantically crawled toward the closed hatch.

Another mooring bolt cracked loose.

Glancing over his shoulder, he found bolts now popping like Champaign corks spitting from bottles.

The far edge of the platform shattered, becoming a child's slide. Gravity tugged him toward the widening crack.

Reaching out, he snatched the edge of the platform that remained fastened. The floor fell away. Girders beneath the riser groaned, bending, buckling. The weapon careened down the incline to become wedged between the platform and the lip of the roof. The fire of its deadly beam stabbed upward.

The shuddering was severe. The machine would not hold. The platform was tearing apart, threatening to take him and the machine down with it.

Twisting himself around, he stretched out to grab hold of something, anything.

The hatch.

His groping fingers found the handle for the locking mechanism. He grabbed hold.

Just in time.

Behind him, the building screeched as if dying. The machine thumped and jerked in its wedged position. The platform shattered, falling away. The machine with it. In its descent, the beam swirled a lethal arc, slicing, burning, melting everything it brushed against.

The sizzling beam swooshed past Paddy's shoulder, missing him by inches.

The falling machine clashed against the walls of the shaft, the clamor deafening.

Gripping the hatch handle with all his might, he yarded himself up to the roof. He then rolled himself over to the edge of the building.

The weapon smashed into the ground floor with tremendous force. An explosion rocked the building. Debris and dust shot up through the opening of the shaft.

Light flashed. The earth shook. Walls caved. Soil and stone gave way.

Paddy blindly threw himself off the edge of the building.

He landed and everything went dark. A deep dark, as if thrown into a well.

Chapter 87

———◆———

Wardenclyff, 3:11 AM

THE CHAOS LASTED LESS than a minute; it felt like years, as if it would never end.

Buck and Natalie burst through the laboratory door, diving for the ground as an explosion jarred the surrounding earth. Rolling onto his back, Buck caught the image of Paddy Tooke falling from the sky. He and Natalie scrabbled up to their feet and ran to where he fell. He lay motionless in the dirt.

The world continued to shake. Pebbles bounced atop the gravel. The soil beneath their feet crumbled, becoming granular, like quicksand being sucked downward.

"We need to get him away from the building," yelled Buck over the clamor.

Each grabbing an arm, they dragged Paddy's limp form across the gravel in a hunched run.

The block building buckled and shifted. Fissures snaked up its walls. Cement blocks cracked and fell. Walls toppled. The ground caved in, like a black hole sucking up the surrounding molecules, dirt, and rock with it. The noise was thunderous.

They scampered down the driveway as quickly as Paddy's dead weight would allow. Chunks of the road gave way under their tread. They sprinted until the ground felt solid again. The noise behind them grew muffled. The shuddering tapered off. Halfway down the driveway, they fell into a heap, their chests heaving breathlessly.

Turning back, they watched as the ground swallowed the block building whole. Cinderblocks, girders, wall panels, machinery, doors, and windows disappeared down the hungry throat. The tremors dissipated. Dirt sifted into the gaping hole. Clouds of dust kicked up. Lingering.

And the night fell quiet.

Staring back at the flattened wreckage, Buck and Natalie found nothing left. No building, no automobile, no bodies in the parking lot. Just a massive indentation. As if swept clean.

Panting with exhaustion, they looked over at each other. Both were caked with murky gray dust and scratched with minor wounds, but neither appeared to have any major injury.

"You came for me," said Natalie, her lips quivering.

Buck stared back as if she were a phantom of his imagination. "Of course."

A thin trail of a tear slipped down her soiled cheek. "Oh, Harry...I..." The words caught in her throat. "When I was in that car...I was sure I would never see you again."

Then a thought came to Buck. "Natalie...the car you came in...I don't think it was in the parking lot when we came out of the building."

A question mark graced Natalie's face. "You're right. It was gone before the building came down."

"Well, who took it?"

"Yegor Volkov," squeaked a voice from the ground.

They looked down to find Paddy's dazed eyes attempting to focus. Lying flat in the dirt, his face was scratched and smeared with grime.

"His body wasn't on the roof," he mumbled. "He's wounded, but he escaped somehow."

Natalie loosened Paddy's tie and opened his jacket, inspecting him for damage. "Are you okay?"

He gave her a weak grin. "I'm fine...just bruised. I'm too old for this."

"There doesn't appear to be any broken bones," she said.

"Anyone ever tell you that you look like Laraine Day?"

Buck laughed. "Natalie Stevens, meet Paddy Tooke."

"You saved our lives," said Natalie, "Making us get out of the building when you did."

Paddy shrugged. "Buck's the real hero. He made me come to rescue you...at gunpoint."

Natalie's eyes lifted to find Buck's. They held each other's gaze for several lingering seconds. Buck smiled. Even as filthy as she was, she looked beautiful. And she was alive.

"I thought you were dead, boy," said Paddy.

"Me too," said Natalie. She reached over to touch his arm. And Buck felt that welcomed hum climbing through his muscles.

"I'm guessing the New Yorker Hotel is still intact," said Paddy. He sat up, his face grimacing.

"Yes, but the laboratory isn't," offered Natalie. "It's buried under tons of earth...and the weapon with it."

Paddy's cheeks curled into a smile. "Good. There are some toys humans shouldn't play with."

Buck and Natalie helped Paddy to his feet. Taking his arms around their shoulders, they hobbled towards the Nash still parked at the mouth of the driveway.

"We better get hold of Deputy Director Carver right away," said Paddy. "He'll want to know what happened and why we left our posts."

Buck knew there would be hell to pay, but he didn't care. He couldn't take his eyes off of Natalie. And she couldn't stop smiling back at him.

"He will not like that we let the microfilm get away," mumbled Paddy.

"Microfilm?" wondered Natalie. "What microfilm?"

"For the weapon," said Buck. "Right now it's on a plane headed for Soviet Russia. We...I...had to make a choice, to get it back or...to save you."

Natalie stopped dead in her tracks, bringing all of them to a halt. "Do you mean the microfilm of the Tesla notebook that the Soviets have?"

"That's right," said Buck. "I was supposed to steal it from Anatoli Yakovlev's office safe, but unfortunately the film is in a diplomatic pouch as we speak."

Natalie stared, wide-eyed. Then, to his surprise, she laughed.

"I don't think it's funny, young lady," said Paddy. "The Commies will be able to build one of those blasted machines now." He glanced back to where the building had been and shuddered. "Not only that, lover-boy here is going to be in a heap of trouble."

"You don't understand," said Natalie. "The Russians are welcome to that microfilm. You're forgetting that I was the project manager for the particle beam weapon. Yakovlev gave me the job of photographing Uncle Niko's notebook. I overexposed the film."

"You mean the microfilm is useless?" asked Paddy.

"When they develop the negatives, all they will find are blank pages. I learned my lesson from the first time I photographed the book a year ago. On that occasion, I shot perfect photos but left out a couple of key pages. Even so, I stole the film back from Dr. Peshkin. I gave the rolls to my SOE handler that night at the New Yorker Hotel."

Then it dawned on Buck. "Wait a minute...that's how the OSS could make a copy of the notebook—from your photographs. Carver told us we had help from the British. It was you."

"The OSS made a copy of Uncle Niko's notebook? Why?"

"It's a fake, with a few formulas changed. To keep the Ruskies chasing their tails."

"Sounds like we were working toward the same end."

"That's why I was at the Consulate tonight, to swap the fake notebook for the real one in Yakovlev's safe."

Natalie thought for a moment. "Yegor Volkov has a notebook now. I saw Anatoli Yakovlev give it to him. Which one does he have?"

"The fake one," said Buck. "I switched them in time."

"After photographing the notebook this afternoon, Yakovlev put it in his safe. He said I could have it after the gala. That was before he knew I was a double agent, of course. I'd planned on destroying the notebook before Dr. Markovitch could see it. He was so determined to build the weapon." Paddy grunted. "Was that the fellow who became smoke up on the roof?"

Buck shot a look his way at the use of the word, 'smoke'. His sobriquet. "Yes," said Natalie sadly. "Poor Dr. Markovitch. Being underground all this time drove him insane. The man was a genius in his own right. I guess it wouldn't have mattered if I'd destroyed the notebook. He didn't need it."

"You would have destroyed the fake one," said Buck. He pointed to his chest and the shredded satchel. "Here's the real notebook...or what's left of it. It saved my life when Volkov shot me."

They drew up to the Nash parked off to the side of the driveway. Paddy glanced into the car, his eyes combing the front seat as if looking for something.

"We need to contact Carver," he said, "But I'm sure the walkie-talkie is out of range."

"We could try it," offered Buck.

He opened the car door and retrieved the device. As he handed it to Paddy, he sensed a hesitation. A guarded look came into Paddy's face, a hint of remorse. Paddy briefly held Buck's eyes. He then pressed the button and made the call to Carver. Within seconds, a response came back.

"Finally Tooke! Why the hell did you take off? You have some explaining to do!"

"Circumstances beyond our control happened."

"Please tell me that the Teleforce notebook is secure."

Paddy peered over at Buck's chest, and the tattered pages bleeding through the satchel. He grimaced. "Yes, we have *Teleforce* with us."

"And the microfilm?"

Paddy glanced at Natalie, who smiled back. "The microfilm has been taken care of as well."

"Good. Stay put. We're coming to you."

Paddy gave a start. "What do you mean? How—"

"We have a tracking beacon in the walkie-talkie. We've been following your movements for a couple of hours. I don't know why you took a trip out to Long Island, but we're almost there. We started late—spent half the evening looking for your trained monkey. We'll be there in a few minutes."

Paddy closed off. He stood staring at the device for a few seconds, irritation climbing over his face. "Damn OSS R and D." he muttered.

Buck laughed. "I've never heard you swear before, Tooke."

Paddy's glare cut his laughter short. A sense of alarm in his eyes caused Buck to squirm.

"Buck, I've got to tell you something, and it's going to change everything that happened tonight. I hate to tell you this, but Carver plans to send you back to Sing Sing."

"What?"

"Sing Sing?" cried Natalie. "That's a prison, isn't it? Harry, are you an escaped prisoner?"

Buck could see disappointment registering in her face, maybe from the accusation, or maybe from the thought of losing him again. Hard to tell.

"No," said Paddy. "He didn't escape. The OSS freed him for this operation. They promised clemency."

Anger flared in Buck. "Did you know about this?" he demanded.

"No, Buck, I did not. I wouldn't have made the promise if I'd known. Carver didn't tell me until tonight. He had a team of men waiting outside the consulate to arrest you the moment you came out."

Buck reeled. He had spotted those men while chasing Natalie's car down the alley. He'd almost gone to them for help. He shuddered. If he'd done that, Natalie would be dead right now.

"We had a deal," uttered Buck.

"I know," said Paddy sadly.

Buck turned away. Hands on his hips, he stared back at the pile of rubble that had been the laboratory. He felt just as devastated. A moment ago, he'd been elated. The mission a success, he'd swapped the notebooks, saved Natalie, and even the microfilm issue fell his way. For five minutes he'd been a free and happy man. And now prison loomed in his future.

"Oh Harry," said Natalie, stroking his back. "I..."

He slid a stricken look her way, as if she were an illusion about to fade from sight. A stone formed in his throat. Just when he had her back in his life again, a set of iron bars was about to separate them.

Paddy stepped up to the two of them. "Buck, it's not in my nature to kick against the goads of authority, but I also don't go against my word. From the beginning, I told you what the bargain was. That's on me. I trusted Carver and Davies. I can't let you pay for my mistake."

"What are you saying?"

"I want you to take off...now."

"What?"

"Just go. Start walking. Lose yourself in the countryside. I'll stall with Carver. You can call me later and I'll come to get you...tomorrow, next week, whenever."

"But you'll get in trouble with—"

"I don't give a damn."

Buck looked back at him. "That's the second time I've heard you cuss tonight."

"Some things are worth swearing about."

Natalie stepped between them. "Harry, I'm coming with you."

Buck's heart nearly stopped. Their eyes locked. "I can't let you do that."

"You can't stop me. I walked out on you once, I won't let you go now."

"But the SOE. You need to..."

Buck never finished. It was too late. An automobile pulled into the mouth of the driveway, its headlamps washing over the three of them.

They were already here.

Chapter 88

Wardenclyff, 3:27 AM

BUCK FLYNN FROZE, SQUINTING into the brightness of the headlamps. Should he run? Or stay and take his chances? Natalie's hand touched his shoulder. Warm. Comforting. He sensed her trepidation seeping through the coveralls he'd worn since climbing into the dumbwaiter—a lifetime ago. He felt his heart dissolving within his ribcage. The two of them were about to be separated once again.

For several seconds, no one moved. The car's engine turned off. The headlamps remained on, bright and blinding. Beyond the halo of light, the dark countryside fell quiet, absorbing the hushed ticking of the engine cooling in the night air.

Paddy stared at the car. Intently. As if penetrating it with x-ray vision.

"Any chance they'll change their minds?" Buck asked.

Paddy didn't respond.

The driver's side door swung open. A man stepped out. His form lost behind the glare of headlamps.

Paddy's right arm was suddenly moving, easing into his jacket as if reaching for his weapon.

"Paddy don't," cried Buck in a whisper. "I'll take my chances with them."

"Shut up, boy," spat Paddy from the side of his mouth. "That dent in the front bumper...I saw that same Ford at the consulate tonight. It's..."

Henry Blacksmith Stewart brought up his own pistol from behind the opened door and pointed it at them.

"Keep your hand right there, Detective Tooke," he yelled. "I want every hand in the air, even you, sweetheart."

Paddy hesitated.

"If I say it again, I say it with bullets," snarled Blacksmith.

Paddy lifted his hands in the air. Each of them stood stunned.

"Good. And now that I know you have a weapon, Detective, slowly take it out and throw it on the ground. Don't play hero. My gun is pointed at Dr. Milosh. If you move suddenly, she goes down."

Buck peered over at Natalie. His throat went dry. Her face was placid, as if having a gun pointed at her head was commonplace.

From the corner of her mouth, she whispered, "Isn't that Arlene's date...from the consulate?"

"Yes. German spy." Buck whispered back.

Paddy threw his weapon down.

Blacksmith's pistol swiveled toward Buck. "Next? Mr. Harry Flynn?"

"I...I don't have a weapon," he reported. He no longer had the pistol he'd taken from Yakovlev's safe. Did it get swallowed up in the hole?

Blacksmith studied him, deciding if he was lying or not. The silence grew.

Finally, he said, "Okay, this is how it's going to go. We're making a trade. Simple as that."

The group remained silent, their hands up.

"I want two things. I know you have the Tesla notebook—"

"You're mistaken," interrupted Paddy. "There is no notebook."

"Don't lie!" yelled Blacksmith. "I know that's why your thief here was at the consulate tonight. He stole it from the Russians. I want it on the hood of the car immediately."

"I don't think so," said Paddy, his tone firm, defiant.

Buck could tell that he was stalling, waiting for Carver to show, but he worried it could get him shot.

"Oh, I think you're going to do exactly as I say, Detective Tooke, or you'll deeply regret it."

Blacksmith took three careful steps back toward the rear of the Ford. He swiped the gun in an easy arc away from the group to point it directly at the trunk. The three of them stared, perplexed by the move.

"I have a gift for you in the trunk," said Blacksmith, his teeth gleaming red in the glow of the taillights. "Her name is Dorothy, but I understand you call her Dottie."

Paddy's face flushed. He took a fearless step forward. Blacksmith's wicked grin stopped him cold.

"Do it," he challenged. "Take another step."

Buck could see Paddy trembling.

"She's asleep at the moment. Poor Dottie's been asleep all day. Sometimes with chloroform, but mostly from sleeping pills. I'm sure it hasn't been pleasant for her, and she'll have a miserable headache tomorrow. But if I don't get that notebook on the hood of the car within ten seconds, I will unload every bullet I have into the trunk.

An angry growl hissed from Paddy's lips.

Buck stepped forward, cautious, his hands in the air.

"I have the notebook," he said. "It's in this satchel I'm wearing."

Blacksmith's grin widened. "Hood of the car...five seconds."

Buck pulled the book from the satchel. As he did, his caddy of lock-picking tools tumbled out, clattering on the gravel.

"What was that?" yelped Blacksmith.

"Just my tools," said Buck.

"Tools? What tools?"

"Lock-picks."

A terrible gleam struck Blacksmith's eyes. "That's what you used. You stabbed me with a lock-picking tool. I wondered about that. You made me lame. Put the notebook on the hood."

Buck approached the vehicle and placed it down. He was close to him now. A car's length away. The pistol looked ominous. He did a three-quarter turn to retreat when...

"Stay put," Blacksmith demanded.

Buck looked him in the eye, the icy blueness frosting between them.

"I told you I wanted two things. A fair swap for Mrs. Tooke. The notebook...and you."

"What do you mean?" asked Buck.

"It was because of you I failed in my mission last year. And I promised myself two things: I would get the notebook back...and I would kill you, Mr. Flynn."

Natalie let out a mournful whimper.

Blacksmith raised the gun. The black eye of the barrel, cold and menacing. Buck steeled himself. Anything to keep Natalie safe. A night of swaps. A fake notebook for a real one. The real notebook for Mrs. Tooke. His life for Natalie's.

Movement stirred behind him. Subtle. Swooshing. Like the rustling of an evening gown.

Blacksmith fired.

Buck felt the hissing wind of the bullet streak past his neck. A cry shattered the night.

Spinning around, he saw Natalie standing limp and hunched, a handgun drooping at her side. Yakovlev's gun. A blossom of red graced her left shoulder, growing across her powder blue evening jacket.

She toppled.

"No!" yelled Buck. He dove, catching her before she struck the gravel. The two went down together, Buck crumpling beneath her to keep her from hitting the dirt. The pistol clattered over the stones.

To his left, Paddy was moving.

Another shot rang out.

From the corner of his eye, Buck saw Paddy drop. He hit the driveway hard.

Cradling Natalie in his arms, Buck turned toward Paddy sprawled in the gravel, clutching at his knee, writhing. Blood seeped through his fingers. He glanced up at Buck, his face fierce, pleading. A signal for Buck to do something. Anything.

But he felt helpless. The pistol Natalie had dropped was six feet away. Encumbered beneath Natalie's limp weight, he'd never be able to get to it before Blacksmith got off another shot.

He looked into Natalie's silvery eyes. She smiled back at him. A tear glistened her cheek. The warm wetness of her blood spread into his garments.

Blacksmith approached.

"They're both just wounded, Mr. Flynn. I could have killed them. I didn't think to ask the woman for a weapon. She looked so innocent in her evening gown. That was my mistake." He gave a humorless chuckle.

He hovered above them.

"I'm going to kill them both, anyway. I just wanted them to see you go first."

Buck refused to look up at him. *Where was Carver? Shouldn't he be here by now?*

With Natalie in his lap, he slipped his concealed hand into the pocket of his coveralls. *Was it there?* He had transferred it earlier. His fingers fumbled. *Yes.* He found it.

Blacksmith crouched down. Two feet away. Then, for effect, or to mock Buck's futility, he set his pistol on the gravel.

"As I was saying before, I've waited more than a year to kill you. You ruined everything for me."

Buck looked into his eyes. Blue. Cold.

"I have something for you, Harry Flynn." His voice like slivers of glass. "The perfect solution."

He brought up his left hand. It surprised Buck that nothing was in it. He opened his palm as if to stroke Buck's face with a caress.

Buck slipped his hand from out of his pocket.

Blacksmith leered. His lips curled back on his teeth. His hand swiped Buck's way.

Off to the side, Paddy moaned a warning. "His ring, Buck...watch out for..."

Buck lurched back, bringing up the cigarette clamped between his ring and middle finger. His thumb rolled the trigger. The Stinger fired. It was the perfect execution of the weapon—that hour of practice at OSS headquarters paying off. Except...

He missed.

Mostly.

The cigarette exploded. A crack in the night. The bullet kissed the side of Blacksmith's neck.

The startled Nazi gasped. The bullet merely nicking a tendon. But, in his surprise, Blacksmith grabbed at his neck, as if to check the wound and staunch any blood there.

Then the bazaar took hold.

Buck watched amazed as Blacksmith's face did a series of reactions. Shock, bewilderment, panic, and finally...pure naked fear.

His body jerked stiffly, as if being pulled by cords in opposite directions. His pupils dilated, eyes bulging. His tongue swelled into his gaping mouth, purple, veined, frothing. Demonic spasms yanked him back onto the gravel. He kicked and bucked.

They watched in horror. The Nazi in agony.

Two minutes later, he lay dead as a stone.

Chapter 89

Wardenclyff, 3:33 AM

BUCK CLUTCHED AT NATALIE, dumbfounded by the spectacle he'd just witnessed.

The body lay obscenely contorted in the dirt. The quiet around them thick and eerie.

"He scratched himself with his own ring," said Paddy Tooke, amazed.

Buck turned his gaze to Natalie, as if the German spy was of no consequence. "How are you doing?" he asked.

She winched. "He got me in the shoulder. It hurts, but I'm okay."

He looked over at Paddy. "And you?"

"Get Dottie out of that trunk...please."

Buck eased Natalie to the ground. He stripped off his satchel and coveralls, balled them up into a pillow for her head, and gently propped her up. Her blood had stained his dress shirt pink.

Grabbing the keys from the Ford's ignition, he opened the trunk, fearing what he'd find.

Dorothy Tooke lay in a fetal position beneath a blanket. Motionless. In the twilight, she appeared deathly pale. Buck shuddered. He feared the worst. His mouth went dry, dust-dry. He didn't like what he saw. He reached down to brush back strands of auburn hair from her face. Her skin felt icy to his touch. So cold. Buck swallowed a lump in his throat, refusing to look at Paddy.

And then...

She twitched. Her head turned toward him, blinking, bewildered. "Wha...what's happening?" she asked, her speech slurred.

Buck lifted her from the trunk to carry her over to the Nash, setting her down in the back seat and wrapping her in the blanket. Paddy managed to stand and hopped over to the car on one leg. His face pure anguish. Buck couldn't tell if it was from his mangled knee, or from seeing his wife under such conditions. Probably both.

Paddy sat in the open doorway at her feet. She cocked her head, confused.

"Paddy...you're hurt," she mumbled.

"Oh Dottie," he whispered, laying his head in her lap.

Buck kneeled over Natalie, stroking her hair and face. They held each other's gaze. For a full minute, no one uttered a word. And then Paddy said:

"Carver will be here any minute, Buck...you better go."

"What?" cried Buck, shocked at the suggestion. "I can't leave now. Look at the three of you."

"There's nothing you can do for us. Once Carver gets here, he'll get us medical attention. You need to go. Or be sent back to prison."

Dorothy Tooke lifted her groggy head to squint at Buck. "Prison? Is this the one?" she slurred.

Paddy patted her hand, giving her a weak smile. "Yes, Dot...he's the one."

She flashed Buck an addled grin. "Do as my husband says, Mr. Flynn. He's looking out for you."

Natalie gripped his shoulder. "They're right. You must go."

He gazed down at her, his expression pained. "I can't leave you."

"You're not leaving me. We'll be together soon."

"But..."

"Go...please. For us."

Buck leaned down and kissed her. The caress of her lips ignited that wonderful hum, spreading through his bones. Reluctantly, he released her from his embrace. He eased himself up from the ground, biting his lower lip. It didn't seem right. It felt as if he were abandoning them.

"Take Blacksmith's car back to the city," said Paddy.

Buck turned to him. "But...what will you tell Carver?"

"I'll make something up."

"You'll be telling no lies while I'm around, Paddy Tooke," exclaimed Dottie.

Paddy barked a laugh. "Yes, Dot." He looked back at Buck, a stupid grin stretching from ear to ear. "Looks like she's going to be just fine." He gave a chin jut. "Go."

Chapter 90

Manhattan, New York, Saturday, 6:08 AM

THE DRIVE BACK TO the city was a blur. Bleak and lonely. A stew of emotions boiled inside. He didn't know whether to be elated or troubled, relieved or distraught. He was driving away from everything he wanted. It felt cowardly. All wrong. Staying would've meant prison, but he could suffer prison now, knowing that Natalie was safe.

He cursed himself for allowing them to persuade him to go.

He met cars along the way—possibly even Carver and his team. He prayed they would get there soon. All three of them needed attention.

As he crossed the Queensboro Bridge, the first rays of morning light came bleeding into the eastern sky. He found an empty parking lot, wiped the car of fingerprints, and abandoned the vehicle to find a taxi. With no jacket, the winter morning air chilled him to the bones. His clothes—the formal wear from last night—were soiled with dirt and blood. His face and hands scratched.

"You okay, buddy?" asked the cab driver, looking him over in the rearview mirror. "You look a little worse for wear."

Buck gave a meager grin. "Rough night."

"Must have been some party," offered the driver.

"Yeah...some party."

"Where to?"

Good question. He'd lost his apartment after going to prison. He didn't dare hide out with any of his old contacts; Carver and his crew would be watching his former haunts.

Then he had a thought.

"Is the New Yorker Hotel still standing?"

The cabbie shrugged. "Why wouldn't it be?"

Why indeed? But he wanted to see for himself. He checked his wallet — the one with the ID for John Humphrey Clark — it contained some money. Not a lot, but enough.

"You want to make some extra cash?" asked Buck.

The driver squinted with suspicion. "Doing what?"

"Getting a room for me at the New Yorker."

A questioning look loomed in the rearview mirror.

"I can't very well go in looking like this," Buck offered, although the real reason was that he didn't dare use the fake ID the OSS had given him. They'd be watching for that. "I'll give you thirty bucks if you register for me," he said.

He watched in the mirror as that just perfect dimwit expression changed into a greedy grin.

An hour later, after showering and ordering room service, he stretched out on the bed to wait for his meal. His chest was bruised from being shot. He thought of Natalie. He wished she were here. He recalled the last time he'd been at the New Yorker, while in the Grand Ballroom waiting for his mark to show, he'd mistaken Laraine Day for the woman he loved. He'd wanted to throttle her then, his bitterness so strong. Now he only wanted to hold her. Caress her.

He'd come full circle—a room at the New Yorker under a borrowed name. The last time he had drifted in as *The Smoke,* and came away with nothing; worse than nothing, he came away wounded and arrested.

His Pops would say,

No matter how much you plan it, life is a crapshoot. Keep your shoes on and be ready to run.

Your shoes squeaked, Pops. It got you killed. Maybe I should listen to new advice. Paddy had told him:

You're a better man than your actions.

Am I? I think I want to be. But with everything that happened, I still came away with nothing.

Well, almost nothing.

He reached down to his tuxedo slacks, crumpled on the floor. He fumbled in the pocket, withdrawing the item. Admiring it. Other than Yakovlev's pistol, it was the very last item he'd stolen...and possibly the very last item he would ever steal.

Did you leave the safe exactly as you found it?

Yes, exactly.

A better man than his actions?

I'll work on that.

And with that, Buck Flynn smiled and flipped Nikola Tesla's Edison Medallion in the air.

————◄O►————

Coming Soon

How do you catch a spy that has no face?

A deep cover spy has infiltrated a top-secret atomic enrichment facility in Oakridge Tennessee—the so-called Secret City. And the OSS find themselves in need of the cat burglar known as *The Smoke*.

Crucial intelligence concerning the Manhattan Project is in jeopardy, however, the undercover spy has a lethal protector. Watching his back is the Russian assassin, Yegor Volkov.

Can *The Smoke* expose the spy and protect American secrets before an assassin's bullet guns him down?

Stealing the Secret City

a noir thriller of espionage

JONATHAN CALL

Jonathan Call is the author of noir thrillers and mysteries. He is also a fine artist, illustrator, and ever-improving musician. He lives with his wife in North Carolina.

"I love the noir world of black and white heroes, antiheroes, and strong-willed femme fatales. At the drop of a hat (make that a fedora) I'll stop to read a pulp mystery or watch a hard-boiled flick from the '40s. Ah...a simpler time of trench-coats, snub nose .38s, and mysteries lurking in the shadows."

Made in United States
North Haven, CT
27 March 2023

34610757R00275